Praise for **SIN**
(*prequel to* **BLACK SILK**)

2006 National Readers' Choice Award Winner for Erotic Romance/Romantica

"How do you have an orgasm without sex? Read *Sin* by Sharon Page! . . . Thoroughly wicked, totally wild, utterly wanton and very witty in its execution, *Sin* is the ultimate indulgence."—*Just Erotic Romance Reviews* (Gold Star Award)

"Strong, character-driven romance . . . extremely sensual and erotic."—*Romantic Times*

"Sinfully delicious. Sharon Page is a pure pleasure to read." —Sunny, *New York Times* best-selling author of *Over the Moon* (anthology) and *Mona Lisa Awakening*

"Sharon Page blends history, emotion, and hot, hot, hot sex within an amazing love story. Blazing erotica!"—Kathryn Smith, *USA Today* best-selling author

"*Sin* is a perfect example of exquisitely rendered erotic romance . . . this book caught my attention with the opening lines and never let go . . . definitely a book for the 'keeper' shelf." —Kate Douglas, best-selling [illegible] of the *Wolf Tales* series

[illegible] **BLOOD ROSE**

"Page's ***Blood Rose*** has scorching love scenes to make you sweat and an intriguing plot to hold it all together."—*New York Times* best-selling author Hannah Howell

"The female protagonist is completely believable, and the two vampire-slaying heroes . . . are simply hot! This is a thoroughly entertaining read."—*Romantic Times*

"Buffy the Vampire Slayer meets Regency England! Two sexy, to-die-for heroes, a courageous heroine, and a luscious ménage make ***Blood Rose*** a sinful treat."—Jennifer Ashley, *USA Today* best-selling author

BLOOD RED

"A blazing path into forbidden dreams . . ."—*Romantic Times*

"Ms. Page weaves an erotic and suspenseful tale that . . . puts you on a sexual roller coaster and doesn't let you off . . . If you're a lover of vampire romance, curl up on a cold winter night with ***Blood Red*** to warm your heart!"—*Just Erotic Romance Reviews* (Gold Star Award)

WILD NIGHTS

"***Wild Nights*** delivers . . . I highly recommend this anthology to anyone that likes wickedly hot sex, action, dominant males, and feisty heroines."—Coffee Time Romance

"Page's story is sensual and sensitive."—*Romantic Times* on *Wild Nights* anthology

A GENTLEMAN SEDUCED

"Sharon Page is a lady to watch out for . . . Sharp, sexy . . . will seduce you from the first page."
—Just Erotic Romance Reviews

"Witty, wicked and wonderful . . ."—*Romantic Times*

Black Silk

Sharon Page

KENSINGTON BOOKS
http://www.kensingtonbooks.com

APHRODISIA BOOKS are published by

Kensington Publishing Corp.
850 Third Avenue
New York, NY 10022

All Kensington Titles, Imprints and Distributed Lines are available at special quantity discounts for bulk purchases for sales promotion, premiums, fundraising, educational or institutional use.

Special book excerpts or customized printings can also be created to fit specific needs. For details, write or phone the office of the Kensington Special Sales Manager: Kensington Publishing Corp., 850 Third Avenue, New York, NY, 10022, attn: Special Sales Department, Phone: 1-800-221-2647.

Aphrodisia and the A logo Reg. U.S. Pat & TM Off.

ISBN-13: 978-0-7582-1471-3
ISBN-10: 0-7582-1471-5

First Kensington Trade Paperback Printing: April 2008

10 9 8 7 6 5 4 3 2 1

Printed in the United States of America

For Gertrude

Prologue

The Scavenger Hunt, Vauxhall, London, September 1819

At any moment, five men would emerge from the bushes and make her submit to the most scandalous erotic pleasures.

Juliette's slippers danced lightly along the path that wound between masses of dark trees. She had left the famed illicit Dark Walk for this narrow, unlit path—and her heart tripped in terror and arousal in her chest. Footsteps crunched behind her, and the heavy breaths reminded her that Lord Hadrian was following.

She was not entirely alone, yet the hairs at her nape prickled, and her spine felt as if buckshot rolled down it.

This had been Hadrian's idea. He wanted to watch her be ravished by five strapping bucks. Yet she trembled at the thought of actually doing it. Of having him act as voyeur. . . .

And beneath that ladylike tremble coursed a fierce flame of excitement. She'd always fancied being on the stage—she certainly could outperform the doe-eyed, large-breasted actresses her late husband had been addicted to. Tonight she would prove it. Tonight she would play the most provocative part. . . .

Her thighs were beginning to ache. Really, she must have tramped a mile by now. How far was she expected to walk? Where were these men?

Or were there no men to be found here?

Had they interpreted the clue correctly?

> *Where risk and scandal frolic beneath man's brilliant sky,*
> *Five rogues await to make a fair lady cry*
> *Her pleasure to the stars as she explodes with heaven's light*
> *And lets her love witness an orgiastic delight*

Hadrian had grasped the meaning very quickly for a gentleman who had drunk an entire bottle of port. The liquor seemed to sharpen his wit rather than dull it and gave a bewitching boyishness to his devastating smile. Her heart had tumbled foolishly as she saw once again that he was more than a handsome (though lined) face, a superb seat in the saddle, and an admirable, though often wilting, cock.

His logic had made sense. Where else did risk and scandal frolic but on Vauxhall's famed Dark Walk? And finally Juliette was walking in that notorious area, experiencing the thrill of erotic anticipation. All those years of being a dutiful lady, first a blushing, charming debutante, and then that decade—her youth!—wasted on Farthingale.

Now was her chance to snatch with both hands the sexual pleasure she'd dreamed of.

Five rogues . . .

Man's brilliant sky must be fireworks. She had guessed that, and it seemed to bear out Hadrian's deduction that they must go to Vauxhall.

Strange that there were no other couples here. Had no one else deciphered it? Juliette frowned. It was not that difficult a clue, really.

She had nothing. Not a penny! She must capture Hadrian's imagination; she must coerce him to make her his mistress.

What other young widow would deign to play these lewd games with an aging rogue? *Any one of the hundreds of young widows left destitute and desperate,* Juliette thought with a wry grimace.

She must give him a grand performance.

She shivered and tightened her grip on her shawl.

"Mamselle—"

The voice had growled from behind her, slurring a version of "mademoiselle" in an accent that bordered on Cornish.

She swung around and almost fell back as wide lips parted on a white-toothed grin and flashing black eyes leered at her.

A black stubble-covered jaw. A dimple. A naked chest. . . .

A naked crotch.

He wore no clothes, her seducer, and looked boldly proud of the fact. He stood, arms crossed, blocking the entire path, blocking her retreat.

He was all firm muscular planes, his stomach as flat as a board, and hovering in front of his navel, like a sword held aloft, stood his prick. She'd never seen such an enormous male appendage, and she heard a gurgling sound from the bushes, which was no doubt Hadrian, shocked by his competition.

"Have you a name?" she asked that dark-eyed man, despairing of what to say. She flicked out her fan and gently brushed aside the warm spring air.

"Trev," he answered, grin broadening.

He took a step closer, slid his hand around her waist, and though she dug in her heels, he pulled her tight to his large body. Her fan tumbled from her hand and clattered to the ground. Dark hair mashed against her white dress—the dark swirls on his chest, the thick line down his abdomen, the mass of coarse black curls surrounding his thick, erect cock.

And that beast nudged her belly, turning her insides to pure heat as though a candle had replaced her heart and the warmth of the flame had become the blood pumping through her.

He kissed rough and coarse, mouth open wide, tongue demanding. He tasted of onions and smoke and small beer, and he grappled with her breasts as he kissed her so hard her spine creaked in protest.

She had never known such beastly behavior, such an invasion. This man didn't care about her squirms of desperation or the grip of her fingers on his iron-hard forearm as she tried to struggle back. He intended to take her without mercy, and her body was becoming a puddle of simpering desire at the thought.

No!

This was an assault, and she was no lily blooded—no, lily-livered—chit who would sob silent tears after having her thighs forced apart by a brute whose victory was his climax.

She kicked his shin, but that merely prompted him to press his massive leg between hers, trapping her in her own skirts. She clawed at his neck and shoulders with her fingers, but she wore gloves, and he merely laughed with pleasure into her mouth.

The bushes whispered, and branches snapped, and Trev, the black-eyed Cornishman, let her free. She stumbled back as the others came out—four other men, all big, with bodies hewn by labor. Farmwork or dockyard work. Bodies touched by the sun, still carrying the sweat and grime of the men's day, but primitive and elemental and sensual all the same.

Juliette skirted away from Trev as a man's hands landed on her shoulders and turned her. She had played this game as a child—putting a smaller girl in the middle and spinning her about and taunting her until the tears streaked down.

She stood in a puddle of moonlight, feeling lost and foolish in the middle, and she swatted helplessly at the hands gripping her arms. The men were encircling her. . . .

She didn't like this. But this man's eyes were a midnight blue, and they twinkled in appreciation at her thin dress, her dipping neckline. "I didn't expect an angel tonight, lads." A genuine appreciation burned in his eyes, and that flame whisked her breath away. "I am Rivers, my lady." He groaned and bent to her hand, ripping off her glove and pressing his wet and hot mouth to her knuckles. He lifted, eyes pools of shadow, and paused with his gaze locked on her breasts.

Hands clumsy, she slipped her hands to the ties that looped around the small buttons to fasten the gown. Beneath the fluttering white muslin, she wore petticoats—which she quickly dropped to the ground—and a corset. She knew, with the sense of a mistress, that the men would not bother to remove her corset.

Her breasts filled the formed linen cups, plumped up by boning, surrounded by fanciful embroidery of vines and rose petals—but all in white. This was the ravishment of the innocent, after all.

Huge hands—Rivers's hands were large, with blunt fingers and black hairs on the knuckles, and they covered even her admirable breasts. His thumbs plucked and strummed, and she quivered like harp strings, and her quim grew wet at his clever playing.

Wrong. Wrong. You mustn't.

She shut her eyes, standing like that forlorn girl in the meadow as their hands slid over her and explored. Rough hands pawing, stroking, caressing her—covering all her skin. Neck, breasts, arms, thighs, and one intrepid man lifted her foot, cast aside her shoe, and began to tease her toes.

This was a harlot's game. This was the fall from desperation to outright sin.

But wine and lust sang in her blood along with anger. She had foolishly grown jaded and lazy—she didn't wish to bat her lashes at boring men and stroke their egos with more enthusiasm than she would stroke their cocks.

Now she must play the most illicit games. . . .

Her lashes lifted as Rivers claimed his kiss. His hands slid down to her bottom, pushing aside other hands there. He lifted her and cried one word as he juggled her with one hand and found his cock with the other.

"Beautiful."

It rang in her ears as he guided the head to her wet nether lips, as she waited, limp and lusting and afraid and wanting all at once. His hips drove forward, and it was done. He filled her, this man she didn't know. He was inside her, thrusting into her, sending all her thoughts and her hopes and her fears skittering into darkness, and she held on to him and let herself be nothing more than her body, imagining him as nothing more than his.

He carried her, jostling his massive organ inside her with each stride, and she clung to him, unable to say a word. She knew his scent now, and she clung to that as tightly as she held him. She turned her head, startled to see Trev stretched out on a bench, holding his cock to the air.

They both meant to make love to her.

Games. Harlot games.

She could run. Perhaps she could marry another Farthingale and drape diamonds around her neck she bought for herself and let the weight and coolness of jewelry take away the yearning for warmth and love.

Harlot games.

How it happened, she did not know. She was laying on Trev, and his breath was hot on her ear, and his member was entering her bottom with exquisite slowness, and she had forgotten how to breathe.

Two men, both with dark hair that glinted with red in the moonlight, attended to her breasts. She shut her eyes, felt hands slide on her thighs, felt the blunt caress of a cock to her quim. She bit her lip as Rivers—for she knew his smile, knew his whispered endearments—filled her.

She kept her eyes closed tight and thought of Hadrian, who must have his eyes open wide—

They were thrusting into her, splaying her wide, and each ruthless thrust tugged her clit, touched every sweetly, agonizingly sensitive nerve. Men at her breasts, her mouth, men filling her impossibly full—

Oh!

She screamed as the climax tore through her. Heavens, she'd never expected—

Oh, good lord, she was about to die—

Aah!

The men drove hard into her, grunting and bucking. Hot semen rushed into her quim, her rump. A spray splurted over her naked breasts. Then—oh, goodness!—the man who'd pulled out of her mouth gave his shaft a rough jerk, and a stream of white cum hit her mouth and cheeks.

What a frightful mess. Hadrian had better be enjoying this; she wanted to cry suddenly, now that the pleasure was gone, now that she was sticky everywhere. Tears dripped to her cheeks.

"There now, lass," said the man on top of her as his softened cock slipped free. The man below her grunted and withdrew also.

She felt a fool as he helped her up, but no one offered her a cloth to clean herself. Finally one picked up a white handkerchief, and she reached for it gladly, too embarrassed to look at any of the men. She focused on that white cloth—

It pressed sudden and hard into her face. Over her nose and mouth. Juliette clawed at the giant hands holding it there. She couldn't breathe!

Hadrian!

Was this part of the game?

A man grabbed her arms and wrenched them back. Rope wound brutally around her wrists, clamping her hands, biting into her skin.

Were they going to force her? Rape her? Why, when she had been so willing?

A black cloth jerked over her eyes and was pulled tight. Someone knotted it, capturing her hair, pulling at her scalp.

No—!

Notation in *Winslow's Volume for Wagering* at Winslow's Gentlemen's club, the upstart of such clubs: *Fifty pounds that the widowed Lady F—, who has been missing from Mayfair for two weeks, has run off with a footman rather than share the bed of Lord H—.*

1

"You spend a night allowing a woman to drip molten wax on your chest, and afterward everyone casts you as the villain." Dashiel Blackmore, Lord Swansborough, leaned back into his leather club chair and grinned.

His friend, Sir William Kent, Bow Street's magistrate and a gentleman who could remain composed while handing down a sentence that sent a youth to a prison hulk, blanched in shock and embarrassment at this casual remark.

"Good lord, you're depraved, Swansborough." Sir William shook his head as he lifted his brandy and drained the last half inch. He adjusted his spectacles over intense blue eyes, his fingers brushing the long-healed scar from a footpad's attack. "What sort of madness was that about?"

"The anticipation of each burning drop." Dash crooked his fingers, then made a snuffing motion, and an obedient, well-trained girl immediately leaped to do his bidding.

Winslow's, the newest of London's hells, combined the tradition of the gentleman's club—venerable location, card tables, a strict control of membership, a slab of beef for dinner—with the pleasure of London's brothels.

Ironic that Sir William had tracked him down to this place, had used his name to gain entrance.

The girl, a plump temptation with honey-blond curls, approached, carrying a candle. Around the crowded, smoke-hazed room, two dozen whores bestowed their charm and favors on various gentlemen. All the women were blondes, all voluptuous with lush mouths and succulent tits.

Wearing a hopeful expression, the girl sashayed toward Sir William and him. She pursed her rouged lips suggestively and gave a tiny puff of breath—enough to set the flame flickering and the pooled wax spilling.

Turning back to Sir William, Dash gave a devil's smile. "Care to explore dangerous sex?"

"Bloody hell, no." Sir William waved the girl away. She gave a pretty pout and spun, setting her shortened skirts whirling around her plump thighs. He leveled a serious gaze, filled with fatherly censure. "Still dressed head to toe in black, I see. Even a black cravat. Swansborough, *are* you the villain of this piece?"

It never ceased to be strange to hear Sir William use his title. Sir William had known him since he was "young Dashiel," had sometimes teased him by using his middle name, Lancelot. He picked up the brandy bottle to refill their glasses. "If you believed me to be the villain, wouldn't I be in Newgate by now?"

Sir William raised his glass briefly in agreement. "Where were you on that night?"

"Tied to a bed, I expect. I cannot remember."

"Four witnesses saw you on the Dark Walk just before the woman disappeared. One insists she saw you dragging a reluctant woman with you—a woman hidden by a black cloak."

Dash leveled his gaze at his friend, the one man who had believed his story about his past, his unbelievable tales about his uncle. He took a long drink of the brandy. "I do not kidnap women."

"Was it part of a game? A bedroom game?"

"I was not at Vauxhall. But I can offer no proof of it."

Sir William raked back his white hair and studied him, without speaking, with the cold, impartial gaze of justice.

Beside them, the blond girl with the candle returned and

flung herself back onto a hard-backed chair and drew up her frilly skirts. A black leather harness was strapped to her hips and her thighs, and a long black rod rose from the juncture between her creamy thighs. A brunette woman straddled her, her skirts caught up in her hands, and she began pumping on the dark dildo, moaning and cooing with abandon. The brunette caught Dash's eye and ran her tongue lavishly around glistening, rouged lips.

His cock stirred, lengthening, thickening. Hell, he was being accused of abducting women to use in perverse pleasures, and he was growing aroused by the calculated display of prostitutes.

He watched the brunette on top, her breasts heaving beneath her snug bodice, her face reddening. Her sexual scent filled the air like candle smoke. The other lass clutched at her breasts, tweaking the nipples through taut silk, thrusting her leather-bound hips.

"I need details," he said even as he watched the courtesan close her eyes in ecstasy and grind mercilessly on the thick, false cock. Blond and brunette curls bounced. Both pretty faces flushed pink. The gasps and moans were like squeezing fingers around his shaft. "The names of these witnesses. The names of the family of this woman. I was not there. Why would my name be used?"

"Reputation?" Sir William suggested.

He knew Sir William had pursued these thoughts himself, but was allowing Dash to talk—to either reveal evidence of his innocence or drape the noose around his own neck. "The woman. What was her name?"

"Juliette, Lady Farthingale."

"Hadrian's mistress." Dash drank deeply again, listening to the brunette courtesan's anguished cries. Her head lolled back, her fingers clutched the other girl's shoulders, and her lover drove up from the chair to spear her.

He noticed that Sir William had turned his seat so as to avoid the view of the copulating women, away from the display that could wipe all rational thought from a man's head. Fantasy presented on a silver salver, the promise of escape for the price of a few coins.

He could bid farewell to his friend and lose himself in that pleasure, but Dash forced himself to ask, "What did Hadrian have to say? If he believes it was me, why hasn't he called me out?"

"Hadrian claims he was watching his lady indulge in some sport; he was hidden in the bushes along the Dark Walk. He heard a sound behind him, something smashed into the back of his skull, and he woke with the dawn—wet, bloodied, and alone."

"And who does he think is responsible?"

"He thinks the . . . er . . . five men employed to ravish his mistress are the culprits."

"Five men? So whoever has copied Lord Chartrand's erotic scavenger hunt is trying to be as inventive."

Sir William gazed awkwardly ahead—at the safest scene in the club, a group of men playing cards, too intent on deep play to entertain women.

"Oh, sweet heaven, I'm going to come!"

The blonde's cry ripped through Dash, igniting lust. His hands clenched to fists; his cock jolted in his trousers. Dash leaned back in his chair, laughing as the young blond girl's body began to spasm with her orgasm, as she cried, hoarsely, "Fuck me hard. Drive yourself on me."

Calculating and clever, the brunette on top saw her partner had reached her critical point, pulled down her bodice and shoved her breasts forward so that as the pretty girl gulped for air in her explosion, she swallowed the soft, warm flesh of fat breasts instead.

God, it was a beautiful display.

The solution to the mystery appeared logical to Dash, but he proposed it with respect. "Have you considered Hadrian as a suspect?"

"Immediately. But he has been watched." Sir William shook

his head. "I can't imagine why Hadrian sought a mistress. The man's a sodomite."

"To deflect suspicion. And Hadrian is not discriminating about the gender of his partners."

The plump, heavy-breasted wench on top held her mate to her tits, lushly smothering her, and gave a loud, happy sigh of pleasure. She watched Dash beneath coy lashes. He watched, amused, as the pretty blonde on the bottom struggled to free herself from her prison of plump tits.

"It's possible," Dash pointed out, "that Lady F discovered her lover also kept a stable of young boys. For a hopeful mistress, that would have come as a shock."

Sir William gave a brief twist of a smile. "Lady F guesses his secret, and he has her removed? He could have paid her off—but then, she may have come back for more. It's all possible. Except for our witnesses who saw you."

"Paid, I assume."

Sir William's gaze settled on the two women, naked and slumped together in bliss, and a red flush coasted over his grizzled face. For all he passed judgement on the sins of fallen women, he apparently was shocked by the sight of them. Clearing his throat, he said, "Hadrian suspects the men took Lady Farthingale for money—that she will be ransomed."

"So why use me for a simple scheme of blackmail?"

"I don't understand it," Sir William admitted. "But then, you could have employed the five men."

"Indeed." Dash watched, amused, as the pretty blonde surrendered and began to suckle a long, generous nipple. Sexual agony rippled through him as the girl's cheeks hollowed, and her graceful hand clutched the enormous white mound.

He'd forgotten his train of thought.

"Did you?" Sir William prompted.

Did he what? Hire the five men. "Bloody hell, no. Give me the names, Sir William. I need to speak to these people."

"I've already done so. I've had some of Bow Street's runners follow them."

Coos and sighs and desperate feminine gasps washed over Dash. Women were such a delight. They could die in an orgasm that would leave a man drained and limp and within seconds happily start bouncing toward their next explosion.

Sir William tapped his glass on the table. "Miss Eliza Charmody."

"And who would she be?"

"An actress. A week ago, she partnered Lord Craven in this game."

"I assume you mention her because she was also abducted? Lady F wasn't the first?"

"No, Lady F was not the first."

The woman on top now galloped, wild and merciless, on her partner, plunging furiously on the dildo filling her creamy quim. He had no doubt each thrust sent the harness rasping against the clit of the girl on the bottom, for she was squealing around the nipple filling her mouth. She gripped the fat bosom with desperate fingers and sank her teeth into the plump tit.

Dash's blood drained from his brain. What in hell did he care if Sir William wanted to arrest him? He knew he'd die young.

Hell, Sir William would probably be satisfied with banishment. Send him to the Continent or the East where he could serve out his punishment surrounded by lush women.

But he was an innocent man.

"I reexamined that case," Sir William explained, his face red, his breathing unsteady. "It took place at Covent Gardens, another clue in this mad scavenger hunt. Two courtesans came forward to say you had enticed the woman away from Lord Craven. And two gentlemen—Sir Percy Whitting and Lord Yale—saw you hand her up into your carriage."

"And again, interestingly enough, I wasn't there." Dash scrubbed his jaw, gave a shake of his head as the voluptuous jades returned to earth, gulped hungrily for breath, and began to eye him. The promise of sliding his rod into a bubbling cunny began to pound through his brain. "Easy enough to pay courtesans to lie. As for Sir Percy and Lord Yale . . ." Christ Jesus, Dash loved the sight of two women's breasts pressed together. He shifted in his seat, searching for a more comfortable position. "Both are young, can't hold their drink, and are gullible. Whoever convinced them they saw me is clever."

"Indeed." The magistrate's face remained impassive.

"And is likely involved in the white slave trade."

Grimly, Sir William nodded. "It is possible this is related, given the disappearances of the women. Though the ladies were not country virgins."

"It might be the reason my name has been used. Revenge." The woman on top winked at him, but, groaning, Dash shook his head. Not now. Later he would spend the night losing himself in mindless sex. Spend the night escaping his nightmares with an orgy, or bondage, or candlewax dripped onto his vulnerable skin.

"Or it is Robert," Sir William suggested.

Guilt rose, black and sickening. "My cousin is not like his father. He doesn't covet the title. And he doesn't know the truth."

The magistrate said nothing.

Dash watched the cavorting women as they winked at him and wriggled together. "So it could be a member of my family—my uncle, my aunt, my cousin. What of my uncle's mistress? Should I include her? Or Craven or his partner, Barrett, who I suspect are involved in white slavery." Dash drained his port—the last of his bottle. "So I talk to your witness. And the other suspects. Then I join the scavenger hunt."

Sir William drew a card from his jacket pocket. "Bloody surprised you weren't in it already." He laid the folded white square on the polished table.

"What is this?"

"Your next clue."

Whereupon he ripped open his breeches, releasing his great purple-headed pecker. He pushed me forward, almost sending me toppling to the crowd below, and he threw me skirts over me head.

"My lord Wooderton," gasped I, startled by the fury of his passion.

"Silence, wench," he cried, and in one thrust, he drove his magnificent lance within me. My scream of submission shocked the theater into silence. Only my desperate cries of pleasure could be heard as Wooderton pounded his cock into my cunny. Then applause thundered from the crowd below us, and in front of all those snobbish ladies of the ton, I received the most wondrous fuck from the most desired gentleman in London.

Having added the last required comma in the chapter, Maryanne Hamilton laid down the manuscript. She ached. And burned. Her heart danced in her chest like a bird beating against glass. And there was sweat . . . unladylike sweat trickling down her bodice.

She leaned back against the ironwork back of the bench. The last of the roses tumbled all about her. Their sweet scent enraptured her, and she closed her eyes and turned her face up to the warm autumn sunshine. Here, in this secret garden behind her brother-in-law's London mansion, she could imagine she was in the country and Almack's and the marriage mart didn't exist.

Her first Season had passed without an offer of marriage.

Thank heavens.

She glanced down at the pages, the corners fluttering in the September breeze.

Miss Tillie Plimpton's spelling had improved remarkably over the last three manuscripts. With her royalties, Tillie had bought herself a nice cottage near Devon, and her three illegitimate children now attended a country school.

The thought of three children with warm beds and gardens of their own made Maryanne smile.

It terrified her to think of children destitute. Of innocents being forced into workhouses. Or worse. She'd been so close to that herself. And she knew what it was to be illegitimate—she and her sisters were the illegitimate daughters of the erotic artist Rodesson, though their mother had spent a lifetime hiding that truth.

Maryanne sighed. Unfortunately none of the books had sold enough copies to pay for the royalties she had advanced to her authors. She was certain they would. Someday. But that day appeared determined not to arrive. And now she was in debt. Very much in debt.

"Penny for your thoughts."

At her sister's words, she muttered, "Five shillings would be more the thing." Or five hundred pounds. Or five thousand.

"What?" Venetia, her hand resting gracefully on her rounded enceinte tummy, strolled along the path. She paused to press one blossoming rose to her face.

Maryanne tucked the manuscript to her side. "Nothing," she murmured even as she felt the familiar plummet in her stomach.

Five thousand pounds. It was an impossible sum, and she still couldn't quite understand how she had spent that much. But there had been so many women in need, so many children without futures. And Georgiana had "borrowed" far more money from their publishing house than she'd imagined. . . .

The breeze flirted with the leaves and with the ribbons on her bonnet. But it did not toy with Miss Plimpton's manuscript. No—it picked up those pages deliberately, tossed them up on the stone path, and sent them tumbling end over end toward her sister.

Fortunately for her, Venetia could not move quickly, and she certainly could not bend.

"Oh, heavens!" Maryanne darted after the fluttering white sheets and stomped her slipper-shod feet on two of them. She dropped to her knees and scooped them up.

"Are you working on another book?"

"Now and again," she gasped. It wasn't a lie after all. She was *working* on the book.

The stones bit her knees as she reached for the sheets, as she crumpled the pages in her haste to group them together. Venetia had supported them by drawing erotic pictures, using the talent she'd inherited from their scandalous father, Rodesson. But Venetia would have a fit if she learned Maryanne was editing erotic novels and in partnership with a notorious courtesan. Novels of passion, Georgiana called them.

They sold very well. Gentlemen loved them.

In truth, she could see why. The books were like ripe cherries—eat one and you craved another.

She couldn't upset Venetia. But she could not stop her work—not when she was in such trouble.

As she gathered up Tillie Plimpton's magnum opus and struggled to her feet, she saw Venetia carefully settle on the ironwork bench. "May I take a peek?"

Maryanne ducked her head. "Oh, no. It's not finished yet."

Venetia nodded, as though she understood, but of course she had no idea. And Venetia would not understand the truth. Venetia had saved their family—she had married Marcus Wyndham, the Earl of Trent. As a result, Maryanne now possessed a dowry in a sum that sent shivers down her back and made her legs quake. And of course she could not touch any of that money, even though she needed it so desperately.

A large portion would stay in her name once she married. But that would require leg shackling herself to one of the eligibles she danced with at Almack's. And men who danced at Almack's were not the sort of men one could imagine making love with naughty, roguish abandon in the middle of the theater.

"You needn't be afraid to let me see. After all, someday you will have to let a publisher take a look."

Maryanne choked on a giggle. She was a publisher! At least, she was running Georgiana's business because Georgiana had vanished once again. No doubt her partner was in pursuit of a new lover, who had probably left town for the hunt, but she couldn't help but feel again that sensation of her tummy dropping away. Usually, within a day or two, Georgiana sent her a letter. Either a glowing report on the charm, wealth, and allure of her new gentleman or a letter filled with fury, disappointment, and jaded regret.

It had been a week, and there was no letter.

"Lord Bainley sent hothouse orchids this morning, I noticed." Venetia brushed back the red-gold tendrils that waved around her face. Her hazel eyes glinted with the mischievous delight she always took in assessing her sisters' romantic successes.

Maryanne stared down at her hem and nodded. Her Season should have been a "success." Six gentlemen had shown interest. Cards and flowers had arrived with diligence, and the men had squired her for dances. She had ridden in curricles in Hyde Park. She had stumbled through so many awkward conversations on the weather she had begun to think she could make a career in predicting it.

"But obviously the orchids cannot compete with a manuscript?" Gentle amusement rippled through Venetia's question.

Guilty, Maryanne looked up. "Lord Bainley is not the right one."

"I see. Have you found one that is?"

She shook her head. "Do you want me to accept Lord Bainley's suit?" She prayed the answer would be no. Many gentlemen were fascinated with Grace's loveliness—why couldn't one of them have proposed to Grace this Season and divert the attention? With her sister Grace in the country with Mother, Maryanne was on her own.

Venetia tapped her lip. "Have you not found anyone you admire?"

A start, a twitch, and three manuscript pages slid to the ground again. Blast.

"There is someone, isn't there?"

Collecting her pages once more, Maryanne nodded. Now, this was a secret she could safely reveal. It would be humiliating, but it would certainly distract her sister. "Lord Swansborough."

In answer, the roses shivered with the breeze, and a flurry of pink and yellow petals leaped into the air.

"Lord Swansborough! You can't be serious."

A hot fire raced over Maryanne's cheeks. "Why not? He's delicious."

And she could see him in her thoughts—his wickedly tempting smile, his darkness—black hair and eyes and dressed in his signature black dress clothes from head to toe.

She noticed an equally pink blush touched her sister's cheeks. Now she was intrigued. Of course Lord Swansborough was a rake. She had no doubt he had done many of those exotic acts her courtesan authors described with such lusty wit. And Venetia had drawn erotic art, for heaven's sake. How could she be *embarrassed?* Why?

"Tell me, Venetia. What do you know about him?"

"Stories that aren't appropriate for—"

"Venetia! I am also Rodesson's daughter." It was still so hard to say that aloud, after so many years of pretending, even to herself, that she was not. "You are not the only one of us to see his artwork. I need to know the truth about Swansborough."

"You truly are serious about him?"

"What did he do? How scandalous can it possibly be?"

"It is rather difficult to describe—"

"I have seen your pictures, Venetia." This was the first time she had admitted it.

Venetia's grip tightened on her shawl. "I had no idea."

"I am not as innocent as you think. Even Grace has had a peek."

At the mention of their youngest sister, Venetia's fingers played with the fringe of her shawl. "Fine. Reputedly he had a woman drip hot wax on his chest."

Maryanne dropped her graphite pencil to the walk and knew the lead within had shattered. Hot wax on his chest? How could that be erotic? Despite her confidence, she felt at once aroused, shocked, and unnerved. "You saw him at that orgy you attended, didn't you?"

Venetia gasped. "How did you know about that?"

"No one notices me when I sit quietly to read. You were speaking with Marcus, and you obviously didn't notice me. What exactly did Lord Swansborough do at the orgy?"

Venetia wore a full blush now. "I saw him pleasuring a woman with another man."

Maryanne gulped, but it was nothing more shocking than what she had read. It appeared men enjoyed the sight of other people making love. It stimulated them. "Hasn't every rake?"

"The woman's ankles were bound, and she dangled from the ceiling. He . . . he pleasured her that way."

Maryanne felt her quim clench suddenly, and a warm jolt of sensual agony washed through her. Her cheeks were definitely aflame. "All men are rakes before marriage. A successful woman is able to determine which one can be tamed by love." She had heard Georgiana utter this phrase numerous times.

An auburn curl danced across Venetia's cheek. "Once, I didn't believe any man could be tamed by love."

"But Marcus fell in love with you and has been the most devoted husband in the history of England. Has he ever even left your side for a night?"

Venetia laughed. "He has. But I would not exactly describe Marcus as 'tamed.' "

"And that is what I want!" Maryanne cried. Perhaps Venetia finally understood. "I want a dangerous man. A sensual, uncivilized, passionate male who merely dresses up as a gentleman but is utterly primitive inside."

"And that man will not be Lord Swansborough. He is too dark, most definitely too dangerous, and too . . . too . . ."

"Experienced? Exciting? Arousing?"

"Lewd. That is the most appropriate word for Lord Swansborough. He is entirely too lewd for you."

Maryanne bristled. Venetia always knew best, always gave orders. There was no reason to argue, but suddenly she couldn't resist. "But what if I were to allow him to bind my ankles and dangle me from the ceiling?"

Her sister's auburn brows arched. Venetia motioned to her stack of pages. "Let me see that manuscript you are working on."

That she hadn't expected! Maryanne slipped quickly to her feet and darted a few safe yards down the path. "No!" She sighed. "You needn't worry about Lord Swansborough. I'll never even dance with him, much less marry him."

She turned abruptly. That thought shouldn't upset her. Not when she had no intention of marrying. Jane Austen had produced marvelous work from her lovely cottage. Surely having a husband underfoot would have made that utterly impossible.

Now that Venetia thought marriage was quite magical, she was determined to foist Maryanne into one.

Maryanne stepped through the back door into the cool house. Sweet kitchen scents beckoned, but she ignored the plaintive rumble of her tummy. She had to get her manuscript hidden away.

She had it safely stowed in its hiding place when a quick rap came on her bedchamber door. A letter by the afternoon post.

The return address was Miss Beasley in Oxford Street, but the writing was Georgiana's. Thank goodness. Surely Georgiana would be returning to London. She could cope with the creditors.

Maryanne tore it open and read.

I'm in terrible trouble. You must come tonight to this address. You must be masked, but you will be admitted, I'm certain of it. Be careful—this house is part of an erotic scavenger hunt, but I know you will keep your wits about you, and I have no one else to turn to.

G

Maryanne stared at the letter. She could see at a glance the address was unsavory.

Excitement shot through her.

Madness to go.

But what about Georgiana?

She could hire a Bow Street Runner.

And pay for him with what? Free copies of works of erotica?

Besides, having been given a glimpse into the sordid, shocking, naughty world of Lord Swansborough by Venetia, she was awfully tempted to have a closer look herself. To have an experience of her own.

One glass of champagne for courage.

Maryanne handed her empty flute to a bare-chested, masked footman who whisked it away. She couldn't help but stare at his finely hewn, bronzed muscles, such a startling contrast to his immaculate powdered wig and black breeches.

Her invitation had gained her entry to Mrs. Master's salon, but she rather felt as if she'd walked into hell. Surely hell was as hot, as raucous, and smelled as strangely. Decorated in Eastern fashion, the salon was a sumptuous den of gold and scarlet, velvet and silk. Pillows spilled everywhere on daybeds and on the floor. Couples and groups explored pleasure in sensuous and astonishing positions.

Behind her mask, Maryanne's cheeks heated. She pushed aside a spray of glittering red beads that dangled from a swinging lamp.

Most of the women strolling about were completely nude, and they encouraged the handsome gentlemen to paw, pinch, or kiss them in any place desired before inviting them to play on the cushions. A few wore virginal gowns of pale silk, like hers, so she did not look out of place, at least.

How would she find Georgiana in this crush?

"My dear, you must be parched."

Another glass was thrust into her hand. She half turned, and the gentleman bowed. Lord Craven. She almost dropped the glass. Lord Craven had been featured in many of her authors' books. The acts he enjoyed gave her nightmares.

He plucked the glass from her fingers, his smile dazzling. Craven was a handsome man, a fair-haired gentleman with angelic blue eyes, long lashes of gold, and a lean, sculpted form. He held the glass to her lips. "Such a delicious brew is not to be wasted."

This was a smaller glass than the one that had held champagne, and the fluid within was a deep burgundy. What harm in a sip?

But Craven tipped up the glass, and the liquor was sweet, intoxicating, and tempting. She continued to drink. At his laugh, she saw she'd drained the glass.

He gave her a leering wink and raised his hand. Instantly another tray of champagne was presented. "To cleanse the palate."

It was true. The drink was . . . clinging to her tongue, sickly sweet. She took the champagne. He grabbed a flute and drank it in a gulp. "Do you dare, my dear?"

His smug smile irritated. "I'm not a fool, my lord." She thrust the glass back, untouched, on a passing tray. She did not have to do as Lord Craven asked.

"Ah, the timid and pretty kitten is now a lioness." But his smirk became a beaming grin of delight.

Understanding dawned. Most jades would not be concerned about becoming drunk. She had given away a clue that she was not a lightskirt.

Blast.

Lord Craven raised his hand. In the blink of an eye, men

surrounded her, gathered by Craven. They made a circle—eight of London's most desirable gentlemen. All dressed in the austere black and white of evening dress. All were taller than she, and as they stepped forward, tightening the ring, cold fear raced through her veins.

One man muttered something to Lord Craven—and the suggestion passed around the circle.

The sweetness on her tongue turned sour. She spun dizzily. She must escape.

But the circle was too tight. There was no way out.

A low, dangerous laugh sent a prickle down her spine. She gaped at the men facing her.

They were unfastening their trousers!

Her feet felt as if she stood on a roiling sea.

Each and every man reached his hand in his trousers and drew out his cock. She almost gagged on the smell of masculine sweat, the intimate aroma of their privates. They began touching themselves, stroking their lengths, squeezing and caressing the heads until each rod became stiff and fat and shocking.

"How dare you!" The high-pitched feminine shriek exploded from the beyond the circle. "Fancy! Snaring eight delicious gentlemen. How selfish!"

A blowsy, drunken woman shoved two of the men aside and stormed into the circle. Before Maryanne could move, the blond woman's hand hit her shoulders and sent her stumbling back.

"A woman requires abundant . . . skill . . . to please so many men." With that, the woman pulled off her chemise, revealing large breasts and plump hips. The men began pulling harder on their members at the sight of the nude woman, who lifted her nipples to her own mouth. Her tongue snaked out and touched the very tip of the erect, long, dark brown length.

For a moment, Maryanne was dumbstruck.

But there, between two dark tailcoats, was a glimmer of light.

She ran.

She ducked under arms and slithered around bodies, artfully dodging through the crowded corridor. At least she was small and slim.

Georgiana . . .

Maryanne stumbled over someone's boot and almost fell into a half-naked footman. She glimpsed the young man's face, beautiful with full lips and startled eyes. Behind her a woman laughed and then squealed.

Two people were copulating in the corridor. The man's bared buttocks were pumping, and plump white legs jiggled around his. He was grunting, the woman screaming.

If this was Georgiana's idea of a joke—for Georgiana had often said it would be amusing to take her secretly into the demimonde world—if her partner had lured her into this nightmare for a diversion, she would . . . would . . .

Throw ink on Georgiana's gowns. Toss her jewels in the Thames. Put a bag of flour over her bedchamber door. Pour treacle in her shoes—

A male hand snatched at her breast.

She bared her teeth, pushed a drunk, swaying woman at him, and then raced down the corridor. At the end, she left the crowd behind. There was no one but her, which meant there could not be any perverse entertainments here. Her corridor abutted another, and at the junction there was a closed door. No sound came from behind the door.

Perhaps this was a safe place to hide. To decide what to do.

Laughter, moans, and screams echoed behind her, pounding in her dizzy head.

In this case, how could the unknown be any worse than the known?

The doorknob turned easily in her hand, and the door swung open to darkness.

She shut the door firmly behind her. Gasping, she braced her hands on it and turned the key in the lock.

A small *snick* startled her, along with the quick sulfur smell of a light being struck. Her heart almost extinguished itself. Shaking, Maryanne turned as flame touched wick and a light caught.

It reflected Lucifer's dark eyes and wickedly handsome face. "Good evening, angel. Are you the night's entertainment?"

2

At one glance, Maryanne knew he was drunk.

And knew, of course, he was not Lucifer.

Lord Swansborough sprawled on a wing chair. His shirt was open at his throat, and curling hair, soft and black as night, peeked out of the black-dyed lawn of his shirt. Cast aside, his elegant coat and his shimmering black waistcoat lay in a jumble on the floor by his feet. The light of the single candle glimmered on his thick blue-black hair.

Every night when she edited an erotic scene by candlelight, Swansborough became the hero of the scene. He was the man of fantasy who stripped off his clothes and lowered his naked body over hers. He was the one to boldly lift her skirts in the theater, or suckle her breasts in a carriage or even—and it was delicious madness to think of it—to tie her to her own bed, arms and legs spread, prisoner to his pleasure.

But here he was, in the flesh, winking at her!

And dressed in his usual shocking fashion—entirely in black.

He caught her staring and gave her a most wicked grin. Enticing lines bracketed his firm, wide mouth, and adorable dimples shadowed his cheeks. "You came in here to seduce me, didn't you?"

With a crook of his fingers, he motioned her to move toward him.

She stayed at the door. "N—no."

The Oriental motif had not ventured past the door. This was an Englishman's study, resplendent with wood and leather, comfortable yet austere.

Both settings suited Lord Swansborough.

"Who are you?" he asked, and he tipped the decanter—the entire decanter—to his lips and took a swallow. He quaffed the drink—likely brandy—the way men in the country drank ale. Some spilled down his chiseled jaw, and he lowered the lovely glass thing and wiped at his beautiful mouth with his shirtsleeves.

His lordship was the first man here who was interested in her name. And she floundered helplessly—she had a creative mind, but all she could do was stare in astonishment.

He settled himself on the back of a chair, one booted foot dirtying the arm. The position displayed the long, lean, muscular power of his legs.

"Your name, puss," he prompted.

She knew men used that name to describe a woman's quim, and she knew she must suggest another name. But what did she want to suggest? Availability or the truth—that she was not allowed to touch a man like he? "Verity."

Truth. Why had she thought of to call herself that—the opposite of what she would speak?

He saluted her with the decanter. "Imaginative. Where is your partner, Verity?"

"I don't have one." Which was, at least, the truth.

"I see." Amusement, chilling amusement, showed in his rakish grin. "If I ravish you and make you explode in the most intense climax, will you give me my next clue?"

A jolt of shock raced, cold and startling, through her veins.

He thought she was a courtesan, employed to work in this bizarre scavenger hunt. She'd heard couples speaking of clues and hunting in the salon. "I came here to find a friend."

The brandy decanter was almost empty. Had he truly drank that much? How could he still be conscious if he had? Her two glasses of champagne and that sickly drink had left her disorientated, and the giddy feeling was now a pounding inside her skull.

"Did you indeed?" he asked. His tone spoke ominously of a man's awareness that he had a trapped female in his possession. But there was a teasing note underneath, and she knew she would much rather be trapped in this study with Swansborough than out in the rest of the house with the other scavenger hunters.

Tearstains itched on her cheeks, and she was certain she looked disheveled. How much did her mask obscure?

"Come here, Verity." His voice had sobered, and it rumbled with bewitching erotic promise.

Verity. Which sounded like her sister's name, Venetia. Had she thought of the name because her sister had had adventures and she had yearned for her own?

But Venetia had told her that Swansborough was exactly like the men who had surrounded her. And he was drunk, therefore dangerous. Logic told her that, but her heart skittered at the gentleness in his black eyes. They were hazy with drink, but not wild with lust.

"Come."

A confident, autocratic command. She knew the other meaning of the word, and a shiver of anticipation, hot, electric, weakening, shot down her spine.

Her feet obeyed, and she closed the distance between them, and with each step, her heart tightened. Sweat trickled down her bodice, and her throat felt aflame. She felt exactly the way she did when reading erotic manuscripts.

She stopped—a little more than a sword's thrust away—and he grinned. "Who is the friend you came to find, sweetheart?"

He was Marcus's good friend—he had seen her perhaps a half dozen times. She was so close she feared he would know who she was. That he could see behind her simple white mask and guess the truth of her soul. That she was Maryanne Hamilton, ordinary virgin, here in Hades to find a courtesan.

"Georgiana," she admitted softly.

His black brow lifted. "Do you belong to her, sweeting?"

Mystified, she asked, "How do you mean that, my lord?"

"Do you know who I am?"

"A viscount. And you expect me to answer your questions, but you will not answer mine." She smiled and dipped her head. Heavens, had she just said that? "You are Lord Swansborough." Surely that was safe enough to admit. He would think her a jade who knew him from brothels and Cyprian balls.

She still wasn't certain what role she should play. Should she pretend to be experienced? Should she admit she was an innocent in trouble?

"I hardly expected to find you in here alone in the dark, my lord."

"But I often drink alone, sweet. There's no pleasure in drinking alone in the middle of a crowd."

He was foxed. Absolutely. "But why—?"

"I encountered a man. He spoke of a tragic incident that happened a long time ago. It is something I like to forget. And I needed a way to help me do that." His lordship lowered the decanter, let it drop the last inches to the table, where it rattled. "You are lovely, Verity. But then, the truth is always beautiful. Dangerous but beautiful."

"I'm hardly dangerous, my lord."

He reached out his hand—bare of gloves. A perfect, long-fingered gentleman's hand. She had never touched the naked hand of a gentleman. He meant to kiss her fingers. Uncertain, she moved forward, for good breeding dictated it, and let him sweep her hand to his lips.

Lovely lips. Firm and delectable and brushing her gloved knuckles. The champagne inside her bubbled up once more at his hot, seductive touch, at the caress of his full lower lip over satin.

He drew her closer, his hand casually holding her fingers.

She took one look into his dark eyes, at the sculpted curve of cheekbones, the autocratic nose, and lost her breath.

Shadowed by dark stubble gracing his jaw, a dimple teased. She looked closer. Beneath his thick, black lashes, his eyes focused in two different directions.

"In you, sweeting, would I find truth?"

In her?

Before she could even gasp, his mouth slanted down over hers, and his broad back blotted out the light. She fell into black shadow and reached out to him. She should not allow this, but she was here, and he expected it and—

No. She was Verity. Truth. She wanted to kiss him.

His lips pressed to hers, his tongue parted her lips and slid inside her mouth. She tasted him—*delicious* was too mild a word!

She tasted brandy, too much brandy, and the warm flavor of him that was so erotically male. His hand cupped her breast. He must know her nipples were indecently erect.

His large body surrounded her, his scent—brandy and shaving soap and witch hazel and the earthy hint of his sweat—washed over her, yet all she wanted was to kiss him deeper. Beneath her fingertips, his shoulders were solid lines of muscle and bone. Daringly, she trailed her fingers toward his neck. She left the almost propriety of his shirt and touched his bare flesh.

And moaned wantonly into his mouth.

His tongue teased hers, and he toyed with her, letting his tongue thrust lazily in a promise that made her heart hammer and her quim turn to liquid honey.

She went rigid, suddenly uncertain.

He eased back from the kiss, bending forward to bestow kisses to her nose, her right cheek, her chin. "Do you want to give me what I want?"

Oh, yes, he was drunk. She tried to make sense of his words. "W—what is it you want?"

He stepped back and yanked his shirt out of his trousers. Before the hem could settle around his hips, he pulled his shirt off, over his head.

Oh, dear lord.

His skin was the color of brandy, like a laborer's, and she couldn't imagine why. What could he possible do out of doors with his shirt off?

"I want you to make me forget."

"Forget what?" she asked. A blush crept over her cheeks that she had been so bold as to ask the question. She normally listened. Tonight, with his kiss singing on her lips and champagne bubbling through her blood, she truly was Verity—someone else other than mousy Maryanne.

Swansborough paced around her, arms folded over his massive chest. Soft black hairs curled over hard planes of muscle. The sight of his nipples left her hot and embarrassed. She felt the sweep of his gaze, the assessment of breasts, of hips, of bottom. She felt like a mare on display at Tattersalls.

"You're slender."

Reed thin, compared to the women here—the women with large bosoms, plump arses, and generous thighs.

He paused long enough to kick off shoes—he had prepared to undress, he hadn't worn boots. With lazy motions, he undid the buttons of his trousers.

This time, with this man, she did not want to run.

"Lovely."

Her heart soared at the word, heaven help her. She liked this. She liked to be stared at by lustful Lord Swansborough.

He peeled down his trousers. She'd thought—she'd been certain—that men wore undergarments beneath their trousers.

He didn't.

She was faced with his cock, and its thicket of black curls, and it, like the rest of him, stole her breath away. He gave her a smile, mischievous and boyish and utterly endearing. "Does it please you?"

"I've no idea." Truth again.

He laughed at that, not the usual laugh of a man who was in his cups. Deep, erotic, his laugh was filled with naughty promise. "Most lightskirts 'ooh and ah' over the size, my dear."

"It is large." Her first thought had indeed been astonishment, and now she knew one did mention that to a man. In all the erotic books she edited, men always possessed members that lasted for one carnal bout after another. Georgiana had laughed about that and had confided, with a wry smile, that such cocks were creatures of fantasy.

"I think," Maryanne hazarded, "it is a creature of fantasy."

He wrapped his hand around the shaft, and this time the sight of his large hand over his enormous staff had her hot and panting and giddy with desire.

"What do you want to do to me, my sweet?" he asked with a strangely vulnerable air, the way a shy man asked a lady to step into his curricle for a jaunt around the park.

She didn't know. She couldn't find words! Her thoughts were a tumble of nebulous fantasies. Of imagination and dreams. Of lust and foolish madness.

"What do you think would please me? I like an inventive woman."

She had no idea, knew she could not hope to fool him, but the challenge heated her blood. "I would like to . . . kiss you. Again."

"Kiss me where?"

"On your lips."

"And I would like to kiss your lips, your breasts, your quim, your arse. Would you be willing to do such things for me?"

"You haven't got breasts."

His deep, throaty, wicked laugh washed over her, more intoxicating than champagne. Surely Lucifer laughed like this—before tempting a woman to surrender her soul.

"Indeed I don't. Disappointed? Do you enjoy suckling another woman's breasts? Tell me—I enjoy inviting a crowd into my bed at times. Have you experience there?"

She felt as if she were being interviewed for a position—she supposed she was. He thought she wanted to be his mistress. Suddenly the realization of what she'd come for stopped her cold.

"I can't. I must—I must go."

"To find Georgiana? She isn't here, love. She's left London."

"How do you know?"

"I know everything, sweeting. The lovely Georgiana is pursuing an earl. She's left you alone. Now, tell me, have you enjoyed sexual sport with another woman?"

Maryanne reeled back on her slippers. She had to grab the back of the chair beside her.

Georgiana had left London! But what of her note? That desperate note? Had Georgiana written a plea for rescue yet left town with another man?

It would be like Georgiana. To forget she'd begged for help, to forget she'd put a friend at risk when a man offered rescue. She'd strangle Georgiana. When she found her.

Her heart twisted in her chest. Her friend had forgotten all about her. She was so very forgettable.

"Other women?" Swansborough prompted.

Startled, she looked up. His lips were parted, and his breath came fast. He was waiting on her answer as if he needed it to live. He was exquisite, beautiful, yearned for by unmarried ladies who dreamed of a charming husband and a stallion in their beds. And he wanted her answer.

"N—no."

She saw his slight stumble, a reminder of how much liquor he must have drunk.

"Any objections, though?" he went on. "I can think of several women who would love to nibble your breasts or suck the honey out of your quim."

She saw his cock jolt upward at his own words. The head glistened as though moist—in all the books she edited, the cocks were always dewy, or dripping, or slick. Lord Swansborough's certainly was. She stared at it, unable to answer his question—she'd read Sapphic scenes, had been intrigued. What would it be like to suckle a woman's breasts to please her? Or lick another woman's wet cunny?

But she wanted him. Only him.

"Touch me."

Two simple words, spoken in a voice hoarse with desire. In a heartbeat, his teasing nature had dropped away.

"I need you," he said simply. "Make me forget. Touch me."

Tentatively she let her fingers brush—and touched the mythical velvet-over-steel she had read about so many times. Nothing could describe the marvelous sensation of his intimate warmth against her skin. And it was truly satin soft yet rigid, and it jumped beneath her touch with a mind of its own.

Her heart leaped into a frantic rhythm.

She clamped her hand around the shaft as he caught her in another kiss, a long, slow kiss that melted her like wax to a flame. She was gripping his poor cock to keep herself from pooling to the floor.

Brandy taste tingled on her tongue as he broke the breathless kiss. Laughing, he took a staggering step. Terrified she'd hurt him, with her hand wrapped around his remarkably pulsing member, she moved back, too.

His hands pulled up her skirts, and she gasped at the sight of satin wrinkled by his hands as her hem rose higher and higher.

His hot breath danced against her ear. "I promise, Verity, when I want to use fucking to make me forget, I am very, very good."

What did he want so much to forget? His hand cupped her inner thigh, and she struggled to think. The roughness of his palm, the strength of his fingers, the reverence of his touch—all conspired to send her wits whirling, shattering.

A man's hand was on her thigh.

Lord Swansborough's hand was on her thigh.

Sliding up, up to the juncture between. His palm cupped her hot, wet nether lips; his fingertips delved inside her cunny.

His hand shifted; the heel pressed that magical place all the courtesans wrote of. The clitoris. Obviously Lord Swansborough knew exactly what he was—

Oh, lord.

Hazily, through shattering pleasure, she saw his smile, saw the roguish curve of his lips. She clung to his arm, to the chair beside her. Oh, it was so . . . so much. Beyond words . . . so far beyond her skill with words—

She tried to back away as he flexed his hand and slowly, torturously increased the pressure and slipped his fingers between her damp nether lips. Her juices were lush, thick, bubbling from inside her.

In her fantasies, she had gazed into his magnetic black eyes and shared the deepest intimacy. Never had she dreamed it could be real. That she would see how long his sweeping black lashes truly were. That she would see his eyes sparkle for her.

He bent to the swell of her breasts, the lightly freckled curves, and ran his tongue over them. Heat washed over her as though a thousand wicks had caught flame at once. She was gazing down at Lord Swansborough's silky black hair while he licked her breasts!

Thick and gleaming, blue-black beneath the soft candlelight, his hair tempted her to touch. She coasted her palms over its softness, barely touching, gasping at the tickle across her hands. Even at that light, feathery caress, he began to suckle. His beautiful mouth left a trail of warm wetness over her tingling skin.

Emboldened, she slid her fingers into his hair. Savored the silky feel.

It was dizzying to touch him so.

She wanted to touch more.

Beneath her lashes, she saw his naked body—his wide shoulders, the lean line of his abdomen, and his magnificent, amazing cock bobbing as he kissed her. As his fingers stroked and teased between her thighs.

She tried to cling desperately to sense. But all she wanted was more stroking, harder stroking, rougher, faster—

His mouth slanted over hers as the pleasure became almost unbearable. She knew this . . . had read it so many times . . . had brought herself to this wonderful, exquisite point. She'd learned through naughty touching how she liked her release, but it was so much more intriguing to have his masculine fingers rasping between her curls to rub her clit.

His touch made her tremble, made the perspiration spill between her breasts, made it almost impossible to breathe. But she needed . . . just a little different rhythm. He was in control, but she rubbed hungrily against his hand. Oh, yes, she loved his touch, but she was hurtling toward climax, and his caresses were not . . . not exactly the rhythm, the speed to take her to ecstasy.

She knew she loved his touch, but she knew her body.

"Yes, my lady of truth, take yourself there." He urged it against her ear, and his lips lowered to play sensual magic against her neck.

She grasped his hand. Not quite so direct a touch . . . a little higher . . . more of a tug—

Perfect!

What must he think? Was he offended? He let her guide his hand; he even smiled—lips kicking up on the right side, his cheek dimpling.

What did she care if he was angry? She wanted . . . needed . . .

She drove toward her climax like a madwoman.

She cried out as it took her. Barely heard his raw, masculine laugh as she rocked with it.

"Come against my hand, my love."

She did, crying out, a slave to the pulsing muscles, the waves of sheer pleasure pounding through her. Her head tipped forward, her mouth opened wide.

Was this the lure of sensual writing—not the orgasm, but the deep joy, the wonderful sense of intimate connection with a gentleman she'd longed for over months?

It was ending, the waves dying slowly away. He scooped her up, her skirts hanging about her hips to the floor. Floating still, in pleasure, she locked her hands around his neck. Her fingers grazed smooth, sensually enticing skin.

"This room is filled with intriguing devices to enhance pleasure."

Dazed, she met Swansborough's amused gaze. Midnight black and twinkling. "Devices?"

"If you are part of the treasure hunt, love, you are supposed to be tied up and whipped."

She hadn't realized that. Even though she was still boneless from her climax, she felt color drain from her face.

He settled her on the chaise, and she let go of his neck to drop on the silk-covered, elegant surface. She realized, still catching her breath, still throbbing deep in her quim, that his cock was hard, rigid, and he must want his pleasure now.

She thought he would mount her.

She couldn't tear her gaze from his blunt-nosed cock pointing toward her, so long and thick and intriguing. One thrust, and she would be ruined.

She didn't care.

She touched his jaw, let his stubble ignite her skin and send magic coursing through her veins. Her skirts spilled over her hips; her legs were bare. She could see her brown intimate curls below crumpled petticoats and the snug front panel of her corset. She parted her legs wide.

I want you.

She couldn't say it. Didn't dare say it.

Still, she wanted him to understand.

But he didn't mount her. Instead he paced over to a simple box standing on the desk, at the edge of the light.

A proper young lady didn't look at a man's naked bottom, she thought wildly. But she couldn't help but look. He possessed the most perfect taut derriere. The muscles of his flanks hollowed deeply as he walked, lithe and graceful.

Grinning in the way that made her throat ache and her quim pulse, he flipped open the lid. "Playthings."

Toys? Why would a gentleman have toys on his desk?

She had time to run. Time to flee to preserve . . . what?

Before she could work up the courage to ask, he returned. He splayed his hands beneath her lower back and lifted her. With the corset, she didn't bend, and he gave her a smile of sympathy. "This will be worth it, love."

Something pressed at the puckered entrance of her bottom. The most wonderful, exhilarating sensation shot through her. It was so wickedly sensitive there—just as her authors said.

He held a small glass vial before her eyes, poured a stream of gold liquid to his fingers. It poured slowly, like honey, and dripped off his fingers.

Her heart hammered.

She was masked. He most definitely did not know who she was. He would not touch his slicked fingers to her bottom if he knew she was the Earl of Trent's sister by marriage.

Ooh!

Slippery, his fingers traced around her entrance, leaving her skin oiled. His finger dipped inside, and her bottom opened for him.

Never had she imagined it could feel so good.

He held another thing before her eyes. One of the "playthings." A small, slim rod with a rounded end. With circular strokes, he teased her entrance with it. With her legs splayed wide, she could only arch with the shock.

"Do you enjoy anal play?"

He was studying her bottom, displayed to him, and she felt a flush of embarrassment. Yet he only appeared . . . intrigued . . . as though he enjoyed the sight of her entrance, her plump cheeks squashed by the chaise beneath.

The slender rod slid in, and she knew at once that she did enjoy such play. Heart in her throat, Maryanne nodded.

"Relax, love. Let it slip inside," Dash murmured.

Dash nuzzled pretty Verity's slender neck. She lay on the chaise with her legs up and spread wide, the picture of carnal welcome. Brandy-laced blood raced down to his rigid cock, and he had to hold the edge of the seat to stay upright.

Verity. Pretty Verity, promising the truth in her pleasure.

Her hair tumbled around her, fallen from her pins, a shimmering honey brown in the golden light. With her skirts around her waist, her shapely, trim legs were revealed. Lovely slim hips and a nipped-in waist beneath her corset.

Behind the mask, her wide eyes were the color of coffee. He'd tasted champagne in her kiss. As with him, liquor fired her blood. With the white silk strip of a mask, he could see only brown eyes, the plump curve of her mouth, the point to her chin.

She wore a blasted awkward gown for a courtesan, yet it was enticing to try to slide his hand inside the bodice to tease her nipple. She squirmed in frustration, and he pressed his lips to the crests of her breasts beneath the satin.

Lovely.

Wrapping his fist around his shaft, he forced his prick down. Even just his touch on his shaft almost hit the trigger and sent him firing. God, he was hard—he needed to fuck, to fuck wide-eyed, lovely Verity—and escape his truth.

He should leave. He'd come to prove his innocence only to be struck in the gut with his guilt. He should—

Don't think.

She smelled like heaven, ripe and creamy from her orgasm.

A kiss. He slanted his mouth over her parted lips as he used the swollen head of his cock to part her wet nether lips.

Hot. Wet.

Beautiful oblivion.

Bracing his arm on the chaise, Dash guided his cock to her snug, velvety quim and sank inside.

3

He was going to make her come until she begged for mercy. Until she pleaded with him to stop because she couldn't bear more pleasure. He would hear her scream for him.

"Oh, dear god!"

Dash chuckled at Verity's shocked cry as his thick cock nosed its way into her quim. Her fingernails clamped into his bare shoulders. Her teeth sank into her lower lip. Like hot cream, she flowed around his rigid shaft. His chest brushed her tightly corseted breasts, his mouth grazed her forehead as he began the slow, easy rock of his hips.

Damn, but she was tight. A mere inch inside her slick, tight cunny and his brain wanted to shatter into a thousand pieces. His famed control was fleeing, and he fought to hang on to it.

A girl this tight was new.

He wouldn't hurt her. But he needed to intensify the game.

Dash caught her hands in his and lifted her arms over her head. Panic flashed in her dark, massive eyes. Her legs were splayed on either side of the chaise. With his weight between her creamy thighs, his length positioned over her, she was trapped.

He read at once her fear at loss of control, but sex was best when accompanied by powerful emotion—by fear, by vulnerability, reputedly by love . . .

He pumped deep, rewarded by her gasps and moans with every thrust. Her cries were so sweet, so bewitching, so delicate. Verity's fetching cries had a truth to them that spoke deeply to his heart.

She was so tentative beneath him.

Afraid of him? Because he was drunk? Because he'd shattered every tumbler in the room into the fireplace? She must have seen the shards of glass.

Her right leg hooked around his calves, her left around his hips.

"Yes," he groaned, and he thrust deep as her hot, bubbling core accepted his cock until he nudged the entrance to her womb.

She cried out then, as women did when he gave that shocking thrust, when he filled them completely. He wasn't buried to the hilt—it didn't matter. Her cunny was snug around the head of his cock, pleasuring that spot on the shaft that was so sensitive.

He had to be gentle. God, that was the pleasure of it—fighting to be gentle while wanting so much to ram, to pound, to pump himself senseless.

He could slip off her mask, see her, but it would destroy trust. Her brown eyes sparkled at him; she gazed at him as if he could give her heaven with a sweep of his arm.

Yes, angel of truth, let us fuck our way to heaven.

Dash let his groans of mounting pleasure join with hers. Growing louder. An intimate chorus that sang in his head.

The slim rod in her derriere made her cunny incredibly tight—it was a trick many courtesans used to enhance their lover's pleasure. Each bounce would pleasure her anus as well as her lush quim.

His brain began to fog. His eyes shut, and he drank in their luxurious scent, the scent now coating his cock and ballocks and her soft, sticky inner thighs. He was leaking into her, his balls ratcheting tighter, tighter, his body aching to burst.

Let her go.

Instinct told him to free her hands, and he braced his weight on one of his. He slid his other hand beneath her bottom, grasping a cheek. It tugged her anus, and she moaned in surprise.

Deep. Go deep. Climb inside.

His groin collided with hers, his jet-black nether hair crushing against her silky, chocolate pelt. Lovely. A shift of his hips, better aim, and he heard the cries that rewarded his success. His cock was stroking her clit with each plunge.

Yes.

He needed her climax. He was going to get it.

Her change was so subtle. Her hands skimmed down his back. Never once had he been caressed that way—so slowly, as though she was memorizing him by touch.

"What is your truth, love?" Why was he asking? Dash wondered. He didn't want to give his truth. But he wanted hers. "Who are you really, Verity?"

Maryanne heard his lordship's question but ignored it. She ran her hands down the broad expanse of his hard back, and her fingers dipped just inside the valley of his bottom.

She was touching Lord Swansborough's arse!

His cock shaft, veined and thick and wet, slid along her clit, and her toes curled. Her hips arched. She wanted to find the rhythm. The perfect rhythm.

She'd read so many times about pain. Pain the first time. There'd been a twinge, almost nothing. But now it was the sweetest agony to be filled by such a big cock. Yet that little tweak of exhilarating pain with each thrust only excited her. It didn't hurt, it excited her. She rose up to him, meeting him halfway, her legs flung over his.

Ruined. She was ruined.

How perfect ruination was.

She closed her eyes. He was a stranger, this man pounding into her. A man she'd dreamed of, yet his every thrust pounded one truth into her head. *You know nothing about him. He doesn't even . . . even fuck like you guessed he would.*

She'd dreamed that he would be sweet. He would call her magnificent, beautiful—she had no idea how a man really behaved.

But this was so very, very good.

Swansborough was raw male hunger and pure graceful skill. A gentleman at the core, carefully balancing his weight, carefully gliding his slick cock over her teased, throbbing clit. But a beast at the heart of him, a man who hammered his pelvis into hers, who drove his cock as deep as he could, and sent shock waves of delight to her brain.

She loved each bang. Loved the blossoming soreness of each collision. Loved the deep, full feeling of being ripped apart by wild Lord Swansborough.

His big hand slid in between their bodies, his long index finger lying across her clit. Her bottom was invaded with each bounce of her hips, her clit stroked, her quim filled.

Sweat dripped onto her face from his brow. A drop hit her lips, and she tasted cool salt. His eyes looked ravaged, and harsh lines ringed his mouth as he gasped and panted.

As he fucked her.

God, she loved it so—

The patter of her heart ceased—like the stillness of nature just before a natural disaster. Her body paused, poised, and the orgasm roared over her like a crushing wave. She clung to shoulder and arse and screamed her pleasure at his ear, and closed her eyes shut, and knew how lovely it was to be ruined and a woman.

Lovely.

She was sobbing with it. Moaning. Gasping.

He surged forward, one last impossibly deep thrust, a bang that sent so much hot ecstasy through her she tore at his skin. His hips bucked, she felt his buttocks flex with it as he shot into her. He growled low in his throat. His body jerked with his orgasm.

It was exquisite to hold a climaxing man.

Marvelous. Perfect.

She couldn't move. She could only hold him and hear his soft groan and the pounding of her heart.

His head lowered toward hers, his damp black hair hanging around his face. She couldn't see his eyes, but he was panting like she was.

He'd come inside her.

She'd done what foolish ruined girls did—she'd risked everything for a fleeting moment of intimacy. And he'd come in her, and she couldn't take it back, and even now, she might be just about to become pregnant.

The horror numbed her.

She stayed absolutely still as he slid out of her. As his hot, thick semen rushed out, too. Her inner thighs, her curls, her buttocks were sticky with it.

What if he saw blood? Her blood on him? Or, dear heaven, would he offer marriage?

No, he was drunk. He wouldn't notice, and if he did, he wouldn't care.

He was a reprobate. A rake. He must have torn maidenheads before.

He'd asked who she was. She'd said nothing, she'd only moaned, and he hadn't asked again.

He slid the toy from her sensitive derriere, wrapped it in a handkerchief. "Did you not enjoy yourself, sweet?"

Even with her mask, had her every thought shown in her eyes? In the cast of her mouth? "I—I . . ." Now was the time to race away. To push down her skirts and run for survival. Another moment longer, he might . . . guess. Not who she was but what she was. And once he'd guessed that, she feared her mask would have to come off.

He kissed her cheek. Gave a smile, but it only curved his lips and left his eyes unfocused and strangely blank.

"I have to go, love."

"You can't!" Her outcry shocked even her. It was the best solution to let him go. But she was afraid to be alone here. She wanted—

What? For him to escort her to safety? For him to take her home—foolishness, that. She could make him call her a hackney—payment for the tupping on a chaise.

She struggled to sit up, and she stared at his back. He'd gone over to his clothes, had pulled on his shirt and was now straightening it.

Without turning, he said, "Sorry, love. But I have to pursue this hunt. I can't stay."

Her brain was a mess of exhaustion and pleasure, champagne and raw fear. "I'm not safe here."

That made him turn. "Are you a professional or not?"

"New. I'm new at this. It wasn't . . . wasn't what I thought. I came only to find Georgiana."

Shrugging on his waistcoat, Swansborough paced back over to her. With his raven hair, midnight eyes, bronzed skin, and black whorls of hair, he was so dark, like a moving shadow. Firelight danced across his face, painting the sharp planes of cheekbone, jaw, and nose with gold. "What do you want with her?"

He could intimidate even while foxed. She guessed it was second nature to a viscount. He expected her obedience.

She took a steadying breath. "How could you know she's gone after an earl? That can't be true."

As he sat down on the chaise beside her, he didn't answer. He wore only a shirt. Glancing down, Maryanne could see his now slumbering cock—so adorable she wanted to touch it. Why shouldn't she touch it? Desperately, fearing what she might start again, she looked up. Into his face. Best to look there, not at his cock, which she felt, foolishly, belonged to her.

His lashes lowered, brushing his cheeks—heavens, she saw the hint of freckles on his cheeks, across his nose, and her heart lurched in her chest.

Slowly he tilted his head, met her gaze. His eyes were so black they shocked her. She couldn't tell where the pupils stopped and irises began.

"How could you know?" she repeated. Could he give her a sensible answer? He looked unsteady, as though the drink was affecting him more now.

He cupped her cheek, nuzzled her neck. His hair brushed her earlobe.

She fought the urge to squeal in shock and laughter—it tickled! "Tell me."

He lifted. He had no scruples about touching her. He pinched her right nipple through her gown. Casually ran his thumb in a circle around the nipple poking hopefully at her dress.

"It's the *on dit*, love."

She drew back. She could barely find her voice with his hand making erotic magic on her breast. "What do you mean?"

He splayed his legs. Reach down and scratched his ballocks.

Good heavens—one fuck and they'd reached the intimate level of her sister's marriage. She knew Marcus did such things thoughtlessly in front of Venetia, her sister laughed about it with other married women. Maryanne hadn't expected the sight of Swansborough scratching an itch to make her heart somersault in her chest.

"I was looking for Craven," he said, as he rearranged his ballocks to his satisfaction. "The story is that Georgiana pursued him to the country, and he left her there while he returned here."

"Georgiana would never have stayed if Lord Craven returned." Her hair. She really should try to fix her hair. "She sent me a letter. She said she was in great danger."

"Indeed. And you came here to rescue her?"

Her hair was a snarl. Exhausted now, she felt on the edge of tears, but refused to give in to them. "You needn't sound so amused. Of course I came to help."

"In a place like this, a novice comes to rescue Mother Superior?"

A novice nun? Had he guessed she was a virgin?

She waited, as taut as a wound-up clock, but he said nothing more. He flopped back, the devil, onto the chaise.

To think she'd feared his first instinct on deflowering her would be to offer marriage. What a romantic fool she'd been. Of course, all who knew her expressed that sentiment behind their hands. *Maryanne always has her nose in a book—and not the improving sort. Really, Maryanne has no practical sense at all. Maryanne must learn that romance is all very well in the pages of a book, but . . .*

The champagne was making her thoughts a jumble. Could sex do that, too? She felt so boneless still, and her quim ached and throbbed in the most wonderful way. "She must be here. She sent the letter. I'll have to go back out there. I have to find her."

Doubt crept in at the edges of her conviction. Several times Georgiana had offered the chance of naughty adventure. A man to make love to her or to do everything but! She'd refused—more out of the fear of giving great leverage to Georgiana. If Georgiana knew she'd made love, she would be a slave to her partner, willing to do anything to protect her secret.

Though, really, one hint from Georgiana that a Miss Maryanne Hamilton edited erotic books and her entire life would be devastated. It was only the certainty that Georgiana needed her that kept her feeling safe. She'd grown up learning not to trust. Not anyone.

Rodesson, her father, had made so many promises and had never kept a one. They were never suitable for him, never convenient, and she'd learned, of course, that one rushed to keep promises for someone one was determined to keep.

"I had to assume her letter was the truth. I couldn't turn my back on Georgiana's plea."

Swansborough got up from the chaise and patted her head. Even gave her a scratch behind her ear like a favored pup.

"You aren't going back out there, sweetheart. I promise you that Georgiana was not here when I arrived."

She heard the hesitation and pounced. "But she could have been here. They find clues, don't they? And go from one scandalous place to another. What if Georgiana went to the next place?"

A thought struck. What if Georgiana had planned such a thing all along? Instead of revealing where she really was, she went to the next place in the hunt and directed Maryanne here. All Maryanne needed to know was where to go next.

She needed one of the clues.

Swansborough gave her a lazy smile, the sort a lion would to a gazelle trapped beneath its paw.

"You have the most dangerous look in your eyes." He had his trousers in his hands. "And considering I can see it even though you are masked, it definitely strikes fear in my heart."

Determined, fighting nerves, she got up. Smoothed her skirts—as hopeless as that was. "I need the clue," she said and gave her explanation.

His dark brows lifted. "Georgiana is that clever?" At her nod, he shook his head. "Astounding. You do realize you have to be whipped to get that clue."

"What?"

"The lady of each couple is to be tied up and whipped. The gentleman is to receive some anal play from willing wenches while the whipping takes place."

Georgiana had sent her here to be whipped?

"Do you still want a clue, sweetheart?"

"I don't want to be whipped!"

"At the hands of an expert, it can be quite a sensual experience."

"You're mad! No!"

"I've never had a jade be quite so blunt, love."

A mistake. Perhaps women readily agreed to be whipped if the suggestion was made by a man like Lord Swansborough.

What if Georgiana's life depended on her submitting to a lash?

"Not to worry, love." That generous smile again, this one lighting up his eyes.

Easy for him to say that.

"I will get you a clue."

"How—"

"Lock the door behind me, lass," he continued without pause. "Barricade it if you wish. When I return I'll knock three times and serenade you." He fumbled with the buttons on his trousers.

"You're drunk."

"Not enough to stopping thinking, alas." He picked up a wing chair and carried it to the door. He wore shirt, trousers, shoes, and an open waistcoat. "Shove the back under the knob," he instructed.

She certainly knew how to barricade a door. She had both an older sister and a younger one.

The instant he closed the door behind him, and she was alone, Maryanne sprinted over, turned the key in the lock, and jammed the chair in place.

Now all she could do was wait.

And think about how exquisite it had been to hold the broad vee of his back and surge up to meet his thrusting cock.

Or she could think about being ruined. Think about being pregnant, possibly.

Think about how gloriously she had thrown away her life.

He had promised her the clue, and now he must live up to his promise. Besides, he needed the clue, too.

The brandy began to taste sour in Dash's mouth, and his head buzzed with the descent from lust and alcoholic madness.

He'd thought his cousin hadn't known.

Murderer.

The word still rang in his head. His cousin Robert thought he was responsible for an innocent man's death—for the death of Robert's older brother, Simon.

He needed to shove aside those thoughts. He wished he could go back to Verity to obliterate his memories with ecstasy. To obliterate his mind.

There was drink to be found everywhere—carried on silver trays by half-naked footmen. He threw two glasses of champagne into his belly. The dull roar in his head focused once more.

The couplets of the clue that brought him here danced in his head:

Dark pleasures on the fringes of Mayfair for the daring, the bold
Bindings at slim wrist and ankle fair, the flick of a lash to behold
'Til torment and ecstasy shatter the voluptuous lass
And willing wenches use clever tongues to pleasure a gentleman's ass

The last line was raw, blunt, designed to titillate. He enjoyed anal play, especially from a woman's tongue—it was a treat rarely bestowed. A soak in the tub followed by a woman lying between his thighs, licking cock, ballocks, and anus. Such a rare boon, he had to admit he'd be almost tempted to take Verity to the dungeon, if she were to enjoy the same fun and avoid the whipping. But genuine horror had shown in her brown eyes at the thought of birch work.

Scavenger hunters—in couples—held the clue cards and raced toward a plain wooden door set in the wall of one of the back rooms of the town house. He'd been here months ago—Dante's Dungeon was famed amongst those who sought dark pleasures.

As he followed the crowd down the narrow, twisting staircase, he overheard snippets of conversation. All the women expressed the same fear: "Am I really to be bound? To be whipped?" And the men laughed about their fate with the wicked jades awaiting them—a pretty pink tongue thrusting in their asses.

Dash joined the crowd that stood in the shadows of the punishment cell. One nude auburn beauty was being shackled in place. She gave her partner a fetching smile. A proper little submissive, she would accept her whipping with pretty grace.

The men who bound her were footmen dressed only in black breeches, with massive codpieces of gold. Two attended her, one on each side, locking the iron bracelets around her wrists. They bent, locked up her slim ankles. Her back was to the expectant crowd—full hips, large derriere, small waist.

She sighed delightedly as the footmen pinched her nipples and spanked her bottom. "Oh, yes. I have been naughty. I do need to be punished." She half turned, face enraptured.

He scanned the crowd. Craven stood with a buxom blonde on his arm. Hell, he wanted to break Craven's nose. No sign of Barrett, Craven's partner.

And, damn, Robert was there—he saw the back of his cousin's head, candlelight touching the curls as black as his own. A man stood beside him, a man who drew pensively on his cheroot—Jack Tate, the gaming hell proprietor who owed him twenty thousand pounds.

A woman walked forward, dressed in only a dyed-black corset and Hessians tailored to fit her shapely legs. The Queen of Dark Pleasure. She wore a mask, of course, with feathers of purple, the face encrusted with diamonds. Her lips were smeared with creamy crimson paint, her smile superior and cruel. A towering powdered wig disguised her hair.

Many speculated she was the Dowager Duchess of Derby.

All around him, the waiting women caught their breath. The Queen flicked the whip, sending the tail snapping against the stone flags on the floor. All jumped. One woman squealed.

The victim, the auburn woman, tipped her head back, letting her curls spill down to her lower back. She then bent forward, exposing the line of her spine. Her hands fisted, and she betrayed herself with a flinch that sent the chains rattling.

Though he'd been in the same position himself, naked and spread-eagled, he had to fight the urge to free the auburn girl. He knew he could tolerate any pain, any torture—he had before. But a delicate, innocent, trusting woman . . .

He saw them then. A woman with a robe tossed around her, loose and flowing. A gentleman walked at her side, holding her hand and speaking in soothing tones.

Dash followed them back to the stairs.

"A thousand for your clue."

Startled, the man paused and halted his lady, who held the robe and gaped. The woman gave a small gasp, a flutter of her lashes.

Had he made love to her one night? He couldn't remember. He did recognize the man now. Viscount Braxton.

Braxton give a high-pitched laugh. "The prize is twenty thousand and a private harem trained in the erotic arts at Eden Manor."

Eden Manor was a notorious country estate. Rosalyn Rose ran the place and taught her girls not to shy away from any sexual game—no matter how perverse. Reputedly the girls were innocents when they began, from impoverished gentility, desperate enough to go willingly to their fates. These were prostitutes who could not be purchased for money. Rosalyn knew her trade—she had made this "harem" exclusive and legendary.

Did it mean Rosalyn was involved in the disappearances of the Lady F and the other? Dash's throat knotted as he remembered that Eden Manor was only a dozen miles north of his family seat.

"But you have to win to claim the twenty." Coolly Dash let his tone remind Braxton that he would likely not win. "But I will pay five."

The girl trembled. Her back must be stinging and raw. Her eyes spoke volumes, yet she dutifully did not speak.

"Five, eh?"

Braxton was in dun territory, close to having his credit refused.

With a shrug, Braxton pulled a card from a breast pocket.

"What does this mean?" Frowning, Maryanne again read the four-line clue.

Ascend to heaven to find true delight
But as you each take on orgasmic flight, you must remember to hold on tight.
The clue will be won if lovers find the position that lets them soar
And below, serpent's river and thundering horse will hear the roar.

"You truly only paid for this—you didn't do those things?"

"No, sweetheart. No whippings. No clever tongues pleasuring my arse."

She knew her cheeks were flaming. "How much did it cost you?"

"Enough, love." Swansborough lounged on the chaise again. His eyes were shut, his long legs sprawled off the end of the ivory silk cushions.

"How does one ascend to heaven?"

"One comes, love."

"There must be more to the clue than that." Suddenly Maryanne realized she had spoken to him the way she would to her sisters. She had forgotten who he was, his status, his station. Quickly she added, "My lord."

He laid his hands on his chest, fingers entwined. Black curls peeked out in the open vee of his white shirt.

"To what would you hold on tight . . . ?" she mused.

"In orgasmic flight? Depending on the position, your lovely

plump tits, your sweet derriere, your slim ankles . . . ah, I could go on."

"You are not helping." But her quim grew wet at his words, and her heart lurched at the way he teased her. They were strangers, yet making love had somehow made them friends—

"Serpent's river," he muttered. "That could be the Serpentine. Which fits with 'thundering horse.' I've raced horses in Hyde Park. But what about ascend? To go up. To fly. To—"

"Balloon ascension!" Maryanne cried. In London, they had all gone to see one in a park. "Goodness, people are going to make love in a balloon?"

4

Torches burned in a ring, flickering in the summer's breeze, licking at the dark sky. At this time of night, Hyde Park was quiet, and, of course, at this time of year, many of the *haute volée* were not in town.

The flames crackled softly, sending a smoky, warm scent into the gently roiling air.

Maryanne gazed upward at the taut ropes illuminated by the soft light. The bottom of the enormous balloon could be seen, gaudily patterned, but the top disappeared into the star-flecked darkness. The woven basket beneath looked precarious and impossibly small.

She faltered. She couldn't go up in the air in that!

Lord Swansborough's fingers cupped her elbow. Sandalwood surrounded, tempted. "We appear to be the only couple here." A soft rumble by her ear, his voice buoyed her courage. Yet they were not really a couple. Not really partners.

"You needn't have come with me. I could have taken a hackney myself."

His hand released, then slid around, and he held her the way a man held a dockside tart, with hand locked around her waist, and her body snuggled tight against him.

"You, at least, I can protect, love." His voice was low yet intense. A deep, dangerous sound.

Did she want his protection? Did she want a partner?

Georgiana, her partner in publishing, caused her nothing but trouble—had brought her into this dangerous game. And her mother had once believed Rodesson would stand at her side as the most intimate partner—husband. Her mother had been left to rely on herself.

The torchlight lit up the faces of the men attending the balloon. Red-gold light caught a beaked nose, a hollowed cheek, even the scarring of a man who'd lost an eye. They looked like demons in Hades, drinking and smoking, laughing raunchily in the quiet park.

Was Georgiana here in the park? Had these men seen her?

And below, serpent's river and thundering horse will hear the roar, the riddle read.

Maryanne stopped, and Swansborough halted with her. His aristocratic face gazed down in concern. Painted by golden firelight, he was utterly breathtaking—his face a sculpture of sharp cheekbones and firm, sensuous lips. Darkly shadowed, his eyes reflected both silver moonlight and bright torchlight.

"Gentlemen usually ride in the early morning, don't they?" she asked. "Doesn't that mean we will have to wait? Aren't there supposed to be thundering horses?"

"We will see. Your madam might already be there."

"Georgiana is not my madam. She is my . . ." She could not say *partner*, not without piquing his interest, prompting questions she didn't want to answer. "My friend."

"Friend," he repeated. His lips lifted in a smile. "And you hesitated a very long time."

"Why are you not like other drunk gentlemen?" What foxed man would listen so intently to her conversation? What sober man, for that matter? "Any other man would have fallen asleep by now."

"Well acquainted with drunk men, Verity?" He sounded amused, but with his face in shadow, she couldn't be certain.

"As most women are." Which was true. Any woman who spent time around men, even in a country setting, in the most innocent of contact, would become acquainted with foxed men.

"You are very intriguing, Verity. Most women would be wondering what they could obtain from me. We made love, after all. What did that mean to you?"

Everything. But she knew it meant nothing to him. It had been merely an amusement.

A rattle behind sent her heart hammering. She spun around as a curricle drew up and two grays tossed their heads. Long white plumes waved on a lady's bonnet, and Maryanne felt both hope and fear. The lady was clad entirely in silver and white. Georgiana did that on occasion. Who was the gentleman driving the carriage—was he a threat?

But as the tall gentleman, attired in a heavy, three-tiered greatcoat, jumped down, Swansborough murmured, "Lady Yardley and the Duke of Ashton."

Lady Yardley waved a greeting at Swansborough. "Dear Lancelot! Have you completed the task?"

Lancelot?

Maryanne gaped as he released her waist and swept a bow for the Countess of Yardley. "Not yet, my dear Sophia."

The countess smiled wickedly and toyed with a silvery blond curl. Though she was not young, she was exquisitely lovely, and her lines gave fascinating character to a charming face. She was compelling, seductive, alluring.

Her soft, melodic laughter was enticingly feminine. "It looks treacherous."

"Only for the intrepid," Swansborough agreed, and Maryanne felt him direct her toward the balloon with a gentle push on her bottom. She swallowed shock—they'd made love. How could she be startled by a caress on her clothed derriere?

Maryanne's chest tightened. She took a deep breath, remembering the feel of Swansborough's hot, wide back as her hands had skimmed over it. Remembering the scent of his skin, the taste of his neck . . .

Her heart ached at the thought of other women touching

him that way. It had been everything to her. It hadn't mattered to him.

"Are you all right, love?" Deep and concerned, Swansborough's voice cut through her horrified thoughts.

She fought for calm. "Lancelot?" she asked. A pet name from a lover, perhaps? How could she, untutored and country bred, compete with such a beautiful woman? Of course, she couldn't—and she wouldn't be. She was his partner for this night—this one night.

Swallowing hard, she realized the truth. That might have been her one chance to make love. She couldn't marry now—which was what she'd wanted, of course—but now the realization stunned her. She couldn't take lovers—that could cause scandal, and she didn't dare hurt her mother, her sisters, and Venetia's coming child with scandal.

Her heart was pounding into the silence. He didn't answer, so she pressed. "Why Lancelot? Confide."

"Verity wants truth, of course." They'd reached the circle of torches, where the smoke was thick and sweet, and the light showed his wry grin.

What woman could resist that slightly self-mocking smile? It made Maryanne's legs turn to treacle.

"It's my name," he admitted. "Dashiel Lancelot Blackmore. Dashiel was my father's choice, a family name, to him a sign of longevity. Lancelot was my mother's flighty wish."

She nodded in understanding. Rodesson had bestowed Venetia's name upon her, but her mother had named both her and Grace, determined not to give in to romantic fancy.

Though she couldn't explain any of that, he smiled. "My father gritted his teeth every time he heard it," his lordship continued. "It amuses Sophia—Lady Yardley—to use it. She pretends I am a noble knight, which, of course, I am not. My sister's name is Anne Persephone—once again, my parents came to an odd compromise."

"Aren't you a noble knight?" she teased and marveled at her bravery. The few times she'd met Lord Swansborough, she'd managed an awkward curtsy but almost no conversation.

"No, sweetheart, don't fancy me to be Lancelot, because I'm not. I wish I could charge in and rescue damsels."

He moved away, and though the summer's breeze was warm and humid, she shivered at the loss of contact. He hailed one of the men, who lurched forward. Aware of the leering gazes of the other men, Maryanne fiddled with her mask. Push it up a bit? Bother—now she couldn't see. She slid it back down. Had she loosened the strings?

Groping behind her head, she stumbled into Lord Swansborough, who was now in low conversation with the man.

"Sorry, milord. I can't tell you naught unless you go up and perform. It's the rules, and they'd 'ave me hide if I cheat."

"All I need is information. I'm looking for a courtesan."

With a lecherous laugh, the man pointed to the basket. "Only enough room fer you and the one tart, milord. Along with our man Tanner who sees to the balloon. Threesome pleasures won't do in the basket."

"I'm seeking a blonde named Georgiana Watson. Brazen and voluptuous."

The man inclined his head—his hair was as dark as his lordship's beneath a brown cap, his skin swarthy, and he wore a red kerchief at his neck. "Ye'll have to go up, milord."

"And make love with my lady up there?"

A chortle was the answer, and Maryanne took a deep breath. The sky was a blend of deep cobalt blue and rich violet, and pink touched the edge of the trees. "The balloon goes up in the dark?"

"Aye, lass, it can." The balloon tender's baritone was gentle and respectful as he spoke to her, which surprised. But then *Lady Yardley* was taking part in this event. Perhaps, as Maryanne was masked, the balloon man thought she was a lady, like Lady Yardley. "You'll be tethered. We let it rise, you complete yer task, and ye're brought down."

Swansborough drew something from his pocket—a pouch, and from that he drew notes. "For your information."

But the balloon tender shook his head, with a look of pained regret.

A young man with bronzed skin and gleaming white teeth, doffed his cap, winked, and bowed. He must be the man who controlled the balloon. Maryanne swallowed hard. How could she make love in front of a stranger?

But what if Georgiana was in danger?

"Then we'll go up now."

"I can't!" She backed away, staring at the bright balloon, trim fluttering in the breeze, and the flame beneath, stark and golden against the dark.

Swansborough swept his arm about her shoulders and turned her away from the sight. "Why not? Afraid of heights?"

"I can't . . . Not in front of . . ." She faltered. A courtesan wouldn't mind—in the stories she edited, courtesans delighted in having two men at once, for most men preferred a lady to make a threesome and not a competitive cock. Had she revealed herself?

Dark and searching, his eyes captured hers. "You truly are a novice, aren't you?"

An escape! She nodded so hard her curls struck her cheeks.

"Then we go up alone."

The man scratched his dark-stubbled cheek. "Tanner's needed to fire the flame and to vent the balloon to bring it down—"

Lord Swansborough silenced him with a wave of his black-gloved hand. "I've seen balloon ascensions and have an idea how it works. Have Tanner explain it."

"Aye, milord, but we have to witness that the couple carries out the act."

Swansborough gave a jaded shrug. "You'll know."

As he strolled over to Tanner and then followed the young man's directions, his lordship's eyes gleamed with boyish enthusiasm. He tugged at ropes, fiddled with the fire, chatting amiably to Tanner all the while. Maryanne crossed her arms before her chest. He seemed more fascinated by the art of ballooning than with the thought of making love.

She strained to see into the dark—but saw no sign of Georgiana.

Suddenly his lordship was at her side. "All right, love. We're ready."

Maryanne watched her raven-haired Lancelot elegantly climb into the basket. Of course, he could do it easily—he had endless legs and wore trousers. Just as she stared helplessly at it, he scooped her effortlessly into his arms. In a froth of hems and petticoats, she was hoisted over the wicker wall and into the basket. As her feet touched the floor of the basket, it came up to meet her. "Ooh!"

The flame illuminated the sculpted planes of his face, his wicked grin as the balloon went up. The basket tilted to the right. She clutched the side. "Goodness."

Swansborough laughed. "But as you each take on orgasmic flight, you must remember to hold on tight," he quoted. He wrapped a hand around the stays that secured their small basket to the enormous balloon and kept the other near the fire box and the ropes that worked the vents. Below, illuminated by the torches, she saw the men gripping the tether ropes, feeding them through gloved hands.

A lurch to the left, and she tumbled back against his lordship. His large body pressed against her, his arm locked around her waist, and she felt safe—though if the basket tipped, they'd both fall. Why should the thought of falling to their deaths together, sharing disaster, make her feel better?

"Magnificent, isn't it?"

With her hands gripping the basket, she stared down.

Far below, the torches looked like tiny candle flames, and she could no longer see the men. Men who thought she was going to rut with a viscount here. Men who thought her a courtesan.

Don't think of that.

The Serpentine caught the moonlight, water rippling in the sweet breeze. Dark trees bobbed and swayed, the leaves silver, and the park was a stretch of dark velvet.

She gazed up. Stars dotted the violet skies above the park. And London's lights were spread out before her. "It's beautiful." The basket swayed. "And terrifying."

His mouth touched her neck, a brush of heat, and she squealed in surprise. Her giggle made her blush—girlish and thoughtless. His hand skimmed up to her breasts as his lips skated over her nape. Delicious sensation rushed over her skin.

This was truly flying. She felt as though she floated on air—weightless. But she didn't dare let go of the basket.

Out of the corner of her eye, she saw him tug a rope, and the basket dropped a startling few inches.

"The clue will be won if lovers find the position that lets them soar," he whispered.

"I know." She spoke to the whole of London, laid out before her, and to the stars that seemed so close she could gather them if she dared to reach. "I don't dare move."

He curled his long, elegant fingers around her left breast, lazily stroking the curve beneath, where her heart hammered. "I won't let you fall."

"Lord Swansborough, that is a promise you cannot make."

His thumb, gently stroking her nipple, stilled.

"We will hold on together," she whispered, half turning. He stood so close her cheek brushed his, his stubble rasped lightly against her skin.

He let go long enough to sweep his arm across Hyde Park, and Mayfair, and London's vistas. The balloon basket jerked, and she swallowed another squeal.

His voice growled beside her ear. "Verity, you are more magnificent than all of that."

In an instant her skirts were up, her legs bared in front of

London, but they were in their private world, far above Mayfair. She loved the thought of being in public yet being utterly private and free. Her skirts spilled down in the front, pooling on the rim of the basket. His hands caressed her thighs, her bottom, coaxed her to take tiny steps to part her legs. "We cannot."

"But you want to, don't you?"

How she did.

Magic coursed through her skin, a spell of desire cast by his powerful fingers crooking into her wet cunny, by his harsh, heated breath coasting over her neck.

"If you came here seeking Georgiana, you are a woman who doesn't fear risk. Yet you are too shy to have a man watch us."

She froze. Did her every action reveal her character? He was still trying to decipher her identity, she was certain of it. Why? Why couldn't he just discount her as another lightskirt?

Because she wasn't behaving like a lightskirt.

But even if Swansborough guessed she wasn't a jade, he thought her a fearless rescuer—he'd never realize she was Maryanne Hamilton, shy and retiring bookworm.

"The only risk here," he continued in a honeyed growl that spoke of sin and temptation, "is trust."

Trust! She couldn't trust him—he was a notorious rake, a man so thoroughly debauched it was rumored he had never spent a night alone. He couldn't trust her, after all—he didn't even know who she really was. And she'd already dropped him into trouble. Marcus would have Lord Swansborough's ballocks if he learned she'd surrendered her virginity.

"You have the most luscious and tempting derriere." Swansborough released her waist, grabbed the stays and dropped to his knees. The floor of the basket almost dropped out beneath her.

"What are you doing?"

Before her stomach stopped its flip-flops, she knew. A hot

kiss teased the skin of her rump. Suspended in a balloon above Hyde Park, he kissed and licked the cheeks of her bottom.

"You must stop." Though she wanted him to do this forever. "We'll fall."

The balloon dropped a little as if in answer.

He stopped his kiss long enough to promise, "We are perfectly balanced, love."

She wished she could trust him on that. They rose again, and she went rigid. "How far will they let us go up?" With the startling view, she could see the threat of sunrise, the warm pink and gold of dawn just touching the horizon.

Dawn. She would have to get home. Someone might come into her bedchamber and discover she had disappeared for the night.

But she hadn't found Georgiana. She couldn't flee yet.

She was high in the air in a balloon with Lord Swansborough. She couldn't flee at all.

She should stop him, but what did it matter now? Her barrier was broken and couldn't be mended.

"I've no idea how far they will let us go." Hot, solid, lean, and long limbed, his body pressed along hers as he stood again. He used the fire to heat the air again, and they rose. Just as her heart lurched up with the balloon, his hand slid between their bodies. Something hot and hard bumped her bottom. His cock. She arched back, stroking her warm, naked rump against his length.

His hand moved between her thighs, parting her hot nether lips. She was soaked still from their lovemaking, bubbling with her creamy juices and his.

"I'm going to slide my cock into your snug cunny."

"But is this the correct . . . position?"

"Ah, love, would you be willing to move into another one?"

He was laughing at her, but she couldn't resist joining him. "No."

Thick, hot, his cock slid between her legs, and she choked

on her laugh. Good lord, he was enormous. He sawed the massive thing between her thighs, the broad head nosing through the lips, the shaft rubbing her aroused clit.

"Go inside me," she whispered. "I need you inside."

"Yes," he groaned.

In a burst of bravery, she let go of the basket and guided his cock into her. Her fingers barely closed around the full shaft, and with a whimper, she stirred her passage with the head. She took charge, tipped her hips, and took him in. How she loved this, the first slow thrusts. His body, controlled and graceful, arched forward. She moved back, seeking his rhythm, moving slowly and carefully. She was slick now, opening so easily for him, welcoming his cock inside.

She clutched the basket again and it jostled as he pumped into her. Fear lurched inside her, but she was hot and wet and loving this so.

Madness! Delirious madness.

His groin smacked against her bottom; the head of his cock bumped her womb. Her cheeks vibrated with each slam of his lean hips. Pleasure rippled through her from each thump, and she thrust back as hard as he pounded forward. The basket rocked precariously, and shouts below warned that the men had to strain to hold the ropes—he'd forgotten to control the balloon.

She didn't care.

Never had she imagined anything like this.

This was soaring.

Powerful strokes lifted her onto her tiptoes as he thrust his cock deep inside her. Expertly he shifted his hips on each plunge, changing angle, making her gasp as fire-hot delight roared through her.

Her clit ached like a slippery trigger. Did she dare—?

It meant trusting him completely, for she wasn't holding on, but she unfurled her fingers from the braided wicker rim. She touched her clit—just as his fingers slid there.

"Yes," he groaned. "Let me hold you while you play with yourself."

His hoarse command sent a spike of delicious agony through her legs as she stroked her own clit. Gently at first, to draw out the exquisite pleasure. Her hand between her thighs made him pant hard as he watched her. Out of the corner of her eye, she saw him open the vent, controlling the balloon while making love to her.

She arched her rear back, wild and wanton. She had to widen her legs to push back against his hard, incredible power.

Oh, heavens, it made him go so deep.

"Rub yourself now, sweetheart. I want to feel you come around my prick."

Men were blunt and forthright while they fucked. It was just as her courtesan authors' books described. Men didn't waste time making pretty claims of love; they gave directions to their women on how to be erotic and enticing.

What would he think if she did such a thing? "Touch me, too," she whispered. "I want you to touch my clit."

"God—" He groaned sharply. His long fingers nudged hers aside, his touch so different than hers. The feel of his hands there was pleasure unsurpassed.

"Harder," she directed. "I like that."

"As do I." His hips sped up again, and his fingers rasped her, igniting pleasure. Blending strokes—the wild thrusts of his big cock; the slow, sensuous touch of his fingers. Tension wound in her, and she sought it, grinding clit against fingers and derriere against hard, male abdomen.

"Come now," he murmured in a hoarse baritone that excited as much as his touch. "Come for me."

He was close—she knew that in the tightness of his voice. He wanted her to climax first; he was holding on to his control to please her. She was making it impossible for him to hold on.

The thought of that—

With him—

She rubbed hard against his hand, and pleasure burst inside. Her cunny clenched around him, pulsating. Her eyes closed as she tumbled into delight. He knew, of course, and let go of the ropes to caress her sensitive breasts. Her nipples . . . oh, yes. He plucked them, and she arched.

"Be merciless," Maryanne hissed, for it was so good.

He laughed, drawing his cock back, and he pumped again.

Her cries spilled out into the night sky and flew out over London. Her screams shattered the quiet of the park—below came male laughter, and then cheers.

She should be shocked. Embarrassed. But she was still rocking with her climax.

Dash knew he couldn't last longer, and the basket jerked as he grabbed the stays again and braced to fuck hard. Verity was tight and wet and still coming around him, and her screams were loud enough to wake slumbering London.

Raucous shouts of congratulations came from below, but he ignored them. He never let another man's chants urge him, affect him. This wasn't a competition or sport, this was blessed heaven—he focused solely on fucking, and his reward was escape from pain.

Her bottom was slick with their sweat and juices. It would be rubbed raw from the rough hair on his groin, but she was urging him. "Hard and deep. Yes!"

One more . . . just once more and he could surrender.

"Oh!"

The signal he could let go. His orgasm exploded inside, ripping through his brain, shooting down his back, roaring from his balls. God, it took him so ferociously he almost stumbled. His eyes shut, his face contorted in agony, and his body bucked as his seed shot out.

Deep into his luscious Verity.

He felt the jerk of the basket, the fight of the balloon—it tossed them about.

He wrapped one arm tight around Verity and moved his hips back. On a flood of hot juices, his cock slid out.

"What is happening?"

"They are lowering us, love. We've completed the task."

Even after two passionate climaxes, her mask was in place, keeping her a secret. She possessed an air of innocence—she was most definitely an ingenue but not untutored. And even the most willing virgin knew to barter that precious barrier.

So why had he never encountered her before?

Dash opened the vent, leaned over the edge of the basket, and saw the torches come closer. The basket shuddered, swayed, and his gut jerked with the motion. Christ Jesus, his head swam and began to pound again.

He had to stay focused. He had to discover who had been here. And he had to control the blasted balloon as they descended.

Verity was a warm bundle in the crook of his arm, her heartbeat pounding deliciously against his palm. Alive. Still recovering from the little death. Her scent was rich with sex aroma now, but he still caught the trace of demure lavender. A simple perfume, when most courtesans used exotic brews to entice.

He wanted to push everything aside and delve into the mystery of Verity.

He wanted to forget about that night when he had let his cousin Simon die—when he had been blind and soulless with rage and had let an innocent man die.

Dash saw the ring of men in torchlight and realized Verity was trying to smooth down her skirts. Beneath his hand, he felt her heart speed up; it was now fluttering inside her chest. She was truly frightened. Perhaps she feared the other men would want her now? If it frightened her, he wouldn't allow it.

"Easy," he murmured by her delicate ear. "I won't let harm come to you."

They were close enough to see the men's laughing, leering

faces. The gypsy's face was like reflective bronze, dark eyes alight with admiration. "Congratulations, my lord. Madam. In truth I didn't think it could be done."

"Blast, you mean we're the first?" Dash asked as young Tanner swung into the basket to replace him at the flame.

"Aye, that you are," the balloon tender answered. "You and her ladyship"—he jerked his head toward Sophia, who sat in her carriage giggling with Ashton—"are well ahead of the pack."

Dash stared thoughtfully at Ashton. Did the duke still hold a grudge over the time he'd shot Ashton's leg in a duel? The duke looked interested mainly in nuzzling the swells of Sophia's breasts.

"The blond courtesan—was she here?" he asked.

"No, my lord."

Dash drew a bundle of notes from his pocket and allowed only the gypsy to see them. He eased them back into place. "I believe I am to receive a clue?"

With his arm around Verity's waist, he lifted her out of the basket. Poor sweet—she held tight to the basket and gave a sigh of relief as her slippers touched earth. He took her hand and led her back toward his carriage. The gypsy, as he'd hoped, followed.

The other men restrained the balloon as Sophia swept down from her lover's carriage to experience what had been Dash's most unusual setting for lovemaking.

"Who employs you?" he asked the gypsy. "I want the name of the man who pays you and where he can be found."

"Mr. Phibbs." The gypsy rattled off an address in the City.

"What is he like, this Phibbs?"

"Slight and pale. Wears spectacles. A rabbit, milord."

"So I expected. And who employs him?"

"I don't know, milord. Not my business to know. And here is your clue, milord."

As the card was thrust at his hand, Dash slipped a few notes to the gypsy. Tipping his cap, the swarthy man turned and sauntered back to the scene at the basket. Sophia was laughing with delight, lifting her skirts to climb aboard.

Verity was nibbling her lower lip. "She must be in trouble. Why else would she not be here?"

"Because she's on her back with a lover? I've never known Georgiana Watson to claim a friend amongst the female sex. I wonder what exactly she had planned for you."

"What do you mean?" Fire flashed in her eyes, dark and mysterious behind the mask.

He leaned close, wrapping himself in her scent—simple and pretty and combined with the earthy smell of sex. A feminine allure that provoked his libido, even in his sated, exhausted state.

A wave of his hand brought his carriage forward, horses snorting, traces ringing melodically as hooves clattered on gravel. Impulsively he tipped up Verity's chin, held the point of it between thumb and forefinger. "Come home with me—for an hour or two. I don't want our night to be over yet. I'll tell you then."

5

"Remove your mask, love." Lord Swansborough dropped his black tailcoat to the floor. His waistcoat followed.

Her mask! She didn't dare take it off.

Maryanne took an unsteady breath, still shocked to look around and think *I am in his lordship's bedchamber watching him undress. . . .*

What had she done?

She had agreed to come to his home. He had asked, his dark eyes had been so intense, and she had lost her head.

He wanted her to stay.

He could not bear to let her go.

She had thought those mad things and had said yes.

"Your mask," he prompted as he pulled down his trousers. With a smile, he fell back on the bed and sprawled on his soft, white sheets. His long legs were splayed, the lightly tanned skin and dark hairs a startling contrast to the silky white. His hand lazily stroked his half-erect cock, his thick, dark curls. "No secrets between us, Verity."

"But isn't the truth dangerous, my lord?" She was stalling and let her gaze dart desperately around his room. Draped in soft velvet curtains of black tied with crimson ribbons, his bed looked as if it belonged to Lucifer. Thick crimson drapes hung at the windows. The firelight cast a cozy, reassuring glow and kept the room wonderfully warm, but she felt ice cold. He could, if he wished, tear off her mask. She would be unable to stop him.

"And you told me you weren't dangerous," he teased.

She turned away and almost collapsed. His room held a secretary, but instead of pens, a blotter, and correspondence, the ornate piece held coils of silken ropes, gleaming lengths of silver chains, and slender ivory rods very like the one he had used in her bottom.

Never would she dream of touching such intimate things, but it gave her an excuse to avoid his request. She strolled to the desk, though her legs trembled beneath her skirts. She picked up a length of black silk, obviously used to tie up one partner for carnal pleasures.

"All right. But you must close your eyes and allow me to prepare."

"I trust you, sweet."

She turned to find his eyes closed, and her heart dropped to her toes. How adorable he looked, lips curved in a smile, thick black lashes lying on his cheeks.

As soundlessly as she could, she approached, the length of black silk held taut between her hands. She held it over his lovely closed eyes. Heat flooded her at the result. At the black mask that highlighted his autocratic features and tempting mouth.

Her cunny grew wet and aching at the sight.

She lowered the cloth.

He jerked as the silk landed on his eyes, then lay still. Trusting. He laughed. "Clever woman. So you will remove your mask because you have blindfolded me."

Maryanne nodded and then realized he could not see. "Yes." Would he agree to it?

"Since you outwitted me, I have no choice but to acquiesce, love. But tell me, is your identity such a secret? You can trust my discretion."

Yes, and she could also trust he would be shocked and horrified to learn whom he'd deflowered. He and Marcus were friends.

He levered up onto his arms, then sat up, and she had to scramble to keep the strip of silk in place. Would he trick her? She'd grown up with two sisters, after all—she knew to trust his honor but not to think him above deception.

A quick knot at the back within his raven hair secured the black silk blindfold. She held her hands an inch above his shoulders, moved to lower them, but stopped. Did she dare touch as she wanted to? Those shoulders made a straight line of smooth skin, tinted gold with firelight. Glinting light skimmed over fine hairs, bronzed skin.

Holding her breath, she touched her fingertips to the edges of his shoulders, touched hot, satiny skin. She had to stretch her arms wide to do it. Solid and powerful, his muscles flexed beneath her touch.

Flattening her hand, she coasted her hands down over the large muscles that defined the broad, tapering vee of his back. A jolt of sensual agony hit her belly, weakened her legs.

He groaned softly and half turned, so the light danced on his profile, made exotic by the blindfold. "What do you plan to do to me, my sweet?"

She crawled onto the bed, still wearing her rumpled gown. Tentatively she traced the line of his spine, down, down to the sweet hollow of his low back. Just before the tempting cheeks of his rump.

"I don't know." And she truly didn't. "Doesn't it make you nervous because you cannot see?"

"No, sweetheart. I can concentrate on everything else. The enticing pleasure of your warm, erotic touch. The scent of you—and I can still smell my scent on you, love."

So could she. And it meant every breath aroused her.

"Mmmm." He sighed. "And I love the sound of your breathing—how quick it became as you stroked down to my arse."

Trembling, she touched down there again. Let her fingers dip into the valley of his bottom. A glance over his shoulders showed his cock slowly growing.

"Your mask, love. Our bargain was that you would take it off."

"We didn't actually make a *bargain*, my lord—"

"I thought we did." He spoke with aristocratic command.

Hesitantly she reached for the ties behind her head. "And you will not remove yours."

"On my honor."

She dropped her mask into his outstretched right hand. He frowned. "So you do trust me, Verity?"

He was blindfolded. It gave her remarkable freedom. She would touch where she wished—explore his tight, hard buttocks or climb about and play with that intriguing cock and his furred balls. Strange that because he couldn't see her, she felt so much more brave.

"Did you truly let a woman drip wax on your chest?"

He laughed and let her mask dangle from the strings. "Does all of England know that story?"

"But did you?"

"Yes."

"Why?"

"Sweetheart, the very reason you are asking the question is the answer. It fascinates and frightens you, doesn't it? You think it madness but it stirs you at the same time."

"No, I simply think it madness."

He twisted beneath her hands, caught hold of her arms, and tumbled her down to the bed. How he moved so quickly, she didn't know, but he had her pinned. "Take off your gown, my love. Sleep with me."

Sleep with him?

She couldn't.

He rolled her onto her tummy. Heavenly to be caught between his hard, naked body and the soft, freshly scented sheets and mattress. Her lids flickered. She was indeed tired.

But she couldn't fall asleep. She didn't dare.

By feel, he was undoing the buttons of her gown, loosening it. He certainly had an adept touch with women's clothing.

She couldn't leave now, though. He might insist she used a carriage; and even if she summoned a hackney, how could she leave without revealing where she wanted to go? And she could hardly tell him she lived close enough to his house to walk!

Her corset dug into her, her gown an uncomfortable tangle of skirts and sleeves. It felt so good to help him to strip it off. Her fingers bumped his long, strong ones. He grinned at her, even though he couldn't see.

"Too drunk and tired to get hard enough again," he admitted.

A glance down showed his reluctant statement to be true. His shaft had softened, as if slumbering itself, lying along the sensuous join of thigh and groin.

He gave a yawn that made her giggle.

"But one last taste of your cunny before we sleep."

Even though blindfolded, he parted her legs with an expert's ease and bent to her quim. Perhaps he actually could see?

But he bumped his nose to her pubis and muttered, "Blast."

Before she could let her nervous laugh escape, he lay between her thighs and kissed her vulva. His tongue slicked out.

She should try to escape.

Oh, but not now.

It astonished how quickly she relaxed beneath him. She knew to trust his touch, knew to let him pleasure her. But still, she did shift her hips just a bit . . . because she wanted that wet, firm tongue to hit just . . .

Oh, yes. *There*. . . .

She arched to him, lifting in the rhythm she wanted, and without even a word between them, he knew. He stroked her clit with his tongue.

Tension built, tightening her muscles. She gripped her breasts, hard, needing to squeeze, to roughly knead.

She pinched her nipples, pinched hard, pulled on them as his tongue licked her clit with hot, velvety strokes.

He stopped to promise, "I could do this for hours, love. Taste you. Enjoy you."

Desire and panic exploded in her chest. That sounded like heaven. In her authors' books, some gentlemen did not even do this to their ladies, preferring instead to have the women pleasure them with lips and tongue. Lord Swansborough appeared to take great pleasure in it. She felt him chuckle against her nether lips, and a blush hit her cheeks.

But she couldn't stay in his bed for hours!

"Play with your breasts," he urged. "Pleasure yourself."

In the stories she read, jaded courtesans made knowing jokes about gentlemen who thrust their tongues in a lady's passage and assumed it would make her come.

His lordship's tongue filled her cunny, sliding inside. She gasped at the luscious sensation, the ripple against her snug walls.

She clutched silken sheets, dug her heels into the downy soft mattress. She met the thrusts of his tongue.

But the authors were correct—this was so wonderfully intimate, so deliciously good, but not quite—

He moved. His warm mouth covered her pulsing, swollen, eager clit. As his mouth suckled, his fingers slid inside. Two fingers opening to fill her passage. One finger gently teasing the puckered rim of her anus.

Her climax was a delicious wave of pleasure, like biting a chocolate to discover a sweet, melting, sticky filling. It was no sudden burst but just a gentle wash of delight.

She gasped with it. Cried out with it. Surrendered to it.

Her every muscle relaxed, and his bed felt like the balloon's basket, dancing on soft currents of air. She closed her eyes, now immersed in the dark like he, reached for his soft hair, and filled her senses. Savored the silky beauty of his hair, the scent of his sweat and her juices, even the taste of her perspiration, salty drops on her upper lip.

"I do love a woman who doesn't just lie there. Who makes demands and knows what she wants."

That made her eyes open wide. She'd made demands? She certainly had succeeded in fooling him. Normally she was indistinguishable from wallpaper—with her mousy brown hair, ordinary brown eyes, and mousy manner.

But here with him . . . well, when she had felt her orgasm building, she'd become determined to reach it. She couldn't bear not to.

She didn't want him to think too much about who she was.

His lordship rose up over her.

Naked, she felt exposed, as though he'd guess from her form. But how would he? Maryanne Hamilton wore proper dresses—the only skin he'd glimpsed of hers had been her neck, her upper chest, the swell of her breasts, her arms, but nothing more. He couldn't possibly guess who she was from touch alone.

Still, she wanted to distract him.

And with him blindfolded, she wanted to explore.

His hand lifted—

Her heart stopped. "Don't peek!"

"An itch on my cheek." With a graceful motion of his long fingers, he scratched. How could his every movement be so enticing? So seductive?

"Now you," she whispered.

Even with the strip of black fabric over his eyes, she saw his surprise—in the arch of his brows, the crinkles in his forehead, the sweet lines bracketing his mouth.

His astonishment gave her the advantage, Maryanne thought as she pushed him onto his back.

Dash let himself fall back into the embracing softness of his bed. Verity clambered over his thighs. He knew what she wanted to do, and a rush of blood went to his cock, but not enough to make him respectably rigid. Her sticky nether lips brushed his leg, and he groaned.

He wanted to yank off the mask. Wanted to see Verity's slender body without a stitch. His imagination supplied a luscious picture—small, pert breasts that bobbed as she moved, a stretch of ivory belly, and slim, nubile legs.

As her wet, magical mouth took his cock inside, he knew the one advantage to being so damned exhausted he wasn't hard. She could take him deeply into her mouth, surrounding his prick with sensations that exploded in his mind.

He had never realized how erotic it would be to lose the sense of sight. He couldn't anticipate what she would do, what he would feel. Each lick of her tongue, each hard suck in her mouth took him by surprise.

"Do you know, I've never let a woman blindfold me before."

She stopped sucking, and he knew he should have kept his mouth shut.

"Never?" she asked. "Even though you've let them tie you up?"

"Never." He couldn't explain why that was one proof of trust he could never give. As a young man he had awoken to find a pistol pointed at his head one time, a knife at his throat another. Any woman who wished to cover his eyes raised an instinctive warning—*she's been paid to kill me.*

As for the bondage, he'd learned techniques to tense his body, then relax to allow ropes to loosen. He had never once been truly bound.

Why in blazes was he thinking this way when—

Christ Jesus! Her tongue lapped at the head of his cock. Then the bewitching woman paused again. "What do you like?"

"Licking. Sucking. I love my ballocks tongued and sucked."

His voice rasped from his throat. "Sweeting, any way you want to suck my cock, that's the way I want it."

Endearingly sweet, her giggle floated to his ears.

A giggle that cut off abruptly as her luscious mouth slid over his length again. Damn, he was thick and big now. She was taking him in only part way. But it was good . . . so incredibly good. . . .

Her quick, bobbling sucking had his cock swelling in her mouth. She clasped his balls, and his hips arched up. Hell, he'd asked her to do it, but he was on the precipice—tense, downright scared because he couldn't see what she was doing.

Eager sucking. Lush stroking of his balls.

"Sweeting—god, I'm going to—"

He fired prematurely. He'd intended to give her warning. Like a bolt of lightning, his orgasm shot through him, melting him.

In time with his pulsing release, her mouth milked him, and she took all his cum into her lovely mouth. He heard the soft sound of her swallowing.

"Sweetheart—"

Her weight settled on him. Silky curls brushed his right shoulder, his neck, his chest. He wrapped his arms around her lithe body and held her tight.

"Did you enjoy it?"

Such worry in her voice. "Surely you know I did, love."

"It's just . . . I've never done that."

"Never? What lightskirt has never sucked a man's cock?" Dash felt her stiffen at his words. Was her tension sexual arousal at the blunt expression? Or a different fear? He reached for the silk covering his eyes.

She clutched his wrists to hold his arms down. "The truth."

Cold gripped his heart. "The truth, then. Let's have it."

"I'm not a lightskirt. I'm a widow."

"A widow?"

"Yes, and of course a proper wife does not perform such indecent acts on her husband."

He had the distinct sense she was mocking someone, but he wasn't certain whom. "And you chose me as your first?"

"Y—yes."

"Who was your husband?"

"I mustn't say. A member of the country gentry. I dare not let it be known that I am in London, that I have done these scandalous things."

He heard the soft sigh—the sigh of relief. For finally giving him the truth. "Where are you staying?"

"I cannot tell you that either, of course."

"So how am I to send you home?"

"We'll worry about that later, my lord."

"Dash. Call me Dash, pet."

Maryanne could think of a thousand reasons why she should not. Such intimacy now could mean disaster later if she forgot herself. Dash . . . even more intimate than Dashiel. It occurred to her then that he had not recognized her voice, even though he had spent a few evenings in her presence. Well, a few minutes out of those evenings, but nonetheless . . .

Maryanne Hamilton had made no impression on him.

And, in truth, had Verity? Tomorrow night he would find a new partner, and that woman would share his wonderful bed.

"Lie down, sweet. You've been awake all night. You need to sleep."

"But what about Georgiana? You told me you would tell me about her."

"Georgiana would sell an innocent to the highest bidder, Verity. And how do you know Georgiana Watson?"

She swallowed hard.

"Now lie down, love."

She did as he asked, drew up the sheets. She couldn't help but sigh in pleasure as they settled against her sweaty, naked skin. His lordship lay on his side. Smiling, still blindfolded, he snuggled against her, and her heart gave a soft pang. His muscular arm lay across her tummy beneath the covers, as though he knew she wanted to run away and he wanted to keep her by his side.

Oh, how she wanted to sleep like this.

But she had to wait until he went to sleep. Trent House was so close . . . a little farther down Park Lane—it was safe enough to race there. Since her sister and brother-in-law spent their nights exploring sensual intimacy, they often slept late. At least her mother and sister Grace had stayed in the country after summer.

She closed her eyes. It was so easy to stay awake. Her heart tumbled about in her chest as she remembered every intimate thing he'd said. *Tomorrow night he will say those things to someone else.*

Had she failed Georgiana? Guilt sat in her belly, acrid and heavy. Or had Lord Swansborough—Dash—been correct? Had Georgiana, the wretch, gone in pursuit of an earl after putting her at risk?

Was Georgiana really in trouble? Was she in danger?

What was her next step?

Georgiana's house. Tomorrow, or rather today, she would have to slip away and try to get into her partner's home. Where else could she hope to find the name of the gentleman Georgiana had pursued?

His eyes opened to complete darkness.

Panic hit Dash first. The pounding of his head second. Christ, why couldn't he see? Brandy. He remembered it splashing into his mouth, down his chin.

He remembered the sweet, simple, erotic perfume of Verity.

So much for taking a peek at his mysterious partner, which had been his plan. He'd passed out asleep beside her.

He rolled onto his back. Fumbling, he reached for the silk that still swathed his eyes, caught it, and pushed it up. His sheets stretched out beside him, rumpled but empty. She'd left him.

Where had she gone? Hell, not to the next clue—it would be too late.

Now, a glance at his mantel clock told him it was after ten o'clock in the morning.

Groaning, Dash sat up.

His gaze fell on the folded sheet of paper that lay on his night table. A parting note from Verity? Then he remembered. Anne's letter. Anne's irritation. Dash reached for it, smiling even at the neat, crisp folds his sister had made. It was so good to know she was safe, now Lady Moredon. He owed Sophia the world for taking in Anne and protecting her. If his mad uncle had had the chance, he would have used Anne as a pawn.

Hell, it was long in the past. But he felt the cold grip of fear on his heart.

For reassurance, he opened Anne's letter and read it again in the daylight filtering through gaps in the drapes.

> *I do not want to come to London and subject myself to a physician's expertise. I shall be perfectly fine under the watchful eye of Mrs. Castle, the midwife. Really, you do fret too much. And it is far too late for me to journey to London. I can barely move.*
>
> *And Moredon is anticipating the hunt—he is quite concerned that his child is refusing to make an appearance and might delay his season. After all, heavens, his heir was expected a week ago. He is both concerned and elated that this shows his son will have a strong character. Of course, I believe this evidence of decided opinions indicates our child will be a girl. Though, as is expected, I do hope most sincerely for a boy, and then I shall*

> *not have to listen to much well-meaning advice on how one begets a boy.*
>
> *You must put your attentions to securing yourself a bride, my dearest brother, and filling a nursery of your own. I do think that is the solution, for then you will hardly have the time to be issuing orders to me. . . .*

He could almost hear her laughing as she wrote it, along with the unladylike snort she made when doubled up with mirth. She didn't understand. He'd spent his life concerned about Anne's protection, taking care of her. A man did not relinquish care of his family so easily.

Not even to the care of a good husband.

Would she write such lighthearted letters to him if she knew what he'd done? If she knew the truth? Would she forbid him from seeing his niece or nephew?

He would be an uncle, and the term *uncle* brought bile to his throat.

He still couldn't push aside the sight of Simon's dead face. The stunned expression, the glassy, lifeless eyes. Some perverse need to punish himself had driven Dash to stand in the distance as his cousin had been interred. And he had been haunted by the sight of his uncle's ashen face and sunken posture, strangely haunted by the fact that the man who had once terrified him was now weak and paralyzed by the shock of the loss of his eldest son. He hated his uncle, but he couldn't forgive himself for Simon's death. Ten years—thousands of nights of perverse sex and excessive drinking—and he still couldn't forget.

Dash stretched to reach the bellpull and tugged. Shut his eyes and relived that moment in Mrs. Master's salon. . . .

He'd thought Robert hadn't known exactly what happened to Simon. Then, at the salon last night, when Robert's hand had clamped down on his shoulder and Dash had turned to have the word *murderer* spat in his face, he'd thought justice might finally be done.

Robert, blistering drunk, should have challenged him to a duel last night. Dash had already been thinking ahead. What would he do? Fire into the air, spend his shot uselessly, and wait to see if his cousin's aim was true, if fate would mete out punishment?

Robert had tried to shake him, but he'd shrugged off his cousin's hand. "No more than your father," Dash had answered coolly, to Robert's accusation.

"Someday you'll pay." His cousin's voice had been shrill with drunken fury.

"For ten years, I already have." And he'd moved on, tense, waiting for the shout behind his back, waiting for anger and youthful pride to set them on a course that would end in his death.

But Robert had let him walk away.

He'd thought there were only two people who knew he had let Robert's older brother Simon walk into the death trap intended for him. Sir William and his uncle—the bloody fiend who had planned to kill him for the blasted title.

He could have stopped Simon. He could have shouted, "It's a trap. You aren't supposed to be here. Stop." But Dash had thought of his mistress, who had been cut with a blade and left to die. He'd thought of Anne. . . .

He'd known what would happen if he didn't die in his uncle's trap. His mistress had almost died in someone's failed attempt to kill him. Anne could be next. His sister's life had been at stake, and he was willing to do anything to protect Anne. Even let his innocent cousin die.

Dash jumped out of bed, landing on the cold floorboards, naked.

Verity. Last night, mysterious Verity had given him a night of pleasure, had helped keep his demons at bay. He hoped she hadn't gotten herself into trouble by slipping out of his house—London's streets could be deadly in the early morning.

At least she hadn't been paid to kill him.

Dash pushed back those thoughts.

Who was Verity? Who were her people? Was she a widow who had slipped out alone for a night of dangerous adventure? Why did she seem respectable, yet she claimed to be a friend of Georgiana Watson, who had served England's noblemen in various positions for more than twenty years?

At the knock on the door, he slid on his robe and shouted, "Enter." Expecting his valet, he was surprised to see a wide-eyed footman standing in the doorway.

"Sir William Kent is waiting in the blue drawing room, milord." The young man's eyes gleamed. "There's a rumor that a lady's body were found in Hyde Park this morn, milord."

"Christ Jesus!" Dash's shin slammed into his dresser as he spun. "Verity!"

6

"Where in blazes have you been?"

Maryanne clutched her cloak as the soft breeze ruffled its hem and fluttered the ties. She faced her sister squarely, though she tried desperately to look innocent. "I woke early and went for a stroll in the park. Foolish to go alone, I suppose, but it is so close, I thought there could be no—"

Arms folded across her chest, Venetia barred her escape to the scullery door. A dab of dark blue paint stood out on her sister's freckled nose. "You were out all night."

At least Venetia had kept her voice low. Where was her brother-in-law?

"Of course not." She'd had at least the presence of mind to rumple her bed before sneaking out the night before.

"Then you will not object to opening your cloak."

Bother! Was it pregnancy that had suddenly made Venetia as astute as their mother? Who was fortunately in the country.

"It's rather cold—" Maryanne began, but her sister tapped her booted foot.

The erotic novels she edited always glossed over the consequence of sexual adventure in the haste to move on to the next one.

"In my condition, I have to use the chamber pot frequently. Hourly." Venetia's brow tipped up as she lifted bare, paint-smeared fingers to brush away a curl. She yawned. "I am well aware you weren't in your bed all night."

Maryanne waited. She had no idea what to say. It was obvious what had happened—she'd ruined herself. She would wait and see what her punishment would be. After all, she now lived at her sister and Marcus's pleasure, thoroughly dependent on their compassion and generosity of spirit.

Venetia pursed her lips and waited, too. Maryanne could count the seconds with fevered heartbeats.

Finally Venetia sighed. "A letter arrived in the post for you."

She hadn't expected that. Georgiana! Terror took hold. "I suppose you read it."

Venetia put her hand to her heart in mock horror. "You were not in the house—you could have been dead at the hands of a cutpurse, for all I knew. Of course I read it."

"And what did it say?"

Slipping her hand into her practical skirt pocket, Venetia pulled out the folded sheet.

Maryanne scanned the few lines of Georgiana's letter.

> *All has worked for the best. The earl has taken care of some of the bothersome issues with finances. I could not slip away last night. If you went, you are the dearest, most loyal friend. I am sure you fared well. Sleep with ease, my dear, I have solved all our problems. But as I must leave London now for the country, you must take care of things with the help of the capable Mr. Osbourne, the man of affairs I have hired—*

"And what problems might you share with a notorious courtesan?"

"A lack of good modistes?" Even as the words escaped her

lips, Maryanne couldn't believe she'd uttered them. She was provoking her sister—she never provoked anyone.

It had been her night with Lord Swansborough. She had emerged as an entirely different person. A person who was tired of being mistaken for wallpaper. And Georgiana's note had left her in turmoil, her heart pounding. She had gone to slay dragons to protect a friend, and it had been exactly as Dash—Lord Swansborough—had said.

Georgiana had begged for her help, then had forgotten her in an instant. *Forgotten her*. Hadn't cared one whit about her. Some earl—possibly Craven or even someone else—had crooked his fingers and her friend had not even thought enough to send a note.

A cold, sick tightness gripped Maryanne's stomach and twisted it.

Her sister cared. She was pushing away Venetia, who did care, because she'd risked everything for beastly Georgiana, who didn't.

This time, when Georgiana returned with bitter tears, she wouldn't care. She was finished with her friend. Finished.

"I'm sorry," Maryanne whispered. "You deserve the truth."

Firm hands caught hold of her shoulders. Maryanne let Venetia turn her and let her slipper-clad feet coast over the cobbles to the bench.

"I might deserve it." Venetia's voice held rueful mirth. "Whether I am prepared for it, I am not entirely certain."

How did one explain a particularly awkward truth? Maryanne sank to the seat and covered her face with her hands. At this moment, fading into the wallpaper would be an advantage. Through slightly parted fingers, she told all.

Silence deafened.

Seated at her side, Venetia turned away and gazed toward the back of the magnificent house. Maryanne felt a spurt of anger. Venetia had behaved just as scandalously to save the family, and Maryanne refused to be condemned for her own adventure. She dropped her hands to her lap.

Of course, it was a lovely morning, resplendent with sunshine and crisp autumn air. The day had no idea what trouble she was in.

Finally her sister faced her once more. "You are editing erotic novels to provide employment for aging courtesans?"

"I know how terrifying it is to face poverty."

"I remember," Venetia remarked with cool sarcasm. "I was there. And what happened last night?"

The simplest truth again. It was the only solution. "Georgiana wrote that she was in trouble, and she told me to meet her at a certain address."

"Oh, good lord. And you went alone. Even prostitutes don't travel London alone—they have protectors."

"No, they pay men not to abuse them, but that is beside the point. I'm here. I'm alive. I survived."

Venetia reached for her hand. "Yes, cause for celebration indeed. Your little nephew or niece is leaping about in delight, I can assure you."

Guilt crashed in. "I—" What could possibly explain how thoughtless she'd been to frighten her sister in her condition? No doubt the baby was thrashing about inside because Venetia was upset.

"Where did you go?"

Even with an excited child in her tummy, her sister was relentless, practical. Taking charge. "Mrs. Master's salon," Maryanne admitted.

"I don't know it. I presume Marcus would know what it is."

"Oh, dear heaven, don't tell him!"

Venetia pursed her lips. "I see. That sort of place."

"You might as well know. I'm ruined. Do you wish me to pack a trunk and be out of the house before tea?" How strange to toss out her greatest fear as a dare. It was exhilarating.

Not quite as thrilling as handsome, delicious Dash pleasuring her from behind in a balloon, but close.

Venetia's eyes went wide with concern. "Of course not!"

Her sister's tummy was a sweet bump beneath her gown. A tremulous smile touched Maryanne's lips. She had thrown away the chance for a proper marriage, a loving husband, children—for what decent man would accept a ruined wife? Suddenly her determination to remain alone felt like a noose around her neck.

"Who was he?"

"A man. No one." It would be easiest to say she did not know his name, but she couldn't force that lie from her lips. It sounded so . . . foolish. So awful. "It was entirely my choice."

"Who was he? A man you love, I hope."

Maryanne nodded. "But one I can't have."

Her sister's face blanched in what must be complete shock. "Not . . . married?" She slumped back against the bench.

Maryanne released Venetia's hand. "Heavens, no! I would never do that! He . . . he didn't know who I was. I wore a mask, you see, and he had no idea he was ruining me. He was . . . well, reasonably drunk."

"Oh, Maryanne. . . ." Myriad emotions passed across her sister's hazel eyes, none of which Maryanne wanted to identify. "But he will have to—"

"No! Don't you see?" She took an unsteady breath. "I can hardly insist that he marry me. I didn't give him a sporting chance to escape the leg shackles."

"His name. What is his name?"

But she shook her head, her mouth dry.

"Did he use a sheath?"

"No." Maryanne spoke airily, even though her head buzzed and she wondered if she would slide off the bench into a foolish swoon. "I thought if I was to ruin myself, I should do it quite thoroughly and in the most dangerous way I possibly could."

* * *

Dash threw open the doors and burst into his drawing room. "Who is she?" he demanded.

Sir William stood at the window, head bowed. One gloved hand rested against his chin, the other fisted behind his back, his spectacles gripped in his fingers. The sunlight touched his silvery hair, cast shadow on his grim expression—the look of a magistrate about to pass sentence on a friend.

"So you have heard." Sir William turned slowly, his voice infuriatingly calm.

"Of course, I bloody heard. Do you have her name? What does she look like?"

"The woman found was Eliza Charmody."

Not Verity. Relief shot through him. With her blue eyes and golden hair, the actress Eliza Charmody could not have been his brown-haired, brown-eyed Verity. The sense of escaping doom was so strong, it felt like brandy in his blood. He felt drunk with it. But in the next breath, guilt clenched at his gut.

Eliza Charmody. The actress who had been Craven's partner and who had disappeared from Covent Garden.

He hadn't known Eliza Charmody, but her abduction had led to death, and he hadn't been able to save her.

A vision flashed before his eyes—his mistress pleading, tears streaking down her face. A terrified woman who'd hurt no one, begging for her life while a man enjoyed her fear—

Dash hadn't actually seen the attack on his mistress all those years ago but he could imagine it. His hand belied his memories by shaking. Only after he'd reached the brandy decanter and splashed some in two glasses did he pivot and look at Sir William. "You think I did it?"

No answer. Just patient silence. Dash held out one glass. "Where was she found?"

He realized Sir William had not told him, perhaps expecting him to incriminate himself. Which meant his friend really did believe he could have done it. As Sir William took the glass, Dash drank down the entire contents of his. This man, who had known him since he was a boy, who had been one of the few to show him kindness, thought him capable of murdering women.

Sir William took a sip of his drink. "Hyde Park."

"And how had she died—or let me guess, she fell from a hot-air balloon's basket?" Anger put the sarcastic edge in his voice.

Sir William stared at him, both astonished and wary. "No. Strangled. The murder weapon had been left with her body. A dyed black cravat."

Dash's trademark. No other gentleman dressed entirely in black. None used a black cravat. "I was not alone in Hyde Park last night."

Verity's testimony could exonerate him. But would they believe Verity? A courtesan could be paid to say anything. So, of course, could a lady, he thought wryly.

But then . . .

"When was she found?"

"By the balloonists as they prepared to leave the site. They had been instructed to stay until half past six."

And Verity had been with him until a quarter after six, at least. He'd glanced at the time when he'd snuggled up to her. How long had she stayed with him after he'd passed out?

But he didn't know who she was, had no idea how to find her.

"I saw my cousin last night. He's not taking part in the hunt, but he was there, foxed, and he accused me of murder."

"You are not a murderer."

"No? The way you look at me, I believe you're wondering if I am. Why else are you here, if not to wait until I make a slip of my tongue and incriminate myself?" Dash's grip tightened on his empty glass. "You told me two courtesans claimed I enticed Eliza Charmody from Craven," he continued. "Georgiana Watson was one of the them, and now she has left London in pursuit of an earl, reputedly Craven. The other courtesan vanished without a trace. As for Sir Percy Whitting and Lord Yale, they were not what you would call reliable witnesses. It appears they did not actually see me take the actress in my carriage. They believed the story of another man—a man they didn't know and cannot now identify—who claimed *he* saw me take her."

And Verity, who claimed to be Georgiana's friend, had had no idea her friend was gone. Was that proof Georgiana Watson was part of this plot to incriminate him for kidnapping and murder? Was that proof Verity was innocent?

Sir William placed his glass, the brandy barely touched, beside the decanter. "Let us go to the park, Swansborough. I want you to see her."

Yellowing leaves rustled around the murder scene, a bizarre and gut-wrenching sight in the beauty that was Hyde Park. A group of men waited, two in the scarlet waistcoat of the Bow Street Runner, Bow Street's professional police force.

The circle opened to allow Dash to enter its core, and then closed around him.

Even as he looked down on the sprawling body, that phrase hammered in his mind. *Not Verity. Not Verity. Thank the devil it wasn't her.*

With gloved fingers he touched Eliza Charmody's hair, a tangled mass of blond curls mashed into the dirt. A blanket lay over her body and face. A flick of his fingers lifted it, revealing blue and purple bruising at her throat. She lay on the grass, naked, her head tipped back to turn her vulnerable throat into a long white column.

Dash's gut clenched as he saw the red scratches and bite marks that covered her bare breasts. A glance lower, and he almost tossed up the brandy swimming in his gut. She'd been sliced open with a blade, with a long straight line that ran from navel to pubis.

He dropped the blanket. Christ Jesus, what kind of sadist would do this to a woman?

Boots crunched on the grass, and he glanced toward the sound. Those boots—belonging to Sir William—rocked beside a strip of black.

One of his cravats, or one dyed to look the same? It mattered. If it was his, it meant it came from someone with access to his home. Or someone demented enough to break in with the sole intent of incriminating him.

He glanced up at Sir William, squinting from the sun. "She was strangled, but why didn't you tell me about the . . . the rest?"

"You asked how she died. The mutilation was performed afterward."

The cravat was cool, damp with dew—he searched for his mark but could not find it. "It's not one of mine."

"Who have you questioned, Swansborough? Who, on the hunt?" Sir William had drawn out a linen handkerchief to clean his spectacles.

"You think I made someone nervous—that they retaliated with this?" Dash let his glove-covered knuckles brush the woman's cold face. Facing death—his own death—was something he could bear. He'd done it before. But he couldn't stand this—was this defenseless women killed just to hang a noose around his neck?

"Twenty couples are now taking part in this blasted hunt," Dash continued, his voice raw and hoarse. "Hadrian has dropped out, but I took his place with—" He broke off. "I have a list of each peer, his partner, and how far they've progressed in the hunt."

He straightened, with the cravat draped over his open palm.

Sir William inclined his head. "Let us walk, Swansborough. Talk of this."

Out of the corner of his eyes, Dash saw the other men bundle the body to move it as he walked toward the spot where the balloonists had been the night before.

"Who is taking part? Would any of those involved have reason to want to throw suspicion on you?"

"You want to know which ones might have a particular grudge against me?" The park was quiet; the morning hour was early, and many of the *ton* were in the country. "Difficult to speculate," he growled. "Craven was there. As you know, I've been investigating him for involvement with a draper's son named Barrett in the white slave trade. And Craven's one of the few with a worse reputation for debauchery than me."

Dash's strides lengthened as they reached the clearing. Sir William walked silently, hands clasped behind his back.

"Ashton was there with Sophia—Lady Yardley. He's likely never forgiven me for putting a ball in his leg in my first duel, even though that was ten years ago, when I was . . . about twenty. Each time he limps, I'm certain he thinks about killing me. But then, so do many."

He laughed at that. Remembering . . .

He'd never understood why his uncle James hadn't just done the job with a knife or a pistol. Easy enough to blow him away. Instead, Uncle James had arranged accidents—and when he'd survived, his uncle had stopped for a while, only to create another ingenious death trap months . . . or years . . . later.

He had to remember it like this. Dispassionately, as if it had happened to someone else. He couldn't let himself really remember what it had been like. . . .

"Jack Tate was there."

"Aye." Sir William nodded. "I heard the rumors he owes you a king's ransom from the gaming tables."

Dash shrugged. "He had to lose, even at his own tables, just to prove he wasn't cheating. I've got a pocketful of his vowels, worth twenty thousand pounds. It's possible he thinks he can avoid paying the debt if he can force me to flee England. But it's a mad way to go about it. A shot in my back would be more expedient there. No reason Tate couldn't arrange to have my throat slit on a dark night."

"Anyone else?"

"Several ladies who took offense to me leaving their beds, but nothing worth murder. The most likely man is my cousin

Robert. Growing up with my uncle would turn anyone mad—I can attest to that. Since he believes I murdered his brother—" Dash broke off. "Uncle James still wants the title for himself, but he has to kill me to get it. It would be much easier to have a footpad slice my throat than to kill innocent women and hope to hang the crime on me."

He stood in the center of a circle of crushed grass, where the balloon's basket had rested. Metal hooks protruded from the earth where the tether lines had been knotted, where the ropes had strained as he and Verity had soared to the stars—

"Blast! Verity!"

Sir William, unlit cheroot in hand, paused at the edge of the circle. "Verity?"

"A woman I met last night. The woman who joined me on this task in the scavenger hunt." Dash's hand tightened on the cravat. "I spent the night with her, which meant I wasn't out murdering Miss Charmody. But now I realize blasted Verity was sent to distract me."

Sir William, who had struck a light for his smoke, yelped as the flame burned his fingers.

"And bloody fool that I was, I didn't get a look under her mask. Or learn her real name." Instead he'd wanted to bury himself in her warmth, hold her breasts, feel her heart hammer beneath his palm, and use pleasure to make him forget.

Would she be here tonight?

That night, hours after he'd come here to see Eliza Charmody's body, Dash was in Hyde Park again. Blowing a wreath of smoke into the crisp, still night air, he strolled amongst the couples waiting for their turn to have sex in the balloon's basket.

Verity had taken the clue—which belied the suspicion she'd been sent to distract him. Why not leave him the clue so he could follow it to the next event, where she could entice him into another mind-melting fuck?

Bitterness touched his throat. Would another woman die

tonight, gruesomely arranged with clues pointing to him? Hell, this was madness.

Drawing on his cheroot, Dash paused in a cool pocket of darkness beneath an oak. From here, on a slight knoll, he could scan the crowd.

No sign of his cousin—though, of average height, with brown hair and brown eyes, Robert Blackmore was difficult to spot in a crowd.

Jack Tate was in the thick of the group, kissing a buxom woman with abundant henna-red curls. His hand roughly caressed one of the plump tits, his other groped her bottom. Ashton wasn't here. Sophia and Ashton must have completed this event last night. Were they trying to decipher the next clue, or was the duke plotting murder?

After exhaling, Dash took another long draw on his cheroot, a pleasure he normally savored, but he barely tasted the smoke tonight.

Hell, what if it *was* Ashton?

Sophia had refused to believe she was in danger. Dash had gone to see her today. She'd had him sent up to her music room. As her fingers had danced precisely over the keys, she'd listened. Then had insisted, with a woman's loyalty, that Ashton couldn't be the murderer.

Dash groaned as he remembered. Against the dark crowd in the park, he could almost see the scene. . . .

Her fingers had lifted from the keys. "I'm not in danger," she had whispered. "But you are." In that moment of pain for him, her age had shown on her lovely face.

"If it's Ashton, my dear, you could be."

"He doesn't bear a grudge over an ancient duel, I can assure you. And you are certain that all this is true—"

"Would a magistrate and a friend lie? He's been trying to protect me. If it is my uncle or cousin, we're dealing with a madman, and, yes, sweetheart, you could be in danger. You were one of the few who recognized how insane my uncle is—you believed me then. Believe me now, Sophia. Let me protect you."

She'd thoughtfully played a series of high notes, the sound as delicate as bird song.

A cold dread had washed over him. "Do you think I did it? Do you think I've gone mad?"

The last note held, shivering in the air. "Of course not. But you must be very careful. So very careful."

She knew more, he was certain, than she was willing to reveal. . . .

Dash jerked himself back to the present. Sir William had sent runners, or hired men, to watch Sophia's home, to follow her wherever she went, to protect her.

From the shadows beneath the thick oak branches, he spotted blond hair beneath a tall beaver hat. Craven.

The lady on Craven's arm was heavily veiled. They walked with arms linked on the edge of the gathering. With a glance in all directions, Craven abruptly turned, and the couple hurried between the trees.

Dash dropped his cheroot to the path, ground it with his boot heel. A man detached from the crowd and followed Craven and his lady. A man who moved calmly but deliberately through the moonlit dark.

He had no choice but to follow. He'd been a voyeur at countless orgies, and he'd always enjoyed watching other people find pleasure. He'd needed to immerse himself in sex and sin until he couldn't think. But, tonight, following Craven while hiding in the shadows left him feeling damned dirty.

As Craven and the woman reached a small grove hidden by closely spaced trees, Craven wrenched off the lady's veil.

Dash bit down to stifle the hiss of surprise. Harriet. Lady Evershire. Sister to his brother-in-law Moredon. Married, of course, but Dash was surprised by his shock. By the spurt of indignation he felt.

Craven wasted no time. He pulled Harriet into a rough kiss, mouth open, as he yanked his breeches wide. He pulled out his cock with equal roughness as she desperately tugged up her skirts.

Blast Harriet. Was she without sense? If Craven was involved in the white slave trade, he was callously having children—female and male—stolen from their homes, brought to London, and shipped off to live in harems. He sold children to service masters who no doubt killed them when they grew, when they were an encumbrance, not a pleasure. What in blazes had possessed her to choose London's most perverse rake for a lover?

A crunch of twigs had Dash drawing back into the cover of the bushes. The other man sauntered up to Craven and Harriet, undoing his own trousers. Moonlight splashed onto the scene, painting the sexual agony on his sister-in-law's face and revealing the identity of the third.

Barrett.

The handsome, charming draper's son who was the worst bloody blackguard Dash had ever encountered.

Christ, was Harriet to be a victim?

Was he going to have to stand guard while she had her naughty threesome, to ensure she didn't end up being strangled and slit open?

As Barrett and Craven wasted no time in pulling up her skirts, he knew he was. Harriet obediently positioned herself on all fours, and Craven slid into her from behind, pumping wildly while she suckled Barrett. He thrust fiercely at her face, smothering her cries of pleasure.

Dash turned his back on the scene, his heart pounding in arousal at the sounds of Harriet's delight. Harriet's moans and shrieks floated to him—the sound of a woman in ecstasy had him hard and aching immediately. And ratcheted up his irritation.

Bloody fool, Harriet.

Her final squeal brought a terse command from Craven. "Switch positions. I want to pound my rod into her luscious mouth."

Dash groaned in frustration.

* * *

Dash stumbled into his bedchamber and fell onto his back, shutting his eyes against sunlight. At least Harriet had enjoyed her night. He bloody well hadn't. He'd been forced to stand in the bushes for half an hour, while they engaged in three raunchy bouts, trying not to watch but act as protector.

There had been no sign of Verity, not even at the next location on the scavenger hunt—a private box at the theater where two twin courtesans provided oral delights for the hunting couple.

What more did he know for spending the night on the hunt? Nothing. One of Sir William's most trusted, most effective runners had spoken to Phibbs. Stevens was the name he'd given as the man who had employed him.

Dash raked his hands through his hair. Stevens would likely point them to some other insignificant name; the man at the top, the man behind the hunt, would have surrounded himself with a maze of underlings and lackeys to remain hidden.

And finding the man who had organized the scavenger hunt might tell him nothing. He might be innocent himself. One of the participants could be using the event to capture women.

Dash let his hand rest on the silky covering of his pillow. With eyes shut, he felt as if he were with Verity again—blindfolded while she matched wits with him, surprised him, and sucked his cock deep into her mouth. And made those delicious sounds of pleasure.

Hell. With his eyes shut, Dash gave a coarse, deep laugh. He needed Verity. And not just to find out who she worked for and whether she had been paid to distract him. He needed to escape in a rowdy sexual bout with her.

He forced himself to sit up, to open his eyes to daylight.

Eliza Charmody had had no escape. The poor lass must have been terrified. Just as the virgins were who were loaded on boats, taken to the East, and sold.

There was no longer any escape for him. Dash knew that now.

Groaning, he reached for the bellpull and gave it a yank. But instead of his valet barging in and disparaging him for his late hours and bleary countenance, someone rapped at his door.

"Enter," he barked.

The door swung open, and Manning stood there, salver in hand. The salver trembled. "A letter, my lord. From Lady Moredon."

"Good news, I pray," he muttered as he strode over to take the letter.

Had the baby come? Or was she still waiting its tardy arrival?

Damn, why couldn't he just open it? Cut the seal and read.

His hip brushed the chair by the secretary, and he stopped. The letter opener lay on the blotter, sunlight a gleam along the blade. The handle was a cool weight in his palm, but he still could not bring himself to slice.

In her last letter, she had begged him to stop his worrying and had demanded that he let her make her own decisions. But he knew Moredon was too indulgent, too doting. Anne should have been attended by a London physician. She should not have been relying upon a country midwife. But it was her wish, and Moredon indulged it.

It would be good news. She would have a boy . . . or a girl . . . to hold in her arms. To dote upon. To love. It had to be.

Have courage. He slid the blade between linen edges and cut through the seal. A flick sent the folds tumbling open.

Lancelot . . .

His heart lurched—her last letter had been written with a tone of reprimanding. To use his middle name . . . she was begging to reconcile.

His gaze dropped. Which would it be? Son or daughter?

There was nothing that could be done.

They say it is a miracle I lived. But it isn't. It hurts so much. I don't understand what I did wrong. I keep thinking and thinking . . .

Nigel said I was not to write . . . I was to rest. But I had to let you know.

Lancelot, I lost the babe. She was stillborn.

The words were blurred as though drops of water had pattered onto the page before the ink had dried.

To hell with this bastard who was trying to make him look like a murderer—he had to go to Anne.

"I sent a note to Lord Swansborough's home."

Maryanne's book slid from her fingers. Pages fluttering, it tumbled to the edge of her window seat and then fell on the floor, upsetting her teacup.

"Oh, god, Venetia, you didn't—" How could her sister do this—waltz into her bedchamber, throw her life into chaos and disaster, and announce it so calmly?

Maryanne would not admit that her heart was racing with hope. Three nights had passed. Each night she had gone to this window in her bedchamber and looked out toward Hyde Park. Her fingers had dallied on the locks—easy enough to slide the window open. More dangerous to climb down the tree whose branches touched the wall, but not impossible.

But her adventure was over, and all she could do was wait.

Now she saw Venetia's purpose. "You wrote to do what? Send him an invitation to his own wedding?"

"No. I invited him to an innocuous musicale."

Her sister carried a small canvas beneath her arm. With a heavy sigh, Venetia settled onto the chaise arranged cozily by the fireplace and laid the untouched canvas on the floor. The tea tray sat on a small octagonal table, and Maryanne hastened to make tea. Tea was always to be served—even in the heat of battle.

Venetia took the cup with a sad smile.

"He refused, I take it."

Venetia's cup rattled slightly on the saucer. Beneath brilliant sunlight, Venetia's face turned an odd shade of gray. Pale with a distinct tinge of green. Maryanne looked about for her empty chamber pot, though her sister had not been troubled with morning sickness for several months now.

She felt queasy, too, queasy with apprehension.

"I received a reply from his secretary," Venetia said. "Swansborough has had to hasten to his sister's home. He has left immediately for Buckstead."

Curdling fear knotted Maryanne's tummy. "What has happened?"

"His sister was in childbed. The child was stillborn, and his sister was very nearly lost herself."

"His sister lost her child? Oh, my goodness." The ground roared up beneath Maryanne with a sucking sound that rang in her ears. Shock and horror rushed up, and she raced to go to the chamber pot. She held it in her arms and was noisily sick.

7

December 1819

Maryanne put her hand to her queasy stomach and nibbled a dry biscuit. There was no denying the truth anymore. She had missed her monthly courses for the third time.

She'd been sick that afternoon when she'd learned about Dash's sister's loss. That couldn't have been her pregnancy. Not so soon. But this roiling sensation in her tummy definitely was.

She slipped her fingers around the doorknob that led to Venetia's studio. She would have to admit the truth. Venetia had waited to act while Dash remained away from London. At least for once Venetia had respected her wishes and had not written to him.

But now . . .

She wasn't going to force Dash into marriage. All she hoped was that her brother-in-law would allow her to have a little of her dowry. Enough for her to go and live quietly in the country. As her mother, Olivia, had done, she would pretend to be a widow. She would live with complete respectability.

For the sake of her child, there could be no more adventures.

And thank heaven Venetia had agreed that they would not reveal anything to her mother yet. Though her mother intended to arrive soon, for the birth of Venetia's baby. What would she do then?

She should open the door, but her hand stilled on the cool metal of the knob. Her shawl slid a little off her shoulders. Dash's sister had lost her child. These tragedies happened. . . .

It would be easier.

Heaven help her, how could she think that? There were ways . . . potions that could be drunk, the use of hooks . . . there were several ways she'd heard whispered about, even though she'd always been hidden away in her world of books while Venetia had helped her mother with womanly duties in the country. She knew a little about the desperate measures women used to rid themselves of babies.

But she couldn't do it. She would have to face her fate.

With a shaky hand, Maryanne opened the door.

Her sister wasn't alone.

Her brother-in-law, Marcus, was stretched out on a chaise. A strangled gasp escaped Maryanne's lips. Sunlight touched his black hair, his handsome face, and fell lovingly across his naked chest. Good heavens, his muscular legs were bare. A linen cloth was draped over his private bits, thank goodness, though there was a distinct bulge beneath the white drape.

Rendered in soft light and shadow, Marcus, with his raven hair and powerful build, looked just like Dash. But his eyes were brilliant turquoise, not mysterious midnight black.

Her throat dried. Dash had looked so beautiful beneath the sheets of his bed, the silk in a tangle around his body.

"Do you know how much it delights me to watch you do that?"

Maryanne almost leaped out of her skin at the sudden seductive purr of Marcus's voice. Gentle amusement rippled through his words, and his gaze at Venetia spoke of pure male desire.

The way Dash had looked at her . . .

What was Venetia doing that delighted? Maryanne, standing with face pressed against the slight opening of the door, looked to her sister. Venetia was sucking on the end of her paintbrush. Her soft red lips pursed around the painted wood shaft as she studied her picture with a frown. Drenched in sunlight, her hair was a mass of flame, and her amber brows drew together in concentration.

Venetia wore the unusual gown she'd had made for her last month of pregnancy. It was like a shift, or a nightgown, with scooped neck and long sleeves. It fell in soft drapes from the neckline, and as she sat on the stool, the neckline revealed the tops of plump breasts.

Maryanne tightened her grip on the doorknob. Soon she would look like Venetia. There was no denying it—in five months, she would have the large, rounded belly, and Dash's child would be wedged inside. No doubt, like Venetia's child, hers would be growing discontented with the situation and would be kicking, squirming, and punching with vigor.

She could try to hide the truth for a couple more months. . . .

Would she be better to do that, rather than face the disaster now?

It would be so much easier.

"No, indeed, that shoulder is not broad enough," Venetia muttered in a breathy voice, tapping brush to lower lip. "Definitely your shoulders are broader . . . straighter . . . hips lean and narrow . . . decidedly trim, and I haven't quite caught the lovely line where they . . . ooh."

"Sweeting, that soft little sigh at the end was almost my undoing." And indeed, the drapery at Marcus's hips almost fell away. He caught it quickly and rearranged it. "Is it too late to pull a chair in front?"

Venetia and Marcus shared a laugh, and Maryanne felt a pang of pain. She had never thought that marriage could seem so intimate; she had seen her mother's distress after time spent with her father, the tempestuous, demanding, flamboyant artist Rodesson. Her mother would speed to the encounters like a moth drawn to beautiful, deadly flame. And after, her mother would return and cry, alone.

There were so many unhappy marriages—even in marriage, happiness seemed to come from finding one's own life. Depending upon another for company, for joy, seemed a dreadful mistake.

"What are you staring at, my love?" Marcus's voice, though teasing, was strained. "Not assessing me for length and girth, are you? If you are scrutinizing the family jewels to record them for posterity, I might just ravish you on the spot."

"As you do every time," her sister answered coyly around her paintbrush.

"Could we take a break?"

Venetia pulled her brush from between her lips. The tip of her tongue dabbed the very end thoughtfully. "You've not been posing for more than half an hour, Marcus."

"I'm stiff—"

"But it will take weeks to complete the work if we stop every time you are . . . stiff."

Maryanne moved to pull the door closed—

"Marcus, there is something we must discuss. About Maryanne."

Maryanne paused. Guiltily she glanced behind her—the corridor was empty. No one was spying on her as she spied on her sister and brother-in-law.

"What is it, my love?" Marcus asked. "From your tone of voice, I fear there's a reason you waited until I was nude to bring it up."

Pressing into the narrow gap between door and frame, Maryanne gulped. Venetia was going to tell him; she had indeed waited until he was naked, so he couldn't storm out and . . . either box her ears or challenge Dash. Marcus had never raised a hand to her, had never been anything but welcoming and warm, but Maryanne knew he'd shot a man to protect Venetia.

Her stomach lurched, but the stump of biscuit she still held wasn't going to help that. This wasn't morning sickness. This was fear.

"It is not the easiest thing to discuss," Venetia hedged. She set her brush into a glass of turps and slid off the stool, hand on her belly.

Marcus was on his feet at once to help his wife, which meant the cloth dropped from his loins. Maryanne shut her eyes.

"Then I can guess. Who's to blame?"

With eyes tightly closed, Maryanne marveled at how calm he sounded. Perhaps, as she was not really his sister, he was not going to be upset after all.

"That doesn't signify," Venetia said.

"I can assure you it does."

Maryanne shivered at the cool, silky danger in Marcus's voice. She had guessed incorrectly. Upset was going to be too mild a word.

"For I need to know who to drag out, whip within an inch of his blasted life, and then drag before a minister."

"There is not to be a marriage."

"I won't whip him that badly. I'll ensure he is able to stand and do his duty."

"That is not what I mean! I was not going to let myself be forced into marriage—as you might remember, we married for love, not for ludicrous societal rules. I certainly will not push my sister into unhappiness."

"The girl is owed marriage—and I want a name, Venetia."

He was obviously going to be as bullheaded about that as her sister had been.

"You will see at once how inappropriate marriage will be."

"She should have thought of that before getting into his bed."

"Men are such appalling hypocrites!" Venetia cried, for now that she was expecting a child, she shouted more often than she used to. "You were more than willing to entice me into yours."

"I proposed marriage immediately after I enticed you into my bed, as you might remember." Instead of sounding contrite, as he should, her brother-in-law sounded as though he was barely clinging to self-control. "You turned me down. I brought you to my bed—"

"The carpet. I do believe our first was upon the carpet."

Venetia's adventures, Maryanne knew, had been as wild as hers.

"Regardless, I knew I had every intention of marrying you. And so will this gentleman—he was a bloody gentleman, I hope—"

What had she done to her sister and Marcus? They normally lived in such harmony it inspired awe.

"It was Swansborough."

There was silence. A horrifying stretch of it, but Maryanne did not dare open her eyes. She suspected she would get an embarrassing eyeful of a naked, enraged Marcus if she did. But she had to know what would happen.

"There, do you see how impossible it is? She cannot marry Lord Swansborough!"

"A whip isn't in order." There was a creak of floorboards, and Maryanne let her lids flicker. No one was walking toward the door, but she gently closed it so only a crack remained. Enough to listen through. "A brace of bloody pistols is."

She froze at Marcus's words.

"Marcus, there will be no duel." Venetia's voice took on a frightened shrillness on the word *duel*.

"Swansborough should have been at my door immediately, begging for her hand. So that's why he vanished from London—"

Maryanne had heard enraged men before—truly enraged ones, not the husbands who blustered and bullied—and there was most definitely danger behind Marcus's calm tones. Was he truly going to call Dash out? She couldn't allow it. She had to stop—

"It is not, and well you know it!" Venetia cried in Dash's defense. "His sister had just lost her child. Anyway, he didn't know who she was!"

Marcus gave a weary sigh. Chair springs squeaked in protest, and wood legs skidded across the wood floor. Obviously he'd slumped into a chair. Maryanne's legs felt like India rubber, and she wished *she* could fall into a chair.

"A mask?" Marcus asked.

"Yes. Yes, she wore a mask, just as I did."

"And where did it take place?"

"That's beside the point. She will be unhappy. You know what a scoundrel he is. I suspect there is going to be a child, but—"

"Oh, good Christ, a child!" Marcus groaned.

So Venetia had guessed! How . . . ? There were many ways, Maryanne realized. Her new habit of eating almost all the time to keep nausea at bay. Or had her maid revealed that she hadn't bled for three months?

"Then it's marriage." Her brother-in-law spoke as if announcing death.

"No. I cannot permit this. There will not be a wedding."

"There will. I am head of my household. The girl is my responsibility."

"She is my sister. I will not bow to you on this!" Venetia cried.

Maryanne shivered. She had never heard such fierce conviction in her sister's voice.

"Oh, you will, my love, I assure you."

"Do not call me your love if you are going to behave like such a pigheaded—" Venetia broke off. "Oh, goodness. I think . . . there's rather a lot of water . . . I'm not certain but . . . it's dripping down my legs."

Maryanne froze.

"Oh, blast!" Marcus cried out, heralding the upcoming arrival of his first child with a curse.

Maryanne swayed. She had caused her sister to begin laboring. Aghast, she turned the knob. She had to hurry, had to . . .

She wasn't certain what to do. She had never helped in births. But she burst into the room anyway.

"Maryanne, what in blazes?" Marcus stood behind Venetia, his body hidden, his arms around her, hands resting tentatively on her tummy.

Venetia giggled—the last thing Maryanne expected her to do. "Fetch your robe, Marcus. And both of you must stay calm. I've been warned that this will take a long time, for the first."

How could Venetia giggle? She had written letters to her unborn babe just the week before, letters to be opened in case she didn't survive the birth.

"Are—are there pains?" Maryanne was standing helplessly, her hands tangled in her skirts.

"Not yet. They're to come, though. Unfortunately Mrs. Collins has been most blunt about what to expect."

"You must be terrified," Maryanne gasped. She took care not to look at Marcus, though she felt him return and saw the swish of dark blue silk—his robe.

Venetia cradled her belly, and she paced, with Marcus following. "I'm not. Nervous, but I will survive. I think. Women do. Many women do. Do you think it will take days? There are women who've labored for three days."

Three days! Maryanne's jaw dropped. Three days of pain? How could a woman survive? Her hands strayed to her own tummy. She knew—each woman in the village knew—of a woman who had died in childbed. And Dash's sister had lost her baby. . . .

She had to stop thinking such terrible things. Shaking, she met Marcus's gaze.

"Send for the physician," he ordered.

He'd never been so terse with her.

"And Mrs. Collins, the midwife," Venetia added.

Maryanne looked to Marcus and whispered, "I . . . I heard. I don't want you to be at odds over me. Not now. I . . . I'll marry him."

Venetia's stern cry of "Maryanne" followed her as she darted to the bellpull and gave it a sturdy yank.

"Marcus!"

Maryanne spun on her heel. Her brother-in-law had swept Venetia into his arms, and Maryanne's heart gave a jump in her chest. He looked at her sister with such deep love.

"Marcus, I am quite capable of walking. It is preferable if I do!"

But Marcus nuzzled Venetia's cheek. "Save your strength, my love." He hastened toward the doorway, holding her sister tight in his arms.

Venetia put out her hand to stop them, and, groaning, he did.

Maryanne expected direction from her sister—instead, Venetia frowned. "You can't marry Swansborough, Maryanne."

"What if that is the only solution that won't hurt either of you?" And it was true. Anything else would risk bringing scandal into Marcus's house, tarnishing her sisters, and that she could not do.

"You must think of your happiness. Oh! This wetness feels terrible."

Maryanne gulped—there was a puddle of water on the floor. Her leg muscles clenched at the thought of that coming out of her. Her happiness didn't matter now. This business of birth must come first, though Maryanne felt awkward and useless as she watched Marcus vanish down the hallway with his long strides, Venetia in his arms. A young footman with large eyes answered the ring of the bellpull, and Maryanne gave instructions.

"Summon Dr. Plim of Number Ten, Harley Street. And a carriage is to be sent for Mrs. Collins—her direction is Number Six, Crofton Lane."

The boy nodded, and she waved her hand at him. "Make haste."

He turned and loped away, clearly excited by the urgency.

Then she went in search of Mrs. Dorset, the housekeeper.

The severe woman took charge at once, and Maryanne trailed in her capable wake as she gave orders to the maids, to the kitchen staff, and to a bevy of footmen.

Useless. In this situation, Maryanne truly was, but she didn't know where she should go. What she should do. And she wanted to keep busy. When she paused, she slipped into frightening thoughts. Thoughts of Dash's sister and her lost child.

No amount of wealth smoothed the business of childbirth.

Two years before, the Regent's daughter, Princess Charlotte, had died giving birth to a precious child, who was also lost.

Maryanne raced up the stairs to Venetia's bedchamber. To her surprise, she saw Venetia pacing the hallway, with Marcus holding her hand. Mrs. Dorset nodded in satisfaction. "Wise, my lady. The doctor will advise you to lie down, for they want the patient where they won't be troublesome."

Hurried footsteps sounded behind, and Maryanne stepped to the edge of the corridor. Maids hurried past, arms loaded with sheets, towels, and basins of steaming water.

No one was paying attention to her, thank heaven.

"Now, my lord," Mrs. Dorset said to Marcus, "it will be a long wait. You—"

"I will stay with my wife," Marcus growled, and Maryanne knew he would. The midwife would be exasperated; Maryanne had overheard her say how useful it was that men took refuge in their studies and their port and left the important work to women. The physician, Dr. Plim, would be shocked, too.

Maryanne joined the line of maids rushing into the bedchamber.

But Mrs. Dorset stood in the doorway. "No, dear. You're an unmarried miss and have no business in here." Firm hands turned her and directed her out the door. Marcus led Venetia in, so Maryanne had to stand aside. And the door closed firmly in her face.

* * *

She'd had no idea the business of laboring would take so long. Had Venetia truly been suffering and enduring for eight hours? The pains had been coming every few minutes—how did a woman endure that for hours on end? Poor Venetia must be exhausted.

Maryanne could take it no longer. She gathered her skirts, crumpled and worse for wear, left her bedchamber, and raced down the hallway. At her knock, the door opened.

She caught her first glimpse of it. Venetia was sitting up on her bed, Marcus at one side, and Mrs. Collins at the other. "Now rest for a minute, my lady," Mrs. Collins soothed. "You must relax, breathe, and make ready to push again."

Dr. Plim was washing his hands in a basin. "Have her push once more—I will turn the head this time."

"Oh, oh—it's coming again," Venetia gasped. Her soaked hair was pulled back, but red tendrils were plastered to her face. Her skin was flushed, and perspiration gleamed on her cheeks. Her white shift was soaked through and bunched up to the top of her thighs.

Struck mute with shock, unable to move, Maryanne stood in the doorway. Her sister's panting turned to cries and then a startled scream.

Venetia!

"Oh—oh! I'm sorry . . . I didn't mean . . . it just came out," Venetia gasped. "Oh, I'm so embarrassed."

What had come out? The baby? No, not that . . .

"Not to worry, my lady," Mrs. Collins reassured. "It's the pressure of the babe. Now, breathe. Relax before you must push again."

A body stepped directly into her line of sight. Maryanne blinked, facing a simple gray dress, and took a step back. It was Mrs. Dorset.

She gripped the doorjamb before the housekeeper could shut the door. "How . . . how long will it take?"

Mrs. Dorset frowned. "As long as is needed, Miss Hamilton. With the first, it can be a lengthy business, but it shan't be much longer. Now, you must go."

She wanted to—wanted to retreat to a book and a nice cup of tea. But in a mere six months, she would be the one doing this!

And for all Mrs. Dorset's reassurances . . .

Her sister's grunts became a cry. Through the space at the door, Maryanne saw Dr. Plim move between her sister's parted legs. She couldn't bear to look. Marcus squeezed Venetia's hand.

"There," announced Plim with a satisfied air.

Mrs. Collins moved, positioning Venetia's bare foot against her hip. "Now push, my lady. As hard as ye can."

Heavens, Mrs. Collins was directing Marcus to place Venetia's foot at his hip. Face straining, Venetia braced herself and let out a cry of pure determination.

Maryanne felt her hand clasp to her mouth. She would be doing this? But she would have no loving husband at her side stroking her forehead and brushing back her damp hair.

Neither did many women, she reminded herself.

Shakily she withdrew and let Mrs. Dorset shut the door again. In six months, she would be suffering like Venetia, paying a high price for her one foolish night of adventure and pleasure and sex.

It wasn't fair to force Dash into marriage, but how could she let Venetia and Marcus fight over her future? Could she face giving birth, having a child, all on her own?

8

"You should be resting, you shouldn't be doing . . . this."

Following her sister toward the west drawing room, Maryanne fiddled with her embroidered shawl. It offered little warmth, but the warm colors—russet and gold and pink—suited her, and she knew her face was starkly pale.

"Baby Richard is napping now." Venetia yawned, and a soft smile played on her lips. "And a proposal of marriage is a rather important event."

A shiver tumbled down Maryanne's spine. Dash wasn't going to propose marriage—he was being told to make himself available at the church on a certain date to marry a woman who had told him a pack of lies.

So many lies. Dash did not know about her editing works of erotica. Fortunately neither did Marcus. Only Venetia knew that and had agreed that even in a sound and happy marriage, some secrets were best kept from the man.

Maryanne caught a glimpse of herself in an ornate oval mirror as they neared the drawing room doors. She looked so terribly ordinary—a girl with bland brown curls and wide brown eyes filled with nervous fear. A glow touched her chubbier cheeks. And much larger breasts stuck out in front.

She looked enceinte . . . and guilty.

Venetia did not know she had carefully continued to edit

naughty books for the last three months. She discreetly sent the works to Mr. Osbourne, the aging man-of-affairs hired by Georgiana, who tended the typesetting, press, and distribution of the works to their booksellers. It had been so easy to continue—since Venetia and Marcus had stayed in London for the birth of their baby, and she had stayed with them.

And no one, not even Venetia, knew about the debts she and Georgiana had incurred to publish books to support their authors. Georgiana had promised her it would be paid, and some was, but only enough to mollify creditors and landlords.

Maryanne's steps faltered. "He was with Marcus for hours. What do you think happened?"

"There were no shots."

"But we wouldn't have heard a whip, if that was your husband's weapon of choice." But then, Dash might not object to a whipping. . . .

Hand on her elbow, Venetia towed her forward.

Surely he had refused to marry her, pointing out that he was not about to be forced into marriage with a wanton tart. Had Marcus persuaded him?

Dash knew she was quite capable of making love in a hot-air balloon . . . in public. Proper, decent ladies didn't do what she had done. The sort of lady he would expect to *marry* would not be willing to do that.

He knew of her friendship with Georgiana—what if he learned about her publishing business and the debts?

She took a steadying breath. Venetia would never tell Dash that Maryanne was Georgiana's partner. There was no possible way he could find out the truth on his own.

The ornate double doors loomed before her, painted in cream and touched with gilt. Behind those doors, Dash was waiting for her. Alone.

In a niche beside, a water nymph bowed her head in demure innocence. Maryanne longed to hit the simpering statue with its water jug.

Impulsively she hugged Venetia. "I'll go in alone."

Venetia nodded. "Good luck."

Maryanne gave her sister a fleeting smile. Luck!

She'd forced him into marriage, and she couldn't—*couldn't*—let him know how she had published erotica with a courtesan and now owed four thousand pounds to creditors! If society learned about that . . .

He'd hate her. Perhaps he could even use the truth to divorce her and bring terrible scandal onto Venetia and Grace. At least the winter weather had given Venetia a reason to dissuade their mother from coming to London just yet. Maryanne swallowed hard. Once she was engaged, she could admit her mistake to her mother.

But first, she had to agree to marriage with a stranger. And she had to concoct an incredibly cunning lie to convince this experienced, dangerous man to surrender four thousand pounds to her—she needed it from her dowry to pay the rest of the debts.

Expanding her chest on a deep breath, Maryanne pushed open the doors.

What was delicious Dash doing right now? Who was he fucking?

Harriet, Lady Evershire, paced the bedchamber of Mrs. Master's, awaiting the nude young wench who would remove her clothes.

No more dreaming about Dash!

Once, with Craven, she'd almost cried out Dash's name. It was preposterous. How long had her affair with Dash lasted? A mere fortnight. And it had been five years ago, before Moredon and Anne had married.

Poor Anne . . . Harriet had visited Buckstead to be of some comfort to her brother and sister-in-law . . . and then he had come. Dash. And she had been driven mad with wanting him. It had been like a craving for opium, a hunger she couldn't fight or ignore. And Dash had rebuffed her every subtle flirtation. She had turned to pointed barbs and biting wit—for their arguments had been the flame that ignited their passions years ago. Yet this time, he barely seemed to notice her.

And she had been forced to give herself pleasure—in her bed, in the bath, on illicit walks out into the woods—and once she'd caught a group of young men watching her after she'd lifted up her skirts. They thought she'd been about to pee, not diddle herself. She'd run the little buggers off, though for once she'd reached climax without thinking of Dash. How lovely it had been to imagine four young men making love to her, awestruck by her breasts and arse. Four men with straight young cocks to please her.

Dash had stayed for three months, and she'd stayed, too, drawn to him by irresistible desire. He had left a few times—his estate of Swansley was only two hours away by carriage—and she'd barely been able to breathe each time, awaiting his return.

When had she become such a fool?

Harriet stopped by the wall of restraints—where ropes and whips hung from ornate gold hooks.

This was what she wanted—the flail with its six leather tongues. The grip filled her palm, hard yet pliant enough to mold to her hand.

With a smooth arc, she cracked the whip against the bed-post.

Why did Dash possess her thoughts so?

Thank heaven, Barrett had turned up while she was at Buckstead. He'd taken a room at the village inn. How naughty it had been to walk there, to spend her afternoon being fucked senseless by that brute of a man. He had introduced her to the most wonderful pleasure—he'd tied her to the bed, slid one of his dildos inside her, and then had pushed his own thick penis inside. It had been marvelous!

He'd guessed her obsession with Dash, though, and that had terrified her. He would blindfold her and make her speak about Dash, what he had done that day, all sorts of silly details. She would grow soaked with arousal, and finally Barrett had begun spanking her for her foolish preference for Dash. Oh, how she had enjoyed the punishment.

Harriet lashed vigorously with the whip until her cheeks glowed a healthy pink. She caught sight of her reflection in the cheval mirror.

She had hoped Dash forgotten once he had left for London, yet now, blast it, she dreamed of him at night.

She turned in front of the mirror and slowly drew up her skirts until she bared her rump. The plump, round cheeks looked so fetching reflected in the glass. She flicked the whip around so the splayed tail struck her arse.

How delightfully naughty it looked to see the tendrils of black leather against her pale peach skin. Wouldn't Mr. Barrett love to watch her do this? He would want to be the one to wield the whip, but she would refuse.

Lazily she flicked the whip, letting the ends dance over the deep, shadowed valley between her cheeks.

A knock at the door stopped her, and she let her skirts slide down before calling, "Enter."

She waited with impatience as the young girl slipped in and bobbed a curtsy. "My lady."

Harriet glanced around. There would be peepholes, and Craven would be fastened to one set, excited by her play with the whip, ready to watch her be undressed by this large-breasted girl. Harriet pulled up her skirts. "You have been tardy, and I am impatient. Suck my cunny. Immediately!"

But as the girl obediently sank to her knees, and Harriet clasped the back of her chair to hold herself up, the door opened again.

Not Craven, but Barrett. "Not yet, my dear." He gave a roguish grin and sent the girl away.

"I was expecting the delights of her tongue in my slit, Barrett." Harriet drew herself up in autocratic splendor.

Barrett produced a length of black silk. "A man will enter the room in a minute, my dear. You will suck his hard, eager cock until he climaxes down your throat."

His large hands pulled the silk over her eyes. He tied a tight knot behind her head, pulling her hair. The jolt of pain had her on the brink of climax.

"Do you understand?" he demanded.

"Yes," she breathed.

She would play any game Barrett suggested—she was not afraid of him. And she stood like the countess she was as he roughly pulled her hands behind her back. Coarse rope touched her wrists, and she caught her breath.

"Perhaps it is even the man you cannot have. The staff you suck might belong to Swansborough."

9

Maryanne squared her shoulders and walked into the drawing room.

Dash—Lord Swansborough—stood at the window, apparently looking out upon the bleak winter world. Water and mist hugged the panes, and gray clouds cast gloom into the room. Three burning lamps, along with a half dozen candles and a cheery fire, filled the room with light and warmth. Still, for her, all those flames barely fought the feeling of chill.

Of foreboding.

Maryanne stood still, the door open, knowing his lordship would sense her if she stared, but she couldn't resist. His head was bowed, his gloved hand resting on the cool pane. Even in the gray light, his luxurious black hair gleamed.

Was he mourning his fate? In the daytime, most gentlemen wore a coat of color—green or blue—but he wore black. Nothing but black. A coat of black tailored to fit perfectly to his magnificent shoulders, his broad back. Snug trousers that cupped his muscular derriere. She thought of his back, naked and burnished with the hint of warm daylight, and how exotic and seductive his black silk blindfold had been against his slightly tanned skin.

And she thought of his rump, how it had flexed as he thrust in her, and how the light dusting of hairs had tickled her fingertips—

Before she could even shut the door, he turned. Her breath raced out in a whoosh.

She had not seen him for three months.

One dark brow arched, and his dimple appeared. "Verity." He bowed to her.

She pulled the door shut, turned the key in the lock. Was she locking herself in with a panther? His lordship moved with the graceful stealth of deadly wild cat as he turned from the frosted window and walked toward her. Nervously she curtsied. She had no idea where to begin or what to say. She might be pregnant, but she was not wronged, and she felt her chest tightening.

She was not going to hide in propriety and offer him tea.

She straightened, finding the courage to glance up at his eyes. Beneath thick raven lashes, his gaze dropped to her waist, which meant he knew everything.

"What did Marcus say to you? What did he write in the letter he sent to you?" Maryanne felt her cheeks grow warm. Nerves had made her voice sharper than she'd intended. "I wasn't allowed to look, of course. I apologize if he insulted you in any way. No one seems to accept that I am entirely to blame."

What was he thinking? With his coal-black eyes shrouded by those lush lashes, she couldn't tell. Last time, he had been drunk.

He stopped by the fireplace, his back to it, and he rested his beautiful hand—in a black glove—on the mantel's corner. "Do you want this? Marriage?"

Seductive and deep, his voice reminded her of a growl—enthralling, dangerous, and sensual. That husky baritone brought her back to the way he'd spoken to her when she'd been in his bed. So teasing, so heart-wrenchingly intimate . . .

"Verity?" His lips lifted on the right in a brief smile.

She did—she had to want marriage, but at the sight of that smile, she blurted, "Not a forced marriage, no."

"If it wasn't forced, would you want to marry me?"

Yes, yes, yes! But her face burned hot, and she couldn't admit it. "Wouldn't any woman?"

He pointed to the settee, obviously insisting she sit. "That's not an answer, Verity. This time, I want truth."

She didn't want to sit and look up to him. It was bad enough that he towered over her when she was standing. She had to tip her head back to look at him. Just as she had in the balloon's basket when he'd bent over her, his body pressed to her from behind, surrounding her, protecting her, scandalously making love to her. . . .

"In truth, I didn't think I wanted to marry at all," she admitted.

His brow went up. "But you obviously enjoy sexual pleasures."

She flushed at that, which was silly, considering what they'd done.

You must marry him. It's the only way out. You must. You must. . . .

But there was no solution. To protect her family from scandal and disaster, she was forcing Dash into one. She couldn't make anyone happy in this—Venetia would be furious when she wed out of duty, Marcus would be enraged if she didn't, and Dash would be forced into either a marriage or a duel.

"Please sit, love."

Love. A casual endearment. Was Dash using it to control anger?

She didn't want to sit, but she realized she was shaking. Nothing in his stance—elegant hand resting on the elaborate mantel, booted ankles crossed—told her what he truly felt. With his face turned toward her, away from the fire, his dark eyes were hidden in shadow.

She moved to a wing chair by the fireplace, but she stopped behind it, the tall back between them like a wall of safety.

"I didn't mean to trap you." Her voice was a mere squeak.

"But you did, sweetheart."

"And I'll pay the highest price—I'm the one who will bear a babe!"

Pain contorted his handsome mouth, and she regretted the slicing words. His sister's loss must still be a raw wound.

"Venetia and Marcus were at daggers drawn over this. They were arguing just before . . ." She floundered. "I can't have them fighting about it—I can't! I think the fighting brought on the birth."

Fire roared into the quiet, and the clock marked the endless wait. Her tummy made pirouettes inside her. She needed a biscuit.

Finally he spoke. "And so, despite the fact you don't want to marry me, you would agree to spare her any more distress?"

Despite his light tone, Maryanne shivered. She nodded. "I'm sorry—it isn't very considerate of me. But it wouldn't help. Venetia doesn't want me to marry you."

"And why in blazes not?"

"You . . . you're too lewd."

A raw, masculine laugh rang in her ears, a laugh that made her skin suddenly aware of sensation—the brush of warm air, the pulse of her own blood, the nearness of him.

His smell teased her, reminding her of how delectable it had been to hold him close and bury her nose against the sweaty hair on his chest and the warm, shaved skin of his throat.

Beneath lowered lashes she saw him move from the fireplace. Foolishly she shut her eyes.

His blend of sandalwood and leather and clean skin surrounded her—a scent that made her nipples harden and her quim pulse. For her, it was the smell of desire. She let her lashes part a bit, enough to see his gloved hand approach. His fingers touched her chin, tipped her face up. "Thank you for the truth, but where is your fire, Verity?"

Mystified, Maryanne stared into those black eyes—as dark and gleaming as jet, as unfathomable as a dark lake.

"That night, you were a fireball, love. Every bit as lewd as

I was. And now you're cowering before me—when I'm the one who ruined you."

"My fire?" Shame and fear and confusion sat like a cannonball in her belly. Or rather, like a baby growing in her womb. "My fire burned too brightly and left disaster. You should reject me. You should walk away. I've no right—"

He abruptly moved his hand back. "I would never walk away from responsibility."

Dear heaven, she'd offended him. Offending him by implying he would want to take her offer to run. She didn't understand what he wanted. He wouldn't want to marry a wanton—why was he worried about her fire?

"Why did you go there, love? Why would Trent's sister-in-law go to the rescue of a courtesan?"

Helplessly she looked into midnight eyes. "That was just a story. I heard the . . . the courtesan's name and . . . and used it."

And how are you going to explain why you need all that money?

"Then why did you go? What did you want?"

"Excitement," she breathed. It wasn't entirely a lie. "Adventure like Venetia had."

"So I was an adventure?"

"You were . . ." How to explain what she didn't know? "Temptation. I just couldn't resist."

A purely wicked, utterly heartbreaking smile touched his lips. It vanished quickly. "How are you feeling? Are you sick?"

"Yes, but I'm told by my sister it's good to be sick."

"Sweetheart, my child is in your belly. Neither of us has a choice about marriage."

"But it wasn't your fault. And you know nothing about—!" She clapped her hand to her mouth.

"About what, sweet?"

Around her hand, she whispered, "My father. Who he is." She'd leaped at the first lie she could think of—she couldn't tell him about her debt. "No, that's silly." She blushed. "Of course, you do. You know he is Rodesson, of course, because you know Venetia, but—"

"I can assure you I am not worried about your parents. Or your illegitimacy."

She cringed. It wasn't the stigma that made her spine jerk at the word. It was what it meant—that her mother had surrendered to love and made a dreadful mistake.

"What will your family think?" She must be mad. She was trying to talk him out of marriage, when marriage was exactly what she needed.

Venetia had been accepted by the *ton* but only because no one in Society—except Dash—knew Rodesson was their father.

"My sister won't care. As for the rest of Society, no one will dare insult my wife."

His wife. "No—I can't. This is wrong!"

His dark brows shot up at that.

"It is. Wrong." She was floundering again, lost in the harsh set of his mouth. "You have to make do with someone so . . . inappropriate simply because you . . . bedded me—"

"Hush."

How could he make such a soft word sound like a curt command?

He took two strides and stopped at the other side of the chair. "We will marry. And make the best of it."

It was the command of a peer, and she knew it. Her shin bumped the wing chair, and she realized it was like a wall between armies—they were using it as a defense while they sized each other up.

Dismay rose, and she bent her head to blink away sudden, silly tears. Was this to be their future? Anger, duty, and awkwardness?

Dash's warm fingers brushed her arm, and she quivered at the intimate touch. No glove now—he'd taken it off. Just his bare, long-fingered hand, stroking.

The curved wood back of the chair dug into her right hand. Her fingers drove into the silk cushion.

She belonged to him now, and he was caressing her.

Could she enjoy his caress, or should she feel guilty?

She was going to marry him, and she knew nothing about him, nothing except the warnings she'd heard, the rumors of debauchery and wickedness and scandal. *He hung a woman upside down and pleasured her that way*, Venetia had admitted.

Matrons gossiped, and girls whispered about him. *He wears black because his heart and soul are black, because he is like Lucifer, because he is dark and tragic. . . .*

He had made love to a woman who dangled from a hook in the ceiling. He was willing to have sex in a hot-air balloon.

But then, so was she. And it had been glorious.

"In truth, I never planned to marry either," Dash said.

That startled. It made sense for her, a penniless country girl born in scandal, with a shocking father who painted erotic art. It did not make sense for a peer of the realm. Did she dare ask why?

"And I'm loath to force you to enter my world, love."

His world? He'd said she would be accepted by society. "You mean your . . . orgies and brothels?"

"My family, love. Not my sister—the rest of them. Anne is mourning now, which worries me, but she's got the warmest heart of anyone I've known. She's the only one in my family who is sane. I'm worried, love, that it will be hard for you."

"W—what do you mean?"

"I'll give you the truth, Verity," Dash murmured. "What you need to know."

His fingers stroked along her neck; the gesture of simple possession made her cunny throb.

"My uncle is mad. He was a tyrant when I was young, filled with thwarted ambition, and he hated me. My cousin wishes me dead. My aunt lives in a world of her own, and my uncle's mistress, a lady he has kept for twenty-five years, lives in their home. She rules the west wing, my aunt the east. On top of that, my sister-in-law is having an affair with Craven, who makes me look like a blessed angel."

His intense, dark eyes watched her. Was he waiting for her to turn and run?

Perhaps, because in a silky murmur, he asked, "So which of us has trapped the other into disaster, Verity?"

But then she saw the lines around his sensual mouth, the tension there. She saw his throat move as he swallowed hard. He was afraid of what she would think. He, a wealthy viscount and wild libertine, feared her rejection.

She couldn't credit it. "My mother ran away with Rodesson to Gretna Green but, in the end, they did not marry. Perhaps because both knew that an earl's daughter who hoped for love and a wild artist wouldn't suit. My mother's father, the Earl of Warren, disowned her, of course, because she was ruined and pregnant. She lived in a small village and invented a sea-faring man named Hamilton to be her husband and our father. I grew up pretending to be the daughter of a fictitious man while my father lived an artist's flamboyant life in London and Italy. You might bring dotty relatives, but I bring a fabricated past built entirely on deceit."

Dash laughed, natural and deep, as though truly entertained. "Then perhaps, sweeting, we were meant to be. It wasn't chance that sent you careening into that study at Mrs. Master's. You are owed marriage, Verity." His voice washed over her, as potent as his touch. How could simple words make her chest so tight?

His finger followed the neckline of her gown, slipping in to skim across the swell of her breasts. She knew the sensation of soaring again, as she had in the balloon basket, with stars surrounding her and the world at her feet.

"We enjoyed making love," he murmured. "Marriage is to produce a child, which we've certainly proven we do very well. There can be more—we'll enjoy that. And children will give you pleasure."

Even as his hand cupped her neck and she whimpered in desire, she abruptly dropped back to earth—like the balloon's basket landing with a bump. She knew what he meant behind those words. Children would give her the love he could not.

His hand slipped into his pocket, and he drew out a small pouch. "Though it's anticlimatic, I should do this properly."

Before Maryanne could blink, he had dropped to one knee. He spilled something from the velvet bag into his palm. Something that reflected candlelight like faceted glass.

He reached out and gently clasped her fingers. "My dear Miss Hamilton, will you make me the happiest man in England?"

It wasn't glass, of course. The large, clear stone was most likely a diamond. Venetia possessed such things now, and Maryanne saw again how she was a product of her country upbringing. A noble lady would have thought "diamond"—not "glass"—at once.

So, however, would Georgiana, and that gave her courage.

"Goodness," she teased. "You're asking me to change my mind even after you've produced the ring."

Frowning, he stared up at her. Oh, no—he thought she was serious. His lips cranked down.

She dropped to her knees in front of him, getting tangled in her skirts. "I meant it as a joke. A play on your words—you'd be the happiest man in England if I said no. I'm so sorry. I bungled it."

"You didn't, love." The dimple returned, and his wide grin whisked away sensible thought. She struggled as she looked into his black eyes. The irises were as velvety black as the pupils. Surrounded by dark lashes, they were hypnotic.

If she took his ring, she would be the fiancée of this handsome, seductive . . . stranger.

He cupped her cheek, and the cool gold of the ring's band

touched her skin. A mere inch from her mouth, he smiled; then his lips softened and she knew . . .

A kiss to seal their fate.

It should be proper, brief, the touch of people who should understood they were strangers, who were embarking on marriage out of honor to correct a mistake.

But it wasn't.

His fingers slid into her hair. Hot, beautiful, his mouth slanted over hers. Lovingly his tongue teased hers, and she soared between desire and tears. She'd worn no gloves, and she fed her senses on the feel of him beneath her fingertips. The soft silk of his hair. The roughness of his strong jaw. The slight rasp of stubble on his neck.

They would be wed. He would be hers.

Romantic foolishness. He never truly would be hers.

But she slipped her arms around his neck and impulsively pressed her breasts to his chest. In answer, he moaned into her mouth and melded his lips and hers. Fire burned inside her again. This heat could melt her, scorch her.

Dash leaned back, drawing her with him. He broke the kiss and sprawled onto his back upon the patterned carpet. With his arm crooked as a pillow beneath his head, he smiled a wicked invitation. "Climb on top, love. Pin me to the rug and have your wicked way with me."

His hand pressed to the vee between her thighs, bunching her skirts between her legs, pushing against her cunny. Even that, even just that was maddeningly good. He rubbed there, against her aroused clit, until she was panting and moving against him.

He needed a wife, not a wanton, but she couldn't stop.

Hiking her skirts to her hips, she straddled his legs—scandalous sin, this, in her brother's home—and bent to press her kiss onto Dash's full, firm, delicious mouth.

He coaxed her mouth wide, their tongues tangled. Her hair tumbled free of her prim chignon, ordinary brown curls dangling before her eyes.

Footsteps? Had she heard that? The creak of the door? Panic raced in her heart, and she jerked back.

A fevered glance behind proved it was only conscience. The door was still closed and locked, of course.

Strong fingers threaded into her mussed hair, and he drew her back to his mouth. "I want you now. I need to hear your cry of pleasure—it will be sweeter than even your 'yes' to my proposal. Or did you ever say yes?"

"Yes. I mean, I don't know if I did. But yes, of course."

"Of course." Dimples bracketed his mouth as his fingers delved into the slit of her drawers.

She gasped as his fingers plunged up her cunny, his tongue invading her mouth. She feasted on his mouth and thrust against his hand as furiously as he tormented her.

Rough fingertips found her clit. She needed her release so much. She jerked against his hand, rubbing, exploring, seeking what she needed—

His fingers crooked, rubbing her clit so hard she saw stars. She grasped his wrist, stopping him.

He broke the kiss to laugh harshly against her lips. "So sweet and demure but such a wildcat about getting your orgasm, aren't you, love?"

"Don't stop," she demanded. She kissed him again and rubbed against his hand—

Oh, yes.

"There will be no propriety in our bedroom, sweeting," he promised. "Only the most inventive lovemaking for us. The delight of marriage is that we can explore whatever we want."

Whatever they wanted? And he would know so much.

"Whatever you want, love. Bondage. Spankings. Dildoes in your creamy cunny and up your tight little arse."

All his throaty promises excited her. Titillated, thrilled.

"Yes, Verity, fuck hard against my hand—I'm yours to use. Make yourself come." Harsh, gritty, the words whispered against her lips.

"What if I want to soar across London in a balloon, f—fucking all the while?"

He cupped her breast, pinching her nipple. She was biting him, her teeth on his soft lower lip, biting and banging hard against his fingers.

"Ow! Blast, yes," he groaned.

Oh! Like the crack of a whip, her body jerked in orgasm. It flooded, it overwhelmed, like plunging into cream and velvet and silk and sweat and joy and bliss. . . .

She was falling—

She was. He'd lifted her and flipped her over, with one hand at her back to keep her safe. The rug rasped her bared legs. His hand was still at her cunny, which clenched madly, wanting his cock inside.

Dash was up over her, blotting out candlelight. His hand was at his trouser buttons. She arched up—

"Wait, love," he groaned. "The babe. We can't risk hurting the baby."

10

"In the last three months, no more women have vanished," Sir William said from the wing chair beside the fireplace in Dash's bedchamber. "None have turned up dead."

Dash tugged at the cuffs of his tailcoat, his gut in a knot. "This is the morning of my wedding, and you want to discuss missing women?"

He glanced at his reflection in the cheval mirror as he strode by—the nervous groom in a snowy cravat, ivory waistcoat, black topcoat, and immaculate trousers. Lines bracketed his mouth, and even he saw the tension in his eyes. In a quarter hour he'd leave for church, marry by special license, and brave the snowy roads to bring his reluctant wife to Swansley, his estate, for Christmas.

Sir William blew a ring of smoke. "It has to be discussed," he returned, grim-faced.

"No women disappeared in London while I was away in the country with Anne." Frustration forced Dash to snap, "You keep hinting at my guilt. Do you think I did it, Sir William?"

"Someone is going to great lengths to make it appear so."

"I'm getting fed up with this. If you aren't going to arrest me, give me some damned help. What do you suggest I do?"

"Stop pacing, Swansborough, for a start."

"Any man facing his wedding is nervous. Are you planning to arrest me after the vows? Will you let me kiss my blushing bride first?"

"I don't believe it's you, Swansborough, though an arrest must be made. The *ton* is still horrified by that brutal murder in Hyde Park. Even though the victim was an actress."

"You had the runners investigate Eliza Charmody's death—her family, her former protectors—but you found nothing?"

Sir William gave a curt nod. "Nothing. And you pursued Lord Craven and his partner?"

"I'm to be married. I don't want to discuss this now." By the end of the morning, he would be married to Maryanne. Who had lied to him about her reasons for going to that salon—he had read it in her eyes. After spending his childhood with his mad uncle, he knew when someone was lying.

Surely Maryanne Hamilton, Trent's sister-in-law, was not part of this plot to destroy him. Or was she? He couldn't trust his uncle or his cousin, who were bloody family—why trust Maryanne, the stranger he was about to marry?

"This needs to be discussed, Swansborough."

"I've already written to you about the details." Dash groaned. "Craven keeps a small estate for notorious orgies, which I visited, but if he keeps ladies chained up on the premises, he's damned good at hiding them."

"What about your uncle?"

"He's old and ill. Essentially bedridden."

"But still able to employ people to carry out his wishes."

Dash stopped his pacing by the fireplace. "Dangerous to hire others to murder women—too easy to lead to blackmail."

"But your uncle isn't entirely sane, is he?"

Just those simple words brought back Dash's memories of a childhood of terror. But he refused to be a slave to fear, anger, and hatred on his wedding day.

Even if he wasn't certain he could trust his bride.

"No, he isn't sane," Dash agreed. "And he's willing to kill

to get what he wants. From Buckstead, I hired men to watch his home. Trustworthy men, ex-soldiers—solid and thorough. I hired them to watch everyone in my uncle's home, including my cousin Robert."

"Did you go yourself?"

Hell, how could he admit the instinctive fear that had gripped him at the thought of seeing his uncle again? He was a grown man, not a frightened boy.

"Anne asked me not to," he admitted.

"She knows someone is trying to frame you for kidnapping and murder?"

"Of course not. She overheard me discussing the trip with her husband."

"Does Anne know about the past?" Sir William asked softly.

"She knows my uncle tried to kill me—she caught him at it once." Dash's cool, jaded tone belied the gut-wrenching jolt of fear that slashed through him at the memory. When he'd later caught Anne, terrified and hiding in the shadows, he hadn't known if his uncle had seen her. He'd lived in terror for a fortnight because he knew if James Blackmore had thought his nine-year-old niece had seen him attempt to commit murder, he'd kill her to silence her.

At the time, Dash had thought Anne hadn't understood what she'd seen. All the more dangerous, for an innocent slip of the tongue would have ensured her death.

Desperate, he'd turned to Sophia, who had assured him Anne would have her protection. And she had taken Anne away to live with her.

He owed Sophia a debt that would last a lifetime. She'd provided Anne with a safe home. With love.

"Lady Farthingale is still missing," Sir William said. "We've found no trace of her after she was taken from Vauxhall."

Dash rubbed his temple. Even though Lady F had been missing for three months, her only family were the children from Lord F's first marriage, who did not care where their stepmother was. Her disappearance meant she wasn't asking them for money.

"Potentially alive then," he said hopefully.

"Or buried in a shallow grave."

Dash's gut lurched again, but he shook his head at the magistrate. "I doubt it if the plan is to make me look guilty."

He had one lead—on a dark-haired Cornishman who had flirted with a pair of prostitutes and had mentioned a jape involving sex and a fat fee. A runner had found a man named Trevelyan Ball, who had been seen at Vauxhall and then had taken the Great North Road, but the trail went cold quickly. No one had seen a woman with him.

Three months had passed, and Dash was no closer to proving his innocence.

"Why are you marrying Trent's sister-in-law?"

The question caught Dash by surprise. And he glanced up to a smile on his friend's normally taciturn face.

"And in such haste?" Sir William added.

The answer was obvious, and he shot his friend a quick look. All of Society could easily guess the answer, given his reputation, but it was his duty to preserve his wife's reputation.

"Love," Dash answered. "What other reason drives a man to irrational measures?"

Sir William's brow arched. "*You* have fallen in love?"

"Absolutely besotted." Dash went to his desk, slid the small key in the uppermost lock, and opened the drawer. Pulling out a bundle of papers—copies of notes taken over the last three months—he tossed them to the polished surface. "Take these. I should have sent them to you, but I decided to propose as soon as I returned to London."

He caught Sir William's amused smile.

"I see you are not wearing black from head to toe for your wedding day."

Dash felt his lips twist in a grimace. "No, on my wedding

day I've no desire to proclaim my purgatory." The mantel clock chimed the half hour. "It's time for us to leave for the church."

Soon, soon he would see his bride in her wedding gown. He started pacing again, suddenly eager to see her, as eager and nervous as a virgin schoolboy with a courtesan. He gave Sir William a jaded shrug. "I'll be leaving for the country immediately after the ceremony—which should mean that no more women in London will be at risk. Thank heaven for that."

Firelight glinted on the magistrate's spectacles, hiding his reaction.

Soon he would be alone in a carriage with Maryanne. At the thought, his cock stirred. Swelling, straightening, leaking precoital juices into his linens. He remembered how tempting she'd looked as she straddled him, lust fierce in her normally gentle brown eyes.

But he couldn't do anything to risk their child, which surely meant he couldn't have lusty, wild sex with her. But he hungered to make love to Maryanne. To relive that moment in the balloon's basket when he'd exploded inside her and felt like he was flying.

But hot sex would have to wait until she'd safely given birth.

Six long months from now.

A rap at the bedchamber door signaled that his carriage stood at the ready.

Time to tempt himself with a bride he hungered for but could not touch. A bride he desired but didn't trust.

Sir William picked up the bound sheath of pages. "I never thought I'd see the day you put on the leg shackles, Swansborough."

"Neither did I."

Did all brides start their wedding day on their knees before a chamber pot? Maryanne set the pot aside and stood on shaky legs. Steam rose from the water in her basin, and she sighed in relief as she splashed it onto her face.

She threw another handful at her eyes and cleaned her mouth. With a soft towel at her face, she turned. Her silk gown lay on the counterpane covering her bed. A tug of the bellpull would fetch Nan, who would help her dress. For some reason she could not bring herself to start.

There was so much to do. . . .

And she would be wed, even if she were fetched up at the altar wearing only her shift, with hair tangled and face still wet. Marcus would insist on that, no matter how hard Venetia fought him.

She couldn't bear to cause them to fight. She had to wait and say it was her desire.

A glimpse of her cheval mirror showed a woman who looked as if she were facing the gallows.

In mere hours, she would kiss Dash as his wife. She would caress his broad shoulders, rest her hand on his powerful chest, she would undress and go to his bed.

Heat coursed through her. At once her nipples tightened beneath muslin, her breasts—already tight and full—ached. Another ache, deep and intense, began in her belly and flooded to her quim.

To protect the baby, to ensure she didn't lose it, Dash had refused to make love.

He must hate her for trapping him.

Swallowing hard, Maryanne picked up the latest note Georgiana had sent—under a false name.

> *My goodness! Viscount Swansborough? How magnificent! How mad! How delicious. For there is no greater lover than he—his reputation is legendary. What a wonderful marriage bed you shall have, and I am so green with envy that my earl has taken to purchasing me emeralds by the score. But however did this come about, my dear? You must tell me all.*

I have sent you the first pages for your opinion, for you can't leave me now, not when we are in such dire straits! I've had no chance to have paste made of the jewels, so I have no funds as yet, and we must publish another book, though that blasted printer has sworn he'll burn the next one unless he is paid. Please, please, please, my good friend—we are partners. You cannot forsake me now—

Five manuscript pages had been folded and tucked in the envelope. The beginnings of a new novel by Tillie Plimpton.

Maryanne shuddered. If their publisher was threatening to burn a book instead of print it, Georgiana had probably lied and the debts hadn't been eased at all. Georgiana needed money.

What would happen if she wrote back to Georgiana and insisted she could no longer edit erotic manuscripts? Would her friend reveal all to Dash?

Would she demand money to keep her secrets?

Georgiana—blackmailing her. Why had she not thought of this possibility before? She'd thought they had been friends. She'd never thought a friend would turn against her.

What a fool she was.

Maryanne's trembling hands tore the letter in strips, and she dropped two as she struggled to tear those into tiny chunks. She swept them all up, crumpled them, and then rushed to the fireplace. Her stomach tipped as she dropped to her knees and threw in the pieces. Even as the papers turned red and curled, she shivered with fear.

Dash would want to throttle her. He'd be furious—and they wouldn't be able to fight the nasty rumors, for they would be true!

Given he enjoyed tying up women, heaven only knew what he'd do to her.

"Why are you not wearing your dress? What in heaven's name have you been doing?"

Maryanne leaped unsteadily to her feet as Venetia swept in, her tiny son, Richard Nicholas Charles Wyndham, cradled in her arms. The room seemed to lurch beneath Maryanne's feet.

Venetia knew about the letter. . . .

No, of course not. Maryanne shook off the paralyzing guilt. Her sister had come because it was time—time to leave. And she was still standing in her shift and stockings with her hair tumbling loose down her back.

Her sister wore a lovely gown of dove-gray velvet with a lace-trimmed muslin blanket thrown over her shoulder to protect the dress from any baby accidents. Her sister, despite lack of sleep, glowed with delight as she stroked her baby's tiny form.

"I was being sick," Maryanne protested.

"I'm not surprised." Venetia moved into the room, closed the door, and then marched to the bellpull. Even as she juggled wee Richard in her arms to free one hand, he slept on contentedly, dark lashes brushing cherubic cheeks.

Maryanne's heart gave a pang. Soon she would be a mother holding a baby. . . .

If she survived the horrible mysterious experience of childbirth. She'd heard Venetia's screams. And Marcus had been at Venetia's side to protect her; Dash wouldn't do that for her, would he? He didn't love her.

The maid would come soon—she only had a few moments to ask Venetia her question.

Didn't you and Marcus make love while you were pregnant? It can't harm the baby, can it?

But Maryanne couldn't find the courage to put her question into words.

She must.

Dash wouldn't wait six months for her. He would go to another woman's bed. "Venetia—" Her words died away as she saw her sister's pursed lips and serious eyes. Her heart gave a leap—Venetia's expression could only mean trouble. What more could there be?

"Rodesson has come," Venetia said. "To give you best wishes and a kiss before you wed."

"No!" She'd spoken without thought, and the vehemence surprised her.

"Are you certain? He won't go to the church, of course."

"I know." Marcus would give her away—he was her guardian, after all, and her father was supposed to be dead. Rodesson, the scandalous artist of erotic paintings, could not attend the wedding of a decent, proper young woman, a woman protected by a noble family. It would drench them all in scandal.

"I don't wish to see him. He never wished to see me." Maryanne wished that hadn't sounded so petulant and young.

Shushing her stirring baby, Venetia met her gaze with a frankly surprised expression.

Of course she would be astonished. Maryanne had always lived to make peace. All her life, she had bit back every tear, every scream, every pout. But this was her wedding morning, and for once she could not think of pleasing everyone else.

"He couldn't come and see you, Maryanne. It would have been a scandal."

How angry Venetia's calm and patronizing tone made her. "You don't understand!"

Venetia settled on the chaise, babe in arms, glowing and happy and lovely. "Then tell me."

Once she would have mumbled something meaningless. But not this morning. "I was Mother's mistake. I knew it. She might have made her peace with Rodesson, but I've made my peace with neither. I can't wipe away a lifetime of crying into my pillow with a few smiles and hugs. I won't."

Venetia stared at her. "Mis—"

"Of course I was a mistake," she broke in. "Do you really think she wished for another child? But she couldn't resist him and went to his bed. I was her folly. I was proof of her weakness to passion. Her foolishness. I heard her speak of it!"

"You didn't blame Swansborough for seducing you," Venetia reminded her.

"He didn't seduce Maryanne Hamilton, he bedded a whore. Or so he thought." It twisted inside to say that, sharp as a knife. Venetia began to protest, and Maryanne rushed on. "It's quite different. And I'm not Mother. Even if my marriage turns out to be a nightmare, and my life is torture, I will not consider this child a folly. I will give it nothing but sunshine and smiles and love, for any mistake is my cross to bear, and mine alone."

"It's perhaps a little naive to think that babies are only sunshine and smiles. . . ." Venetia gave a rueful smile.

Perhaps so, but Maryanne rushed on. "I can't go to him. I won't. I have to marry a man I don't even know, but he doesn't ask me to pretend I love him. Don't ask me to go to Rodesson and pretend love and forgiveness."

Her maid, Nan, knocked and then opened the door. Not just her maid—a bevy of them, all preparing to transform her into a bride fit for a peer.

She swallowed hard. Tears were too close to the surface.

Venetia nodded. "I will tell him and then come back to help. Mother and Grace wish to see you also."

Her abigail was carrying her clean shift, and the question she must ask Venetia couldn't be spoken now. She thought Venetia and Marcus had enjoyed lovemaking while Venetia was enceinte, but she needed to know for certain.

She couldn't bear to wait six months to make love to Dash again.

Outside her door, Maryanne heard Venetia speaking in a low voice. The voice that answered she recognized as her mother's, and she took a deep breath to prepare herself.

Grace rushed in first, her pretty face alight with happiness. "Your husband is so wonderfully handsome, Maryanne!"

"He is not my husband yet."

Grace hugged her. "I am so happy for you. You are so deserving of a good marriage. You have always been the most good-natured of all of us. I know you will be very happy."

She wished she could be as certain. Grace stepped back as their mother came into the room.

I was a mistake. Her folly.

Why was that all she could think of as her mother came toward her, smiling? Her mother's silvery white hair was elegantly dressed and Maryanne realized she had never seen Olivia look lovelier.

"Congratulations, my dear." Her mother hugged her.

Maryanne felt so awkward hugging her mother back.

Then Olivia straightened and turned to Grace. "Please go and help Venetia, dear. I wish to speak to Maryanne alone."

Maryanne felt her tummy churn as Grace left. *Please, don't let me be sick now.*

"I hope you are very much in love with Lord Swansborough." Olivia moved aside as the maids bustled about, organizing the petticoats, the corset, and the dress. "I always dreamed you would all find happiness in marriage."

Maryanne guiltily touched her tummy. She had not yet told her mother about the baby.

"I am sure I will be happy," she said. She needed something to nibble on. Desperately.

"Is there something wrong?"

Maryanne jumped at her mother's question. Venetia had looked shocked and surprised when she'd claimed to be her mother's folly. But it was true. Her mother had been expecting to marry Rodesson when she'd become pregnant with Venetia.

But then she'd learned he hadn't been faithful. He was too wild. Olivia had known she would never marry Rodesson, that he would never be the husband she'd hoped for. But she had still gone to his bed again and again because she loved him so much. And then she had become pregnant with Maryanne.

So of course I am proof of her mistake—her mistake of loving the wrong man.

But mousy Maryanne would never speak of such things, she thought ruefully. She could not be honest and say, *I know that every time you looked at me you saw the hopelessness of your love. You saw your broken heart. I saw it in your eyes.*

Instead, she went to her mother and hugged her once more. "Just wedding day nerves."

Morning sunlight streamed in through the church's modest windows. Not St. George's for this simple gathering, but Dash was glad of that. Cool air settled in this one, though, and when he'd first entered, he'd seen his breath.

Logs had been heaped on the fires, warming this sacred place, while he stood at the altar, waiting for his bride.

With thoughts anything but pure.

He was an expert at torturing himself, and he was doing it now.

Visions of Maryanne straddling his hips tormented him as he looked out on the small gathering sitting in simple pews. His cock throbbed at the memory of the sultry way she'd lifted her skirts to bare her shapely legs. He could remember the hot, silken feel of her pussy on his fingertips. He could remember her taste, her primal smell.

He was rock hard, and he needed to shift to find a more comfortable position for his thickening rod. He'd been naked at orgies, made love before dozens of witnesses, but he felt damned embarrassed to be erect in front of his marriage's witnesses in a church.

He had no family watching him. Anne had been furious—she'd wanted to come, but he'd refused to let her travel as far as London, especially in winter, and he'd sent a terse note to Moredon damning the man to hell if he relented and brought her. Anne insisted she would instead make the short trip to Swansley later, but at Dash's wedding, only Sir William stood to represent him.

His bride's mother dabbed at her eyes with a handkerchief. In joy or sorrow, Dash couldn't be sure. Rodesson was not here. Maryanne, like Venetia, was entering high society—and the connection to a scandalous artist could never be revealed. A slender blond girl sat beside Olivia Hamilton. His new sister-in-law, Grace, whom he'd never met.

Where in blazes was his bride?

Fear curdled his gut. Was she ill? Seriously? While Anne was pregnant, she'd told him the early months were worrisome, for there was always a chance of losing the baby.

Carrying a babe was dangerous business. What could he do? Ensure Maryanne kept to her bed and never moved? He'd suggested that to Anne, but she'd firmly refused and told him that it was better for a woman to be up and about.

Where was his bride?

Mad thoughts plagued him. Had she run away? Had she fled to Gretna Green with someone else?

The doors at the rear opened, welcoming more sunlight and brisk air. And his bride. Head bowed, she was breathtaking in a shimmering white silk dress. A fragile white veil fluttered about her face.

He felt a jolt of guilt over his doubts, a spear of desire at the sight of her.

Her full breasts wobbled as she moved, but in her dress, she didn't look pregnant. Slender and willowy, she looked lovely and pure and delicate. Not at all like the wanton woman who had been determined to climax with him in the hot-air balloon.

How could Trent's shy sister-in-law be the same woman who had made love to him at Mrs. Master's salon?

Her lips, pink and soft, parted with fragile uncertainty. He remembered that mouth. A wanton mouth that had tangled with his, had pressed to the swollen head of his cock, an erotic frame to the lovely tongue that had licked his shaft from tight, aching ballocks to throbbing tip.

In a house of God, about to say his vows, was he supposed to be thinking about sex?

Maryanne moved down the aisle, and the light seemed to

brighten around her, as if she shone more brightly than the sun. Her brown eyes glowed. She ducked her head and blushed.

Thank the devil there were vows to follow—otherwise he'd be tongue-tied.

Her white dress flowed over her slim hips and slender legs. He watched her hips sway with each step, his throat dry. She looked so innocent.

Some lunatic was trying to make him look guilty of murder. Was he putting Maryanne at risk, bringing her into his life? What choice did he have? He was honor bound to marry her.

And if she was innocent, honor bound to protect her.

Shoving those thoughts away, he smiled at Maryanne. Her lips trembled as she returned the smile. He'd never anticipated having a wife; now his fantasies ran riot.

He would scoop her up as she reached the altar, draw up her skirt, and bury his cock deep inside her. Bury himself in her heat. Hear her lovely moans next to his ears.

He imagined her soft brown hair—scented like field flowers—tumbling down her back. Her skin would be satin beneath his touch, warmed with dewy sweat. He could cup her plump bottom, cradle full breasts, pump her along him until they both shattered, came—

Blast, he was in church. And the minister had just muttered something about taking her hand.

Eyes cast down upon the book held on his outstretched hand, their bald minister mumbled the beginning of the ceremony. Dash had insisted on a quick ceremony, a request the mumble-mouthed man of the cloth seemed to be adhering to. They reached the part where objections were called upon—at least Dash assumed they'd reached it. There was a long pause, the minister glanced up for a second and then sought refuge again in his page.

Dash caught Maryanne's eye. She was fighting a giggle.

She glowed—she carried his child, she was going to be his, and she sparkled like a diamond.

Silence stretched around him. Pews creaked, feet shuffled. A throat cleared. He tore his gaze from Maryanne's, looked helplessly to Sir William, who mouthed *your vows*.

He was supposed to repeat the mumbling minister? Heaven help him.

He fumbled through, though he could barely speak to repeat "take thee, Maryanne Estella Hamilton." Estella. Like a star. His name Lancelot had been his mother's fancy. Was Estella her mother's desire? Or a concession to Rodesson, the artist?

Soft, lovely, Maryanne's voice carried through the church as she pledged herself to him. *I thee wed.*

The ring was pressed into his hand. He slipped it onto her finger and lifted her hand to his mouth, touching a kiss to her soft skin and the cool ring.

They were married.

How they reached the carriage, he didn't know. Her bouquet flew through the air, landing at her mother's feet. Venetia cradled her son in her arms, and Marcus stood with a hand at his wife's waist, which brought a pang to Dash's heart.

He hadn't been able to protect Anne from loss and sorrow and disappointment.

He had to do better for Maryanne.

Still, he leaned out of the carriage, waving as she did, and the carriage lurched as it started.

They hadn't shared a word yet. He cleared his throat. "I'm sorry I'm whisking you away before breakfast."

She jerked around, her arms wrapped around her chest, as though she was cold, despite her sable-trimmed pelisse and the heated bricks beneath the carriage floor. She blushed. "Oh, I've eaten so many biscuits this morning, it shouldn't matter."

He leaned back, hoping he looked more at ease than he

felt. "I wanted to get out of London. Quickly. I had a basket brought to the carriage—food for us to share."

"Th—thank you." They were trotting up the London streets now, and Maryanne turned to stare out the window.

He stretched his arm along the back of the seat, his hand resting just beyond her graceful neck. She shifted forward, just a little, as though she wanted to ensure she didn't touch his hand.

His heart lurched.

Where was his wit? His reputed charm and rakish wickedness? But guilt sat in his gut like a chunk of lead. If she was unhappy, he was the cause, and he didn't know what to do. Sex was his customary method of escape.

But he couldn't have sex with his bride.

"My sister . . . Anne told me women dream of their wedding. Hurried vows in a draughty church can't have been your dream."

"Women dream of love—" Maryanne broke off quickly.

He touched her chin, and she relented and turned her face to his. He lowered his lips until her eyes widened and her breathing quickened.

"Wait," she gasped.

"It is customary to kiss," he murmured, but his gut tightened. Would his wife reject him?

11

"I would like to kiss." Maryanne managed to smile at her husband. Her husband!

How she wished she could read his thoughts. They were married. Was he angry? He'd been so quiet. And why was he determined to whisk her away from London as fast as possible—because he was ashamed? What other reason could there be?

If he found out she needed almost five thousand pounds for debts, and that a courtesan could blackmail her, he would be beyond furious. Would he tie her up and dangle her upside down, but not with the intention of making love?

Her hands were clasped on her belly, still a small curve beneath her pretty pelisse and skirts. Maryanne took a deep breath—Venetia told her that deep breaths were a luxury she would soon lose. At least, no matter what happened between her and Dash, she had saved her baby the stigma of illegitimacy.

Dash kissed her.

His lips, warm and silky as honey on hot bread, teased hers, and his tongue urged hers to play. She gripped his arms. Blood seemed to rush from her head, leaving her dizzy. Heat surrounded her—from hot bricks beneath the carriage's floor—and her body felt as if it could catch fire.

She wanted to make love. In all the wild ways she'd read about. In every scandalous way he would want.

But as she surged forward and thrust her tongue wantonly into his mouth, Dash eased back. "Would you care for buttered buns?"

"You wish me to spread butter on your bottom?" Would he want her to lick it off? Maryanne gulped at the thought of slathering butter on his tight buttocks and licking there, tasting fresh creamery butter and his delicious skin. . . .

He raked back his dark hair—he'd tossed his hat to the seat across. "You do think I'm lewd, don't you?" With a lithe stretch, he leaned to the seat opposite and brought out a basket from a compartment.

"N—no," she stammered. But she couldn't tear her gaze from his broad back. How she would love to lick him from head to toe.

"But how does an innocent maiden think up such erotic ideas?" With a flick of the hasp, he opened the lid, and she gasped. Dozens of small baskets sat within, along with a few bottles—mild ale and wine.

"I—I don't know."

"I'm sorry I stole you away from family and hot food."

He had apologized once already. "I don't mind," she said again. "I hadn't much appetite." Which was the truth—her tummy was full of flutters and butterflies.

"You need to eat, love." He began to pile grapes on a plate for her. Hothouse grapes, of course, and she took the plate and popped one in her mouth.

Shutting her eyes, she bit and savored the explosion of sweet and tart. "Heavenly."

"And so is watching you eat, love." His strained voice sent a shiver of desire down her spine.

She opened her eyes. He reached for her plate, piled bread and fragrant slices of ham on top. She hadn't expected her husband to serve her, and his simple, thoughtful action left her startled.

He peeled off his gloves; black leather slid down to reveal lean, strong wrists and then his palms, which would be sensitive to touch, to a lick of her tongue, and finally his long, elegant fingers that knew just how to give her pleasure.

On the scavenger hunt, they'd teased and bantered with ease. Now they were married and she had no idea what to say.

His fingers caressed her neck, and all she could do was close her eyes and whimper as goose bumps washed over her skin.

Something slick and greasy touched her lips. She let her lashes rise and opened her lips to let him feed her a piece of bun. Oh, so chewy and fresh and delicious. She took the rest of the piece, her tongue and lips stroking his fingertips to do it.

She grasped his empty hand and led it down to her bosom, pressing his palm to her swollen breast. He easily opened her pelisse. His bare hands curved around the silk of her bodice.

He smiled. "Very full."

That made her think of them being filled with milk. After her baby's birth, Venetia's breasts had grown huge and hard and painful. And putting her baby to the breast had only made Venetia scream. Mrs. Collins had returned to help Venetia learn to feed her baby. Maryanne had caught a glimpse, determined to learn, and it seemed a complicated business. Venetia, who always was in control, had panicked when she could not get it to work.

Maryanne chewed her bread, feeling panic herself. Shouldn't feeding a baby be natural? Shouldn't it happen with ease?

Dash fed her another piece of bread, and before she could thank him, he lifted her onto his lap. The carriage lurched, and she almost fell off, grinding his rigid cock against her bottom.

He held her tight, and she could barely swallow.

What a gloriously naughty position.

From books, she knew men penetrated women this way. Women rode men.

She wriggled against his cock. How she loved the feel of him poking into the hot cleft between her cheeks.

But his large hands stilled her hips. "Don't tempt me too much, my sweet. I don't want to do anything to risk the child."

"But I want to make love," she whispered. "I've heard that women are very lusty during this time, and I do believe it's true." And she wriggled her bottom again, giving an invitation.

"Maryanne . . . don't. It's torture."

She twisted in his arms. His lips were firm and grim, lines of stress evident around his mouth.

"It won't harm the baby. I'm certain it won't."

But she saw at once he was not going to give in. "Six months without climax?" she cried. "I can't."

He gave a rough laugh. The raw, purely masculine sound made her cunny ache. He clasped her breasts again, with both hands.

"I'm certain Venetia didn't suffer months of celibacy." She daringly slid her hands up over his. "And—" She broke off. Was she mad to ask?

His thumb stroked her nipples through dress, corset, and shift. "And?"

"I want to keep you for my own." She knew Marcus had forsaken all others for Venetia, despite his rakish past. But Rodesson had broken her mother's heart . . . ."I will do anything to keep you as mine alone." She looked straight ahead as she spoke, too shy to meet his eyes. What if he thought her a fool? In the *ton*, most wives ignored their husband's love affairs. Fidelity was neither offered . . . nor expected.

"I know how adventurous you are, dear wife." Dash nipped her earlobe, the sharp, erotic tug of his teeth making her squeal in surprise.

How neatly he'd tried to avoid that. He rocked his hips beneath her, his cock a tease against her round bottom, but she couldn't enjoy it. Not while thinking of him going back to orgies, to other women. "How many women have you bedded?"

"What?" He'd been reaching for more bread and dropped it on her lap.

"Why should I not know? I am your wife."

He rescued the bun. "That's exactly why you shouldn't know. You are my respectable, gently bred wife."

He must be teasing her. "But other women know. Perfect strangers know. They gossip about it!"

"How many women do these perfect strangers say I've bedded?"

"The most generous estimate has been five thousand."

"I haven't bedded five thousand women."

"Please don't tell me it is closer to ten."

"If it was, my sweet, may I tell you that you are the most exquisite lover of them all?"

At the tease, she felt her cheeks blaze.

"Did you hear any other gossip?" he asked.

She shook her head.

"You are such a puzzle, love. I believed Maryanne Hamilton was a quiet, demure young lady who always seemed to be holding a book. I am beginning to understand why Marcus speaks so highly of marriage. What man wouldn't want to possess a lady who likes both literature and lusty fucking?"

His hands cupped her breasts, his lips played skilled havoc on her neck. She started guiltily at the word *literature*, but he did not seem to notice.

Why wouldn't he answer her question? She was certain he was hiding his true feelings behind teasing.

"When did you make love for your very first time?"

Maryanne could not believe the words had slipped from her lips. But suddenly she was dying to know. In the stories she'd edited, those first times seemed very popular. Just being the first time made it unforgettable. . . .

Her skirts lifted, and she knew he intended to distract her.

"It is a very important detail of your life, my lord—don't you want to share it with me?"

"Playing Verity again?" He brushed his knuckles along her inner thighs. "Most married couples of the *ton* share a bed now and again. Very few share the secrets of their souls."

"Would you want to share secrets with a wife you loved?"

His hand slid between her thighs into her silky drawers. His fingers touched her curls. He murmured, "Mmmm. Wet and sticky," and she knew she would get no answer from him.

He found her clit and mercilessly wiggled it with his fingertip.

She almost launched up through the carriage roof. "W—what do you plan to do?"

"Tease your creamy little quim until we reach home. But no more, angel. Not until I'm certain it wouldn't risk a miscarriage."

His finger rubbed and stroked her engorged clit until stars exploded before her eyes. Home, he'd said. His home, now hers, and she could barely think.

She rocked against his fingers, grinding her clit against his hand. She was swirling like the snow now buffeting the window, but she was on fire, too. His eyes sparkled at her—the climax hit her. Her mouth went wide, her eyes shut, and pleasure washed through her every nerve.

Oh!

Falling back against him, cunny still pulsing, she knew she wanted more. "Mmmm," Maryanne whispered. "I love having orgasms with you. And I love your hand playing between my legs." Then she giggled in embarrassment, shattering the seductive moment.

She turned, her head bumping his strong jaw. "I want you inside. I want—I want you to come in me again."

"God, Maryanne. No. Stop." He slid her off his lap, depositing her on the seat.

She wrapped her arms around herself. "A letter home can confirm that it won't hurt the baby—or we could ask a midwife."

"All right, sweeting." He cradled her against him. "We will."

Maryanne closed her eyes, floating in pleasure . . .

The carriage jerked, and she blinked her eyes open to gray gloom. She lay against Dash's broad chest, his powerful arms embracing her. A black sable throw was wrapped around her. She pushed it down, her chest dewy with perspiration. She must have fallen asleep once more.

They had stopped for lunch, and he had been effortlessly charming. Polite, yet distant, even as he ensured her every need was tended to. It had been unnerving, and she'd barely been able to eat a bite.

They had spent hours together in the carriage, and after he had insisted they could not make love, it had been as if they were in different worlds.

"Where are we?" she murmured. He'd put out the light, perhaps to let her sleep.

His intimate, tender smile set her heart racing. But how could he care for her? She'd forced him into marriage.

"Traveling along the Great North Road, love," he said. "We will have to stop soon to warm up. We missed tea, so I imagine you're hungry. I hope we're still able to travel in the snow."

Her belly rumbled, the sound so rude she put a hand to her mouth as her cheeks flamed. Nervously she realized they must be close to his estate. Thick, white snow splattered against the carriage windows. Such a heavy fall could only mean a storm brewing. It was so close to Christmas treacherous weather was expected. Maryanne shivered, grateful for warm bricks, the fur-lined cloak, and Dash's arms, warm and strong around her.

Crack!

Even though the falling snow muffled sound, the pistol shot was an explosion that rang in her ears. Maryanne bolt up from Dash's embrace. A shot?

A highwayman?

In a winter storm?

The carriage lurched suddenly to the right, and men shouted. Dash's arms clamped around her as she fell forward, and he hauled her back against his hard chest. Her back slammed into him, her breath flew out, and she drove her fingers hard into his arms to hang on. His booted feet braced against the floor. The carriage swung wildly the opposite way, and then slid, as though across a frozen pond, and everything tipped.

Screams filled the carriage—she was screaming. He held her tight, his arm locked around her, bracing them with his legs and his free arm.

The carriage stopped with a soft *whump*. Tipped, but not precariously so.

Maryanne sucked in a breath. "Have we gone off the road?"

"Yes." On that monosyllable, Dash set her onto the seat and leaned to the door. As he swung open the ornate door, snow rushed in on a fierce wind. Maryanne tightened the cloak around her as wet flakes stung her cheeks. She saw a groom hurrying forward, but then Dash's large frame filled the door opening.

She heard him growl, "What happened?"

A young man's voice answered. "Slid into the thick snow, milord. Some madman was racing his rig down the road, veered toward us, and fired a shot as he passed."

"Was anyone hurt?"

"Naw, but Riggs is cursing a blue streak."

"He did well to keep us from the ditch."

Maryanne found she was still shaking, but Dash was able to calmly praise his servants. She was astonished and felt an odd burst of pride. *This remarkable man was hers.*

In name only, she reminded herself.

Dash eased back into the carriage, and she caught the last of the groom's words. "It'll take a bit of pushing, milord, but we'll have the wheels out in no time. Are ye and her ladyship unhurt?"

Dash nodded and, with a harsh grunt, hauled the door shut, closing out the cold and the howling wind. But as he relit the lamp, Maryanne gasped.

His lips were drawn in a hard line, his eyes heavy lidded and bleak.

He looked . . . haunted.

12

Did she dare ask Dash directly what worried him? Beneath lowered lashes, Maryanne gave a sidelong glance at her husband.

He leaned against the carriage window and looked out, a pistol at his side—a weapon that had meant she could no longer cuddle up against him. Though his arm stretched invitingly across the back of the blue velvet seat, she felt as if a wall stood between them. His great coat had fallen open, revealing powerful leg muscles tensing beneath his trousers. His jaw was set, teeth held so tightly together she could hear them grind.

He was waiting to fight—to fight for his life.

Bad drivers were common enough on the road, why was he so obviously balanced on a knife's edge, waiting attack?

She hated this, sitting with her hands in her lap. Her neck ached with tension; her throat was so dry it hurt to swallow.

"We're here. Home." His voice held a note of humor on the word *home*.

Dash leaned away from the window, and she caught a glimpse of light. Grooms carrying lamps had rushed out to meet the carriage. She craned forward, dazzled by a blaze of light. "Goodness, is every window in your home alight?"

A fond smile touched his handsome mouth. "Quite likely. They haven't had a bride arrive for thirty years."

"D—do you have servants who have been with you that

long?" She wished she didn't find herself stuttering so much with him. With other gentlemen, during her Season, she hadn't stuttered, though she had repeated aspects of her conversation, since she'd been often too bored to pay attention. Why did he make it so difficult to find words?

"Several. Henshaw, the butler, and Mrs. Long, the housekeeper, have overseen all since my father's day."

"So they have known you since you were a boy—"

"And if you think either would reveal an unsavory story about my young years, you are wrong, my love."

But she loved to see him smile now, his eyes brilliant instead of shadowed. And those dimples in his cheeks made her heart pang. "I have heard some of your unsavory stories. I wouldn't have the courage to ask a butler about them."

"I suspect you have the courage to do almost anything, Maryanne."

She flushed at that, astonished. The carriage stopped then, and she gazed through the water-spotted glass at his magnificent house. Swansley stood in somber symmetry, dozens of windows as bright as brilliant stars, the wings curving around like embracing arms.

Her mother had lived in a lavish home like this. She had visited once as a girl, when it was open for tours. She had gazed at—but had been forbidden to touch—the pianoforte her mother had played, the chaise her mother had curled upon with a book, the bed on which her mother had slept. She had even hoped for a glimpse of her grandparents, the Earl and Countess of Warren. But they had been in town, and she, Venetia, and Grace had merely stared up at their portraits.

Would she feel as much an awkward guest in this house?

At her mother's home, she had been so tense with nerves, she almost knocked over a priceless figurine. She had better not do the same here. She must fight her nerves. Women were supposed to follow husbands; it was their duty to leave for a new household, a new life.

But most women she'd known in Maidenswode had married within the village, or at least to men who lived close by, and they already knew the homes they would live in, the lives they would lead.

She knew nothing about what her life was to be in this enormous house.

"It's lovely—" Her uninspired words of praise for Swansley died in her throat.

Dash's smile had vanished, and he looked at his home as if monsters lurked inside.

A soft knock sounded at her bedchamber door, and the door opened to reveal Dash lounging there, lips kicked up in a smile that stole her breath.

Maryanne gave him a nervous twitch of her lips in return. She'd sent away her maid to meet the others downstairs, to give her time alone, to take in the amazing fact that this was now her room in her home.

But practicality now reigned—she must change her traveling dress for her first dinner. With her husband, the man who looked dogged by devils one moment and smiled like Lucifer the next. "Do you want help with your dress, my love?"

Gulping hard, she pirouetted to present her back to Dash. "Yes, thank you."

She quivered at the touch of his hands on her shoulders. Standing in the center of this enormous, foreign room, she felt a pang of loss of her family and her home—and a fear of being adrift.

But Dash's warm breath whispered over the nape of her neck and heated her skin. He deftly opened her dress. As his hands moved over her, her pulse throbbed in her ears.

Why didn't he say something?

As her dress sagged, she drew it down. A roaring fire warded off winter chill. Velvet draperies of crimson were tied to gilt bedposts, promising a cocoon of heat and pleasure in her bed. She drank in the rich scent of the fire, the bewitching sandalwood scent of Dash's skin.

"Do you like it, your home?"

And what choice do I have if I don't?

But she bit back those bold words. She dropped into her usual role of quiet peacemaker. "It is the most beautiful home I've ever seen."

His lips caught her earlobe, causing a girlish giggle to escape her lips. And she flushed at that. She'd met his staff—Henshaw, the aging butler; Mrs. Long, the reed-thin housekeeper who crackled with efficiency; and Mr. Kerrick, the secretary with a Scottish burr and a startlingly youthful face. There had been the steward, maids of every station, footmen—a staff she was supposed to command. Domestic concerns were a woman's domain, and the housekeeper and secretary had tended to those concerns in Dash's bachelor household.

A shiver of apprehension raced over her bare arms. She had lived in Marcus's world for only a year. How did she go about ordering servants? Settling disputes and squabbles and dealing with troubles?

Dash's tongue stroked the rim of her ear. Maryanne arched back. Who cared about duties?

His skillful fingers undid the bow in her corset ties, and he began loosening them. Each tug sent a shiver of pleasure rippling down her back.

She took refuge in sighs and moans, and he kissed down her neck, gently bit and licked. Easing her corset down, he helped her step out of it, and he whisked off her shift, over her head. Winking in the warm firelight, her pins fell out and dropped to the carpet.

"Oh—I didn't need to remove my undergarments."

"An indulgent treat." He pressed close, his erection pressing against her ass. He shifted so her naked cheeks framed the thick, impressive length of his cock.

"I'm not wearing a stitch—in your home in late afternoon. Isn't this wicked?"

Hands on her shoulders, he turned her. A slow grin curved

his lips—it was like watching dawn slowly touch the sky. "More wicked than making love in a hot-air balloon?"

"Yes," she claimed, because it was.

"This is exactly why I adore you, wife."

Maryanne gazed up at his dark, twinkling eyes. "How can you? We are almost strangers."

Dash stepped back to admire his wife's perfect peach-and-ivory breasts and curvaceous hips limned by golden firelight. She was lovely, and she appeared to be blushing everywhere.

One hand shyly covered her pubic curls, the other moved so her arm covered her breasts. He shook his head, mystified once again by how this shy woman could be the same wanton who had soared in a balloon. The woman who fearlessly directed him to give her an orgasm.

She intrigued him. He wanted to unravel her secrets.

"Intimate strangers," he reminded her.

Strangers. The word hammered into his head. He'd brought into his home a woman he knew nothing about. A woman who admitted her life story was a fabrication.

Why trust her? Why even believe her child was his? She was Trent's sister-in-law, but that didn't mean she wasn't being paid, or coerced, by his uncle to kill him.

Since arriving here, to his home, he'd felt that cold, crippling doubt he always did. It was as though he breathed it in from the walls.

Christ Jesus, he must be going mad. How could he even conjecture that Trent would allow his sister-in-law to become pregnant as part of a plot to kill him?

He was twisting himself in knots. And he'd come to his wife's room prepared—with a few toys and lengths of black silk tucked into his pockets. Pulling one out, he dangled the strip of silk.

Her hands still covered her most intimate parts. "What do you wish to do with that? Blindfold me?"

She looked so fetchingly innocent he had to be a madman

to have doubts that she was anything but an untutored maiden who had gotten herself in trouble.

But then there were times he was certain he had gone mad.

He eased her arm from her breasts and caressed her pretty pink nipples with the silk. Her nipples hardened at once, thicker and darker than he remembered.

"You didn't seem too frightened by the accident on the road." An accident that wasn't an accident—he was sure of that.

She brushed a strand of hair back from her cheek, the gesture beguiling and sweet. "It was such a shock, I didn't have time to even think."

"A complete surprise?"

Her brows drew together. "Yes. I didn't even understand what was happening."

Teasing her right nipple with silk, he lowered to take the other in his mouth. He cupped her full breast, lifted it so he could feast, and he felt the fast beat of her heart as he sucked.

She tugged at the silk. "I could blindfold you."

Releasing her nipple, he grinned. "No, sweet. It is time to teach my wife obedience."

Her brows flew up. "Obedience?" Her voice trembled—at first he thought it was with spirited anger, but she swallowed hard. Hell, his wife thought he really was planning to whip her into submission. What in blazes had she heard about him? Apparently quite a bloody lot.

"I meant to tease, love," he reassured. "And play. I want to wipe away your worries."

"Worries?" she parroted.

"About what happened on the road."

"Oh, I'm not worried about that. It was just a madman at the reins, wasn't it? I've seen many gentlemen drive at a neck-or-nothing pace in the country."

He nuzzled the dewy valley between her breasts. Murmured against them, "I'm sure it was. A madman at the reins."

"I saw you were furious," she whispered. "More than furious. You looked—"

"We could have been seriously hurt," he interrupted, not wanting to hear what she'd seen on his face. Haunting memories had caught him raw. "I've had two carriage accidents in my past."

Her jaw dropped in surprise, her eyes wide.

Those two carriage accidents from his past were now stark in his mind. Both had been engineered by his uncle.

"How did they happen?"

"A madman at the reins—and some would say the madman was me." But his skill with the reins had saved him. Though it had shaken him to his soul to almost die in the same way his parents had died.

He dropped to his knees and pulled Maryanne's slick, fragrant slit to his face.

She gripped his head as he suckled her clit. A glance up told him she was watching them both in the cheval mirror. Shy Maryanne watching with frank interest.

Clasping her ankle, he coaxed her to lift her leg, and he settled her foot on his shoulder. This opened her cunny even more to him. He could feel the stickiness of her juices on his lips and chin. Above him, her plump breasts jiggled with her frantic breaths.

Hell, you want to believe in her.

The thought stopped him cold, his tongue poised to plunge deep into her hot, creamy quim.

"Oh, but you can't stop—!"

"A change of position." He scooped her lithe, naked body into his arms.

"But I liked that one."

"Trust me."

With black silk cloths trailing, he carried her to her bed. As she sprawled there, she gazed at him, sighing in delight.

Was she an innocent or a pawn in a game to destroy him?

She caught hold of the silk he held and tugged at them. She wanted to pull him on top of her. Grinning, he tugged back and kneeled between her outstretched thighs.

"You've had quite a day, haven't you, sweeting? Marriage with me, a man you know mainly by black reputation. Then leaving your family behind at my command. The accident on the road. And arrival here at Swansley."

Wide-eyed, she nodded. "I didn't realize you—yes, it has been a strange day." She smiled. Against the deep crimson counterpane, his wife looked like a confection of cream and marzipan, a temptation waiting for him to take a bite.

"I saw your shock when you stepped into the foyer."

"It was enormous, and I didn't expect a domed skylight."

"Installed by my father at ridiculous expense. And I have to admit I was unnerved to see the entire staff standing in a solemn line. Bloody strange ritual—it looked as if someone had died." And Maryanne had looked like she wanted to cower in the corner, not review her household troops.

"You did seem to be in a hurry to get through it."

"I think they hired people from the village to pretend to be staff—I had no idea I employed an under-boot boy."

"There wasn't an under-boot boy!" She giggled.

"And I was rushing you through it, wanting to get you up to bed. I fantasized about it—sweeping you up the stairs, pausing on the landing to lift your skirts and slide my cock deep. . . ."

She moaned. "But you didn't . . . you wouldn't, not in front of your staff."

He waggled his brows, as though to imply he just might, and her cheeks flushed brilliant pink.

"And now here you are," he murmured. "Lying on your bed, awaiting pleasure." He caught his breath. Her dainty hand skimmed down her milk-white tummy and stroked her nether curls. "No, you're too impatient to wait for me, aren't you, love?"

Her only response was a shy giggle. She could play with her cunny in front of him but couldn't speak of it. What a complex lady she was.

The hell with questioning her.

As though attempting one-handed applause, his cock lurched in his trousers.

He stripped off his clothes, tossing them into a heap on the rug. But he kept his lengths of silk. Hell, he enjoyed her appreciative gasp at the sight of him.

He stretched out on the bed at her feet. The silky sheets caressed his chest and belly as he clasped her ankle and kissed her toes, rewarded by more of her pretty giggles.

Watching her beneath his tousled hair, he tongued her big toe.

"Dash!"

"Shouldn't every husband kiss his wife's lovely feet?"

"Of course." Sweet laughter washed over him.

As he suckled her toes one by one, he looped the silk around her ankle. Tied it neatly, the gleaming black a seductive contrast to her pale skin. How naughty it looked around her neatly turned ankle.

"Oh, heaven, what are you doing?" But she squirmed in anticipation.

"Trust me, love."

"You ask for a lot of trust."

"And I expect you to give it."

"No, you have to earn it," she threw back pertly.

How did she do it—stun him with just a phrase? And with a simple action—she spread her legs so he could fasten her to the bedposts. His cock throbbed, his juices bubbling out and dripping off the swollen head. He had to straddle her waist to begin to tie her wrists.

She arched up and licked his dribbling fluid off his rigid cock.

"Sweetheart."

She grasped his rear and pulled him down to her, sucking

him, licking him. Her teeth scraped the head, and he almost cried out in surprise. That had been gentle and deliberate. Damn, she was good at this, his enthusiastic wife.

But he drew back. "Not yet, angel. More fun for you first." And he bound one wrist and secured it. Then the other.

"Come up here, my lord," she urged. She looked saucy but also shy and uncertain. "I want to suck you again."

How could he refuse?

Bracing his hands on the headboard, he lowered and let her feast on his cock.

"You must move up a bit."

He obeyed.

She licked his ballocks. Opened her lips wide to surround one. He felt them tighten and scurry up. Her tongue swirled, tugging at his long, fine hairs. Slid down toward his anus.

But as he looked down on her, he was rocked by the realization he'd never intended to do this with a wife. He moved back.

Astonished eyes met his. "What's wrong?"

"Let me pleasure you."

"What are you going to do?"

He tried to make light. "Being tied up and at my mercy adds spice. And not knowing makes it even more exciting."

But guilt rose. If she was innocent, if she wasn't trying to kill him, he should be treating her like a wife.

But Maryanne had been his partner in wild sex in the balloon. She was game for everything.

And he wanted this.

Try it. Why not just try it?

She was considering. Her soft brown brows dipped in the center, and she wriggled on the large bed. "The bonds do make it . . . thrilling."

He trailed the ends of the last piece of silk over taut brownish-pink nipples, over the curve of her tummy.

Their child was inside, so tiny, not even giving her a bump yet.

Kneeling between her thighs, he licked and laved her clit. She squealed. Bounced her bottom on the bed and set the canopy shaking—

And climaxed on a scream.

God, yes.

He slid his tongue into her, tasting honey. With finger play to her anus and more suckling, she came again.

"Let me please you," she whispered, her eyes dazed.

He was on the brink, but instead he stroked his staff with his hand.

"Oooo, that is . . . arousing to see you touch yourself."

Laughing, he did more, falling into his familiar rhythm, lost in her sparkling eyes. The pleasure built, his body tightened . . .

No, he hadn't meant to—

His cum shot out and splattered onto his hand.

Maryanne blinked, startled to open her eyes to find daylight creeping between the drapes.

She'd slept through supper? And even more shocking, she'd drifted off to sleep while bound to the bed. Dash had thoughtfully untied her, but he'd also left her alone in her bed.

Covering her mouth, she gave a shocked giggle. It certainly proved she trusted him. Or that she was exhausted. Her tummy growled, and it roiled as soon as she recognized hunger.

She breathed in myriad scents—rich bitter chocolate, baked bread, spicy meat. She sat up to see an enormous silver tray on the bedside table, a gleaming silver urn, and an array of covered dishes.

A tray. He'd had a breakfast tray brought up.

And she had missed supper. Her meal would have been thrown out, and the cook must certainly be upset. There was always waste in a great house, but it was unthinkable to simply refuse to go down for dinner.

Had Dash told them she was asleep? Should she explain herself? She was mistress of the house, not the scullery maid.

With a heavy sigh, Maryanne sat up. She wished Dash had come back to her bed. But this was to be their life now—he would sleep in his own bedroom. He would go to town. He would . . .

She didn't want to think of him going to his world there—his orgies and brothels and beautiful mistresses. She'd read enough erotic stories to know that men craved variety and novelty in sex, but knowing it did not make it any less painful.

Why did it hurt so much?

Maryanne swung her legs around out of bed and slid out to land on the soft carpet. Her robe hung by the bed. Her heart pounded—her belongings had been unpacked, her robe and slippers left for her use by her maid. Even Nan, brought from Marcus's house, was embarking on a new life. And probably more comfortable with that thought than she was.

Maryanne padded to the long windows and drew open the drapes.

Drifts of pristine snow swirled in fantastic patterns, sculpted by the wind to look like ocean waves. Sunlight sparkled along the crests of the snow, contrasting with vivid blue shadows. Snow dripped from bare branches, and the lawns looked like a garden for ice fairies. The lawns sloped away from the house; from her window she spied a frozen lake and even a maze, with the clipped hedges covered by drifts. The gardens were severely geometric and terribly symmetrical, a constant pattern of round fountains and linear beds—she could tell from the covered shrubs and the mounds of snow.

A regimented garden in a symmetrical house—one of Dash's ancestors had strongly believed in order. Dash didn't seem like that. A live-for-the-day libertine, addicted to pleasure and vice, was the way she would describe him.

The last sort of man she expected to be married to.

Her stomach growled, and she turned. She hastened over

to the tray and stuffed half a bread bun in her mouth. She gulped it down and swallowed a cup of chocolate.

Was her upset tummy a result of pregnancy sickness or nerves?

She prayed Dash wasn't the one who had wanted the severe gardens and the orderly world. How would she run such a household?

Today she would find the local midwife.

She refilled her cup of chocolate and then carried it to the window. Sipping it, she touched her fingertips to the cool glass, dazzled again by the brilliant white.

A dark figure emerged from a copse of trees. A gentleman wearing a black coat, black hat, and riding astride a huge black gelding.

Dash. Dash riding along a cleared track. She put her entire hand to the pane as though she could touch him. As though he would know she was there, waiting for him.

Impetuously she put down her chocolate and then opened the window to call out. A blast of wintery air rushed through the fabric of her robe. Her nipples stood up, and she squeaked in shock.

Bang!

The roar stunned her. The impossible roar of a gunshot.

Dash's horse reared, stark black against the blue-shadowed white snow.

He fell!

13

What in hell had happened?

Levering up on his arms, Dash winced as his head pounded. He blew out a sharp breath to clear the snow off his mouth. Wet flakes clung to his eyelashes and dripped off his nose. He wiped his face clean with his gloved hand.

At least he hadn't broken his neck, but where was his horse?

Fighting throbbing pain in his chest, he turned to see Beelzebub trying to race through snow. Damn, the beast would break his leg for certain. Dash tried to push to his feet, but pain sucked at him and his head swam, his eyes dazzled by the whirling sea of white.

He had to get Beelzebub. Had to get away.

He fell back into the snow on his side.

Rifle shot.

There could be another.

Lying there, he drew in shaky breaths. The first time he'd been shot at, he'd been six. Careless poacher. His leg had been grazed, his pant leg driven into the raw slash. Damned terrible accident. And there had been the chance an infection would carry him off.

He hadn't known then that his uncle had been the one to pull the trigger.

His uncle, at least, had been a bad shot.

Had that been the case again? A man on a horse against a field of white snow should not be a difficult target for an experienced marksman. Or had the miss been intentional?

He struggled to his knees. Snow had sunk in his boots, making them lead heavy. He fell forward but caught himself by pressing his hands into the compacted snow.

Was the villain waiting to shoot again, or had he run after his first, bungled attempt?

"Dash!"

Maryanne raced toward him from the gallery—she had left the glass-paned door open in her haste. Her fists held up her skirts—she wore nothing other than the traveling dress she'd worn the day before, and the air was sharp and cold. Her hair streamed out behind her like a cape of brown silk.

Her pallor was as white as his lawns, shock and fear written in her wide eyes and tense mouth. Was she frightened he was hurt or stunned he was not?

Then his brain kicked into action. "Get back in the house!" he roared. "Now!"

But she kept running toward him.

"Maryanne, go back to the blasted house!" he shouted as he struggled to his feet.

She stumbled as her slipper-shod feet reached the deeper snow, and she fell forward on a cry. White puffs flew up as she dropped face-first in a drift. In a second, she lifted her head, her eyes, cheeks, and lips iced with fresh white.

Dash bit back a laugh at her frustrated grimace—did he really believe she was being paid to destroy him? Bending low, he waded through the snow toward her. But the tenacious woman got back on her feet as he reached her.

He'd been the perfect target as he'd struggled through the snow. The shooter must have run. And one look at Maryanne's wide eyes made him realize he had to soothe her, ease fears.

He forced a lighthearted tone. "Maryanne, sweeting, you're going to freeze."

"Are you hurt?"

"Knocked about by the fall, but the snow is soft. As you discovered."

"I was so frightened!" she cried.

Water droplets from melted snow ran down her cheeks. Dash put his thumbs to her cheeks and gently wiped them away. Instinct demanded he scoop her into his arms and run for cover, but logic prevailed. If his attacker had wanted him dead, there had been plenty of time for a second shot.

His grooms shouted—one cheered. Someone had caught Beelzebub, and the shout of victory told him his gelding was unhurt.

"Let's get back inside, love, and warm you."

She nodded, licking ice crystals off her upper lip with her tongue. "But why would someone shoot at you? I don't understand—"

"An accident."

"No, it couldn't be. Why would someone shoot a rifle across your lawn in the middle of winter? There's nothing to hunt."

"A jest then." Despite the soreness in his hips, back, and neck, Dash caught hold of Maryanne's waist. He did gather her up into his arms. "I shall carry you across the threshold, dear wife. And we will get you dry clothes."

"How can you be so cavalier?" she demanded. "You could have been killed."

"I wasn't, love. You won't be rid of me that easy, I promise. I've proven in the past that I have more lives than a cat."

Her brows drew down, her eyes troubled. "I—I don't want to be rid of you. Is—is that what you think I want?"

"No, sweeting. Of course not. Now, quiet. Let me concentrate as we wade through this snow, or I'll drop you."

He hugged her against his wet clothes, his snow-dampened greatcoat swinging around them. Waving back the concerned servants, he carried Maryanne to the open door of the sun-filled and now chilled gallery. Curious maids rushed off at once at the housekeeper's command that the fire be stoked in the mistress's bedchamber and hot water be brought up.

"I am capable of walking, you know," she protested, but she shivered in his arms, and he ignored her to rush to the stairs.

Could a fall in the snow, frigid weather, and fear for him harm their child?

"You should rest. You were the one who fell! I'll sit on top of you to pin you down if you won't stay still, or . . ." Maryanne glowered down at her stubborn husband, who lay on her mussed bed.

"Or?" he prompted.

"Or I'll tie you to the bedposts!"

"Is that a promise, my love?"

Dash's devilish grin returned, and she gave a sigh in relief, even as her heart gave that little skip she now knew well. His every smile set her body trembling, her nipples hardening, and an . . . awareness sizzling through her every nerve.

That she understood. She'd read enough descriptions in her authors' books. It was lust—intense, fiery, all-consuming lust.

He was nude now, but he had been wearing his black clothes again. For the wedding, he hadn't worn his usual black. But now he had returned to it, as though he was mourning his life before he'd been forced to wed.

It hurt.

Maryanne turned from her husband. "I should think you would be too sore for games like that."

"Never, love."

Her hand trembled as she clutched the handle of the teapot; a tea tray had been brought by a maid, by one of the seemingly dozens who had swarmed in and out of her room. Her attempt to pour him a cup sent a stream of hot tea to the silver tray. "Clumsy!" she muttered.

She blinked back tears—of relief, not out of grief at wasted tea.

When she'd seen him fall from his horse, her heart had stopped. She'd run like a hoyden down the stairs, not caring about her half-buttoned dress or her trailing hem. She'd run to Dash, heedless of snow, cold, and propriety. Even of being shot! She'd thought her heart would burst of the fear before she'd reached him.

Was this love?

Was she in love with Dash, who was both her husband and a stranger? Love, hopeless love, hurt terribly. She knew that from watching her mother.

Maryanne touched her belly below the knotted belt of her robe. No matter what happened, even if Dash broke her heart, she would never resent her baby. She would never call her baby a "folly." She would never look at her child and see her lost dreams in its face.

"But there's no better cure for any ill than climax," Dash teased from behind her.

She almost dropped the teapot. Gaining control, she poured. This time the tea swirled into his cup. "Where did you go last night?"

At once she regretted the words. Wives probably did not ask.

The bed creaked. "I rode to the village."

"Oh." On her wedding night. Perhaps he kept a mistress there. Or he was a favorite of the barmaids at the local inn. . . .

"To ask if any dangerous drivers had traveled through yesterday."

She jerked around, and a splash of scalding tea on her bare wrist reminded her of the cup in her hand. "Blast!" she muttered, and she ran over to stick her arm into the basin of cooling wash water.

He was on his feet. "Are you all right?"

"I've burned myself with tea any number of times," she

muttered. "I'm fine." Gritting her teeth, she let her skin soak. "But I've read enough gothic novels to know what you were looking for! Evidence—a description of the driver who ran us off the road. Dash, why is someone trying to hurt you?"

His warm body pressed against her from behind, hard chest against her back, groin against her rear. His arms slid around her waist as she lifted her arm from the wash water and toweled dry.

"I was investigating a peer," he said. "And some other men involved with white slavery. I suspect someone could be trying to frighten me off."

She tried to twist in his arms, but they were locked around her middle. "Who?"

"It doesn't matter, sweet. The peer will not be the one who drove the curricle. He won't be the one who pulled the trigger today."

"If you have an enemy, I want to know who it is."

He nuzzled her neck, and she gasped at the warm touch of his lips. "I'll protect you—"

"Tell me." Strangely she needed him to share this with her. She was shaking with the fear he would refuse. Why? She knew to expect that her husband would not want to share much with her. He had not answered her questions in the carriage. They were not a love match like Venetia and Marcus. And Rodesson, her father, had never shared anything with her mother.

"Remember, I have no proof of this, and you must not breathe a word of it. Do you promise?"

She nodded. "Not a word. Ever. It could never be dragged from me."

"Don't say that, even in fun, Maryanne. The peer I suspect is Craven."

"Well that makes perfect sense—the Earl of Craven is a horrible, lecherous rogue! At the salon he was, anyway." She reached down and clasped her hands over his. "It is very noble of you to be rescuing kidnapped girls."

"There is more to me than simple lewdness, love. But I'm not feeling very noble now. I want to make love to you. I *need* to."

His growl sent tremors down her spine. She knew she must remind him of the baby—she knew sex wouldn't bring harm, but he feared it might, and she didn't want him to be angry and regretful afterward.

He brought her fingertips to his lips for a kiss. Then he winced as he moved his arm.

"You are still hurt," she observed. But alive—thank heaven, thank heaven.

He let her hand drop but turned her with a simple but convincing pressure on her shoulders. "Look down," he murmured.

One glance and she couldn't drag her gaze away. She could see how rigid and thick and big his cock was.

"It's hurting me more not to, angel." Black hair, damp with melted snow, fell over his eyes, and he shoved it back with a harsh thrust of his hand. The head of his cock bobbed.

What did it feel like to have a part that jutted out that way? Was it heavy and cumbersome? Did he treat it with paternal pride and detached amusement, as her courtesan authors claimed men did? Georgiana claimed that once a man was erect, it was the small head that did the thinking.

"I want to make love to you." His breath came ragged then.

She couldn't resist reaching out and touching his hard chest. Her hand slid down the sculpted valley between his firm, high pectoral muscles. His dark curls teased her palm. The sensation shot right down to her quim, and she wriggled her hips in response.

"I want to make love to you inside your bottom," he admitted hoarsely. "That should be safe for the baby, I think."

Inside her bottom? She blinked. She had not expected that. As the toy had been?

Her bottom actually tingled with anticipation. It had felt

terribly good to be penetrated there with the slim toy, but his cock was so much bigger.

"You—you can do that?"

A grin spread across his face. "Yes, sweeting. Your bottom would accommodate me, and when I filled you, you would feel incredibly good."

"I know." In the books she edited, women screamed at first at the invasion, but within a few thrusts they were crying out for more.

"You said, 'I know.' Now how, sweet wife, would you know that?"

She certainly couldn't admit the truth, that she'd read several dozen passages of stunning sex where well-endowed men pleasured women from behind.

"It felt good when you . . ." Courage almost failed. "When you put the toy there. And of course, I've seen Rodesson's pictures. I looked at his books. I wasn't supposed to, of course."

She had to distract him. She wrenched her hand from his and scrambled up onto the bed. Tugging at the belt of her robe, she cast off the peach silk.

He was so hard. She marveled at the length of it, the way it curved toward his taut abdomen. Veins, prominent veins shot up the shaft. The heavy head was a blend of purplish red and dusky pink, and his dark nest of hair lush and thick.

His massaging hand rubbed his leaking fluid into the broad head. Such rough ministrations, and he panted harshly as he did it.

Then doubt struck. "You truly don't think you should rest?"

"Sweetheart." His laugh was a raw bark. "You do know how to torture me, don't you? No, this is what I want."

On her knees, Maryanne gazed at her husband beneath lowered lashes. This mattered. Doing this as he wanted, in a way that would please him. She didn't want him to go to other women for adventure, she knew it as surely as she knew her heart would beat. She wanted him to herself.

She was determined to keep him for herself.

And all those books she had edited had told her exactly how she could do that.

Daringly she slid her fingers down to her quim. Foolish, shy, embarrassed—she felt all those until her fingers touched her clit and sensation exploded through her. Then all she wanted was sex. Sex and orgasm. "Now what do you want me to do?" she whispered.

A gentleman did not introduce his wife to anal pleasures by leaning her over in front of her vanity and taking her hard from behind.

No, a gentleman didn't. But Dash did.

"Bend over the table and study yourself in the mirror," he directed. Her round and generous bottom thrust out as she did. His heart pounded as hard as it had when he'd fallen from Beelzebub. He prowled toward her while she hummed innocently and twirled a curl around her finger.

From his vantage, he could see both her face and her reflection. Compelling brown eyes. A freckled nose with a fetching bump on the end. Wide, large pink lips. She pursed them at her reflection, and his preparatory juice bubbled out of his cock.

Picking up a silver hairbrush—her own—she stroked it through her hair. The curls stretched to a length of silky brown and then bounced into lively coils as the brush passed through.

He couldn't take any more.

Forcing his rigid cock down, he stroked it between her cheeks. The mirror reflected startled eyes and her open mouth. "Grab your breasts," he urged. His orgasm hovered—he felt it in the tightness of his balls, the tension of his muscles, the weakening agony shooting through his legs.

The mirror showed him her small hands cupping her full breasts. Reddened and thick, her nipples pointed at the glass.

He should get oil from his room, something to make her slick and soft, to ease this, but he couldn't wait. He couldn't draw his cock away from the hot, tempting cleft of her arse.

She moved forward so her cunny rested against the smooth, rounded corner of the marble-topped vanity. A wriggle of her hips and he understood why. She was rubbing her clit against the smooth, cool stone.

The wicked wench.

Slicking her ass with the wet tip of his cock, he bent forward and nuzzled her earlobe. A pink blush blossomed on her cheeks as she teased herself. Her lips parted as she panted. Rubbing her clit sent her juices flowing—he breathed in the scent.

Nothing compared to the smell of an aroused woman. He could drown in it.

The head of his cock brushed her tightly furled anus, and she moaned in delight. She wasn't shocked or scandalized. She wanted this. What a delightful woman he'd married—

Assuming she wasn't part of the plot to kill him.

Should he have told her about the missing women in London . . . about the actress's body in Hyde Park? If she was innocent, should he give her the truth?

And how in blazes did he do that? Did he lean forward now and whisper in her ear? *A madman is trying to make me look like a kidnapper and a murderer. But it wasn't me. I didn't kill the woman. You believe me, don't you? After all, you know nothing about me other than rumors about my depravity. . . .*

Her bottom pushed back, plump cheeks engulfing his iron poker of an erection.

"Slowly, love," he rasped. "I want this to be good for you." While satisfying his own fantasies. She stood on tiptoe, her legs long and shapely, her bottom lifted and served up for his pleasure. Hair tumbling down her slender back, tiny waist flaring to heart-shaped buttocks, she personified temptation.

His wife. He had never dreamed of gently massaging the

swollen head of his cock against the resistant anus of his wife.

"How's that?" he groaned.

"Oooo—good. I like it—" But a slight push of his prick had her squeaking in shock.

Lightly slapping her hip, he drew back. "Ah, lass, I can't do it like this. Wait for me."

He threw on his robe, his jutting cock tenting the dark blue silk. Without bothering to tie the belt, he darted to the connecting door to the parlor between their rooms. Maryanne rested her elbows on the vanity, her naked arse sticking up in the air.

A quick sprint to his bedside drawer and he had a glass bottle of oil. His heart hammered in his throat as he ran back. He was afraid to find she'd gone. But she was waiting and squirming with abandon against her vanity.

With splayed hand, he slipped the oil between her cheeks, slicked the puckered entrance with his middle finger. She moaned as his finger penetrated—to his nail and then his knuckle. He plunged it in and out, and she moaned with every thrust.

His finger slid in to the hilt, and she arched against him, crying out. Her breasts bounced.

"Was that only your finger? It felt so delicious. I want . . . more," she whispered. She collapsed on the vanity, and he nosed his cock inside her relaxed, slick anal passage. The head eased the tight ring open, and it bit down hard on the shaft as the head popped in.

God, he loved that sensation. The pop and hot bite.

Her throaty moan sang in his head.

Gripped tight by her snug, velvety passage, his cock forged ahead an inch. Instinct begged him to thrust deep and pound hard, and he gripped the vanity to control himself.

Scream for me, love. I need to hear you moan. I need to hear your pleasure.

His cock filled her to the hilt, and two deep thrusts ended on her scream. She came, sobbing as she did, and at the sweet, lusty, throaty sound, he lost his famed control.

Like a shot, his orgasm tore through him, exploding out of his ballocks, through his shaft—he stumbled forward as if his muscles had turned to semen and launched out of him.

He caught himself with splayed hands on the marble vanity and felt his hot semen pulse through him and pour into her. Sharing a low laugh with Maryanne, he nuzzled her neck. They gasped for air together.

"We should bathe again, love," he whispered. But he hesitated, wrapping his arms around her waist. His chest was damp with sweat, and her back was hot with it. He cuddled her.

He'd never known this before.

The desire to stay with a woman. To hold her for as long as he could.

"And now I'll leave you to your day."

Maryanne jerked her head up at Dash's words. Her entire body still tingled, and she wanted to collapse on the bed and spend an hour or two sighing with delight and shock—in Dash's arms.

No wonder so many of her courtesan authors' stories featured that intimate act, so based on trust. It had hurt—only a little, at first, for he'd been so gentle and careful.

And then, when he'd thrust his cock deep, the sensations . . . oh my! She'd wanted more, wanted him to the hilt.

Her orgasm had almost stopped her heart.

And now, now that he'd tenderly cleaned her derriere and his cock with warm water and cloths, he tied the belt of his robe and strode toward the door.

Her day? But what was she to do? Where was she to start? A strangled sound leaped out of her throat.

He turned.

"But . . ." She had no idea what to say. Of course she was now supposed to run his household. Of course a wife and husband did not live in each other's pockets. Venetia and Marcus were not a normal *ton* marriage; in some marriages a husband and wife never even attended the same public events, they despised each other so much.

A husband who despised you would leave you alone to live your life. It would be as if you never married.

No, she didn't want that. To live under the same roof as someone who hated her. But Dash waited, smiling, for her to finish her sentence.

"You will be careful, won't you?" she asked. "What do you plan to do?"

"Nothing too dangerous, love, I assure you."

"*Too* dangerous?" But he was gone, and the door shut behind him.

She swallowed hard. Mrs. Long and the servants would know at once that she was not bred to be a great lady. They would guess at once why Dash had married her. Sniggering jests would be traded from footman to maid. Even the tweenies would know . . . they would know she had been wanton and gotten pregnant by Dash.

She couldn't bear to be surrounded by servants who bowed and bobbed curtsies but smirked behind her back.

But how did she face Mrs. Long without a blush after the naughty sexual things she'd done with Dash? Great ladies didn't have their husbands make love to their bottoms. Did they?

She'd felt her climax in her womb but hadn't told him that. She was certain it couldn't harm the baby, but it was a secret she'd kept from Dash. Another one.

With a tug at her heart and a heavy dose of guilt bearing on her shoulders, Maryanne paused by her window. Water droplets dotted the panes, and she longingly remembered all the times she had curled up quietly in a window seat, a book held close to her nose.

But, from this very window, she had also seen Dash fall, and that jolt of remembered fear made her jerk away.

Squaring her shoulders, she walked resolutely to the bellpull and tugged. It was time to put on a disguise, to pretend to be a viscountess.

So within an hour, fed and dressed by her maid, Maryanne met Mrs. Long in the morning room—the room in which the previous viscountess, Dash's mother, had attended to the morning's business. Just after summoning the housekeeper, Maryanne had run a nervous finger over the white and gilt escritoire, with its many dockets, now empty.

Dash would have been a child when his parents died. Marcus had mentioned once—shortly after she had seen Dash at a ball on one of the few times he'd attended one—that his parents had died together. . . .

In a carriage accident.

She clapped her hand to her mouth. No wonder he had looked so horrified by the accident on the Great North Road. How could she not have thought of that?

What sort of wife was she? In her heart she wanted them to be at least friends—or civil, if not that. But a friend would have understood his pain and helped him share it. . . .

"My lady?"

Maryanne spun at the housekeeper's voice. Dressed in her simple gray gown—but a well-cut one—Mrs. Long bobbed a curtsy, and Maryanne almost tripped over the elegant stool.

She stumbled helplessly for something to say. "Where do we begin?"

It was wrong, perhaps, to admit she didn't know. But Mrs. Long nodded, her hands clasped in front of her. "I would be delighted to give a tour of the house, my lady. And there are the day's menus. I believe arrangements for the arriving guests will be satisfactory."

Guests? Venetia, Marcus, their baby, and her mother and Grace were to come—but not until just before Christmas Day.

"The south wing has been prepared for Lord and Lady Moredon. Lady Yardley will be given her usual suite of rooms—the lavender rooms."

Why had Dash not told her his sister would be visiting? Oh, she wasn't prepared to meet his sister. Not yet. His sister would guess at once that they'd been forced into marriage. A tremor of fear raced down Maryanne's back, leaving her shivering. And Lady Yardley—would her ladyship recognize her from Hyde Park?

Maryanne lunched alone. She toyed with the stem of her wineglass and glanced around. Long windows overlooked the gardens, and between the windows hung paintings of landscapes. Twenty chairs lined the table, yet this was only the informal room where the family dined.

Were there any touches here Dash had added?

Platter upon platter had been laid out for her. She thought of Maidenswode, where the smallest serving of ham would feed the entire household for a week. Here, she had barely touched the roast beef, the serving of fish with dill sauce, the bread.

Where was Dash? Would he join her?

She left the table and slipped quietly from the room as the footmen entered. She was to meet Mrs. Long to discuss menus for the next few days. Hugging herself, as if she could flit unnoticed through the hallways by becoming smaller, she found herself lost and confused.

Bother. Where did this hallway lead?

She heard a flurry of noise. The clatter of footsteps across the foyer floor. It could only mean the arrival of guests.

She was not prepared for this—she'd thought Dash would be at her side!

If she couldn't be found, she wouldn't have to meet his sister. Not yet.

She could go to the nursery on the uppermost floor. She could pretend to be making decisions.

Glancing down the hallway, Maryanne lifted her hems and raced for the stairs.

* * *

"Someone shot at you."

Dash gave a rueful nod as he poured a glass of sherry for Sophia, Lady Yardley. Trust Sophia to be blunt and to speak of an attempt on his life with disapproval instead of horror.

As he strolled over and handed her the glass, Sophia lay back against the plump, silky cushions of the chaise. "And how did your new wife respond?"

"She raced to me across the snow, her hems in her hands." His grin widened at the memory. "She looked properly horrified. Of course, she then tripped and fell into the snow on her face."

He felt Sophia's gaze rest on him, and he turned and began pacing. He didn't want to discuss his suspicions of Maryanne. Not after introducing his sweet wife to the intense ecstasy of anal sex. She'd trusted him to give her pleasure, not pain. And, Christ Jesus, it stunned him how much he wanted to let himself trust her.

"The fiend escaped?" Sophia asked.

Lush, voluptuous, and dressed entirely in white and silver, Sophia was breathtakingly beautiful. Many assumed they'd had a long-standing affair. When he'd been a young man, he'd wanted to—he'd tried to seduce her. But she looked on him as a son. She had given Anne a home and had always been his friend.

Sophia had kept him sane.

Dash brushed back his hair with both hands. "Footprints were found that led past the pond to the woods. But others have been in the woods today, and the footprints were lost. And apparently, despite a staff of several dozen tripping over each other on this estate, no one saw the blackguard. No," he corrected, "two young undergrooms did but could give nothing better than a vague description of a shadowy figure in black."

"And you suspect one of the Blackmores—your uncle or his son."

He nodded. "Though there are others who would like to

see me dead. Craven and Barrett, to hide their white slavery ring. Jack Tate—"

"The hell proprietor?" She looked startled. "Why . . . oh, I see. You bested him at cards."

"Even Ashton."

Sophia straightened on her chaise, eyes flashing fire. "The Duke of Ashton is not trying to kill you, I assure you!"

"Spoken like a woman in love."

She waved away the sentiment. "What are you planning to do? This entire situation is madness. Shooting at you! Carriage accidents! Kidnappings in London and murdered women!"

From the hallway, where she lurked behind the door, Maryanne gasped, shocked by Lady Yardley's words. Kidnappings? Murdered women? Dash had said nothing of that. She gave a hurried glance down the hallway. It seemed unforgivable to spy on her husband, but she couldn't resist.

And if a servant caught her, she'd look a terrible fool.

Her fingers rested gently on the door handle, holding the door to ensure it didn't swing open. It hurt.

He wanted to speak of something personal, something important—such as the attempt on his life—and he was doing so with Lady Yardley.

Not with her.

What did she expect? Theirs wasn't a love match. And how could he have spoken to her even if he wished to? She'd been hiding from his family and Lady Yardley in the nursery.

At least she hadn't crawled under one of the unused children's beds to hide but, really, just lurking there had been foolish enough.

Why wasn't Dash answering? He paced, his long legs crossing the gleaming floor of the drawing room with strides that spoke of restrained anger and coiled energy. "I'm planning to confront them both," he said. "I spent my life just trying to survive but never finding the courage to face them down. I'm no longer a child and have no excuse not to end this."

Lady Yardley reached out to him with an elegant hand, a careless yet graceful gesture, and Dash was at her side in an instant. Maryanne's feet felt like ice blocks.

"But how do you plan to solve it?" Lady Yardley asked. "Over pistols?"

"If necessary. But first I will extend a warm invitation to gather my family for Christmas."

"And Sir William?"

"Has his Bow Street Runners investigating."

"He will not turn a blind eye if you shoot a relative, Lancelot, my love, even though he knows about your past."

Dash merely grunted.

Her ladyship—though Maryanne realized with a start that she was now a "ladyship," too—leaned back and smiled at Dash with an intimacy Maryanne would never dream of assuming. "As a word of warning, I've already invited Ashton."

"Sophia—"

The woman invited men to his home? A man Dash had dueled with? Bitter, stabbing jealousy hit Maryanne's heart. How could she ever compete with that sleek white and silver cat purring on her husband's chaise? Had they been lovers? Were they *still* lovers?

Lady Yardley stroked her fingers along Dash's forearm. "Ashton knows he was a fool to call you out. And you could have killed him, but you chose not to. I promise you he is on my side, which means he is on yours."

Maryanne knew she had to open the door. Even if they guessed she'd been listening. She couldn't leave her husband alone with this—

"I am quite surprised you brought Maryanne Hamilton to Hyde Park."

"*What?*" Dash shouted.

"Once you wrote to inform me you were marrying her, I knew why your partner in Hyde Park seemed familiar."

"She was masked. How could you have known it was her?"

"Woman's intuition, dear boy. And, of course I could tell at once you were interested in her in a deeper way than usual. But really, Lancelot, do you think it appropriate to have courted a decent girl by taking her to an erotic scavenger hunt?"

14

Alone in her bedchamber, Maryanne reread Georgiana's letter. The butler had given it to her as she'd snuck back to this room.

It had been so embarrassing. And she'd almost ignored Henshaw when he'd called out, "My lady."

Sighing, she set down the new pages of Tillie Plimpton's manuscript and skimmed over Georgiana's plea for money.

Dear partner, I am dire straits. You must help. I am almost mad with worry—I know I must be discreet, but I am so worried about money I could become careless. If you could pay the debts and loan me two thousand pounds—enough to ease my fears, and it would ease yours, too. . . .

It wouldn't stop with two thousand pounds! Maryanne read on, and the last paragraph of Georgiana's letter sent her dropping to the gilt and ivory stool in front of the escritoire.

And if you wish to entrance a gentleman such as Viscount Swansborough, you must play upon your naiveté and your qualities as a well-bred lady. It will arouse him beyond reason if your language in his bed is base and erotic. Admire his cock—tell

> *him his prick is most magnificent. His blood will be aflame with desire. When he thrusts deeply inside you, hook your legs about his hips and beg him to fuck you. Repeat the word over and over, cry, "Fuck me, fuck me, fuck me hard," or some such thing. Be shy in bed and use these phrases while demurely watching him beneath lowered lashes, and I vow you will capture his soul.*

Her legs trembled even as her pulse leaped to a crescendo like harp strings. Did Georgiana know this from specific experience with Dash?

"Good afternoon, dear wife."

Startled, Maryanne craned her neck to find Dash lounging in the doorway—the one that connected through a parlor to his bedchamber.

Hurriedly rolling the letter and manuscript pages, she thrust the roll into a docket, where it jammed. With the smooth, effortless gait of an elegant cat, he strolled toward her.

She must tell him the truth and ask him for almost five thousand pounds.

But what would he do when he learned the truth?

Would he throw her out in the snow?

Would he be less angry to learn that she didn't create the books, that she had only fixed the spelling and added commas? Or would he be disappointed to discover his wife was a grand resource of proper grammar and not of inventive sex?

He reached her and stroked his knuckles along her neck. Electricity prickled over her. Goose bumps rose to greet his roughened skin.

"We must go down and join Anne and Moredon in the drawing room," he said. "Anne is bubbling with excitement to meet you."

Guilt washed over her. "I was . . . upstairs when they arrived. In the nursery."

"Ah. But before we go down, we have some time . . . for fun."

She almost fell off the stool in surprise. She'd expected him to be disappointed that she'd hidden away. Instead he bent until his warm breath coasted by her ear.

"What is your most secret fantasy, love?"

"I . . ." Georgiana's words rang in her head. *When he thrusts deeply inside you, hook your legs about his hips and beg him to fuck you.*

"Th—the midwife," she stammered. "I meant to ask about the midwife. To find out about harm to the baby—"

He glanced to the pages jammed in the slot. "A letter? I hope the news was not bad."

"N—no. It's from my mother," she lied. "Praising the shopping in London."

How had she not thought to ask Mrs. Long the name of the local midwife? She could have had the midwife summoned and found out if they could make love. But she'd been too obsessed with her own awkwardness to even think.

"I spoke with Anne," Dash murmured. "It should be safe to do whatever we want."

Strangely that angered her. One word from his sister and all was right and they could make love. Yet when she had told him she thought there was no risk, he hadn't listened.

What did she expect?

"Your fantasy, love. What is it?"

Should she do what Georgiana had suggested—use lewd talk to excite him? A dozen books flashed through her mind as her breathing sped. She could talk of sharing him with another women—men adored those stories. She could marvel at his cock. She could . . .

Tell him her true fantasy.

She turned to face him, trapped between his tall, hard body and the edge of the escritoire. "You. This. Us. This is what I fantasized about."

Maryanne marveled at her courage and waited breathlessly for his response. Dash grinned, a slow grin that set her heart pounding as fast as it did when he undid his trousers.

He cupped her cheek.

Dash could see his wife had revealed a secret. Her chest lifted with her labored breaths, a blush swept across her cheeks, and she quickly averted her gaze from his face.

They rocked him. Her words. She knew exactly what to say to leave him feeling as if the ground had dropped out from underneath him.

"Indulge me," Dash whispered. "What would be your wildest fantasy?"

Her brown eyes were wide and as dark and tempting as chocolate. "Do you . . . want me to make something up? Something erotic?"

The movement of her full lips over the word *erotic* sent blood surging from his brain. His cock, trapped in his trousers, lifted, determined to straighten.

He laughed. "Sweet lass. How do you understand me so well?"

"I don't know what you want me to imagine. What is your fantasy? That intrigues me."

Clever wench, gazing innocently into his eyes and turning his question onto him.

"You have done everything," she murmured, her words sultry and sweet. "What is secret and forbidden to you?"

His brain ran riot. Tying up his wife in dozens of leather straps, watching her sweet honey pool between her nether lips as he did? Paddling her with a riding crop in playful dominance? Burying his face into her quim and coating his mouth with her feminine juices?

He had to admit he couldn't think of an answer. "This. Discussing forbidden fantasies with you. And thinking of a quick fuck. Before we go downstairs."

Cocking her head to the side, she slipped away from him

and strolled toward her bed. "Do you always fantasize? Do you make up stories in your head? Do you pretend you are somewhere else or with someone else?"

He trailed after her like a puppy on a lead. Even while tied up by a woman, he had never felt truly on a leash. "I never would pretend with you."

Her finger demurely pressed to her lower lip. "With me, you are just fucking *me?*"

"Yes." He hissed it through his tight throat. Was it the right answer? He couldn't think. He yanked his trouser buttons open, took a shuddering breath at the relief of pressure on his cock. Then he fished the beast out of his small clothes and prowled toward his wife.

The post of her bed was at her back. But he knew she wasn't going to retreat.

She glanced down where his prick jutted ahead of him. Full of blood and painfully stiff, it felt heavy as lead.

"It's huge," she said. "Magnificent. You have a magnificent . . . cock. I'm . . . I'm trembling at the thought of such an enormous . . . prick inside me."

He had to laugh. Her cheek twitched as she spoke, and her hands were clenched into fists. Worry wrinkled her forehead as she waited for his reaction.

"My prick is delighted to hear such compliments."

She gave a soft smile. "And are you?"

"Sweetheart, lift your skirts."

Hand on his cock, he guided it to the juncture between her thighs, beneath her dangling white petticoats, and he groaned at her pretty moan as the tip touched her lush, brunette nether curls. He braced his right forearm against the fluted column and stroked the taut head of his cock between her sticky nether lips.

"Are you going to tie me to the column?"

"Not now, love." He shifted his hips forward, pushing his cock into her tight, creamy passage. He couldn't wait long enough to get rope.

Couldn't wait.

Her leg slung up around his hamstrings. "Please . . . please fuck me."

Reaching down, he held her thigh—smooth and plump and soft, bare above her stockings. A thrust of his hips drove his cock deeper into a silken grip that almost stopped his heart.

Slowly he worked his cock inside her until her juices bubbled against his furry pubis and they were joined as deeply as possible. His balls were tight and hard against his body, and sensation thundered through his cock to his brain.

So hot. So tight.

His groin held her skirts up, and he caught her wrists. Lifted her hands above her head. She let him do it.

Trusting him.

He licked the rim of her ear, felt her squirm. "I want to make you come," he groaned, and he gave long, agonizingly relaxed thrusts. Drew his cock out to the tip until his brain screamed for more heat and he surged back in to the hilt.

She rocked against him. "Fuck me."

His thrusts quickened. Sweat beaded on his brow. His nipples stood proud against his shirt. He plunged his cock as deep as he could, his groin colliding with her body, punishing them both.

"Fuck me," she urged.

Gentle. He heard the voice in his head. Distant. *Be gentle with her.*

But she was banging hard against him. "Fuck me hard," she implored.

He reached down and slid his fingers between his cock and her clit.

"Yes!" She ground against him.

He found her nipple with his mouth, sucked it through her gown. He brushed his teeth over it, rubbed her clit, and pounded his cock into her.

She screamed—the scream of a woman falling into a climax that could set her on fire. Her sweet pussy pulsed around him, and she rocked wildly against him.

He drove deep and let her climaxing cunny take him over the edge. He exploded.

Pinned to the column, her arms held above her head, Maryanne kissed Dash's strong jaw. Her tongue rasped over the dark stubble now sprouting there.

He drew back, grinning. "I didn't make too much of a mess of you, dear wife."

Maryanne frowned, glancing down at crumpled skirts. "Are you certain?"

"No—I'm lying, dear love. I think you will have to change your dress."

She felt his seed dribble onto her thighs.

Georgiana had been correct—he enjoyed the naughty words. She'd feared she'd hurt him when he climaxed so hard and for so long. She had moved, to thrust again, and he'd cried out in anguish at the sensation. He'd pressed her back against the column to stop her.

And he'd still pulsed into her. For a while, she thought he'd never stop.

Did that mean he'd enjoyed it very much? Had she been as good as a courtesan?

She didn't dare ask.

He was buttoning up his trousers, and he shared a wicked smile. His tousled hair fell over his brow, and his dark eyes flashed fire.

She slid to the side of the column and sank to the bed. Her legs felt boneless.

She had Georgiana to worry about. And acquiring money. And her husband believed someone wanted him dead yet seemed utterly cavalier about the prospect.

"All right, love?" he asked.

Of course not! She wanted to ask him about kidnappings

and murdered women—but how could she broach it without revealing she had eavesdropped on his conversation? She hadn't meant to overhear. . . .

No. It was too embarrassing. And he'd never trust her if he knew.

"Yes," she lied. "I'm fine."

He bowed in front of her. She let him kiss her hand, her shy smile fixed on her face; her cheeks hurt with it, and she felt her lips might cramp.

"Can you be ready to go to the drawing room in half an hour?"

She nodded and watched him turn. His scent was all over her—the rich aroma of his cum between her legs, the scent of his skin on her neck and face, the masculine smells of male clothing and smoke on her dress.

In half an hour, she couldn't bathe those scents away. Not bathe and change her gown and redress her hair. But she smiled again, even waggled her fingertips at him like a twit when he paused at the door.

As soon as he closed the connecting door behind him, Maryanne went to the bellpull to ring for her maid but stopped with her hand on the silken cord.

His sister knew she was pregnant—he must have revealed that while asking about risk to the baby. Heavens, how had he broached such a thing?

What must his sister think? The reason for their hasty marriage was clear, and Dash's relationship with his sister was obviously close.

Did Lady Moredon hate her for snaring Dash in a forced marriage?

Maryanne saw Dash's fond smile for his sister light his handsome face the instant they walked into the drawing room. He turned that smile to her, and she knew he expected her and Lady Moredon to be friends at once.

She gulped. No matter what, she must make it appear to be so.

But before she'd left the threshold, the slender woman launched forward with a hand outstretched. "Dear sister!" Lady Moredon cried. "How delightful to meet you."

Lady Moredon possessed bewitching beauty—though what else could she have expected from Dash's sister? His sister's hair was a startling blue-black against a peach-toned complexion, whereas Dash's skin was darker, tanned by exposure to the outdoors. His eyes were fathomless black, and his sister's were a fey green.

Maryanne saw Dash's pleased grin out of the corner of her eye and advanced forward. She'd never excelled in social situations. In Maidenswode, they'd learned to discount her. In London, she'd relied on her dowry to speak for her.

"Thank you." Did she curtsy? She must, for Lady Moredon did outrank her. But she found herself enveloped in a hug before she could.

"Come sit here by the fire with me and tell me all. How you met, how he proposed. On one knee, I hope, but he can be dashed thoughtless."

Maryanne let Lady Moredon take her hand and draw her to the settee. Her ladyship wore a burgundy velvet dress—simple but beautifully cut. Petite but voluptuous, Dash's sister seemed to fill the room with her charm.

Maryanne swallowed hard. She should have invented a story. She should have asked Dash what he'd told his family.

"Wait," he called, and she prayed for a reprieve.

"I haven't finished the introductions," he said.

"Bother, that," his sister cried. "I'm Anne. And that, of course, is my husband, Moredon. Nigel Roydon, Earl of Moredon. And lounging on the chaise is Sophia, Lady Yardley—assuming you two have not yet met. You were occupied when we arrived—"

Hiding, thought Maryanne guiltily as she followed beautiful Lady Moredon to the settee.

Her ladyship promptly poured tea as Maryanne peeped over the curving back of the chair. Dash had headed to the brandy decanter, and Moredon was joining him. Lady Sophia stretched like a cat on the chaise and purred a request for sherry.

"Now," Lady Moredon said softly, "I know you are expecting—so I know Dash had misbehaved, which he does, though he is decidedly honorable and kind."

"Oh, I—"

"And he smiles at you in that way."

"That way?"

"That besotted way. I can see it, of course. He tells me Lady Trent introduced you. Marcus and Dash are good friends—friends since childhood—and Marcus has always been so very good for my brother. Kept him out of trouble."

Out of trouble?

"Where are you from? I know you met in London."

"Maidenswode." Maryanne had spoken by rote, her hands tucked between her knees. She quickly gave a description of the village, her heart hammering in her ear. What if Lady Moredon asked about her parents—had Dash told her the lie, or had he given his sister the truth?

"I do hope we haven't imposed by coming down so quickly—I wanted so much to meet you. And I shan't be surprised if I don't see you very often. I'm sure Dash will wish to monopolize you." The green eyes twinkled. Her voice lowered to a melodic tinkle. "When are you due?"

Maryanne gulped. She didn't want to speak about the baby—it would be unkind in front of Lady Moredon, who had lost hers. But she couldn't ignore the question. "I . . . I think June."

"Lovely. Before the weather becomes so unbearably hot. London or here for your confinement, do you think?"

"I . . . I don't know." She felt swept on a wave by Lady Moredon's voluble conversation. She took the offered cup of tea, thankful to have a reason not to speak. She sipped.

"And we must drag out the garlands tomorrow and the other ornamentation for Christmas!" Lady Moredon exclaimed. "I'm sure it's all in fine order—Mrs. Long is most particular. Though she can be a bit of an ogre. I remember hiding from her as a child."

Maryanne tried to swallow the hot tea.

"I didn't live here all my life, of course," Lady Moredon continued. "Once Mother and Father were gone, I lived with Sophia. She felt I needed a woman's influence and wished to ensure I received a proper education—one beyond striking poses in my looking glass." She threw a fond glance to Lady Yardley. Maryanne glanced over the chaise and choked on her tea. Dash sat on the end of the chaise beside her ladyship's shapely legs, outlined by the white skirt.

Anne cheerfully continued, "I remember, when I was just a child, the queen had a tree brought in for Christmas and hung ornaments on it—balls of glass and gold bells and such. It was apparently quite lovely. Do you think we should try something like that?"

"Er—yes. It would be lovely."

A shadow passed over Maryanne, and she looked up, hoping for Dash. Instead, Lady Yardley murmured a greeting and settled on the wing chair opposite with her sherry. Dressed in a complex arrangement of curls, her silver-blond hair sparkled beneath the candlelight. "I have met your sister, Venetia, Lady Trent."

At an orgy, Maryanne remembered. She felt paralyzed again. "Y—yes," she muttered.

"A very resourceful and talented woman—the perfect mate for Marcus Wyndham." Lady Yardley tapped her finger to her cheek. Full, rouged lips curved into a smile. "How surprising to see that Dash so unerringly found the perfect bride."

"Well, he—I mean, I—thank you." But Maryanne impulsively leaned forward. "But I'm not, am I? Not the perfect bride for him. He's . . ." She looked helplessly at Anne. She couldn't say "a rake" in front of his sister.

"He is worldly and experienced, but that only made him more naive about things of import," declared Sophia. "He enjoyed pretending to be dark and depraved, posturing as men are wont to do."

Anne giggled and then sipped her tea. His sister didn't mind hearing the word *depraved* in connection with her brother?

"He needs a woman who finds delight in everyday things."

Untutored and simple, Maryanne thought. *That is what she really means*. "He . . . he seems troubled," she ventured. "Perhaps by something that happened in London . . . ?"

She was taking a terrible risk, and she felt fear and exhilaration.

Lady Yardley desperately looked toward the men. "Ah, here he comes now. And the way his eye is gleaming, I think he intends to whisk you away." She waved to Dash, who was prowling their way. "You two are newly married—you've entertained us long enough," she called to him. "Dear Maryanne is concerned about your troubles in London: I'm sure you would rather discuss those in private. Have you shown her the intriguing collection in your study, Lancelot?"

The use of his middle name again startled Maryanne. But Dash bowed. "Not yet. Are you asking me to do so now?"

"It's rather important, is it not, that you share the events of London?"

It occurred to her then that no one had spoken of Dash being shot at. Or of the carriage accident. Though both would be tender subjects for Lady Moredon.

As she left the room at Dash's side, Maryanne realized that Lady Moredon's happy chatter covered worries. She'd known women in Maidenswode to do that—deny the troubles in their life by busying themselves in the mundane.

Was it just the loss of her child? Or something connected to Dash?

"What is the intriguing collection you keep in here?" Maryanne asked, to set aside nerves as she stepped into Dash's study.

She caught her breath. The room was decorated entirely in

black—a black silk-covered daybed stood in the corner by the fire, black silk pillows heaped upon it. The furnishings were black and polished to a gleam. And black drapes shrouded the windows.

She shivered, despite the warmth of the room.

"Several . . . collections of erotic art and erotic writings." He sat on the edge of desk, his long legs stretched in front of him. Since he wore all black again, he looked like Lucifer.

"Come here," he said.

Once she was close enough, he clasped her hands and drew her to him. Leaning forward, he kissed her. She tasted the brandy on this tongue.

"Do you trust me?" he murmured against her lips.

"Of course. I belong to you now, don't I?"

Standing, he pulled out a black leather chair and helped her stand up on the seat. Her bottom was at the height of his shoulders. Twisting around, she saw his mouth open—he hoisted her skirts and planted a hungry kiss on the cheek of her derriere. And slapped her other cheek.

She could see her reflection in the tall window—errant curls falling down about her face, curling around her dress, and her skirts pushed up once more.

Heavens, they were illuminated.

"Dash—someone might see through the window."

But he laughed and showered hot kisses over her bottom.

He went to orgies. He must be accustomed to people watching.

In the stories she had edited, men did grow aroused by watching other men and women have relations. Women, it seemed, enjoyed it, too.

He turned her with his hands on her hips and pulled her forward. His mouth closed over her clit.

Pleasure swamped her. She closed her eyes and then remembered she was standing on a chair.

His hands held her securely. He licked her, lavishly swirling his tongue around her clit. It felt good. Lovely. Wonderful.

But she couldn't come. She knew the sensation of orgasm, and it wasn't building.

Why? What was wrong?

She closed her eyes and moaned. And moaned again. She mimicked the rising sounds of pleasure she made when she was striving for orgasm. The cries. The gasps of his name. She rocked hard against him, arched up on her toes, and then bumped her cunny against his mouth, the way she would if she'd reached her pleasure.

She was tired. And she couldn't concentrate. And he'd want to give her pleasure—he might think her less pleasing if she didn't come.

She cried out and writhed around in his embrace, acting out an intense climax. As she pulled back, he gave a pleased smile, very contented with himself.

"Now, love. Let me tell you about what happened in London."

15

"I swear to you, before I tell you this, that I had nothing to do with it." Dash knew he had to open with the truth, and he watched Maryanne's eyes widen and her lips part. But she said nothing.

He had insisted she sit by the fire; he'd given her a snifter of brandy, and her fingers clung around the curved glass. A full, generous, rounded shape, like her plump breasts. . . .

Damn. He moved to the warm fire, rested his elbow on the mantel. "The day I met you on the scavenger hunt . . . that day, Sir William, the magistrate of Bow Street, found me in my club to tell me that several witnesses saw me kidnap a woman from Vauxhall."

Her eyes grew even larger, dark circles against her ivory skin, but she just stared at him, speechless. "The woman was Lady Farthingale, and she was a participant in the hunt. She was also the mistress of Lord Hadrian, and he went immediately to Bow Street—"

Maryanne's brandy snifter was sliding from her fingers. Lunging forward, Dash caught it before she dropped it and set it on the octagonal table beside her. He lowered onto his knees before her. Loose wisps of her hair, almost gold in the firelight, brushed her lips.

"Yes, there were witnesses, love, but they were paid to lie.

I didn't do it. You must believe that. I would never kidnap a woman. I would never hurt any . . . never a woman."

"But why you?" she choked out. "Why would anyone wish to blame you?"

"I don't know, love, but it gets worse." He felt his mouth twist into a rueful grimace, and he held the brandy to her lips.

Obediently she sipped. Then coughed.

"There was another woman who disappeared from the scavenger hunt, and again there were witnesses who saw me take her into a carriage. Two courtesans and two gentlemen were the witnesses that time. And again, I vow to you, Maryanne, that I did not do it."

Hades, he could read nothing from her eyes. It was as if she were reading a book, not listening to a protestation of innocence from her husband. "That woman was Eliza Charmody, an actress."

"Had you ever . . ." She let her words die away.

"Did I have an affair with her? No."

"Are you certain?"

Christ Jesus, how bad did she think he was?

He paused. There were times at orgies, when he'd been drunk, that he'd engaged with many sexual partners but couldn't remember any of them. Still, that wasn't an affair—he'd never been the woman's protector. "Yes, I'm certain," he repeated. "I hate to have to tell you this, Maryanne." He cradled her hands in his. Hers were cold.

Was she staring so evenly at him because she already knew this? Was she involved? He'd expected her to burst into tears. Or back away from him in fear. Not to sit calmly, weighing his words.

"Eliza Charmody was murdered," he finished. "And her body left in Hyde Park on the night you shared my bed."

"But, then, it couldn't have been you. You were with me."

"What time did you leave me that morning, love?"

She frowned, forehead wrinkling. "Almost half past six. Just a couple minutes before."

He let out a sharp breath. Maryanne gave him an alibi, but he couldn't use it. Not without tossing them both into scandal.

"Miss Charmody was strangled with a black cravat. It was not mine, however."

Her gaze flicked to the black cravat he wore. Then she stood so quickly he almost toppled backward. Abruptly she marched away from him, leaving him with his hand splayed on the warm, carved stone of the fireplace.

She doesn't believe you. She's heard the stories of you tying up women, spanking them. She thinks you're a murderer.

He *was* a bloody murderer.

He pushed himself up to his feet as she reached the desk. She plucked his pen from the ink fountain. "But you didn't kill her, obviously, and someone did. Do you know who?"

She caressed the length of the pen with her fingertips—he remembered Marcus telling him he could get hard just watching Venetia put the end of a paintbrush handle to her lips.

Dash understood. His cock pulsed as Maryanne fondled the pen.

"No, I don't know who."

"But you must suspect someone. It must be the same person who shot at you!" Droplets of ink sprayed his neat blotter as she gestured with her hand.

"Yes. It's possible."

"So it must be Craven. Or his partner." She shuddered. "Yes, I could imagine Lord Craven doing such a horrid thing."

"It's not as simple as that, love."

"Then tell me!" She turned on him, her curls in disarray, frothing around her pale face. "I'm your wife. Tell me!"

Dash knew he couldn't. If she was involved, he would be revealing his hand to her—she would know exactly what he knew and could use it against him.

If she was innocent . . . she didn't need to know. He would protect her.

The dinner gong sounded, saving him. But she must have guessed his intent. "It's only the first. You have time to talk to me."

"It only puts you in danger to know, love. It's time for dinner. Are you able to go down?"

Maryanne nodded, but she hastened over to the mirror to fix her hair. Dash linked her arm in his. "I believe you," she told him.

And at dinner, Maryanne felt as if she were acting in a play. The five of them sat at the table—herself, Dash, Lord and Lady Moredon, and Lady Yardley. Talk was of humorous gossip and of the past. Green eyes twinkling, Lady Moredon had shared indiscreet stories of Dash—the many times he'd fallen from a tree while sneaking out of the house, the maids who had swooned every time he smiled their way.

But Lady Yardley's words hammered in Maryanne's thoughts the entire time. *He will not turn a blind eye if you shoot a relative.*

She couldn't think. Couldn't follow the lighthearted conversations surrounding her. The words kept distracting her. She'd spilled soup, hit her wineglass with her wrist, and saved it, with her heart in her throat.

Who exactly did Dash suspect of kidnapping women, of shooting at him? Why would he not tell her?

Under lowered lashes, she glanced to the Earl of Moredon. With sandy hair, freckles, and bright blue eyes, he held boyish charm. He looked the least likely man to murder women or shoot at his brother-in-law. But wasn't that what held her glued to the pages of her horrid novels—the twists and turns, the surprise at the end?

Not Anne. Maryanne jerked up her head to watch Anne teasingly sparring with Dash. She could not believe Anne wished her brother ill.

After dinner, she yearned to snare Dash alone—demand that he tell her—but she had no chance. The five of them gathered in the music room. Anne played pianoforte. Lady Yardley's fingers plucked heavenly melodies from the harp strings.

They would expect her to play. And she'd never been accomplished at music. Maryanne closed her eyes. . . .

"You should go to bed, sleepy one," Dash murmured by her ear.

Her heart soared, her nipples tightened, her cunny throbbed—her entire body willed him to join her. But her husband escorted her to her bedroom, brushed a kiss to her fingertips, and returned to his guests.

Maryanne flopped onto her bed. Damn. She was . . . aroused. Shamefully so.

She should be worrying about her husband's life, not yearning to ride him until he roared.

Maryanne jerked up. Dash was downstairs. Did she dare sneak into his room, search for any notes or letters he might have written about his suspicions? She wanted to know exactly who he suspected. She needed to know.

She shook her head. No! It was sinful enough that she'd overheard his conversation with Lady Yardley. She would not rifle through his things. Instead she would force herself to stay awake and go to his room when he retired, and she would demand to know the truth.

Fingers tweaked her nipple beneath her nightgown, drawing on it until it stood erect. Pleasure rushed through her. Something hot and hard pressed against her bottom. The skirt of her nightdress was pulled up. A large hand parted her thighs and unerringly found her tingling clit—

Maryanne jerked awake.

"Sorry, love," Dash whispered. "I didn't mean to wake you."

So aroused she could barely speak, she rolled onto her back. Her cunny felt like a drawn bow—one stroke of his cock would fire her trigger.

"I want you." She couldn't see him against the velvet black darkness, but she sensed him. Smelled him.

His hand cupped her breast, and she spread her legs wide.

"I've hungered for this all night," he whispered.

A rap sounded at the door. "My lord? My lady?"

Dash hung his head—she felt the brush of his silky hair against her cheek and lips. "Damn and blast," he muttered. "Why are we being interrupted at midnight?"

The bed creaked as he shifted, and she wanted to scream as his heat pulled away. Instead she drew up the covers and sat up to strike a light. Dash opened the door to the hallway, and the footman's candle threw light on him. Wall sconces still burned in the hall, and she blinked as light spilled in. "Yes?" Dash glowered.

"L—Lady Evershire," the footman stammered. "And Mr. Jack Tate, my lord. They've made it through the storm, my lord, and have just arrived."

"Jack Tate?" Dash repeated.

"Yes, my lord." The footman explained more, but kept his voice low, and Maryanne could not hear.

Dash gave curt directions—to prepare rooms, to ensure a dinner was laid out, to have servants ensure the guests were changed, refreshed, and then brought to the drawing room. Maryanne swung her legs out of bed as the footman left.

"No need for you to come down, love," Dash said. "Lady Evershire is Moredon's sister. I was not expecting her."

"And Jack Tate?" Though she knew who he was. She'd overheard Dash tell Lady Yardley. Guiltily she murmured, "The name is familiar, but I can't place it."

"Tate owns several London hells. And he owes me twenty thousand pounds. I can assure you he wasn't expected either." Dash's mouth flattened into a grim line. His eyes sparkled, as hard as jet.

"What is it?" she gasped. But she understood. "Twenty thousand. That's enough to kill for, isn't it? He must be unsavory, to own gambling dens. Do you think he is the one who shot at you?"

Dash raked back his hair. "Damned brazen to do it and then show up as a stranded traveler, but possible."

"You can't let him stay."

"The storm is a blizzard now, he has no mount, and I'm not certain I can send him out to die."

"N—no."

"Not when I have no evidence he is definitely the blackguard."

She nodded. Honor again. A gentleman's honor. "But . . . but what of Lady Evershire?"

"She rescued Tate on the way, it appears."

"She has no reason to kill you?"

"Actually she has a very good one. A woman scorned and all that." Then he laughed, his deep, masculine laugh that normally aroused her every nerve. But she only felt cold, uncertain.

"But, no, I don't believe Harriet shot at me." A fond smile touched his lips. "Go back to bed, sweeting. I'll dress and go downstairs."

To a man who might have shot at him? "Wait!" she cried, and she launched onto her feet, dragging the sheets with her.

Framed in the doorway that connected to the parlor, he paused. Turned.

"If Tate wants to hurt you over the money, why don't you forgive the debt?"

Ruefully he shook his head. "It's a debt of honor, love. It would dishonor us both to forget it."

She dropped the edges of the sheets and stepped over them. "Honor is more important than your life?"

His broad shoulders lifted and fell in a casual shrug. "Yes."

Scrambling, she reached him as he moved to step through the door. Hesitantly she wrapped her fingers around his hand. She drew his palm to her belly, beneath the flowing muslin of her nightdress, and sighed at the warm pressure of his hand against her. Saw the smile come to his lips and his black lashes lower.

"I want to ensure you are here to see your child, Dash. I'm terrified something . . ." She couldn't finish, frightened that if she spoke of it, it might become real.

He nuzzled her neck, and her body took fire, her quim becoming juicy and hot. She tipped her head to the side. With his hand on her tummy, his lips on her skin, she gasped at the sizzle that shot from neck to toes.

"You play with sharp blades, don't you?" he murmured.

"I don't understand."

"You know my vulnerabilities. I promise you I'll take care—for your sake and our child's."

"What are you going to do?"

"Welcome Tate and Harriet to my home. Play the generous host."

She pushed back her hair, left loose, not braided, and in a tangle. "I wish to be with you."

"You need to sleep, Maryanne. For both your sake and the babe's." But he removed his hand from her belly as he repeated the words. "You cannot be with me when I speak with Tate. That's male domain."

She rolled her eyes. She couldn't help it.

He tipped up her chin and brushed a kiss on her nose. "And just so you aren't surprised, the Duke of Ashton, Sophia's lover, will be arriving within a few days. As will my family—I'm inviting the lot of them. My uncle, aunt, and my cousin. Along with Marcus, Venetia, and their babe, and your mother and sister, we'll have a full and cheery house for Christmas. Now you'd best go to bed, angel."

With his hand splayed on her lower back, he propelled her to her bed. She wanted to protest, but he lifted the sheets off the floor. Lit only by candlelight, his face bore a cool expression that brooked no argument. She climbed up and slipped underneath the covers.

Remarkably her husband tucked her in.

"Sleep well. And don't worry."

She nodded but implored, "Please, don't keep secrets. You didn't tell me about Tate. Please let me help."

"I want to keep you safe. Go to bed and I'll tell you all in the morning."

She knew she shouldn't let him escape, but she yawned. She was so tired she felt her lids drift down as he moved away.

Oh, he would try to avoid giving her the truth. She knew that, for she would do it in his shoes. But she would pursue.

Snow piled up against the terrace doors, driven by the wind. Tree boughs, loaded with a fanciful, thick white frosting, hung almost to the drifts. Sunlight turned the view to a sea of glittering white, a vista like a cup of one of Gunter's ices. Beautiful, but Maryanne felt no delight looking at it.

Where was Dash?

She'd woken twice in the night to use the chamber pot, and he hadn't been in the room. Should she have searched for him? It was all she could do to balance on the pot and then stumble back into her warmed bed.

She'd thought he'd gone to his room, to avoid her, to avoid having to reveal secrets. But this morning, in her nightgown, she slipped through the adjoining parlor and peeked through his door.

His bed had not been slept in.

And for the first time, she'd seen his bedroom. Her room sparkled in gilt, crimson, and ivory, with lacy curtains tied with golden rope and flocked paper and tasseled, exotic rugs. His was simple, austere. Deep green walls, a bare floor, and an enormous but simple bed.

He wasn't at breakfast—she'd peeped into the dining room, taking care to ensure no one saw her. She didn't want to have to chatter with Anne or Lady Evershire or Lady Yardley. She wanted to find Dash. But the breakfast room had been empty.

The corridor leading off from the doors was also deserted, so she hiked her hems and ran. She turned left, took a branch to the right, and then another to the left. She must be in the east wing. But a glance out a stairwell window revealed she was standing over the terrace doors—she was looking at the same view.

Bother, where was she?

A terse male laugh sounded from behind the double doors opposite. Dash—that must be Dash. She darted over and pulled open one door. Another laugh echoed from below. The ceiling arched overhead, and she stepped into the room onto a gallery. A wrought-iron railing framed it, running around the oval room. A voice, muted, rose from beneath her. Cool air rushed out to her—obviously this enormous room was not kept warm.

Gathering courage, Maryanne went to the edge, put her hands on the railing, and looked down.

A blond man leaped into view, dressed in flowing white shirt and breeches. He swung a foil around and barked a laugh toward the shadows beneath her.

A voice answered. Dash's voice. Though she couldn't hear all the words, she heard the name *Tate*.

Maryanne's heart skipped a beat. The blond man must be Jack Tate.

Was this to be a duel over debts?

A hand to her mouth held back a gasp as she crouched down to watch between the pickets of the railing. Tate moved with lithe grace, slashing his blade at the air, a boyish grin on his tanned face.

Dash moved out of the shadow.

Her hand gripped the picket hard.

She'd seen him nude, but he was just as magnificently arousing dressed in breeches clinging to hard thighs and shapely calves, with an open black shirt thrown on carelessly. Loose at the neck, it revealed the curling dark hair she loved to run her fingers through and his large, sculpted pectoral muscles.

Dash was bigger than Tate, taller and broader. The flowing sleeves of his shirt outlined the bulging muscles of his arms.

Foil in hand, he prowled to a table and lifted a slip of paper. "Your vowels, Tate."

"Suggesting we play for them?" Jack Tate drawled. He brushed back his wheat-blond hair.

Dash ripped the paper in two.

"What in blazes are you doing?"

"They're forgiven."

"You must be joking, my lord. Don't insult me. I'd rather fight for them."

"Blackguard. I've a wife in a delicate condition." But Dash readied himself, blade upright before him, his back to her.

Maryanne caught her breath as she gazed down from blue-black hair and broad shoulders to narrow waist and lean hips. Dash possessed the most entrancing derriere, and each shift of his weight tightened and relaxed the muscles of his haunches, deepening the shadow. Next time they made love, she'd urge him on top, slip her hands down to his buttocks, and stroke those firm hollows.

His rear tightened as he took a step, and her throat dried. She was indecently wet. Never before had she seen men fence or fight.

Tate swept an elaborate bow. "My apologies, Swansborough. If you'd care for another game of hazard, I'm at your service."

Dash didn't answer; instead he paced around, and Tate followed, so they slowly circled each other. Maryanne's nostrils flared at the subtle scent—of male prespiration, of their skin, of their anticipation.

"I'd rather blades than dice," Dash said, and Maryanne's heart plummeted.

How could he?

Why would he prefer to risk his life than gamble and lose? Was it just male pride and madness?

Tate lifted his blade, still grinning. Waiting.

Dash instantly seemed to relax, to become fluid, but Tate carried tension. Did that mean Dash was the better swordsman?

Maryanne pressed closer to the space between the twisting white-painted iron pickets.

Dash lifted his blade in turn, but she could see only his back again. "Did you shoot at me two days ago?"

Maryanne choked on a gasp. How could he be so blunt?

Tate faced her. Surprise registered on his angular features, in the widening of his blue eyes.

"Shoot at you?" Tate repeated. He lunged, grabbing the first blow, but his blade clashed harmlessly with Dash's. "I was in London until yesterday. The blizzard hit before I reached Tremouth, and I encountered Lady Evershire."

They separated blades and retreated. Tate bounced on the spot, his breath a white puff in the cool air. "Enjoy this cold. Been spending too much time in the heated bedchambers of London ladies."

"No doubt." Dash drove forward this time, muscles flexing. Gleaming blades collided again. Dash used his to push Tate's aside, and he pursued the advantage with a quick leap ahead. Tate darted back and brought his blade around to parry Dash's just as the tip sliced toward his chest.

Dash's blade arced so fast Maryanne could barely see the whipping of the thin steel. Clash after clash showed her that Tate was fighting desperately to hold on, that he was always in retreat. Tate reacted in defense. Dash was in control.

Her heart soared.

Dash's hair dangled around him, wet with sweat. His forehead, cheeks, and chin gleamed with dampness, and his fine shirt clung to chest and arms, almost translucent where it touched skin. Yet he barely seemed out of breath. He leaped, darted, drove forward with elegant ease—he sprang faster than she could even gasp in reaction.

Pins and needles raced up her legs, where they were curled beneath her, but she stayed crouched on the floor, clinging to the railing.

Win, win, win, she urged Dash.

"You arranged to meet Lady Evershire in Tremouth?" Dash asked as his blade slashed against Tate's time after time, the clang ringing up to the ceiling.

"A chance encounter. Good fortune for me, for the inn was full of travelers stranded by the storm. I thought I might have to sleep in a stable. And of course, I couldn't allow such a fate to befall such a delicate, cultured lady, so I drove her carriage here. No one surpasses me at the reins."

Tate was still cocky, even as Dash forced him back toward a corner. Desperation glowed in Tate's eyes. He gave a wild leap, landing on the cushioned seat of a chair, and he launched at Dash, blade slashing.

Maryanne screamed.

Dash jerked toward her as his blade flew up to block Tate's blow. He missed, and the tip of Tate's blade slashed his arm. The black sleeve parted.

Blood welled along the line.

"Stop!" she yelled. "Stop at once! I will not allow you to kill each other!"

Tate fell back, staring at her. Dash clapped his hand to his arm, his gaze fixed on her. He knew she'd snuck in here to listen. She'd broken his concentration and gotten him wounded.

What a fool she'd been! And now he was hurt. Almost tripping over her skirts, she clawed her way up to her feet. Blood dripped beneath his hand, leaked into the pristine lawn of his shirt.

She gathered her skirts and ran for the stairs.

She didn't care how angry Dash would be. He needed her attentions.

"Apologizes on wounding your husband, my dear lady."

Startled, Maryanne turned in the corridor outside Dash's bedchamber to find Jack Tate lounging against the wall. His shoulder narrowly missed the gilded frame of an oil landscape. He still wore his open, sweat-soaked shirt and his tight breeches. He swept a bow. "Jack Tate, at your service."

She tipped up her chin. "Do you call dueling with my husband a service to me?"

Tate's bronze-red lips widened in a wicked grin. He moved closer so his elbow rested against the wall and he was towering over her. "I had no intention of seriously wounding a newly married man."

"I doubt you could have. It was obvious who controlled the bout."

He laughed, blue eyes twinkling. "You're captivating. No wonder Swansborough was willing to fling on the leg shackles with you."

"Was that intended to be a compliment?" She had no idea what prompted her to joust with him this way. He might be a murderer, and she was goading him. Yet she couldn't stop.

"Yes." His gaze swept over her, from her curls to her hem. "Pretty in a shy and naive sort of way. I would be honored, my dear, to be at your *service.*"

He lay such stress on the word, while winking, that Maryanne froze in place. "Are you suggesting . . . are you . . . ?" She must be imagining it.

Tate's voice dropped to a seductive growl. "Not an affair, my lady. I would never be so uncultured as to suggest that to a newly married bride while sheltered under her husband's roof. I was thinking of a ménage-à-trois. Three in the bed."

Her lips parted, but only a squeak came out.

"Swansborough's notorious for enjoying crowded beds."

She merely gaped into those laughing blue eyes. Was he trying to shock her? Frighten her? Make her doubt her husband? "Thrown out," she croaked. "I could have you thrown out."

"Are you certain you want that? A threesome would prove a far more pleasurable fencing match than the one you witnessed, my lady. Two swords jousting to be the victor—the one to make you scream your pleasure first—"

"Out! I. Will. See. You. Thrown. Out." She threw the words at him, gasping between each one.

"I expect when you tell this tale to Swansborough, I will be." And he winked.

16

"So, sweeting, why were you threatening to throw Tate out of the house? What did he say?"

Maryanne drew her hand from her fur muff and slipped her arm into the crook of Dash's. Dash had shown her the grounds, the stables, and the snow-covered orchard. Several footmen had accompanied them, men in livery and powdered wigs who now waited, discreetly watching the woods and the house, as Dash stopped by the stone fountain.

Leather brushed her chin as he tipped it up. Serious dark eyes met hers. "What did he say?"

She glanced around; surely the footmen were too far away to hear. "He wanted to join us in our bed."

"I'll run him through."

"No! Perhaps he only said it to goad you into a duel. Perhaps it was intended as a way to kill you."

"It was an insult to you, love. That can't be ignored."

"And so you rush inexorably toward death. I don't care if he stands on a Drury Lane stage and calls me a courtesan, I won't have you risking your life."

Dash crossed his arms over his chest, thrust out his lower lip, and she laughed. "You plan to ignore me, don't you?" She sobered and glanced out over the lawns, blanketed by thick, dazzling snow. "He said you enjoy crowded beds."

"I did. Not now."

She shook her head. "I don't believe that, and you needn't lie to spare my feelings."

"I want to keep you all to myself, Maryanne."

She'd read such fantasies and had been intrigued. Two strapping men, as Tate had suggested, both determined to win her favor with their prowess in bed? And she'd even, shockingly, been aroused by the scenes that paired two women with a gentleman. "I would never dream of doing such a thing."

He growled, "You don't think so, because you've never tried it."

"And you have said I can't."

"Perhaps, if you wished to add another woman to our bed . . ."

She scooped up a handful of soft snow and pushed it against his chest. It clung to his black greatcoat.

"I didn't like Mrs. Master's salon," she whispered, "before I found you there. There were eight men, and it was all very horrid."

He grasped her wrist. "Eight! You didn't tell me about this. Did they hurt you?"

"No!" Maryanne remembered to drop her voice. "A courtesan exposed her breasts, shoved me out of the way, and distracted them."

"Thank the lord for that. And all this talk of crowded beds is making me hunger for our bed." He adjusted his trousers. "We could slip off behind a grove of trees—"

"We can't make love out here. It's freezing!" Maryanne cried.

A boyishly beseeching look lit up his eyes. "We would heat up quickly."

"It's fine for you," she protested. "You only need one part of your body, and you'll be sliding that into warmth."

Dash laughed so hard he lost his footing. His arms waved as he struggled to stay up, so Maryanne shoved on his chest. With a yelp, he tumbled back in the snow, laughing. "True, sweet wife," he admitted in a soft voice. "Outdoor lovemaking generally favors the gentleman. Still, I promise it can be a—" He broke off, staring across the gardens.

"What?" She twisted to look.

"Lady Evershire. Off for a clandestine rendezvous." He struggled to push himself out of the snow. As he jumped to his feet, he slapped at the white lumps clinging to his coat and trousers.

Maryanne squinted in the direction he was looking—she spotted Lady Evershire as the lady passed between snow-covered shrubs.

"Stay here with the footmen, love." He hailed one of the young men over.

She grasped his forearm, coated in sticky snow. "What are you doing?"

"I'm going to follow her."

"Why? Perhaps she just wants a bracing walk on a pretty winter's day."

"I've known Harriet a long time. Only two things can stir her this early."

The footman loped toward them.

"And they are?" she asked.

The words brushed by her ear. "Shopping and illicit sex."

Maryanne waved the footmen away as she tripped up the path to the Tresdale—a small cottage on the neighboring estate to Dash's. Her heart pounded, and not simply from chasing after Dash across packed, slippery snow.

Lady Farthingale kidnapped from Vauxhall.

An actress who vanished from Covent Gardens. Who had been found dead in Hyde Park.

Dash couldn't have done such a thing—not protective, heroic Dash. He'd married her out of honor, and despite his notoriously dark sexual appetite, his sister and Lady Yardley insisted he was the most honorable man. On the other hand, they also believed him besotted with her.

Was he? How could he be? They were veritable strangers.

However, that honorable man was now crouched behind a shrub, peering in a diamond-paned window of the Tudor cottage.

He spied her—his hand abruptly waved at her to turn and go back, but she merely smiled, ignored him, and crept quietly toward the window where he stood.

She wrapped her arms around her chest, shivering in her velvet gown and fur-trimmed pelisse. Her half boots sank into the thick snow. "What are you watching?" she whispered, ensuring she stayed out of the view of the window.

He gave a low groan. "Harriet behaving witlessly with dangerous men."

"Let me see."

His arm embraced her and brought her forward—her boots sunk and stopped, and she arched up on tiptoe to see in. Lacy drapes were tied back and framed the scene—a cozy parlor heated by a blazing fire, a tea service on a buffet by the window. Movement caught her eye.

A naked woman sashayed in front of the window, her gaze directed away, golden blond curls tumbling down her back. A lovely back, with sloping shoulders, ivory skin, and wide, flaring hips that swayed temptingly as the lady walked. This lady obviously knew her allure.

Maryanne gulped as she recognized Harriet and saw two men emerge from the shadows, one possessing straight hair as golden as the lady's and one with tousled brown locks. Both wore their shirts open with tailored trousers. Both held their naked cocks in their hands.

Laughing, Harriet held out her arms in welcome, and the men embraced her. The mirror over the fireplace reflected them. Craven's handsome face, gilded by his pale hair, transformed into the leer of a satyr, his blue eyes narrowing in an almost comically lusty expression. The other man Maryanne did not know—he was dark, his jaw shadowed by dark stubble, his eyes black beneath straight, thick brows. He was not handsome but arresting; her heart beat faster as she watched him nuzzle Harriet's slender neck.

As she waited to watch him do something scandalous.

She didn't wait long.

"That's Barrett. Craven's partner," Dash murmured.

Barrett rested his open gloved hand beneath Harriet's full nude breast. Her breasts sloped forward, impossibly round, topped with thick brown nipples. Abruptly he bent forward and buried his face in between. Goodness, the man could smother himself in those.

Craven approached Harriet from behind, aiming his cock at her curvaceous ass. Barrett shifted to take Harriet's right nipple in his mouth while he brushed his member between her thighs—

Maryanne pulled back. It was rude to watch, but she felt so heated, she must be melting a hole in the snow.

She met Dash's amused gaze.

"So that is a threesome," she observed.

Dash had to smother a laugh at Maryanne's serious expression. Of all the things he'd imagined she'd say, that simple statement wasn't one. He drew her back away from the window, his hand at her waist to guide her over the lumpy snow.

"What do we do?" she whispered.

"I was planning to wait—to make sure she emerges alive."

Shielded by both the cottage wall and a snow-covered lilac, they were in a warm and secluded spot. He felt Maryanne's breasts rise and fall against his chest.

"Have you had many threesomes with another man?" she asked, sotto voce.

"A few," he admitted.

"Was it . . . interesting?"

"I did explore them for fun in my pursuit of mind-melting pleasure." Did he reveal to his wife that the women most definitely enjoyed themselves with two mouths, two cocks, and four hands? What if Maryanne wanted to explore sexual fun?

Given his lifetime of sensual exploration, did he have any right to deny it to her?

Hell, of course he did. Yet most peers kept mistresses, and their wives took lovers.

The thought of Maryanne seeking pleasure and love in another man's bed had his blood running as cold as the melted snow dripping around him. And if another man hopped into their bed and touched her, he'd rip out the bastard's throat.

His arms tightened around Maryanne's tiny waist.

If Tate touched her . . .

"I told you I believe Craven and Barrett are involved in white slavery," he murmured. "But I can't uncover direct proof. And Harriet's love affair with both men has complicated matters. I can't put her at risk."

"But they could be responsible for that shot."

He nodded. "And I suspect they are using Harriet to watch me. What worries me is that they will find her a liability—"

"Perhaps she is the one who wants to hurt you and she brought Mr. Tate to draw suspicion away from her lovers."

"You have a torturous and clever mind, dear wife. I hope you never decide to get rid of me."

"Be serious," she hissed. "Of course not!"

"Why not? I'm beginning to lose count of the people who want me dead. Harriet. Craven and Barrett. Jack Tate. My bloody family—my uncle who inherits the title, my hothead of a cousin. You had a loving family, sweeting. I did not. Power and wealth were all that mattered in my family. My father had it and was reckless with it, and my uncle craved it." He grinned at her horrified expression. "Even Sophia's lover, the Duke of Ashton, holds a grudge because I shot him in the leg."

"Well, I would never hurt you, Dash. Never."

Did she protest too much?

A loud feminine cry sounded from inside the cottage—a

shout of pleasure, not of pain. "Fuck me harder!" Harriet cried. "I want to be stuffed full of both your cocks."

Dash clasped Maryanne's hand. "Come, we should go back to the house."

Confused, she held back. "Aren't you going to stay to ensure Harriet's safety?"

He backed away from the house toward the lane. "Not with you here, dear wife. I'm not keeping you out in the cold where we could get caught. Lusty Harriet will have to look out for herself."

Frowning, Maryanne darted out from the cover of the lilac to join him. Dutifully she walked at his side as they hurried down the lane to the drive back to Swansley.

They had reached the thick grove of woods that bordered his lawns when she stopped. He halted, too, waiting.

She waved her hand expressively, her fur muff slicing through the air. "But, Dash, if you suspect all these people of trying to kill you, why on earth would you want them under your roof?"

He shrugged. "Confrontation. What is a Christmas gathering if not a time for confrontation?"

Fire lit up her brown eyes—his wife was preparing to argue, when a male voice shouted, "Swansborough!" and he looked up to see a gentleman striding their way, walking stick swinging, sunlight glinting off round spectacles.

He grinned first with recognition, but then doubts hit. Why would Sir William have arrived at his home unannounced? What had he learned? Was Lady Farthingale now dead?

But as the magistrate neared, he called out a hearty, "Good afternoon to you both," and greeted Maryanne with a bow; then he straightened, clapping Dash on the shoulder.

Dash made the introductions and saw consternation come to Maryanne's brown eyes. "Sir William Kent is an old friend. A man who was like a father to me."

He'd hoped to use those words to reassure her, even though his own gut was knotted with apprehension.

"And he is Bow Street's famed magistrate." Maryanne tucked her hand into her muff and bit her lip. The glance she threw to Dash was fearful, as if she expected to see him thrown into irons.

Dash shook his head, turned to his friend. "What the blazes are you doing up here, Sir William?"

"Taking advantage of your hospitality, Swansborough. Were you both returning to the house?"

At Dash's nod, the magistrate grinned. "Then let's make haste. I'm in the mood for a warm brandy and a good fire."

At least Sir William did not arrest Dash.

Shakily Maryanne sat down at the escritoire in the morning room. She set her candle on the blotter and drew Georgiana's letter and the manuscript pages from within the folds of the shawl she'd carried to hide them. As she'd guessed, the morning room was empty. Maids had been in and out of her bedroom, and she was too afraid Dash would enter through the connecting door. Here, she could count on being alone. She hadn't counted on the cold.

She smoothed out Georgiana's letter on the blotter.

She had to write to Georgiana, but what could she say? And what of Tillie's book? She certainly couldn't edit it. She couldn't continue to be Georgiana's partner.

Dipping a pen in the inkwell, she drew the pen across a sheet of fresh paper.

I went to your rescue. I risked scandal because I believed you needed help. . . .

She paused, the ink blotting onto the page.

She'd sensed that Sir William wished to speak to Dash alone, and she'd grasped the chance to rush here and write the blasted letter and be done with it.

But now she had no idea what to say.

A cutting letter might hurt Georgiana—and when the flamboyant courtesan was wounded, she sought revenge.

Or should she just stall for time?

Blast Georgiana for spending all their money, though Maryanne knew she was also to blame for merely trying to pay their authors and keep the creditors happy, without confronting Georgiana about her lavish and spendthrift ways.

She wished she had Dash's courage. He welcomed a confrontation with a murderer!

"Who is in here, please?"

Mrs. Long's voice startled Maryanne, and she jumped up from the plush seat, blocking the desk with her skirts. "I am in here."

"My lady?" Pure surprise pitched the housekeeper's voice upward as she entered the room. "My lady, I am sorry, but the morning room is not normally used after luncheon. The fire is not kept lit after that time."

"I—" What reason could she give? *I was hiding from my husband and my maids.* "I wished to write some letters."

Mrs. Long's lips thinned, and her fingers steepled in front of her plain skirts. "This room is not—" She stopped there, as though remembering she was speaking to her mistress. "I will have the fire lit again."

Flustered, Maryanne shook her head. "Do not bother. I—I don't believe I will stay." She turned and awkwardly gathered the letter and the pages. They slid out of her hands, and she had to slap her palm on two to keep them from falling on the floor.

She sensed Mrs. Long waiting. Why wouldn't the woman leave? She could dismiss her; how foolish that she didn't dare, in case—in case she aroused suspicions.

"Letters from my family," she explained needlessly.

But the housekeeper waited to follow her out of the room. In case she set something on fire? Or took something she was not supposed to? Clumsily thrown over her arm, her shawl trailed to the floor.

"Tomorrow, my lady, I wish to review the arrangements

for Mr. and Mrs. James Blackmore and young Mr. Blackmore and the Duke of Ashton, of course. I do wish to ensure that all meets your approval."

"I'm sure what you have planned will be lovely," she murmured. She cringed, though, at the hurried weakness in her words.

"I have prepared menus for Christmas dinner—"

Roast something, how complex could it be? Maryanne muttered under her breath. "Fine. Wonderful. I shall review them tomorrow."

"I shall of course attend to place settings, but there are centerpieces for the dinners. Her ladyship—the late viscountess—had Beadles in London make them."

"Oh, I wouldn't—" Maryanne stopped. "Whatever has been used before will be perfect."

"Of course. I shall leave you now, my lady." And Mrs. Long withdrew.

Bother, why did she feel she had failed at a test?

"We found one of the men who took Lady Farthingale."

After delivering that stunning statement, Sir William sipped his brandy, ensconced in a leather chair by the crackling fire.

Dash leaped up from his chair. "Which one, the Cornishman? Where did he take her? Who the bloody hell was he?"

"Aye, the Cornishman, Trevelyan Ball. However, he claims he took Lady F to the Ox and Swan Inn, near here, and turned her over to a gentleman named Smith."

Leaning against the edge of his desk, Dash groaned. "And the trail is cold after that?"

Haunted by memories of Maryanne on the chair by this very desk, her skirts up, he shook his head.

"Indeed." The brandy was set down with a clink, and Sir William removed his spectacles. Rubbed his temples. "This business grows more complicated."

Dash stretched his arms behind him and supported his

weight on his hands. "Complicated? I'm going to have a half dozen people in my house who want to see me dead."

The magistrate's gaze stayed on him, level, penetrating, neutral but all the more accusatory because of that. Sir William cleared his throat. "A woman's body was found in the woods behind the parish church in the village. She's been dead for a very long time."

A woman's body—found in the village just a mile south of his estate. "How long? Does anyone know who she is?"

"Yes, we know who she is. She wore a locket, on the back of which a name had been engraved." Sir William's spectacles dropped to the carpet, where they bounced, the frames reflecting firelight. "Dash, it was Amanda Westmoreland."

"Amanda," Dash repeated. Glossy mahogany curls and blue eyes that exuded calm and confidence. The touch of her slender hand on his forearm as they strolled together, as she conversed easily and they shared a warm laugh. Amanda had been lovely. Exquisite. "She eloped to Gretna. With the estate steward's son. Left a note."

"Obviously she did not get that far."

A woman he'd kissed. A woman he might have married—if he hadn't been so blasted afraid his uncle might kill her as part of his plan to get the title. "It's been ten years." His voice echoed in the library—it didn't sound like his voice. Too sharp. The words shaky. "Why now? Why had no one found her before?"

"She was buried, it appears, though the grave was shallow. It appeared to have been freshly dug."

"Someone moved her body after all these years? Brought her here? From where?" He pushed himself up from the desk and paced, needing to move. His hands clenched and opened. "You knew her." He swung around on Sir William. "You knew how lovely she was."

"Indeed." The magistrate inclined his head, slid on his spectacles. "She cared for you very deeply, Dashiel."

"What's the idea here? That I did it?" He dropped his head into his hands. "Christ Jesus, it was probably my uncle. He would be afraid I'd marry and Amanda would have borne an heir. I told her I couldn't marry. I was afraid I'd break her heart, but she merely kissed me on the cheek and told me it didn't matter. That there was someone else, someone she was in love with and she wished to marry. And you're wrong, Sir William, Amanda was not in love with me."

Sir William pursed his lips, picked up the brandy snifter. "I do believe you are wrong about that. I would imagine the young lady had a great deal of pride."

Pride? Had that been it? He'd hurt her, but she'd been too controlled a lady to burst into tears or slap him or shout at him?

"And then, within three days, she was gone. As was the steward's son. Did he do it? Or are his bones buried somewhere?" Pain sliced through Dash's head, his heart. He'd thought he'd protected Amanda by sending her away. He'd walked into his uncle's study and told the blackguard he had no intention of marrying, in the hopes of keeping her safe.

But she'd been lost. He hated to imagine what was left of her, buried for ten years. All that life, all that loveliness—lost. A beautiful life cut short.

He shook his head. "I don't understand. I wasn't going to marry her. There was no reason for her to be hurt." Cold fear slid through his veins. "Maryanne," he said. "Maryanne is why I have to deal with this. I have to end this."

"Ah, your wife. Do you trust her?"

He frowned. "Any reason why I should not?" He had wanted to tell Sir William she was Verity. That he wasn't certain whether he could trust her or not. But Sir William's question provoked the need to defend her. "I want to believe her," he muttered. It was the hell of it. Wanting to trust, needing to trust, but hesitating, knowing he could not.

"Your wife is a gently bred young woman," Sir William mused. "I doubt she could be involved."

He must be mad, Dash thought, to have suspected she could be. But he couldn't shake away the wariness. Couldn't lose the fear that the person he should trust most—his wife—was a stranger. And it would be so easy for her to work against him. "You have passed sentence on hundreds of guilty women—women who stole, who murdered, who lied. How can you tell who is guilty or not?"

"I weighed the evidence, Dashiel. And acquired experience from years on the bench. Most of those brought before me were obviously guilty and didn't have the sense to hide it. But there was one time when I was mistaken. One woman who fooled me utterly and completely. I believed her plea of innocence and later learned I had been bewitched." Sir William curled his hands around the carved arms of the chair, his grip hard as though anger still flowed at the memory of failure. "Do you believe your wife is lying to you?"

17

Maryanne woke to the warmth of lips closing over hers. Her lashes fluttered up, and she caught just a glimpse of Dash's enigmatic black eyes before he kissed her.

He kissed her breath away, and as he drew back, she let her eyes open slowly. Drawing out each moment made it more exquisite. Sharing her bed with Dash was the most wonderful pleasure, even though he'd joined her late and had merely cradled her close and fallen asleep.

He hadn't made love to her.

The cloud-soft mattress settled beneath Maryanne as she rolled onto her back. Winter sunlight painted him with silver light touched lightly with gold—he'd obviously opened the curtains and slipped back into bed before waking her with the kiss.

Dash shared her smile with one that heated her to her toes; then he moved over her, easing his lean hips between her spread thighs. She caught her breath. The long muscles of his arms bulged as he braced his weight. Her ivory silk sheets had slid down to lay over the firm curve of his buttocks, revealing his wide shoulders, his muscular chest.

She slipped her hands up to his shoulders and wriggled beneath him, hoping the sinuous motion proved an invitation.

She wanted him so much.

But he wasn't hard. She could tell where his groin pressed against hers. What was wrong?

Had she done something wrong?

Dash nuzzled her cheek, the caress so tender her throat tightened. But he lifted from his caress, his eyes serious. "Do you have any secrets, Maryanne?"

Startled, she caught her breath. She wanted to shake her head, but he stroked her cheek with the back of his fingers. "You can tell me anything, love. Trust me."

"All wives keep secrets from their husbands." She began lightheartedly, but she stopped. Her nipples, hard with arousal or possibly fear, brushed his chest. Fear and excitement and uncertainty made her dizzy. "Yes, I have a secret you should know about." Her heart thudded in her chest, drowning out all sound.

His brows dipped. "You have nothing to fear, Maryanne. Tell me."

If she paused any longer, she'd lose her courage, so she rushed in. "You know Venetia drew erotic art to save our family from poverty. I did something, too . . . but . . . but it only mired me in more trouble." She wasn't explaining well, but she didn't dare stop.

But he made her pause by brushing his thumb along her lower lip. "What did you do?"

She knew she had to go on; she didn't dare stop. "I met a courtesan. Georgiana Watson."

His warm, slightly rough palm cupped her cheek, and sensation spiraled, stealing her breath. "How exactly did you meet a notorious courtesan?" he asked.

"At Hyde Park," she admitted as her face flushed. "I would go there before the obligatory afternoon visits by the *ton*. I went to . . . to write. There was a secluded bench on which I would sit, beneath the trees, and struggle to put words to the page. And then Georgiana began to go, to meet a gentleman—a married earl whom she adored. I saw them meeting,

I saw him kiss her hand and could feel the fiery need and desire between the two of them. She was head over heels in love. Once, she saw me seated on a bench, and she approached me. And we . . . we spoke."

"And you didn't run in preservation of your reputation?"

"No. No one was there to see us. And, given my family, how did I dare judge her?"

"I do adore you, sweet wife."

I do adore you. Did he? He threw the words out with a casual chuckle. Each of Georgiana's titled protectors professed love. At first. And by the end of the affair, Georgiana would be throwing their clothes out of the bedroom window as the gentlemen demanded she move out of the house so the new mistress could move in.

Her mother had loved hopelessly, and so had Georgiana.

"What sort of things did you write, Maryanne? Did you write novels?"

Deep and throaty, his voice mesmerized her, and she said, "Yes. Like Miss Jane Austen," without thinking. "Or so I desperately hoped. But I had not had a book published. I was too afraid to send one to a publisher. Georgiana was intrigued that I wrote and proposed an idea. She knew of so many jades who were growing older and needed to support themselves and their children."

"Did you write books for Georgiana?"

"No, I edited the books written by the courtesans. And I was Georgiana's partner in publishing. I wished to ensure our authors could earn a decent living."

Dash bent and kissed her neck. Against the hollow of her throat, he murmured. "What sort of books do courtesans write?"

"We decided we must publish books that would sell well, so the courtesans wrote of their . . . intimate experiences."

"That explains a great deal."

Her heart leaped. "What? What does it explain?"

"How you could be a virgin who wished to make love in a notorious salon and in the basket of a hot-air balloon."

She feared he'd be furious—instead he smiled as though bemused.

"Dash, I'm so sorry. I should have told you before we married. It all went wrong—terribly wrong. I thought I would help these women and help our family. But at first there was no money. Georgiana had a bit, but we accumulated debts. And our authors needed money, so . . . so I had our man of affairs send them money, rent them cottages, do want they needed to live. I thought the money would come eventually."

"And it did not?"

"No. Any money that did . . . it had been spent so many times over, it barely touched the debts. Georgiana withdrew the money we did earn and spent it again."

"So you have debts, you and your partner?" He slid his fingers down and tweaked her nipple.

Her voice failed her. She just couldn't gaze into his sincere eyes and tell him she owed thousands of pounds.

"Wait here, love."

With a brush of a kiss on her forehead, he was gone. Leaving her to stew. She must tell him. She must. But perhaps she should . . . arouse him first. Georgiana claimed that a woman could ask anything of a man when he was hard.

The door opened with a soft click, and Dash, in his robe, walked back in. Two leather-bound books were tucked under his arm.

Maryanne swallowed hard as he strolled to the bed. A light swing of his arm, and the books bounced onto the counterpane at her feet. Grinning, he dropped his robe and climbed up to join her. He reached for a book, balanced it in his huge palm on its spine, and lay beside her. "This one? Is this yours?" Dash's wicked grin was both hopeful and lusty. "An uplifting read."

"I edited the works. I did not write them. Though there

was a scene or two I suggested—for development of the plot, of course."

She could not tell if he wanted to tease her. His eyes glittered; lines bracketed his mouth, his dimple a deep shadow.

Her heart panged. Who was the author of the work that excited him? She held out her hand, and he laid the book there.

She read the spine. "Madame Desirée. Memoirs. They aren't truly memoirs, you know."

"Aren't they? My innocence is shattered, love."

"She's very talented, isn't she?" she said lightly. "Do you have other books she's written? We published three."

But he lazily stroked the curve of her hip beneath the sheets. "Who did the illustrations? Your sister?"

She shook her head. He owned her books. Why did it surprise her so much? Of course, he had an entire sexual past she knew almost nothing about. Part of her wished she knew everything he'd done, who had he done it with.

The sensible part knew she was better just to imagine.

Dash lifted the book from her hand, flipped the pages, and smiled down at the spread pages before him.

What was he looking at? What was he reading?

"Do you know what I think of when I read these words? When I look at the pictures?" he asked.

"Sex? Fantasy?"

"You. I would imagine us. I would think of sliding my fingers inside you as I read aloud to you. Or suckling your nipples. Or of you sitting on my cock, riding me as I read the erotic words aloud to you. And you, Maryanne, would you imagine yourself in the story? You might be the governess captured as a sex slave for a depraved earl. Or captured in a harem and I would charge to your rescue to find you had become the favorite of the experienced ladies there. And before we escape, we are treated to a wild orgy with a half dozen odalisques joining us."

Maryanne was aflame. Her hands trembled as she accepted the book. On the left side was an illustration. A lady did these—a lady who was a grandmother, who had both her own young children and her grandchildren to feed.

In the picture a new maid was being introduced to the household. The novice was bound hand and foot. Her legs were folded beneath her so that her naked bottom stuck up in the air. Her face was buried between the thighs of a pretty lady's maid who lay on the floor and pinched her own nipples. The housekeeper, who was a voluptuous wanton, held a long, curving dildo pointed toward the new girl's cunny.

The shackles. If she wore her hands shackled and her ankles bound, she could be positioned that way. Completely available to her husband. His erotic prisoner.

She held the open volume out to him, and he took it.

"That picture. That intrigues me."

The book slid from his fingers, pages fluttered as it crashed to the floor.

She'd shocked scandalous Lord Swansborough.

Wearing a grin worthy of a marauding pirate, Dash dangled the cuffs by the silver chains so the diamond-and-ruby encrusted clasps twirled before his astonishing wife. She ducked her head shyly, soft brown curls dangling around her face, but she gamely clambered up onto the daybed in the library and bent over like the maid in the picture. Dutifully she crossed her wrists behind her back, the picture of submission.

The black drapes framed her pale curves—the scoop inward at her waist, the rounded flare of her hips, the heart-shaped lushness of her bottom. All begged him to touch, to feast with fingertips first and then his lips, his mouth.

"Why does this intrigue you, Maryanne?" he murmured as he approached. He knew she would hear his boot soles slowly thunk along the floor, and he saw the almost imperceptible shiver she gave.

"I don't know," she admitted, head bowed. Then she looked up, curls spilling down her back. "Does it mean there is something wrong with me?"

He laughed. "No, love. I know you would not want this for real. But the game intrigues. It arouses you so strongly you can't help but be tempted to just pretend . . . just for a little while."

She nodded. "It is like reading the books, only it is so much more . . . because I am actually doing it."

Stripping off his shirt, he cast the black linen to a chair. Cool air prickled over his skin and his dark nipples tightened. But the dominant was supposed to be immune to discomfort, for that was what entranced the submissive.

He strolled around, crossed his arms in front of his bare chest, and quirked a brow as he towered over his lovely, diminutive wife. "Are you ready to be bound?"

Frank brown eyes gazed at his face. "Yes, bind me."

He crouched and cupped her chin. "If I do anything you do not wish, you can stop me with a word. It won't be 'no,' for that word becomes meaningless in intense pleasure."

Her hands slid off her back, so he tapped her cheek. "Hands."

She put them back, again crossed at the wrists. "What do you wish me to say?"

"This is a word I don't wish you to say, but a necessary one. If you want me to stop, say 'desist.' "

She nodded, and he stood once more. He bent over her graceful naked back—heard her sharp breath—and clasped the shackles around her wrists. Her entire body stiffened, but he bent and kissed the curve of her spine. She relaxed, and he turned the key and slipped it into his pocket. Lined with velvet, the cuffs bit gently into the fine bones of her wrists.

He'd never expected to see a wife in this position.

Did she want to do this, or was she enduring it to please him?

Black silk. Dash twined the length of it around his wrist. Her skin was softer, more alluring than silk. Her beauty more precious.

She waited with her arms locked together and linked by a short silver chain, resting just above the shadowed valley of her bottom.

Maryanne. His wife, who trusted him. Who had revealed her dangerous secret to him—a partnership with a courtesan to publish erotic books.

Hell, unless she was an actress who could put the entire company of Drury Lane to shame, that was her true secret. Her only secret.

Unwinding the length of black silk, Dash looped it around her ankles and bound them together, dressing his arrangement with a bow. Normally he would draw out the torture for his submissive playmate, but this time, with Maryanne, he couldn't control himself.

He slid his fingers between her smooth thighs and stroked her wet cunny. Her loud, surprised moan echoed throughout the quiet room.

"Oh!" she gasped. "It seems a terrible sin to moan in a library."

"No, sweeting. I've known sin, and this isn't it." But his heart gave a pang at the innocence in her rich, soft voice. And he knew he didn't want the game. Didn't need it. He didn't want to use sex to forget. He wanted sex to share intimacy—special, precious intimacy—with Maryanne. He wanted to gaze into her eyes as they joined. He wanted to kiss her lips, feel her hands embrace him.

He needed it.

Click! He unlocked the shackles and took them off. Then undid the binding at her ankles. She twisted, surprised. "You don't wish to play?"

Gently he rolled her onto the silk-cushioned daybed. "Not this time. No games. Just you and I, loving each other."

Her arms locked around her neck, and she pulled him into a kiss.

It had never been like this. He'd never felt so . . . connected to a woman, not even to Maryanne before. He'd never known a woman reveal all her heart to him.

Last night, he'd drunk half the contents of the brandy decanter. Oblivion. He'd wanted to drink until his brain stopped working and the bloody guilt ceased pounding at his soul like a hammer.

He should have taken better care of Amanda. He should never have believed she'd run off to Gretna.

Then his gut had rebelled and he'd retched up most of the alcohol. Disgusted, he'd stumbled upstairs, washed out his mouth, bathed his face, and flopped into his bed. The canopy had been slowly rotating above his head—or so it appeared—as he dragged himself to his feet and lurched into Maryanne's room.

There, stretched out in her bed alongside her warm and lovely curves, he'd understood. Anyone who knew him declared he lived for the moment, immersing himself in wild orgies, unfettered sex, drinking, and gaming. It wasn't true. He was locked in the past. He spent his present trying to escape the past by staying drunk and randy.

Now he drew back from Maryanne's kiss and eased her hands from his neck.

Her forehead furrowed.

"I've done something wrong. It's the debts, isn't it? Are you angry about me publishing erotic books?"

"No, love. Not angry. Impressed by your courage and cleverness, yes."

"I thought you'd be shocked, horrified, furious."

"Why? Because you wished to help your family?"

"No, because Georgiana—"

"Wants money? Now that you've married a viscount, I assume she felt a little blackmail was in order."

She looked so relieved. "I never once thought she'd do such a thing. Of course, I never planned to marry. Marcus settled an immense dowry on me—oh, but you know that."

His lips quirked. "After he was finished shouting at me, Marcus did discuss the marriage settlements."

Maryanne winced. "I'm so sorry he shouted at you. It was all my fault, after all. You didn't even know who I was." She took an unsteady breath. Why did it bother her still that he hadn't been able to look into her eyes at the scavenger hunt and see who she was, despite the mask, despite being in a scandalous place a good girl had no right to be in? "How could you have? Did you even notice me, Maryanne, a little mouse who scurries into her little hole beneath the skirting board?"

"Love, I don't think you were in disguise that night in the salon. It was the skirting-board mouse that was your disguise. Why were you always trying to hide behind a book?"

Maryanne's jaw dropped. Oh, he was too astute, her husband. She'd always used her books as a shield. If she curled up small enough, perhaps she could crawl under one and simply not be. . . .

How many times had she thought that as she'd seen her mother cry over Rodesson?

"But you must be angry. Georgiana has threatened to reveal . . . what I was doing—"

"Publishing erotica," he supplied. "And she'd have me by the ballocks forever, is that what you're worried about?"

She nodded, startled by his conspiratorial tone.

"Sweeting, I have men shooting at me—I'm not worried about Georgiana." He brushed his lips over hers, ignited sparks that sizzled to her quim. "But I am worried that you seem determined I should be angry. That I should resent you. I don't, Maryanne. We'll weather this." Dash laid his hand over her tummy. "There is something I have to tell you," he said. "About a woman named Amanda Westmoreland."

Lover? Mistress? Maryanne's heart set up a patter like a frightened rabbit.

"That's why Sir William came here. They've found Amanda's body."

The words rang in her head like pealing bells, and she almost missed the rest of his words. A woman he'd grown up with, a baron's daughter, a woman Dash had thought to marry. And then they'd parted—for some reason—and she'd run off to Gretna Green.

"Who did she run off with?"

"She vanished along with the steward's son, who was a handsome wastrel with an eye for the ladies and hopes of good prospects. It was assumed they'd quickly return and he'd be hoping for his father-in-law's support. But they never came back."

"Didn't anyone wonder why? Didn't anyone look for her?"

"We assumed she believed she'd been cut off from her family—and her blasted father threatened as much. But it doesn't matter. She never left. Someone killed her."

"But not you."

"Though I seem the most likely suspect, don't I? She tells me she loves someone else, and then, within days, she's dead?"

Confused, she stared. "You can't possibly be trying to convince me you did do it!" But she understood now why he had not wanted to make love or play erotic games. It had not been her. It had been this nightmare from his past.

"Maybe I am." He jumped up and ran his fingers so harshly through his black hair she was certain he tore some out by the roots. "You want to believe me innocent. I'm not. I'm responsible for her death. It's my blasted fault—"

"Why?" She felt so exposed and awkward, naked. She curled up her legs, put her hands across her breasts. "How can it be your fault?"

"She was killed because of me. By my uncle. Or my cousin.

Craven or Barrett. Damn, whichever one it is, I'll rip out the blackguard's heart with my bare hands."

He was striding toward the door and snatched up his shirt on the way. Craven or Barrett? Had he known them all those years ago?

Was he going mad? The attempts on his life, this nightmare from his past—was this horror destroying his sanity?

"Dash!" She reached out to him, even though the motion bared her breast. "Wait. Please."

He paused long enough to turn the key in the lock to open the door.

"Stop! You can't rush off like this!" What if he confronted Craven or Barrett and got himself killed? Slipping off the daybed, she grabbed the silken jumble of her gown. Overwhelmed by skirts, she struggled to find the bodice.

She clamped the dress in front of her in a bronze tangle as he opened the door.

"You could get yourself killed."

He glanced back, his cheeks sharp and hollowed, his mouth a grim line. "But what if I told you I deserved to die? I have killed. I killed my uncle's son. My eldest cousin. He was an innocent man, and I watched him die."

The door slammed behind him.

Curling up with her dress, Maryanne cowered as if she'd been hit. Tears burned her eyes and then flowed like a stream of raindrops down her cheeks.

He was wrong. She *was* just a scared little mouse.

She wanted to hide.

Coughing, Maryanne fiercely wiped the tears away. She wasn't going to cower and let Dash either get shot or go mad.

She had revealed everything to him because he told her to trust him.

Her gaze fell on the jeweled shackles. She was going to force him to trust her and tell her everything, even if she had to shackle him to do it.

* * *

Four little beds stood in a row, stripped of pillows and sheets. And a cradle. Maryanne rested her hand on the cradle and swung it gently, and her heart gave a forlorn lurch as she looked at the empty little beds.

In a few months, she would be gazing down at her baby in the cradle and shushing him—or her—to sleep.

What if I told you I deserved to die?

Of course, Dash wasn't up here—but she hadn't found him anywhere else in the house. As for asking the servants, she'd been far too ashamed. *Excuse me, but could you tell me where his lordship went after he stormed away from me?*

She'd encountered Lady Yardley and had all but turned and ran. And, worse, the Duke of Ashton was arriving, which had the staff in a tizzy. A search hadn't even turned up Sir William; she prayed that meant the baron was with Dash and talking sense to him.

Was he truly in danger of losing his mind? Or was he just confused in his shock and anger, and he'd mistakenly blended the past—Miss Westmoreland's murder—and his present investigation of Craven?

"Maryanne?"

She hadn't expected a voice, and she spun around, her hand colliding with the swinging bassinet. She bit back a cry as Anne walked into the nursery.

"I was looking for you, Maryanne. I'd hoped we could make plans for decorations."

Christmas. Anne wished to make plans for Christmas. Dimly Maryanne remembered promising to do it. And she had forced Anne to come here in search of her—which must be painful. Anne's child should be sleeping here. She should not have lost her baby.

Maryanne snatched her hand away from the ornate cradle. She did not know what to say. By instinct, she almost dropped into a curtsy.

"It's been a very long time since I was in this room." Anne

turned in a circle, her green skirts swirling around her. "I was quite young when I left, just nine. Lady Yardley took me—oh, yes, I told you that."

Maryanne wondered why—from Mrs. Long she'd learned that Dash's uncle and aunt had moved in here after his parents' deaths and had stayed until he finished his schooling. Why had Anne not stayed in the house also? Was his aunt not also a "feminine influence"?

Instead of asking any of those things, Maryanne stood in silence, feeling awkward. "I'm sorry."

Anne swung around to face her and strolled over toward the cradle. Maryanne swallowed hard—it must be wrenching Anne's soul to look at it.

"About our parents? It was a long time ago. I am sorry, it's true, to have lost them so early, but I have good memories."

"Does Dash?" she asked impetuously.

"Of our parents? Yes." Lovely, slender, gloved in fine muslin, Anne's hand touched the cradle and set it rocking. "I have convinced Nigel I'm ready to try for another child." She glanced up, her smile warm and friendly. "You know how men are. They fear we are far more fragile than we are. He's afraid I will have my heart broken again."

"You won't. I'm sure—" Maryanne broke off. It was a foolhardy thing to say. To reassure something that could never be promised. And what did she know of bearing children? Anne must think her a fool.

"Thank you." Anne moved around and linked arms. "It is nice to hear good thoughts for once. And to have hope."

"Put the wretched pistol down, Lancelot."

Dash leaned back into his leather club chair and laid the pearl-handled pistol on his desk. He threaded his fingers behind his head and frowned at Sophia as she stormed into his study.

Sophia never moved with such thunderous anger; she usually floated with languorous grace, her hips swaying seductively. But she slapped her palm onto his desk and leaned over, her eyes flashing fire. "What did you tell her? I saw her race upstairs—to the nursery, no doubt, pale as a ghost. What exactly did you say, Lancelot?"

He straightened. "Who? Who raced upstairs? Anne?"

"Your wife!"

Maryanne had rushed up to the nursery? Was something wrong? He was on his feet—then hesitated. What a blasted idiot he'd been. She was enceinte, and he'd upset her. "I told her about Amanda Westmoreland. Maryanne is in a delicate condition and—"

"She's a robust woman, I assure you." Sophia picked up the pistol and took aim toward the fireplace. "Excellent weapon. Not that I'd expect any less of you. And Sir William spoke of the tragic discovery of the girl's body to me. But why would that affect your wife so much? Surely she doesn't think you responsible?"

Hell, he'd shouted at her as she'd protested his innocence. "Maryanne seems determined to believe the best in me."

"Have you told her about your years with your uncle?"

"I did mention that I killed my cousin."

Sophia swung around, and Dash found his gaze focused on the barrel end of his pistol. He pushed it gently aside; her hand was shaking.

"This is enough!" she cried. "I will not countenance this any more. Go upstairs and tell her about your upbringing. Immediately. For if you do not go at once and find your wife and speak about this, I will tell her. She will never forgive you if the words come from my lips and not yours. Understand this."

"You want her to think me either wounded and pitiable and to break her heart over me, or to have her think me unstable and insane? No."

"You have let your wife believe you are a murderer. I do not understand why you wish to continually seek punishment for what was not your fault. Tell her everything. *Everything.* At the very least, she deserves to know before your uncle, aunt, and cousin arrive. There is danger, and your wife needs to know from whence it comes. Do not be a fool. Whip yourself after. Let her whip you. I do not care, but tell her."

18

Maryanne joined in the laughter as the sleigh skimmed over the sloping, snow-covered fields. She clung to Dash's arm as they swooped down a hill. Sparkling white flakes flew at them, kicked up by the hooves of the black horse in the jingling traces.

In the opposite seat, Anne snuggled against her husband, and they shared a laughing kiss. Maryanne glanced up at Dash—for all he grinned, his black eyes alight, she knew he carried two pistols in his greatcoat pockets. Two because one pistol, once fired, was useless.

But his deep, throaty laughter sounded completely genuine. And for that reason, she wasn't cuddling against him. Would a sane woman caress a wild cat? She couldn't understand him. He had been wild with fury, mad with grief, and now the tempest was gone.

But her stomach was still churning, her nerves still tingling.

And she couldn't stop thinking about those pistols. Weaponry for a jaunt across the snowy meadows to attend supper at a neighboring estate. It seemed madness, but Dash's life was at risk. Yet he had been calm as he had found her in the nursery, as he'd apologized for his "outburst"—an inadequate word for the way he'd almost demanded she think him a villain.

Of course he had said nothing about his parting statement.

And she'd been too weak to press. Meekly she'd slid her arm in his and let him lead her downstairs to meet the Duke of Ashton. Hating herself with every step.

Dash had been wrong—she wasn't truly bold like Verity. She was Maryanne Mouse.

And so, after pummeling herself with those thoughts, she'd been quaking as she met Ashton.

The imposing duke had been charming and had shown no sign of recognition. He hadn't seen Maryanne Hamilton behind the mask, at least. Her fears had been silly and unwarranted, of course. Dash hadn't recognized her, and he'd made love to her. Why would the duke?

Still, she'd made flustered comments about travel and weather, relieved when they joined Lady Yardley, Anne, and Moredon, and she could merely sit and nod.

And within a half an hour she would have to be social again and meet the local gentry.

Maryanne swallowed hard.

Dash slid his arm around her waist beneath the fur throw wrapped around them. "I want to talk to you later," he murmured against her ear. "In private."

She flicked a glance to Anne and Moredon, who had turned to watch the horse canter up a small knoll, and were waving to Lady Yardley and Ashton, who cuddled in another sleigh. Sir William and Harriet sat across from the lovers. Jack Tate had removed himself to a local inn. Apparently Tate felt it inappropriate to stay under his host's roof after a botched attempt to seduce the man's wife.

"Yes," she answered, determined to sound determined. "We will."

Surprise could hardly describe the way his square jaw dropped and his dark slash of brows shot up. Then his dimple deepened, and his wide smile dazzled her more intensely than the white snow. "We will," he echoed.

But what was she to learn? That Dash was actually a murderer?

This man, her husband, was a stranger to her. And what she kept learning was horrifying—men who wanted Dash dead, a mysteriously unhappy childhood, a murdered fiancée, his admission that he had killed his cousin. . . .

She eased away from Dash as the sleigh crossed another open meadow and approached the estate of Lord and Lady Markham, an Elizabethan house set amidst enormous gardens. Frosted with snow, the house looked like Dash's—like a fairy tale setting come to life.

Excitedly Anne pointed to a frozen pond, and Maryanne craned to look. Dash murmured, "No ice skating for you, love."

Which gave them the perfect reason to find a moment alone.

Though it seemed an endless wait before the party gathered skates—curious contraptions with sharp metal blades and tangled leather straps. Standing at the window with Dash to wave farewell to the sleighs leaving for the frozen lake, Maryanne took a deep breath.

Meeting her hosts and the intrigued guests had passed like a whirlwind—Maryanne couldn't remember what she had said. No one spoke of her being enceinte. How many of them had guessed?

Surely her every word and awkward gesture made her hosts, the vicar's wife, and the other ladies aware that Dash had married beneath him. And they must guess the reason why.

She almost wished she could climb on a table and declare it to the room. That would be far easier than waiting, her fingers clenched around a glass, waiting for some sharp-tongued cat to insult her.

They were all so welcoming and nice. Was that truly how these great ladies felt about her? Or was it simply Christmas cheer? Her glass was never empty.

She had slipped away to the retiring room, returning just as Sir William and Dash also moved out of the drawing room into the corridor. Sir William had clapped a hand to her husband's shoulder. "Miss Westmoreland died a long time ago. It's not your fault, Swansborough. You did what you could. Now you have a wife who cares about you. A child. Make love to your wife."

Make love to your wife.

As Maryanne stepped back from the window, the sleighs out of sight, Dash's hand clasped around hers, strong fingers threading between hers. He slid his fingers up and down, and she melted—her spine became hot wax, and her cunny became moist with immediate desire.

They were not alone, of course. Footmen stood impassively about the drawing room. She wished she could send them away. Her legs quivered, and she wanted to stumble to the sofa and pull Dash down on top of her.

"Let us gather our coats and stroll out on the terrace. Enjoy the bracing air."

She prayed it might cool her down, and once they were dressed and out of doors, she selected a cold stone bench to sit upon. Ice crusted the sculpted edge. The instant Dash helped her lower her bottom to the smooth surface, she shivered as cold shot through her thighs and derriere.

At least she wouldn't be distracted by desire. . . .

But he propped his booted foot on the edge of the bench, and his greatcoat fell open, giving her a view of his muscled legs and his crotch.

She gulped. But boldly reminded him, "You wished to talk."

"Yes. About my past." His gaze dropped to her lap. As he cleared his throat and said, "Every child deserves to grow up with love," she knew he was thinking of their child as well as himself. "So many don't," he continued. "You'd think I would have known nothing but privilege, security, safety."

She shook her head. "I know it is not as simple as that."

"You, Maryanne, are very wise."

She didn't believe that, but she laid her hand on his arm. "What happened to you, Dash?"

"My uncle, James Blackmore, always resented being the second son, but he always hoped to inherit once my daring, neck-or-nothing father conveniently killed himself in an accident. My father was wild and bold—he traveled the world as a young man. He raced carriages, gamed for insane stakes, and took any dare suggested to him. Hotheaded, he'd won any number of duels. He was exactly the sort of peer who burns brightly and dies young. All my uncle had to do was bide his time. Unfortunately I was born before my father had the accident my uncle had dreamed of. My father was driving the carriage too fast—"

"Both your father and mother—"

He nodded. "She both loved and loathed his recklessness. Unfortunately her taste for excitement ended in her death, too. Which left myself and Anne alone. But ever since I'd been born, I'd been plagued by accidents. My birth ruined my uncle's plan. But infants—and young boys—often don't survive."

Cold slid over her entire body; her fingers stiffened, her toes were numb, her lips refused to move. "Do you mean . . . when you were a baby, a defenseless baby, your uncle tried to kill you?"

He shrugged. Shrugged! "I can't testify to what happened when I was an infant, though apparently I almost died in my cradle once. After that my mother spent every night with me, watching over me. And when I was a boy, I was the most accident-plagued heir in England."

"Good god." Shivers racked her body; her fingers wouldn't stop shaking. "Didn't anyone realize? Didn't anyone stop it?"

"I think my mother suspected. She watched over me as closely as she could. I think it drove her mad—she was highstrung, often hysterical. Once I saw her hammering my father with her fists, screaming at him. I wondered . . . if that had caused the accident. She hadn't wanted to leave me, and my father insisted they travel. I wondered if she was urging him to race home."

Tears brimmed in Maryanne's eyes, hot against her chilled skin. She understood. He'd felt responsible for his mother's death. The same way he felt guilt over Amanda Westmoreland. She tried to stand, wanting to wrap her arms around him. "Your cousin—"

Her boot slid on a patch of packed snow, and she flailed.

Dash grabbed her and scooped her into his arms. "Come inside. You're cold."

"You didn't kill your cousin, did you?" She clutched his lapels, but in his arms she couldn't shake sense into him. "What happened, Dash? What truly happened?"

An intense fire burned behind his long-lashed black eyes. "I let him walk into my uncle's trap. It seemed bloody poetic justice to let my uncle's greed cost him his beloved eldest son."

His mouth, lips soft and parted, lowered to hers. His hand splayed over her bottom, gently kneading as he claimed her mouth in a kiss. Sensual. Languorous. He plundered her mouth until she thought her spine would dissolve.

Her courage did.

She closed her eyes and lost herself in the kiss. The kiss of a master.

The kiss of a man who wanted to hide from the past.

But she couldn't let him kiss away her senses. She knew what she had to do. She must lure him to bed—and then force him to talk before they made love.

It was a frightening gamble. He might refuse. He might walk out on her rather than tell her more.

He needed to use sex to escape, and if she told him he no longer could, might he go to another woman's bed?

" 'The Countess's Lovers,' " Dash read, and he glanced over to Maryanne, pleased to see the pink blush touch her cheeks. They were in her bedroom, and he was lying on her bed with a book. With one of her books.

While he'd acquired this book she had published, he'd never

actually read it. Still, a collection of erotica came in useful—women, he'd discovered, responded lustily to the written word.

"Come to bed," he urged, "and I'll read you a bedtime story."

He cradled the book on his palm and glanced down to the first page. " 'Chapter One. Her ladyship, the notorious and buxom countess, picked up the riding crop and commanded the insolent footman to present his posterior and drop his breeches. As two perfect, sculpted arse cheeks came into view, she paused long enough to sweep the handle of her crop between her thighs. Artfully she stroked her cunny as the young man's black breeches slid down to his boots. Oh, how she ached for a young man's hard cock inside her, thought Louisa, the countess. But a countess did not stoop to finding her satisfaction with a mere footman, no matter how large his staff, how beautiful his buttocks, or how—' "

Dash broke off.

Two naked breasts bounced in front of his eyes, obscuring his view of the page and the accompanying illustration of her busty ladyship and stiff-cocked servant. Maryanne had stripped off her shift. Berry brown and large, her nipples jiggled in front of him, the perfect complement to her pale, round breasts.

"Georgiana had a secret mission with her books," she murmured. "Even though they were intended to please men and were about male fantasies, Georgiana insisted we depict the complex business of making a woman climax. She refused to let an author write that a man thrust a few times into a woman and that made her come. For it is more difficult than that."

He tossed the book aside, wrapped his hand around his wife's waist, and pulled those breasts to his mouth. "I know, and now I know why you take charge of your pleasure," he murmured before tasting her sweet flesh.

The wicked woman straddled his thighs and wriggled her luscious, hot quim over the ridge of his cock. He loved how playful she became in bed.

"I might be only a viscountess," Maryanne whispered, her breath a tease on his ear, "and you are most definitely not a footman, but your naked posterior makes me mad with desire."

He released her nipple long enough to rasp, "Are you certain? I'm sitting on it right now."

"And I am sitting on you." As though her intent were torture, she clasped his shoulders and danced upon him, her hips sinuously rotating on him, her sweet cunny brushing his shaft.

He dipped his finger into her navel, and she stopped, giggling. "Oh, don't. It tickles." She drew back her hair, revealing wide eyes, starkly honest and concerned. "I was going to deny you. I cannot let you use sex with me to escape the past. We have to face it together."

"We will, darling. Immediately after I've made love to you and we've both exploded like a bottle of shaken champagne."

"Oh, you are impossible to resist. The thought of you exploding that way . . . your body bucking with a violent orgasm, and your face revealing every inch of your agony—"

"Maryanne, love, your words are more exciting than any book. You drive me mad." Dash threaded his fingers in her hair and drew her mouth to his as he struggled to tug down the sheets clamped between her cunny and his cock.

Her plump silken bottom rested on his thighs. Her wet nether lips pressed to his rigid shaft. Her inquisitive hands teased his nipples, stroking his chest hair. Her breath skimmed his skin.

He adored everything about her.

She didn't want him to die, and he sure as hell didn't want to be dead.

He filled his hands with her generous breasts, savoring their weight. She rose on him, wrapped her palm around his cock. Her fingers tightened around the shaft as she guided the blunt head to her plump, sticky lips.

She arched back as she took his rod inside. She plunged down on him so her full derriere landed hard on his thighs and ballocks. He moaned into her mouth, and she kissed hungrily as though she could taste his groan of pleasure. Fiercely she rode him, and each delicious slap of her arse, each stroke of her tight passage drove him wild.

He gripped her breasts, kneaded them, pinched her nipples, ravaged her with his mouth, nipped her ears, licked her neck, drove hard into her, and played with her clit.

"And tell me when you're going to come," he growled, between nuzzling her earlobe and seeking the sensitive places on the delicate line of her neck.

She ground against his fingers, gasping. "Now! I think it will be now—oh!" Sweetly, high-pitched, her cry echoed like a harp's music.

His muscles tensed like an over wound clockwork ready to fly apart. His ballocks tightened, his brain dimmed.

She bounced upon him, a slave to her pleasure, curls flying. And as she began to slow on him, he teased her clit, tweaked her nipple, and took her to climax again.

And again.

Until she screamed, "Dear Dash, no more! You must come!"

Never one to disappoint such a precious lady, he let go of his control. Wrapped his arms around her waist, slammed his hips up hard to seat his cock as deep as he could. His cum shot through him, and he roared with it.

It ravaged him, each thundered pulse. And, after, his muscles became as floppy as the sheets, and he fell back against the headboard. Laughter rose, but he didn't know why. He was so drained he could barely move, and he wanted to laugh. "Maryanne, sweet Maryanne."

She bent forward so her forehead touched his. He threaded his fingers in her silky tresses.

"I don't believe you killed your cousin," she whispered.

He had to face it now. Tell her the truth. He told her about his mistress, Lottie Ashley, and saw the uncertainty touch her eyes. "I kept mistresses, love, but have never loved anyone before you."

"It doesn't matter. I'm not a child. It is a man's actions that speak for him, not his promises."

She stole his breath with her understanding, his wife. "But Lottie was attacked one night after leaving the theater—she had attended alone, in the box I rented, for courtesans do, to display their beauty and entice men. A mistress knows she must be thinking of her next protector."

He took an unsteady breath. Shut his eyes, but he couldn't block out the memory. "They cut her with a knife. Sliced her throat, but not deeply, thank God. Sliced her arms and her . . . middle. And they left her there, to bleed. She was found and saved."

"It wasn't your fault—"

"I couldn't believe it was my uncle. Why should he hurt Lottie? But as Lottie healed, she described her attackers to me. She was a damned observant woman, and I was able to find one of the men, an albino, at a dockside inn. I jammed a pistol barrel into his mouth until he was willing to tell me who hired him. A Mr. Blackmore. But what my uncle didn't know is that his precious eldest son, Simon, had come to see me. Simon knew his father wanted the title, knew how much my uncle hated me. You see, I was invincible. My uncle had tried a half dozen times to kill me, and I'd escaped every attempt. But Simon didn't know his father had tried to murder me, and I couldn't bring myself to tell him."

"You didn't want to disillusion him, make him hate his father?"

"I didn't think he needed to suffer because his father was an evil, immoral bastard—" Dash broke off. Gave her a contrite look. "Sorry for the language. I forget myself."

"It is all right. I have edited erotic stories, you might remember."

"Simon went with me when I went to that dockside inn. I knew it was a trap, but I let him come with me. I let him walk into it without any idea what was waiting. He was stunned to hear the albino footpad claim it was his father who had hired him. He stopped me from killing the footpad, even though I sorely wanted revenge for Lottie. But as he hauled me back, the albino sliced me in the gut with a knife."

He remembered Simon's horror, how his cousin's face had gone stark white. Blood had leaked from between his fingers as he'd pressed his hand to the wound. Simon had helped him out to the carriage. . . .

"He got me home, where a note was waiting for me. They'd kidnapped Lottie and would kill her unless I brought a ransom to a warehouse near Temple Bar. I had an hour to get there, or they'd kill her. Simon wanted to go. I was certain it was a trap, but I couldn't take the risk."

"Dash—"

But he was lost in memory. "I got him to bandage me up as best as he could, and we headed there, both armed with pistols. My plan was to find a back way in—to send Simon in with his coat on and his hat pulled down, in the hopes they'd think he was me. I was still bleeding—it was soaking through the bandage—and I felt so weak I could barely stand. But I stumbled around the back. Saw a light in one of the windows. Two men were waiting in there. There was no sign of Lottie. My first fear was they'd killed her already. But then I realized . . . they didn't even need her. I'd rushed into a trap out of blind terror. My uncle knew I'd do it. He'd counted on it. But he hadn't counted on Simon being the one to walk into the room."

"You didn't warn Simon."

"My legs were going weak from loss of blood. And I knew that next time they might kill Lottie. Or someone else I cared about. Possibly Anne. My uncle might use Anne as a pawn to hurt me. But if Simon got hurt . . ."

"You thought it would stop. Dash—"

"I found the door, though I was barely able to stand. My plan was to let Simon get wounded; then I'd rescue him. I know . . . madness . . . I wasn't thinking straight. I knew Simon was armed. He never even got to that room. Someone shot him through the heart the moment he stepped through the door. Shot him in the dark."

"What did you do?"

"I killed one of them, and then passed out. The other two ran. Losing his son destroyed my uncle. But it destroyed me, too. . . ."

"It wasn't your fault. It was your uncle's evil that caused it." She cupped his face with her small, delicate hands. "What do you plan to do? You can't be planning to meet your uncle over pistols, can you? That's madness."

"I have to make it stop, Maryanne. Amanda Westmoreland was an innocent and lovely girl who had her life ahead of her. Eliza Charmody didn't deserve to die in Hyde Park. And there's Lady Farthingale—she might be dead. And the only way it is going to stop is if one of us is dead."

"But it might not be your uncle this time. It could be your cousin Robert." Heaven knew that living with such as monster as James Blackmore must have made his own children mad.

"It has to stop."

"You don't have to make amends to those women by offering your life!" she cried. "I—I can't bear it, Dash. I want you. I love you! Do you understand that? If you die out of guilt you will take my heart with you. You have no choice but to live. To live for our child."

"Sharp blades again." He rolled her over so she tumbled onto the bed. "I promise you. Nothing foolish. No duels. But I will end this, Maryanne."

Five times. Or six. By morning Maryanne had lost count of the number of times they'd made love. Her thighs ached. Red splotches dotted her breasts from his suckling mouth.

Her head still buzzed with pleasure, and she could do nothing but sigh as Dash rose over her. She shook her head. Surely she would die if she tried to make love one more time.

"No, love. You made me talk. This is the price you pay."

Slick with his juices and hers from a half dozen orgasms, her quim welcomed his rigid cock. He filled her, the swollen head nudging her womb.

She arched with him. Taking him deep. Withdrawing, moving in perfect unison with him, and driving up to take him once more. They reached climax together and fell apart, gasping for breath.

She held his hand, reassured by the loving way he squeezed hers. But could she ever ease the pain he still carried in his heart?

How could she make him move on from the past and look to the future?

19

"The kissing bough will be perfect there!"

Maryanne forced a smile at Anne's enthusiasm as Anne pointed to the doorway leading from the ballroom to the enclosed gallery that overlooked the gardens. Silky ribbons tickled Maryanne's palms as she followed Anne—she balanced the jumble of tangled ribbons they'd been working to sort and knew she should try to at least add a word in agreement. But her throat ached, and her head pounded with a headache.

Tomorrow it would be Christmas Eve day. The evergreen boughs and ivy, garlands and ribbons would be put up. Venetia and Marcus and their baby would be arriving.

Maryanne so wanted to think only of the future. Of the pleasure of seeing Venetia again. The joy in holding her baby nephew and anticipating her own child.

But she couldn't.

Perhaps the future might never come.

Or if it did, it would be like the nightmares that now plagued her. At any moment, Dash's uncle, his aunt, and his cousin Robert would arrive. She dreaded the arrival of the footman, the announcement . . . and then meeting the people who had tried to kill Dash.

In the past three days, there had been no other attack on his life. Nothing else had happened. Surely that meant his uncle was the culprit. That the killer was not Tate, Craven, Barrett, or even Ashton. It must be James Blackmore, and the evil swine was waiting until he was actually in Dash's house to strike the final blow. . . .

Or it meant it was Robert.

Or was it because Dash had kept her almost a prisoner in his bed for most of the last three days? He hadn't been outside to be a target for the killer.

"I think ivy with ribbons beneath each sconce," Anne mused as she swept a circle. Gold ribbons overflowed her hands. She paused, waiting approval.

"Certainly," Maryanne answered. But she wanted to think of her three days in bed with Dash. Her cheeks heated at the memory of the erotic games they'd played. Sensations. Each game had introduced her to a favorite sensation. The husky sound of his voice as he'd blindfolded her. The brush of his fingertips lightly on her nipples, a sensuous contrast to his suckling lips. The scent of him—the clean aroma of his skin tinged with sandalwood soap and witch hazel after a shave, and the heady musky perfume of his underarms, the earthy and ripe allure of his cock.

It had been heaven, but it was as though Dash wanted to squeeze a lifetime of pleasure into just a few days.

Boots clopped across the wide expanse of the floor, echoing to the arched ceiling above. "My ladies," the footman announced, "Mr. and Mrs. Blackmore and Mr. Robert Blackmore have arrived."

Maryanne saw her ribbons tumble from her hands, the ones wrapped on spools rolling along the parquet floor. Anne was at her side in an instant. But Dash strode into the ballroom then. She heard Anne's breath catch, and Maryanne's entire body both melted and froze at the sight of him—nonsensical as it seemed, it was exactly how she felt.

Raven hair draping over piercing black eyes, Dash looked every inch the powerful viscount. An immaculate jet-black jacket enhanced his broad shoulders, matching the black of his shirt and cravat, the perfection of a shimmering black silk waistcoat. His legs stretched endlessly—from his lean hips to the floor—clad in snug trousers and gleaming boots.

He wore his wealth and power blatantly.

To goad, she knew.

Maryanne swallowed hard; the words he'd ground out in his deep baritone pounded through her mind: *The only way it is going to stop is if one of us is dead.*

Her arm linked with Dash's, her fingers resting on his steely forearm, Maryanne stopped abruptly on the threshold to the drawing room. Anne perched on the settee nearest the window. A wispy gray-haired woman sat at the other, her hand clamped on the wrist of a dark-haired young gentleman. The woman's head wobbled gently, and the hand resting in her lap seemed to jerk of its own accord.

This must be Mrs. Blackmore, Dash's aunt. And Anne was staring at her slippers, avoiding gazing at her aunt. Moredon stood at Anne's side, his hip balanced on the embroidered ivory arm of the sofa. He clasped Anne's hand.

Dash drew Maryanne toward his aunt. Panic raced through her. What would she say?

Then she saw him.

The elderly man slumped in the wing chair, a blue wool blanket tucked around him, an elaborately carved cane balanced beneath an enormous, clutching hand.

How offensive to think he insisted on a blanket when he'd tried to hurt a defenseless child! She longed to race forward and snatch away the blanket.

A white shock of hair framed his uncle's heavy face. The thick cheeks made the dark eyes mere pinpricks in the florid flesh. She realized she'd released Dash's arm, and, astonished, she saw Dash walk to his aunt.

He acknowledged the other ladies in the room, Anne and

Sophia, and then greeted his aunt. With exquisite politeness. "It has been a long time, Aunt Helena. I trust you are well and the journey not too taxing."

Dash's aunt's head jerked toward him. "N—no. Well, I am well." She waved a hand toward his uncle, who rapped his cane on the floor in a rhythm that echoed in Maryanne's head and reverberated through her teeth. "He is not well. Did you summon him to ensure he was dying?"

"It is the Christmas season, a time for family to visit. And you, God help me, are my family."

"Do not bully a confused old woman, my lord," Robert snapped.

Yet his aunt directed a flashing glare to her son. "I am not confused. Nor am I old. Whelp."

And Dash astounded her again by laughing. "Touché, Aunt."

His aunt flung her hand toward Anne. "Have you been to town? Tell me all. All the gossip. Please, my dear."

Anne shot a desperate look to Dash, as though seeking his approval. Should she be civil or not? At his curt nod, Anne launched into lighthearted tales of London from the season.

A firm hand touched her elbow. Maryanne almost screamed. Dash led her to a wing chair beside Sophia. She felt as if she had walked on stage in the midst of a Drury Lane play. The mistress of the house should act the hostess—pour tea, summon cakes, and charm with delightful banter.

Instead, she gripped the arms of the chair.

Dash prowled over toward his uncle. She wished to scream *stop!*

"What do you want, Swansborough?" James Blackmore's voice croaked out into the room. "Why did you ask me here? What is your blasted plan?"

"What is yours, Uncle?" Dash threw out the question in a jaded drawl.

The cane tip slammed into the floor. "Mind your tongue,

Swansborough. I will not conscience accusations from a debauched rake. From a bloody murderer." Shakily his uncle rose to his feet, his face beet red, the blanket cast on the floor. "You deserve to rot in hell." He spat at Dash. Spat at him!

Maryanne couldn't hold it in. She couldn't sit as a witness and pretend to be polite.

"How dare you!" she cried. Jumping to her feet, she slammed her hands down to the chair's arms. "He was just a boy, and you tried to kill him for the title. You tried to destroy him, and you gave him a life of terror and fear. You do not deserve to be under his roof. You should be on your knees begging forgiveness."

"Stop, Maryanne." Dash turned on his heel to face her, but she ignored him.

She wanted to run to his uncle and slap him.

"That's all lies!" James Blackmore shouted. "He always was uncontrollable, incorrigible. He was even before my brother and his wife died. Did he fill your head with lies about my evil behavior? Swansborough is the killer. He is the monster!"

It wasn't true. Over three days Dash had revealed a little of what his uncle had done. His uncle was using Dash's pain to hurt him. Maryanne was shaking; her gaze seemed to be tinged with red. "You shot at him with an arrow to make it appear to be a child's accident."

"Maryanne . . ." Dash was at her side, his hands on her shoulders, stroking and soothing her. "You mustn't upset yourself, my love."

Out of the corner of her eye Maryanne saw Anne pale, her green eyes wide. And she saw Sir William move quietly into the room, his cheeks bright with color. He seemed to give her a nod of approval—but she couldn't stop.

"And the fire?" she shouted. "You discovered an old stable in which he used to play and set it on fire."

Dash's uncle clung to his cane, his body stooped, his shoulders slumped forward. It was the result of age, but also seemed as if his wickedness had eaten away at him, slowly consuming him.

"Shut up, woman! It was a candle that caught!" he shouted. "It was an accident. Just as the arrow shooting was. A foolish game played amongst boys. I believe he does think me responsible. He believes these lies." Blackmore waved his fist at Maryanne, tugged at his cravat with his other hand. But his gaze slid away from her, moved to Sir William for just a moment—for a telltale moment, and she saw him watch for the reaction on the magistrate's face.

Liar. He was the liar, of course.

"Stop." Dash's cold, dangerous voice resonated from her side, and she spun on her heel to meet Dash's eyes, utterly black, untouched by candlelight. And she stopped.

Silence reigned except for the curious whistling sound spilling from Dash's aunt's lips. The clatter of Sophia's lorgnette to the floor. The tinkle of the glass jewels on the candelabra disturbed by the fall of Blackmore's hand on the side table.

"It's not your battle, sweeting." Dash spoke with unnatural calm.

But it was. His fight was her fight. She parted her lips, but the pain in his eyes made her stop.

Dash turned slowly to his uncle. "As for you, Blackmore, you have attacked my wife. I demand—"

"No!" Maryanne gasped.

He wanted to duel over this. He couldn't. Blackmore was old, shaky, weak, but she could not let Dash face him over pistols.

Desperate, she reached out to Dash, but he prowled once more toward his uncle. She had forced this by speaking out. He could not let this go unanswered.

How stupid she had been.

"No!" she shouted.

Dash stopped. He faced her, his dark brows drawn together.

She sensed Moredon approaching, perhaps to stop her, so she raced to Dash. Planted her hands on his chest.

"Please, no," she begged, even as she knew it was hopeless. She couldn't stop him dueling, even though it was illegal, and he could not back down now. "He could cheat—shoot first. Dishonorable men do. And a man who tried to kill a child can have no honor, no humanity, no heart." She curled her fingertips hard into his biceps as if she could hold him in place and keep him safe. "Dash, please. If you kill him, a wicked but feeble old man, won't you condemn yourself for it?"

"This isn't vengeance, it's to save lives."

"Let justice be done. Sir William is here. Make him admit what he did, let him rot in a prison for the rest of his horrid life."

"You are correct, Maryanne." Dash's lips kicked up in a smile. "I cannot put a ball in the chest of my own uncle. That is a line I cannot cross."

"It bloody well is not!" Blackmore shouted. His face was red, the blood vessels pulsing in his temple. He leaned on his cane and pressed a hand to his heart. "You killed my son."

Dash took her hands in his but craned his head to face Blackmore. "If you insist on meeting over pistols at dawn," Dash snapped, "I might decide to play the perfect host and give you the pleasure."

She shivered at his chilling tone.

"You will meet me over pistols, my lord." Robert Blackmore threw out the words. "Not my aging father."

"I would prefer not to shoot any member of my family. And as my wife pointed out, we are discussing dueling—illegal as it is—in front of Bow Street's magistrate. We could find ourselves both in Newgate. I thought death would be the only way to solve this, but there will be no duel."

"Your wife began this, Swansborough. My uncle deserves the opportunity to—"

"To what? All here know the past. All here know the truth."

"You killed my brother, you blasted murderer."

"Stop it!" Dash's aunt screeched. "I can't bear any more! I can't bear to lose another son." She dropped her face to her hands and sobbed bitterly. Then lifted her head. Pointed her shaking finger.

Maryanne took a step back, the gnarled finger like an arrow directed at her heart. "You began this, you witch. You whore. What other sort of woman would have Swansborough? Evil, wicked, wanton—"

Dash's hands tightened around hers, but she felt her blood run cold.

"Mother, stop," Robert pleaded.

"She must rest—" Maryanne began. But Helena Blackmore closed her fingers around the rim of a vase on the octagonal table at her side. Even with her shaking arm, her aim was true. Maryanne ducked, and the spun glass vase soared over her head. Shattered.

Dash had his aunt restrained in a heartbeat, his hands clamped on her wrists even as his uncle screamed curses at him. "If you think to hurt my wife, you will regret it." His voice was ice. "Robert, let us take her to her room."

Maryanne froze, expecting Robert to rebel against Dash's command. But the young man nodded and wrapped his arm around his mother's shoulders. Murmuring soothing words, he led her from the room. A wave of Dash's hand had two footmen escorting them and two to accompany his uncle. Maryanne broke her feet free of the floor to follow, but Dash murmured, "Stay."

She did, until he followed his uncle and the two footmen out the door.

She couldn't let him go alone.

Grasping her skirts, she rushed to the door, only to have to dart around a young, doe-eyed footman. "M—milady?" the boy stuttered.

"What?" But she saw that Henshaw was also with Dash, the footman, and his family. And Sir William brushed by her to join. She breathed a sigh of relief. She had nothing to fear. His uncle wouldn't dare try to hurt Dash in such a crowd.

"A lady asked to see you. A Mrs. Watson. She went out to her carriage and left this note."

Mrs. Watson? Georgiana?

Even as she opened the note, she knew what it would say. Georgiana wished to speak to her in private—and if she did not come, Georgiana would come to the door once more. The threat was obvious: her partner would tell all if she did not meet her. And promise money, no doubt.

After his aunt's vitriol, she couldn't bear to have everyone know she had been a courtesan's partner. She couldn't horrify Anne, who wanted to be friends.

But she refused to let Georgiana force her to live a life of fear.

She had to go to Georgiana's carriage as her friend requested. Which, wrote Georgiana, would be waiting at the end of the drive.

And she would tell Georgiana to go to the devil.

Dressed in her pelisse, Maryanne slipped out the kitchen door—the low-arched, heavy-timbered door that led to the kitchen gardens. Blue shadows stretched across the snow, and she stepped from blazing heat into frigid cold. And silence. The sun had dropped, and the sky settled its gray embrace on the estate.

Maryanne tucked her hands into her muff and drew in a frosty breath. Her lungs ached instantly with the cold. She exhaled, and her breath danced in the air. Above her, the terrace curved, and light spilled from the gallery windows. But, here, she stood in the shadow, hidden from sight.

She had to get this done with.

Hurrying, Maryanne kicked up snow as she followed a narrow path around the side of the house. She passed the shrubs on the east wing, evergreens sculpted into fanciful shapes. The dim light pouring from the lower windows sent long black shadows across the snow.

Heart pounding, she raced across them. But she stopped as she reached the corner of the house, for often footmen and grooms loitered in the front yard.

A soft crunch came from behind her. Followed by a sigh.

Not her imagination, she was certain—

A hand clamped over her mouth, stuffing cloth between her teeth. She screamed—useless, of course! She kicked backward, and her heel connected with a hard boot. A huge arm ensnared her waist.

And lifted her.

She flailed her feet, and a rough voice chuckled. The villain's arm squashed harder over her breasts. The stench of liquor swamped her nose, and she choked on the dirty cloth in her mouth.

"Feisty wench, aren't you?" the villain growled.

A second man eased out of the shadows, and he grabbed her swinging feet—gripped them so hard his fingers drove into her calves. Dragging her ankles together, he held them in one massive hand and looped rough twine around her. The wretch wasn't content just to bind her ankles, he trussed her up to her thighs with the rasping rope, sniggering all the while. And the first idiot juggled her to tie up her hands. The cord cut into her skin through her kid gloves. Her fur muff fell to the snow.

Then they hauled her around the house as if she were a sack of grain to be tossed on a wagon. Just her luck; not a servant was in sight—it was too blasted cold. They quickly crossed to the shadowy trees that lined the drive, making speed even as she struggled.

Dash!

But she just choked on cloth for her trouble. He'd see the footprints at least, and find her muff, but it would only lead to the front gate. Was there any way she could leave a trail?

She tried to wrench in the first man's grip—her head was pressing against his hard gut, and she couldn't see for his flapping coat. She had paper in the pocket of her pelisse, but what good would that do? If she'd had ink, perhaps she could have dripped it in the snow.

With bound hands. And how would she drip it from the carriage? *Brilliant.*

They reached the plain black carriage. With a grunt, the first villain chucked her in through the open door. She landed on her chest, arching her back to keep from smacking her face. Behind her, the blackguard clambered up. The second disappeared, and just as she managed to roll onto her back, they were off.

A woman's half boot stood right by her nose.

And she spit out the cloth and gazed up.

Cradled in sumptuous sable, a jaunty sable-trimmed hat perched upon her pale blond hair, Georgiana sat on the blue velvet seat and gazed out the window as though she was terribly bored. Maryanne would not have that. If her friend, her partner, was kidnapping her, Georgiana would bloody well face her. She was not going to let Georgiana escape the vicious immorality of kidnapping her by looking away.

"Why are you doing this?" Maryanne demanded. Fibers of the cloth stuck to her tongue and made her want to retch. But then, so did being with her Judas of a partner.

Obviously startled by an autocratic demand in place of a whimpering plea, Georgiana gazed down at her.

"Well," Maryanne snapped. "This is how you repay me for helping you? For rushing to your rescue?"

With a sigh, Georgiana looked to the dark-haired man. He sprawled in the seat opposite, picking his wretched teeth.

Georgiana waved her gloved hand like a countess. Innumerable bracelets glinted in the low lamplight. "Gag her," Georgiana snapped. "I don't wish to have to speak to her."

"You witch!" Dash's aunt's insults rose up, but the brute

bent over her and jammed the horrid cloth in her mouth before she could truly let loose on Georgiana.

"And blindfold her."

As a strip of folded muslin pressed hard against her eyes, and a knot tugged ruthlessly at her hair, she remembered blindfolding Dash. With him, this had been an erotic game.

Now her heart pounded. It was terrifying to lose her sight.

What if Georgiana's enormous lackey was unsheathing a knife? Or planning to strangle her? What if the fool held a pistol to her head—a jolt on the road could cause him to fire.

Her heart raced far faster than the carriage.

A ditch. They could end up in a ditch.

Her baby. Dash's baby—

The man gave a lusty laugh.

"She's got lovely plump tits. I can think of some fun for the—"

"She is pregnant, you lout," Georgiana snapped, her voice sharp with disgust. "I forbid you to rape her."

"Not that. But a lovely bit of fondling. A little bouncing of her arse on me cock through me trousers—for that's the rump of a lady of quality," he mocked.

"You, Ball, are an irritating fool. Do you not know what happens to a man who thinks only with the little head in his trousers?"

An unintelligible grunt was the response.

"The big head gets blown off his shoulders. Now behave. Or I'll put a pistol ball through your handsome eyes."

"In a moving carriage. Nah, you won't," the man returned jovially. "You'd miss, and I'd have your throat slit. Or I might amuse meself first—by cutting up your pretty tits and your loose, welcoming cunny."

"You'd never hurt me." But Georgiana's voice shook. "The master would kill you."

Imprisoned in darkness and rolling about on the wooden floor, Maryanne felt her heart race so fast she feared it would explode. Could this be the man who had killed the actress in Hyde Park?

She tried to fight the urge to throw up. She didn't dare be sick while gagged. She might choke.

Courage, Maryanne Mouse. Think.

She'd assumed Georgiana had hatched this plan to kidnap her and extort money from Dash. Was Georgiana working for Dash's uncle? Or Robert? It made no sense—would Georgiana do this to secure favor from a man who only had the aspiration of being viscount?

Her brain threw possibilities at her. Did Georgiana owe Jack Tate a fortune? Perhaps Georgiana was a gambler? Or was Georgiana serving Lord Craven? He was an earl, one with fabulous wealth.

She tried to brace her bound feet against the seat to stop rolling. To protect her tummy and her child.

Her child.

If a son, her child would inherit the title. Even if Dash was to die, the title and the estate would not be given to anyone until she bore a child—until she bore either a girl or a boy.

Sick dread wrapped around her, more tightly than the ropes binding her. She fought to breathe. Was she being taken so they would kill her? So Dash's heir would die?

Or did Georgiana just want money?

But why do something so extreme? For money, all she had to do was make a demand.

Maryanne's stomach cramped painfully, and she screamed into the cloth gagging her mouth. She drew up her legs, trying to bear the excruciating agony that racked her loins. It faded but left her shaking.

Was her fear and the rough treatment causing a miscarriage?

Tears leaked into the blindfold.

Courage! She had to quell fear. She had no choice but to be courageous—she was not going to lose Dash's child!

But with every muscle tense, she waited for another cramp. She was jostled about on the floor for an eternity, her head bouncing up and slamming down with each rut.

"I hate to see her smacked about like that," Ball commented. "Let me put her on the seat."

"Fine. Do it then," Georgiana snapped.

One of the beefy paws cradled her head; the other wrapped around her waist. "Not much farther, love," he remarked cheerfully. "And you'll be more cozy in me arms."

20

Melted snow dripped from Maryanne's sable muff onto Dash's hand as he charged up the stairs to his uncle's bedchamber. He slammed his boot into the paneled oak door, and it bowed and then tore out of the aging lock. It slammed inward.

The bed curtains were drawn, and muffled behind the velvet came a confused, weak voice. "What—? Who's there? What do you want?"

"Get out of here. On your feet or I'll shoot you through the bloody drapes." A lie—he had no pistol, but it proved effective.

A wavering hand clutched the drape, and two legs emerged, along with the cane. White as the proverbial sheet, his uncle slithered out from between the crimson velvet drapes, and he cautiously dropped to his feet, but the petulant look on his fat face enraged Dash.

"What did you do with my wife?" Dash raged.

Confusion met his demand. "What in blazes are you talking about, Swansborough—"

But Dash had his uncle by the throat—by the cravat, for he'd obviously lain down for a nap fully dressed. "Maryanne is missing. If you don't tell me what you did to her, I'll rip out your windpipe with my bare hands."

His uncle desperately shook his head. "I didn't touch the girl. I've no idea where she went."

"I don't believe it." He gripped Blackmore's flabby throat.

The beefy hands clawed at his wrist, but Dash's grip was like iron, stronger than even he'd expected.

A surge of power and rage thundered through Dash's head. All his life, he'd feared this man. He'd been vulnerable. Frightened. And now he was physically superior, more powerful.

"It's the truth. God's truth."

Relentlessly Dash squeezed tighter. His uncle's fingers grew weaker.

"Please. Please. I know nothing. Don't kill me. Please don't kill me." Broken, beaten, a weak man in tears. Pleading for his life. All bravado and anger and courage gone.

"Swansborough, stop!" His aunt's voice filtered into his head. He twisted his head to see her in the doorway, her head bowed and her hands clasped. Pleading. "His heart is weak. Any strain and he might be gone. Remembering his son, his lost son might be enough."

Dash blinked, unable to reconcile this controlled woman with the shrieking harridan who had attacked his wife. But he released his uncle and stepped back as she hastened across the floor.

Had the display in the drawing room been a trick? Wrapping her arms around his uncle's sloping shoulders, his aunt soothed Blackmore and helped the shaking man lower onto the bed.

Helplessness hit Dash. He slammed his fist into the gilt column of the bed canopy, knuckles colliding with a furled leaf, but he reveled in the pain that bit into him. "I want to know what he did with my wife."

Straightening, his aunt's resolute set of mouth, sharp features, and unflinching gaze gave her the look of a tower of strength. Even with iron-gray hair in disarray. Vehemently she shook her head. "Nothing. He didn't touch her. You think he plots against you? He is an old, confused man. He lives only for the time he spends with her—his mistress—for she makes him believe he is still a young man. I believe he should accept the truth."

Hell, he didn't care about their marital issues. He wished them both a miserable union. "I do not believe it. I know he would hurt a woman to hurt me—"

"He has changed—the shock of losing Simon, of losing a boy he loved, preyed upon him."

"He was bloody content to kill me."

She shook her head and grasped his forearm. Dash flinched at the touch. "Come," she whispered, and he followed, cursing his dependency, damning the wasted time. "He didn't send the footpads to hurt your mistress; he did not send that ransom note. He did not send the assassins who killed Simon." Her watery gray eyes met his gaze. "I did. I hired them. I paid them. I sent them. And I lost everything. Everything."

Rocked back on his heels, Dash bent over her, his fist pressed against the wall. "Why? Did getting that blasted title mean so much to you?"

"It meant so much to him," she snapped bitterly. She wrapped her thin arms around her chest. "I wanted to be the one to give James what he yearned for."

"You're both mad, but I don't give a damn about either of you." Menace turned Dash's growl into a hoarse rasp. "All I want is Maryanne safe and sound. I'll spare you both if you get her back to me."

But his aunt stood, trembling. "Every night, for all these years, I've dreamed about Simon's death. I've seen his cold, still face. I've heard his death rattle." Beseeching, she gazed at him. "I would never . . . could never hurt anyone again."

Liar. His uncle had played the jovial country gent and kind relative while trying to kill him. But how could Dash get the truth out of her? "On the other hand, such a great loss could make you more determined to get that blasted title."

Panicked, she shook her head. "No. You must believe me, Swansborough."

"That you wouldn't hurt my wife after you insulted her? The only reason you remain in this house is because you know where she is!"

"I don't."

"Then I turn James Blackmore over to Sir William."

"Sir William was a peer of James's. A friend. He would never—"

"He learned about my past when Simon was murdered." He watched her flinch. "He'd had suspicions; he ensured he freed me of Blackmore. The reason I'm alive today is because Sir William intervened."

His uncle had known he had to be clever in the way he destroyed Dash so Sir William could not connect the crime to him. And now he understood why Sir William had been unable to arrest Blackmore for the attack on his mistress and Simon's death. They'd been looking for the wrong culprit—it had been his aunt Helena.

"Who killed Amanda Westmoreland? You or my uncle?"

A blank stare met his question. Did she truly not remember Amanda?

Maryanne. How was he going to protect Maryanne? How could he make this woman reveal where she was? Would his aunt tell the truth to save her husband's life?

The creak of hinges. Dash swung around to catch the sheen of reflected light. Focusing, he realized Sir William had walked into the room. He held a sheath of folded paper.

"Swansborough, I need a word."

Helena reached a trembling hand toward Sir William. "We've done nothing. We didn't hurt her. I have no idea where her . . ." A grimace touched her lips. "Where her ladyship is."

Dash gripped his aunt's arm—for Maryanne he had no choice but to bully a feeble-bodied, feeble-minded old woman. "If you are lying, I will make you both pay."

Abruptly he turned his back on her and strode across the

room, but her plaintive words followed. "There is nothing more you can do to us. We are already in hell."

One of your own making. His heart felt like a hard lump in his chest as he followed Sir William to his own bedchamber. "You looked in your wife's room, but you did not look here. This was left folded beneath your sheets."

What had possessed Sir William to search his sheets? But Dash took the note and read:

Where risk and scandal frolic beneath bucolic sky and
Five rogues await to make a fair lady cry
Her pleasure to the stars as she embraces heaven's light
And lets her love witness an orgiastic delight.

The bloody Vauxhall clue from the scavenger hunt but slightly changed. His pulse roared in his head. *Embrace heaven's light. Five rogues . . .*

Raped and then killed . . .

God no.

A hand clamped on his shoulder. Sir William. "Easy, Dashiel, turn over the sheet."

The grip of his hand had crumpled the side of it. Small, cramped writing scrawled across the top.

Mine to enjoy. Yours to find. But you are to be witness. Whitby Manor. Alone.

Whitby Manor was in the village of Wising not four miles away. As far as Dash knew, it had been empty since autumn.

"You are not going alone," Sir William began, eyes grave behind glinting eyeglasses. "I will bring—"

A knock at his door, the knob turning.

Maryanne! Was it possible she'd escaped?

But his heart plunged like a stone as Harriet stumbled into his bedchamber, alone, her glove-clad palm pressed to her cheek. "Dash! It was horrible. It was a nightmare. Oh, I've been such a fool and—"

"What in blazes happened? Where is Maryanne?"

She halted, her hand leaving her cheek and exposing a swollen purplish patch. "Maryanne? I have no idea where your wife is. Why should I?" She rushed forward again, cheeks pink and blue eyes bright with tears. "I was with Craven, and the gentleman is an utter monster. You warned me at Buckstead about my behavior, and I've mired myself in danger. I have nowhere else to turn, Dash."

"What did Craven do?" he roared. Was Craven behind this, after all?

His vehemence seemed to startle her, and then, blast her, she flung herself against his chest. "Dash—I discovered what he was. He has kidnapped a girl, an innocent girl, to take her to London. I was enraged, and he mocked me. He keeps these girls as his private playthings. Keeps them in a sordid club and shares them amongst his noxious peers. And there are others he has stolen from the country and sold into sexual slavery."

He gripped her upper arms and pushed her back from his chest. "Christ Jesus, I've no time for your games. Is this the truth? Did you see the girl he took?"

She shook her head. "No, no, it is the truth!" she cried. "But I did not see the girl. I saw her gown—it was left in the cottage. I took him to task, thinking it belonged to a tart. He hit me, throttled me until I passed out—and I was certain he was going to kill me! But I woke to find Barrett there. And he told me all. I had a dagger hidden in my dress. I had to stab him to escape."

"Did you kill him?"

"No, but I cut his cheek, and he will kill me if he finds me, I know he will."

"Why were you carrying a knife?"

She gaped. "I always do. A woman must protect herself."

"Especially one who consorts with perverts and villains," he roared. "Where is this bloody club of Craven's?"

"I don't know. It is patterned on the Hellfire clubs of the last century. I believe the men dress as Satan—they wear only breeches and papier-mâché horns, and they hold orgies."

"Bloody hell." Dash's heart hammered in his chest. Had Craven taken Maryanne to use her as a hostage as a way of protecting himself from prosecution as a white slaver? Or was it someone else?

A glance up at Sir William showed the man pondering, likely the same questions. "I think Whitby Manor is the most probable, Dashiel. But you are not going alone. And it is dark—you should wait until morning—"

"Leave Maryanne in danger for the night? Not bloody likely."

And within a half hour, Dash had two loaded pistols in his greatcoat and Beelzebub saddled and ready. He charged out of the front door, jamming his hat on his head. Hail pelted him, and he leaped down the steps.

His boot heel skidded in the slippery snow.

A treacherous night.

But he was going to ride hell-bent for leather to rescue Maryanne. And dying trying was not an option.

"I assume my advice on ways to please Swansborough had him panting with desire for you?"

Silk rustled as Georgiana approached Maryanne's cell, and the careful speech—every *H* pronounced and the accent controlled—had Maryanne gritting her teeth.

At this moment she despised everything about Georgiana. The witch. Was money worth so much to the heartless cow?

Obviously.

"Or were you too much of a mouse to try?" Georgiana appeared at the bars, a tray balanced in her hands. "It is exasperating that I must do this—carry a tray for you like a servant. And I suggest you eat."

Since her ankles were shackled to the damp stone wall and a short chain attached to narrow metal cuffs linked her wrists, Maryanne could not see how she could eat. With her fingers, like a rat—and this hideous dungeon must be full of rats.

Two candles burned in the low tunnel outside the bars, magnifying Georgiana's shadow over tooled stone walls.

Maryanne glared at her former partner, hoping she looked an imperious viscountess, even though she was imprisoned in a cell wearing only a dirty shift and Georgiana gleamed like pure driven snow. The famous voluptuous figure was squeezed into a white gown, her hands clad in white silk gloves, and perfectly dressed golden ringlets framed an artfully made-up face.

Tarted-up old witch.

Insults were fruitless, but they did give some satisfaction.

Georgiana set the items from the tray onto the floor, which was dirt. A cup of weak-looking tea, a hunk of cheese, and a torn-off piece of bread. To her irritation, Maryanne's tummy growled. Sliding through the narrow gap in the bars, Georgiana's wrist tempted—if only Maryanne had a weapon, she could catch Georgiana and hold her prisoner, bargain her escape.

But she could not move without clanking chains.

"My husband would pay you a fortune to release me." There was no point in appealing to Georgiana's sympathy, reminding her they had been friends. "You could escape to Italy and live like a queen."

But Georgiana stood and drew back. "I doubt your husband would let me live. And it is more than money that I want."

"Oh, heavens," Maryanne groaned, shifting her ankles and wincing at the clink of metal on a ragged flagstone. "You are doing this to please a man, aren't you?"

Georgiana whirled, skirts fluttering. She bent and blew out one candle.

"What in blazes are you doing?"

"Preparing." And Georgiana picked up the remaining candle, cursing as the handle of the holder smudged dirt on her glove. "Good-bye."

"No, don't!" Fear rushed over Maryanne. "I'll give you money. Bushels of it. Don't leave me! Don't take the candle!" Pride, who cared for pride? Desperation gripped her like a living thing, choking away her breath.

But Georgiana's affected laugh rippled back as light faded. Dim slivers of light bounced over the stone, and then vanished.

Rats. They'd come out now. On her hands and knees, she scrambled for the food—she felt sick, but she didn't want the smell of it to attract vermin. The shackles bit into her bruised ankles. She could see nothing but spots before her eyes. Damn, she would not cry.

How she wanted to.

Her fingers drove into the cheese, scattering pieces. And then tears fell. She'd never be able to gather the crumbs by feel. It was the final frustration.

First she'd been stripped to her shift by Georgiana's horrid lackey. He'd pawed her breasts through the gossamer muslin, and with her hands bound, her only weapon had been spittle. She'd spit on his face as he tweaked her nipples, as he gave a rude squeeze between her thighs. He'd hauled her down here, and he'd been the one to shackle her—chuckling lewdly all the while.

Where in blazes was she? Blindfolded, she'd used her other senses. The carriage had crunched on gravel before it stopped. Other voices rose around them as the door opened. What sort of house had servants who were not surprised to have a bound woman arrive?

The house of a horrible fiend, she supposed. The sort who would seduce a twit like Georgiana. Well, if Georgiana was helping a gentleman like Craven, Georgiana would surely end up dead. Unfortunately, so would she, thought Maryanne, so she'd have no chance to gloat.

Fumbling, she found the bread, her fingers sinking into it. Dirt coated the crust, but she bit into the clean, doughy top. She devoured it to the gritty parts.

How would Dash ever find her?

Or was his uncle using her as bait for a trap?

She touched her belly. "Don't worry, little one," she whispered. "We will survive." But a scampering sound came from the corner.

Oh, not the horrid rats! The faint light touched their small eyes, and then they slipped into shadow. She sensed the movement, heard it, but couldn't see it.

Where were they?

She jumped up. Pirouetted as she kicked out wildly with her feet. Her toe hit a small furry body. Something scratched her foot.

She shrieked. Teeth or claws?

Footsteps echoed off the stone. The scuttling vanished.

"Good evening, my lovely child. How very delightful you look in chains."

The voice. She knew the voice. A cultured accent. It was the voice of a man younger than Blackmore. And Robert had a softer voice, higher in pitch. Was it Craven? No. He'd sounded more . . . odious. Nor was this Tate's voice, with its insolent drawl and rough edges.

"And how delicious you look when you are frightened." The villain's eerily delighted chuckle sent horror shivering down her spine and bile rising in her throat. She swallowed hard and instinctively curled up.

"Your husband will join you soon—I hope he hurries. My fingers itch to bruise you, my teeth hunger to bite, and my cock . . . ah, but my whip desires lashing you first, splitting your soft skin, flaying you until blood flows."

The singsong quality of his words sent her scuttling back.

But of course the chains gave her away. She knew the voice. It haunted her.

But who?

Clang!

She shrieked as something struck the bars of her cell.

"Swansborough made an excellent choice. This once, his cock did not steer him wrong."

Wising. The tiny village rose up along the road that twisted its way to the escarpment. Snow had blown fiercely against the ridge, piling around the row of Tudor buildings that overlooked a white, sloping stretch of common.

Dash shifted his shoulder, breaking apart the thin layer of ice encrusting his coat. He spurred Beelzebub up the hill as fast as he dared, following directions given by the innkeeper of the neighboring village.

Maryanne.

Please, let her be safe. He'd trade his life for hers in an instant.

And their babe. *Let the babe be safe.*

Ducking beneath tree boughs heavy with snow and ice, he charged up the laneway to Whitby Manor, a simple, symmetrical stone manor. All the windows blazed with light. An unmarked black carriage sat in the drive.

He reigned in Beelzebub. It would appear to anyone watching that he had come alone, but Sir William had rounded up runners to—

"My lord." From the shadows a man emerged, masked and dressed in a black cloak. Dash gripped Beelzebub's flanks with his thighs as the gelding shied. Two other men, also masked, ran out, one carrying a lantern.

"Dismount, my lord," ordered the man with the pistol.

Dash had no choice but to comply, but the instant his boots hit the icy snow, he sensed a whistle of air, a sudden motion.

He half turned as something slammed into his head.

* * *

Bound. Chained. Trussed. Kicked until his ribs ached with every breath.

Dash groaned and lifted his head, clenching his teeth against the pain that shot through his shoulders, back, and chest. Shackled to the wall, his arms were stretched wide, enough so that his tendons ached. Iron dug into his ankles. At least he wasn't suspended on the wall, so his limbs weren't being ripped from his body.

He was stripped naked and shivered in the cold. It stank of damp.

Faint gray light crept through three narrow slits in the wall, and the winter air poured in.

Closing his eyes, he focused his strength and tried to rip his right leg free of the wall. Hopeless, of course; the damned chains held tight, rattling against the stone wall.

"Who—who's there?"

Hope and joy and love and pure terror exploded inside him. "Maryanne?"

"D—Dash?"

"Yes, my sweet. It is me. The gallant knight racing to your rescue only to be hit on the back of the head and thrown in chains."

A shaky sob answered him.

"Courage, sweeting. But are you all right? Are you hurt?" He caught his breath. She'd been locked in this prison for a night and a day.

"Not hurt, but I would rather not be here. I'm in only my shift, so I'm frozen to the bone."

Damn, he wished he could hold her, warm her, protect her. "Maryanne, who holds us here?"

"You don't know?" came her answer.

"Masked and caped. And I think the men who brought me here were servants." Why didn't she tell him, or was she afraid to speak the name?

"I don't know who it is, Dash," she grumbled, sounding more peeved than terrified. "He visited me, but he was also masked and wore a cape. I did not recognize his voice—but I am certain it was not your uncle or cousin—"

He leaned as close to her wall as the chains would allow—being nearer made being bound hand and foot more bearable. "It couldn't be, love. They were still at the house. Are you certain you aren't hurt?"

"Dash, would it help you if I was and I admitted to it?"

That set his heart pounding, and he wrenched once more at the blasted chains. He let out a roar like a boar chained and tormented.

"I'm not hurt," she cried, her voice a trill squeal. She dropped it to a murmur he strained to hear. "Nor did he sound like Craven, though it has been months since I heard that horrid fiend's voice."

"Did he . . . touch you?"

"No. He hasn't handled me in any way at all. He came down here, disguised to mock me, the cocky wretch."

He'd prefer another term to *cocky*.

"He made threats . . . lewd threats, but he has not touched me. He told me you would be coming. I don't . . . I don't understand what he wants. He had Georgiana bring me food—"

"Georgiana?" But he understood quickly as Maryanne explained. Her partner, the betraying bitch, had been the bait for the trap. Dash hung his head—she'd raced out to the carriage alone to protect him, terrified she'd bring scandal to him.

"That woman is a bitch," he spat.

"I think I agree. If a titled man told Georgiana he'd buy her a necklace if she lopped off her hand, she might very well do it," Maryanne snapped.

He marveled. How could she manage humor? Sir William and the other men couldn't be far behind. In fact, he was amazed they'd waited so long to storm this bloody—

Light suddenly knifed down the tunnel in front of his cell. Followed by cheerful whistling. Christ, when he got out of here, he would—

"Swansborough, you rode quickly. My congratulations. You have certainly proven how deeply you care for your wife."

Shock hit his brain harder than the club had.

The voice belonged to Sir William.

21

You were like a father. . . . You were my friend . . . the one man I could trust. . . .

Dash bit back the words. Closing his eyes, he steeled himself. He wanted answers, but he damn well would not beg for them.

The bloody magistrate of Bow Street had kidnapped his wife and imprisoned him in a dungeon.

Fear lanced him—with a crippling blow more powerful than any he'd endured. God . . . this man had carved up Eliza Charmody in that sadistic and brutal way?

Boot heels clicked on stone, and Dash jerked his eyes open. "Watch, Swansborough. You will see my triumph." Sir William stooped to put the lantern on the flag floor. As he stood, he dangled a key. Howling in fury, Dash tried to charge forward; the sharp-edged shackles cut at his flesh, the chain held fast.

Sir William sauntered to the cell on the other side of his—not Maryanne's. Clinking sounds followed, and then, smug, Sir William called, "Come out, slave."

A soft voice answered. Dash caught the word *master.* Sir William backed up until he stood in front of Dash's cage. In his hand, he held a black riding crop. A thin, dirty woman came into view. She wore nothing but a black strip of leather banding her breasts. She shuffled forward on her haunches, her legs and bottom bare. Her hair hung around her in tangled strands.

Sir William cocked his head, mouth curved in a sickly, triumphant grin. "Lady Farthingale." Then he barked, "Touch your forehead to the floor."

She did obediently, her unkempt hair spilling around her.

Bruises of deep blue and purple ringed her wrists and ankles. Bruises decorated her back. As did fresh lash marks. Her skin clung to her spine and ribs. Her hip bones jutted out. Once, Lady Farthingdale had been a lusciously voluptuous woman.

Bile rose in Dash's throat. He had been bound for sexual pleasure, had been whipped and had given whippings. But he'd never tortured anyone.

Lady Farthingale crawled toward Sir William. On reaching his boots, her tongue flicked out. She laved the toes of his boots.

He heard a horrified cry from Maryanne's cell.

Lady Farthingale had been missing for three months. She must have been a captive here for all that time. She looked unwashed. Uncared for. Beaten and subdued. But what sickened Dash was that, in three months, Sir William had destroyed the soul of a once proud and vivacious lady.

"Return to your cell," the magistrate commanded. Bowing, with her hands clasped as though in prayer, Lady F crept back. To Dash's horror, she willingly backed toward her cell.

What had this bastard done to make her submit?

With a grating creak, the iron door swung shut on Lady Farthingale's cell, and Sir William approached it with the key. After, he came to Dash's door and unlocked it. Alone.

Shackled hand and foot, Dash tore at the chains, but they held firm. He wanted to grip the bloody madman by the neck and throttle him. He wanted to rip him apart.

Rage tore through him, but he fought it. His blind fury had led to his cousin's death.

Maryanne . . .

He had to stay in control to save Maryanne.

Letting his arms relax and the chains slacken, he forced his voice to stay level. "Why?" he asked.

Sir William drew out a flint and a stub of a candle. He set flame to wick. "I wouldn't tell you now. Not yet." He twisted the candle in his hand, letting the wax pool. Then, his lips curved in a sickening grin, he walked forward.

"But I would not deny you your usual pleasures, Dashiel."

"You're insane, you bloody beast."

"You dabbled in these games, intent only on a fast release, with no true artistry. You have no idea how I have refined the sexual games we lust for." He lifted the candle over Dash's chest.

Dash watched the droplet gather, translucent white wax. It broke free, changing from teardrop to ball. It hit his chest right between his pectoral muscles. He bit back his roar. His hair absorbed most of the heat and pain.

"You wonder why I enjoy dominating women? Women would stand before me on the dock, awaiting my sentence. Women charged with prostitution, with theft, with running a bawdy house, with stealing children."

Another droplet, higher, seared his skin. Good Christ! He tasted blood as his teeth drove into his lower lip. *Control . . . control . . . stay in control for Maryanne.*

"Those women watched me . . . some with bold and saucy bravado, some in sheer terror. Some with pleading eyes. And some with desperate, wanton eyes that promised me any pleasure, any favor if I spared them."

The candle lowered, the flame skimming his skin. "You killed Eliza Charmody. You cut her open," Dash said.

Holding the flame beneath his chin, Sir William transformed his face to that of a demon's. Behind spectacles, his eyes gleamed with demented delight. "But she is the sort of woman who wants a man inside her. I merely used a blade and not my cock."

Dash jerked back—stunned. A wax droplet struck his soft,

exposed cock. His head slammed back against the wall as pain seared him.

"You've whipped women," Sir William said. "You pay them; you think you control them. But have you known the excitement of holding a woman's life in your hands? Have you tasted a woman's true fear? I promise you it is a pleasure unsurpassed. Do you understand the sexual delight of controlling every aspect of a woman's life—every morsel of food, every sip of water, even warmth is at my pleasure."

Dash forced himself to stay motionless as Sir William brought the candle toward his chest again. "To break a proud woman . . . it is magnificent."

Sir William tipped his hand, and a stream of wax lanced Dash's abdomen. He screamed—hating himself as it echoed in his chamber.

"Stop!" Maryanne cried. "Please stop. Don't hurt him."

"Silence," Sir William commanded, and the mad chuckle at the end of the word did bring silence. "I am going to have the pleasure of watching Dashiel watch the woman he loves die."

To her astonishment, Harriet found herself surrounded by family who cared about her. She sat in the drawing room of Swansley, covered in warm wool throws, surrounded by sympathetic women for the first time in her life.

Anne and Sophia and Maryanne's sister Venetia, Lady Trent, who had just arrived with her husband and baby, were pouring over the perverse clue that had been left for Dash. Maryanne's mother, Olivia Hamilton, had also arrived, along with the scandalous erotic artist Rodesson! Harriet had been astounded to see him—she knew him from some of London's wilder clubs, though she had never had an encounter with him. But it appeared, amazingly, he was Maryanne's father.

Dash had married the illegitimate daughter of a scandalous artist. And Moredon had taken her aside and murmured, "Harriet, you cannot spread gossip about this. It would destroy Dash—it would destroy Anne. Please—"

"Of course I won't," she'd interrupted. And she knew she would never hurt Dash, or Anne, who she realized loved her like a sister.

And then her brother threatened to rip Craven and Barrett apart with his bare hands—once he found Craven in London.

"No, please," Harriet had begged. "You mustn't. I don't want you to risk your life! I want you safe and sound for both me and Anne!" Tears had poured down her cheeks. She'd thought Moredon didn't care less about her. She thought he, like their father, had seen her only as a pawn in the marriage mart—a way to align with another powerful family.

She had been so wrong. Moredon had been horrified. Anne and Sophia had actually cried over her ordeal and her wounds. Even Venetia, who was red-eyed and shaking with shock over the news of Maryanne's kidnapping, had shed a tear for her, too.

She had been a fool to be enticed by the danger of Craven and Barrett.

What would Evershire do if he learned what she had done? Her husband wouldn't care about the sex—after all, he didn't love her. At forty, he was still handsome and virile, and he had more lovers than she could count. He'd never spent an entire night in her bed—he'd always left it to fuck another woman. A mistress, an actress, or even one of the maids in the house.

Would he even care that she'd almost been killed?

"We ride to Whitby Manor, then. Blast—what was he thinking to go alone?" That angry exclamation came from Lord Trent, the darkly handsome earl who looked rather like Dash.

"He isn't alone—Sir William left also and is taking his men to help," Anne protested.

"I'm not going to rely on a bunch of hired lackeys!" Rodesson shouted. "I'm going! I'm not going to lose Maryanne. I'm not!"

Olivia Hamilton dropped the handkerchief from her eyes. "I'm going also!"

Rodesson swung around. "No, Mrs. Hamilton, you are staying put."

Venetia had gone over to her husband, Trent. "Yes, you must go. Dash could be racing into a trap. But I'm afraid—what if Maryanne is not at this Whitby Manor? What if it's a lie?"

He nodded. "We'll send servants out to search."

Anne jumped up. "They can report back here." She turned to Moredon as he gathered her into an embrace. "I think we'll find them both at Whitby Manor, but I can't see what this blackguard wants."

"Dash dead," Harriet breathed, horrified by the very words.

All stopped and turned to her.

Trent grimaced. "I believe she is correct. We need to move now."

"We must move! We must have carriages brought round." Anne raced to the bellpull and tugged it hard.

"You aren't going."

Harriet shivered at the fear lacing Moredon's command to his wife. His love clung to each word, and Harriet felt a pang around her heart. No man had loved her like that.

"Of course I am! But not Venetia, because she has a newborn son."

"I am going," Venetia insisted. "He will be safe with nurses, and I must go and help my sister."

Trent grasped his wife's arm. "No. You need to be here. He could wake; he will want to be fed. And there's danger. I can't let you race into that."

Venetia was a redhead, and she looked ready to let a fiery temper burst free. But then she gave a thin smile. "It's true. My duty now is here—to my own family. It's a startling thought." Venetia gave Trent a push toward the door. "You men! You are all wasting time. Go!"

Harriet impulsively raced forward and hugged Moredon before he could follow Trent and Rodesson out the door of the drawing room. "All of you come back safely and bring them both back."

He gave her a quick kiss to her forehead. "Of course we will," he said like an earl. But Harriet saw the uncertainty in her brother's eyes. Were they already too late?

As the burly servant shoved her into the bedchamber and she fell hard onto the gleaming wood floor, Maryanne's first instinct was to cower in fear. Sir William followed, tapping his riding crop against his gloved palm.

But she couldn't flee into a mouse hole in the skirting board. Not now. Two more servants dragged Dash into the room, past Sir William. Maryanne brushed tears away as she stood. The sight of Dash imprisoned sickened her. Sir William was a beast—a heartless beast.

Iron shackles clamped around Dash's ankles to cobble him so he couldn't run. A wooden bar lay along his broad, naked shoulders like an oxen yoke. His arms were draped over it and chained in place. A leather ball had been forced between his teeth, and a leather strap was buckled behind his head to keep it in place. Even though the servants carried pistols, Dash fought. He swung the yoke like a weapon, plowing it into a servant's chest.

The second servant leveled the pistol at Dash's back.

"Dash!" she screamed.

He spun, stopping dead as he saw the pistol held in the beefy, determined hand of the grinning servant. A sadist who would love to kill a victim, she was sure.

Dash's eyes widened in horror, and she followed his gaze. As she expected, that worm Sir William had a gun trained on her. And Dash immediately adopted a submissive stance—a subtle change that told even her he would not fight.

A wave of Sir William's hand directed the servants to drag Dash out of the room. He turned the key in the lock after them and pocketed the key. He waved his hand around the room. "This is where you could live if you are obedient."

The lavish room was filled with a huge bed of blue and

gilt, hangings of gold silk. It smelled of perfumed candles, and it made her stomach curdle.

She wanted to cry, *I will not be obedient, so I suppose I shall stay in your dungeon!* Brave words after spending another horrible night down there. Christmas Eve! But having Dash in the cell beside her, reassuring her, had given her strength.

She had to have courage—she might be bruised and dirty and hungry and scared witless, but she was no longer bound. There had to be a way to free herself and get to Dash. To escape. She had to stall for time.

Watching Dashiel watch the woman he loves die. . . .

This lunatic, who now stood casually polishing his spectacles, thought Dash loved her, that it would hurt Dash to watch her die.

But their baby would die if she did, and she wouldn't—couldn't—let that happen. Her baby was no folly, no mistake—she loved her baby. She loved Dash. Drawing herself with the hauteur of a grand lady, she peered down her freckled nose at Sir William. "Why? Why are you doing this?"

"It amuses me to toy with inferior creatures, my dear." He turned and sauntered toward the door. He paused in the doorway. "I will return later, but first, I wish to hear Dashiel beg."

The door slammed, and the key turned in the lock. She ran to the door, useless attempt though it was, and of course the white-painted, paneled slab of wood resisted her kicks and her hammering fists. She dropped to her knees and peered through the keyhole. Something black was in front of it, something that moved.

He'd left a guard at her door.

She raced over to the window, flinging open the blue velvet drapes. Her heart sank. Ice sat around the frame, clamping the window in place. And beyond that, closely spaced iron bars made the room a prison. Groaning, she rested her forehead against the freezing glass and looked down. A two-story drop to a swept flagstone terrace.

No wonder Sir William hadn't worried about the window. In one book she'd edited, a gothic about a deformed lord and an innocent lass held as his captive, the heroine had tried every way to escape, and every attempt led to more and more disaster. Soon the poor girl was locked in a small shed and broken until she called the lord her "master."

Maryanne spun away from the window. "Come on, little one," she whispered to her baby, "We won't let a fictional story steal our courage. We will find something!"

But after searching every shadowed nook and cranny, she dropped to her knees on the plank floor to peer under the bed again, ready to scream in frustration.

The bedchamber was completely stripped of anything that might be thrown or swung. No fireplace poker. No shovel for the ash. Not a candle, not even a picture on the painted walls. Only the massive bed and a large chair. She'd tried to lift the chair with the idea of throwing it at the window but it was an ancient oak thing she couldn't budge.

She couldn't even brace the chair against the door, but since she was trying to get out, not lock herself in, that wasn't a great loss. . . .

What was happening to Dash? She slumped back onto the floor. He had shouted in such agony in his cell. . . .

Tears bubbled up, threatening to spill.

No, she couldn't give in to that. She would not be a helpless heroine who screamed plaintively for help.

Scrambling to her feet, Maryanne leaned against one carved bedpost and stared at the bed. Pillows, but what sort of weapon would they make? Sheets, plenty of them, and clean, too, but without an open window, they were useless.

She could hide when Sir William returned, but he'd find her under the bed or behind the drapes.

Perish it—how was she going to get herself and Dash out of this foul house?

She needed a weapon!

She rubbed her hands along her chilled arms. The fire was

low in the grate; obviously Sir William wished to torture her with the cold. . . .

The fire!

Hope, hot and exciting, rushed through her veins.

What better weapon than fire? The damage it could cause . . . and in the confusion, she could find Dash and—

And potentially perish. What if she trapped herself and Dash in an inferno? And what of Lady Farthingale, who was locked in the basement? What if there were other women trapped in this wretched house?

As much as this horrid place deserved to be leveled to ash, she wouldn't set the house on fire.

But she had to do something.

And the fireplace beckoned—there were no flames, only a red glow flickering amongst the charred logs.

Only charred logs were left, but one would be good enough. One piece had broken off and fallen into the grate. She stripped off a pillowcase and then wrapped it around her right hand. Clenching her teeth, she plucked up the smoldering log. Warmth radiated through the cloth. She grasped the log as tight as she could. Holding it like a lance, she charged at the window.

The impact wrenched her shoulder, and she yelled in both pain and triumph. A long crack snaked up the pane of glass. She hit it again and again until it shattered. Small pieces exploded outward, raining down over the terrace below.

Long, jagged pieces stayed in place.

"'Ere!" called a masculine voice outside her door. "What're you playing at?"

The rattle of the doorknob warned she didn't have much time. Gently, using her cloth, she wobbled the largest shard of glass back and forth. The putty holding it broke and crumbled. She worked the spike of glass free.

The door swung wide, and heavy footsteps charged in. She spun, her weapon held behind her back. The florid-faced servant looked as solid as a wall. His gaze snapped from the broken window to her discarded log. "Twit," he snapped. "Those bars can't be broken."

She launched at him, swinging wildly at his neck.

"Bloody 'ell!" he shrieked.

Her baby's life was at stake. Dash's life was at stake. She slashed. She felt the glass hit flesh, but she couldn't bear to look and see what damage she'd caused. Blood splattered her thin chemise, and she fought nausea. Instead, she sprinted past him as he clutched at his throat.

She couldn't have killed him, but she'd stunned him. But as she reached the doorway, she collided with a body racing in.

"Bloody hell!" Maryanne screamed herself as she slammed into a soft chest and rebounded back. The strong scent of sherry hit her. Georgiana stumbled back and wiped her lips, leaving a stain of red on her white satin gloves. She blinked tears and then stared dumbfounded at the guard who had sagged back against the wall.

"How in heaven—?" Georgiana broke off. She had been into the sherry. Remorse? Or too many victory drinks?

Maryanne yanked her hand back as her former friend reached for it.

"I must get you out of here," Georgiana implored as Maryanne darted around her. Yanking up her skirts, Georgiana ran after her. "He's mad. Utterly mad."

"Oh, have you discovered he intends to chain you up and force you to lick his boots?"

Georgiana almost stumbled into a table and clamped her hand brutally tight on Maryanne's wrist. "We must get away. I have a pistol."

Maryanne understood at once. If Georgiana had her as hostage, she had power.

"I can't leave Dash. He'll be killed if I escape."

"I've bribed two grooms to have my carriage ready—I'm stealing my own carriage! And you are coming with me."

"No." She had the shard of glass—nothing else!

She slowed, but Georgiana dragged her forward. Turning the corner, Maryanne gasped. Three large servants were racing toward them.

Georgiana raised the pistol with one hand, but the muzzle wobbled wildly. And as she fired, her arm kicked up in the air.

"Grab them!" one footman shouted, even as the ball shot past his ear and exploded harmlessly into the plaster wall. "The master wants her ladyship now."

Maryanne's hand tightened on her piece of glass, and she felt the pain of her skin parting. The wetness of blood. Georgiana's pistol was spent, and though she clobbered one of the footmen over the head with it, he quelled her with a hard punch to her jaw. Georgiana fell back like a sack of coal.

Two servants bore down on Maryanne—Ball, the man who had captured her at first, and the one who had thrust her into the bedchamber.

She couldn't fight three men with a piece of glass.

To keep the glass hidden meant she would have a weapon when she was dragged to Sir William. She fisted her hands in the skirt of her shift as the men grabbed her.

Courage. She must believe in herself.

"Now, my pretty," muttered Ball, "you'll get to see his lordship whipped within an inch of his life."

Maryanne's legs sagged, and she almost collapsed as her courage dropped away.

22

The lash whistled through the air and struck his flesh, slicing a burning line, a diagonal blaze across weeping vertical wounds.

Bent on one knee, Dash flinched as pain shrieked through him. Given that he'd enjoyed several erotic whippings in his life, he should be bloody able to bear this. Sir William wanted to decorate his back with an artistic pattern of pouring blood.

Maryanne—was she safe? She had to be. The bastard wanted to torture him; Sir William wouldn't hurt Maryanne without doing it in front of him.

He slumped forward on his knees. Hell, what kind of husband was he if he could not get free?

He couldn't lose her.

He'd spent a lifetime waiting for the final blow to fall, waiting to get caught in the trap that would finally kill him.

Now he wanted to live . . . he damn well yearned to live.

He wanted to hold Maryanne. He wanted to watch her grow big with their child. He wanted to watch her hold their baby. He wanted to watch her hair go gray and know they'd spent a lifetime together—

The whip hit again, but the pain—hell, that pain was nothing.

"Soon your wife will be coming to watch this delightful display," Sir William goaded. "She will soon see how helpless you are. She will watch you suffer, knowing she is going to die."

No. No, Maryanne was not going to die because of him. There had to be a way.

"How should I kill her? Like Eliza Charmody?"

Dash fought the rising vomit. "Touch her and I'll tear your heart out."

"Will you, now, Dashiel? I don't think so." The whip whistled—the tail hit the floor beside him. God help him, he flinched, and he gritted his teeth as Sir William laughed.

Dash found the strength to growl, "Why in the name of God are you doing this? Have you hated me all my life? Are you doing this for my blasted uncle?"

Sir William paced around Dash until he stood in front of him. "You have no idea, do you, you arrogant sot?"

"No, you piece of scum, I do not." He had to suck in a deep breath, and he shifted his head to send his sweat-soaked hair dangling over his eyes. To hide the pain they must reveal.

Sir William lifted the whip. The flick of the tale riveted Dash's gaze. He flinched again, and triumph spread across the magistrate's face.

The one man he had thought he could trust.

What sort of nightmare was his life? His uncle, aunt, and cousin wanted him dead. And the man who had acted as a father, a mentor, a confidante—the man who had kept him sane wanted to torture him.

To kill him.

"You aren't going to win," Dash spat. When he'd been a boy, there had been many nights when he'd thought his uncle would win. When Dash had been willing to give up, just to stop the fear.

He had one light in his life. One reason to wake up in the morning.

Maryanne. He was not going to lose his chance for happiness with Maryanne.

Dash threw himself forward, threw all his remaining strength into launching himself at Sir William. But the bastard danced aside.

Two servants hauled him back into place as Sir William propped his booted foot on a low table of iron and oak.

His torture was being carried out in an elegant parlor. Thin lace curtains shielded the windows. Two bulky servants played guard outside the locked double doors.

"Miss Westmoreland."

Dash frowned. "Amanda? If this is revenge over Amanda's death, you have to believe I didn't kill her. I didn't care who she loved, who she intended to run away with—"

Sir William gave an evil chuckle. "Of course you didn't kill her. I did."

"Why—Jesus!"

The whip sliced toward his head, and he jerked to the side. With the blasted wood strapped over his shoulders, he was awkward, unbalanced. He toppled to the floor in a twisted position, the edge of the yoke jammed against the floor.

"I kept her, you see. All these years. I couldn't keep her if she was alive—she loved you. You! You cast her aside, and she still loved you. I offered her everything—my heart, my soul, my wealth, position, children. Everything a woman could want. But she would rather pine for you, be alone and miserable, instead of accepting me. But I loved her. Adored her—the senseless witch."

Sir William had loved Amanda? Dash grimaced as he tightened his gut muscles to pull the yoke off the floor and right himself. "But why kill her? How could you do that if you loved her?"

"It was the only way I could keep her with me."

"You kept a corpse with you?" Dash's blood chilled with horror. Christ Jesus, he had to get Maryanne out of here. How?

"I kept her with me, but I realized I was willing to give her up at last. And I wanted to see your face when Society accused you of killing her. For you did—you captured her heart, and you destroyed her—"

"I had to protect her from my blasted uncle." The irony hit him cold. Anger burned through him. Why did Amanda have to lose her life, her future, because of a madman?

But Sir William paced in front of him. As though considering sentence. "Had you not wondered why I never married, or did you never trouble your shallow, drink-sodden mind to consider me?"

Dash groaned as he straightened so that his torso was upright and he was sitting on his haunches. "I assumed your tastes—"

"You thought me homosexual. Ah, no. I appreciate the beauty of both young boys and young girls—the taste of them, the softness of their skin. But Amanda, with her spun-silk hair, her ruby lips, her sapphire eyes . . . she was ethereal. A treasure." Cold and ruthless, Sir William's eyes glinted behind the spectacles. "Your wife is not as lovely. Common and plain. She hides her fear—it will be a delight to break her."

Maryanne! "Why now?" Dash knew he had to keep Sir William talking. "Why give up Amanda now? Why try to make me look like a murderer?"

"Ah." A playful smile. "It was so easy to torment you. You stole Amanda's heart; she cried out your name as she died, even as she looked into my eyes and I told her how much I loved her." Fury blazed suddenly in Sir William's eyes. "She lied to me. The bitch asked me for advice, hung on my every word, made me believe she loved me and she needed me. And she turned me down for you. I've hated you always for that. I offered love—precious, sincere devotion—and you . . . you fuck whores. You are sick and perverted."

Dash bit his tongue. Sick and perverted couldn't begin to describe this lunatic he had once thought a great and just man.

"And Georgiana—what was she supposed to do for you? Was she supposed to lure Maryanne to me? Why?"

"I needed a distraction for you . . . and Georgiana provided me with an innocent. One with whorish tendencies—"

"Blast you!" Dash roared. He would not listen to this bastard insult his wife.

The whip flayed his chest, and he roared again, curling in to protect his bare skin.

"And then you married her." Sir William chuckled. "It was magnificent. I hadn't counted on that. I needed a victim to turn you once more into a stupid, dashing knight."

"But why now?" Dash demanded, rising, even if it meant another wound.

Sir William threw aside the whip. He strolled to the desk, opened a drawer. Dash knew what the gleaming wood case was even before the magistrate opened it.

Dueling pistols.

But, given the blackguard had no honor, he withdrew them both himself. "Primed and loaded in preparation. One ball for your heart. One for your wife's." The silver barrel leveled at Dash's chest. "You asked me why? Because I am dying, Swansborough. No physician in Harley Street can save me. I will stand on the dock before God and be judged. But I could not leave this earth and let you go unpunished."

"For what sin?" he demanded.

"For stealing the woman I loved from me." Sir William cocked the pistol.

Dash tensed his muscles, ready to jump aside—

The door flew open. "Here is her ladyship," Ball announced.

Dash's heart skipped a beat as Ball pushed Maryanne into the room. Blood spattered her shift and her face. God, was it hers?

She screamed as she saw him.

Another servant rushed in the open door, a scrawny-looking boy. "There's been riders spotted, master. Approaching."

Sir William frowned. He threw aside the whip, drew out a pistol from his pocket. "Ball, take the men and intercept them."

Riders? Hell, could it be men from Swansley? Then Dash's blood ran cold. Could it be Moredon? Christ, if it was his brother-in-law, what in blazes was he doing riding into danger?

Sir William slammed the door. "Now we are alone. Though I suspect you would not mind an audience, would you, you tarty wench."

Fury boiled in Dash as Sir William pulled Maryanne close. She winced and tried to pull away.

Sir William's hand yanked up her tattered skirt. "I am going to cut you to pieces, my dear. And you will feel every slice of my blade—"

"No!" Dash launched forward, swinging the wooden yoke strapped to him.

"No!" Maryanne cried, and she slapped Sir William's face.

Blood ran from a slash across his cheek.

Sir William clapped his hand to his face. "What in blazes . . . ?" He aimed the pistol at Maryanne's head. Grinned. "Stop where you are, Dashiel."

Dash froze.

"Good. Now retreat. Get down on your knees."

Dash's gaze met Maryanne's terrified brown eyes. He knew he had no choice but to go back and kneel.

"I have one shot." Sir William laughed. "Now who should I use it on? Dashiel, I think. Not to kill, but only to maim—"

Footsteps pounded outside the door, voices shouted, and the doors flew open. Sir William jerked the pistol toward the door. Bound, his body screaming in pain, Dash spun, too. Maryanne, thank heaven, had the good sense to leap away.

But Sir William quickly swung the pistol to point at her back.

A shot fired, and Dash's brain almost exploded in panic. Confused, he saw Sir William scream in agony and reached for his leg.

Dash leaped forward, twisting as he did, and slammed the yoke into the back of Sir William's head. The pistol roared, but the barrel pointed at the floor. The ball slammed into the floor at the exact moment Sir William's skull cracked into the low table on which he'd propped his boots.

Deafened by the explosion of the shot, Dash didn't hear the impact of bone and wood, but he saw Sir William roll off to the side. Blood spurted from the wound, and before his eyes, Sir William's gaze turned glassy.

Dead.

"Dash! Oh, Dash!" Maryanne was racing toward him, darting around furniture. Stunned, Dash realized that Trent and Moredon were at her heels. And another man. . . .

A man with a scarlet kerchief tied around his neck and wild, long, gray hair. The man who had fired the pistol at Sir William.

The famed and scandalous artist of erotica, Rodesson.

Rodesson rushed forward to embrace his daughter.

But Maryanne cried, "You must help Dash get free!" She spun and glared down at Sir William's body.

"Don't look, sweetheart," Dash pleaded as he stumbled toward her.

But she didn't scream. Or faint. Or turn white. She stamped her foot. "If he wasn't dead, I'd kill him myself."

"Oh, love." Dash felt a mad chuckle rise in his throat. "And what in blazes did you cut him with?"

"This!" She held up a shard of glass. "I broke it out of the window when he locked me in the bedroom."

"You, my wonderful wife, are the bravest person I have ever known."

She brushed at tears. "You are. You've endured hell. . . ."

He did not want Maryanne to see his carved-up back, so he edged around. He jerked his gaze up to his two brothers-in-law and his father-in-law. Trent's brow lifted—Dash didn't even want to think of how gruesome he looked with the yoke and chains in place and blood running over his flesh.

Trent nodded. "Our men have the servants rounded up—and your steward has brought the runners Sir William was using. They had no idea what was actually happening. And we also have Georgiana. We'll turn the lot of them over to the local magistrate."

Dash lifted his shoulders. "Before that, would you mind unlocking me? I would like to hold my wife."

Several hours passed like a blur. Sir Jasper Dayle was the magistrate, and his lovely, adept wife, Lady Dayle, tended to Dash's wounds. Though Dash protested, Maryanne insisted on helping. He made it damned difficult for her because he kept stopping her to hold her hand, to kiss her lips.

For the rest of his life, Dash was going to keep Maryanne close. He was going to touch her, kiss her, cuddle her. Treasure her. Despite Sir Jasper's invitation to stay the night, Dash knew he wanted to be home. For once, returning home didn't fill him with dread.

Even with his uncle still there.

Home felt like home now, simply because it was the home he shared with Maryanne.

The carriages were prepared, with Trent assisting weak Lady Farthingale, who cried helplessly for her "master" and clutched the clothes given to her by Lady Dayle.

As Maryanne helped Dash down to Sir Jasper's drive, she suddenly whispered, "Come with me."

Surprised, he did. Twining her fingers with his, she led him onto the lawns to the wide trunk of an ancient oak. Gray-brown branches, bare of leaves, reached for the pink-blushed sky as Maryanne leaned back against the tree. Though he felt damned confused, he knew an opportunity when he had one—he pulled her to him, cradled her face, and kissed her.

There wouldn't be a chance in the carriage—they'd be sharing it with Trent.

Dash reveled in the delight of holding her close.

Soft hair brushing his fingertips. Her hot lips on his. Her tongue—a tease that had his cock standing up in an instant. A jolt of pain hit him as the skin wounded by wax drips rubbed against his clothes. He blocked out the pain, wrapped his leg around hers, dropped a hand to her low back, and held her to him.

He was never going to let her go.

Heat flooded his soul from their joined mouths. The dying sun painted the snow pink, and a breeze sent branches clacking together.

He eased from her delightful, addictive mouth. "We should return to the warm carriage," he began, but her lashes swept over her large brown eyes, and the horror of what might have been swept over him.

"Thank heaven Marcus arrived and followed your note to Whitby Manor." She shivered.

"And your father—he charged in to rescue you."

"Yes, he did." Her brows drew together. "He claims you invited him to visit Swansley."

"I did." Dash cupped her face again, his big hands following the point of her chin, her fragile jaw, her pink cheeks. "Maryanne, I love you. I was so afraid to admit it. So afraid that something would happen to you, that I'd lose you, or taint you, or hurt you. As it's happened to everyone I've loved—"

"Stop that! It's rubbish."

He jerked back. He'd poured out his soul. She'd called it rubbish.

She wagged a finger at him, suddenly the bookish Maryanne once more, but a fiery and determined version. "It's not your fault Miss Westmoreland died. Or that Sir William was a mad fiend. Or that Anne lost her baby. Or that your parents died because your father was reckless. Bad things have happened *to* you, not *because* of you. But regardless, you must look forward. You must go on and embrace happiness and pleasure. Don't you see that for all these years, your uncle had won?"

"Won? How?"

"He didn't get the title, but he killed you inside," she said. "And you just cannot allow that to happen. You cannot allow Sir William, or your uncle, or even fate, to win." She took a deep breath, her chest rising. "I did exactly the same thing! I was my mother's mistake. Her regret. I trapped her utterly and completely; I was proof that her love was folly, but one she could never escape."

"That can't be true."

"It is. She was pregnant with Venetia when she ran away to marry Rodesson."

A tear sparkled in her eye. "I represented her recognition that she would foolishly love Rodesson for the rest of her life."

"Sweetheart—"

"No, Dash. Let me explain. My mother lived in Maidenswode, pretending to be the wife of a man who had traveled to India to make his fortune. She also pretended to travel to Plymouth to meet him when he returned to visit, but it was all an elaborate fabrication to explain the times she spent with Rodesson. It was all a terrible risk—the truth would have destroyed her reputation, her life. But she still took that risk. And then she became pregnant with me—"

"Maryanne, I saw the way she looked at you in the church." Dash wiped away her tear. "She loves you. She's proud of you. And Rodesson was beside himself with fear over you. He came to your rescue, he shot Sir William, and even I can see he can barely hold in tears." Sentiments Dash could never lay claim to. His father had been absorbed in his own excitement, and his mother had been devoted to her friends and her social conquests. Dash had wanted Maryanne to find happiness with her father. He brushed Maryanne's damp, full lip with his thumb. Precious. She was so precious to him.

Her large eyes held his, beseeching, honest, filled with concern. No one had looked at him like this—as though she wanted to free his heart and soul.

"Perhaps she does love me," she whispered. "But what I realized is that it doesn't matter. What matters about my life is not where I came from but where I am going. What I will do. Our present, our future—that is what is important. You were forged to be so incredibly strong—forged by your past.

I would wish you a different past, but that would mean you would be a different man. And I love you, the man you are, so very much."

"Our present and our future will be perfect," he vowed.

But she shook her head. "Perhaps not—there will be sad times. There must be—it is part of life. I spent my life insulating myself from the world, living it through the emotions I read in books. Yet I learned from those stories, too; I realized that I experienced the points of view of others, and that has given me perspective. But I know that I want to experience life. Our present and our future will be rich and wonderful because we share it—"

"And it will be filled with love. That I can promise." He kissed her once more. The cold air didn't touch him. He didn't care about the dark or the wind or the snorts of the carriage horses and the creak of the wheels on the snow.

She broke away from the kiss. Astounded, he watched as she undid the lower buttons of her pelisse.

"Do you remember the morning we followed Harriet?"

Threesomes . . . ? It was the first thought in his head. They had spoken about threesomes. Arousal and protectiveness hit him with the force of a blunt object. He couldn't share Maryanne.

She began lifting her skirts.

"It's freezing, love. Stop that."

"We'll be pressed close together, and you can wrap your coat around us both to keep us warm."

She wanted to make love outdoors. The way they'd spoken about teasingly. His cock lurched against his clothes, reminding him of wounded skin.

But he wanted her so much, he didn't care about the pain.

Twilight whispered over the soft snow as he undid his trousers. Closing his eyes, gritting his teeth, he grasped his sore but rigid cock and brushed the head against her wet, hot nether lips. She wriggled, he pushed, she squirmed, and he thrust inside.

Filling her.

Joining them.

Madness, to make love outside in the freezing cold—but their thrusting bodies and wild kisses warmed them. His grunts and her soft moans carried on the night air, but he didn't care if his friends waiting at the carriage heard.

He grasped two handfuls of cloth-covered derriere and guided her along his thick, hard staff.

"Oh, yes. Like that! There!" she cried, and he laughed joyously into the crook of her neck. His bold and determined wife knew exactly what she wanted.

"I'm coming," she whispered fiercely. "Coming! Coming!" She chanted the word as she rocked against him. As her lashes fluttered and her mouth gasped for air. As her tight, creamy cunny clutched at his cock.

He gripped her arse and exploded deep inside her. He had to fall back against the oak to support his shaking legs. Pleasure melted his limbs and his brain and his soul. His climax sent the world rocking beneath his feet, and he shouted up to the stars peeking into the deep blue sky.

Laughing, still shuddering, he found her lips again. But before he claimed them, he understood. "It was worth living my past to win you, Maryanne."

"I love you, Dash." She brushed at tears. "Though perhaps I would have avoided the more scandalous aspects of mine if I'd known you would be my future."

"Don't wish that." Understanding deepened for him. "I love everything you've done—the courage you've had. The strength. Your creativity. I love you for the magnificent and complex woman you are."

She tensed in his arms. "You truly feel that way?"

"Yes, I do."

23

All she longed for was a hot bath. And food! It was Christmas Day, and normally she would begin the day with church, not escape from a sexually perverse madman. Cuddling with Dash in the heated carriage, Maryanne touched her tummy as it growled. Twinges of nausea hit her still in her hunger.

But she whispered, "I am so happy you are safe, little one."

Dash's hand, bare of gloves, pressed gently on top of hers. She glanced up to share his smile. Love. Relief. Joy. Exhaustion. All showed plainly in his dark eyes.

She had once thought his black eyes dark and mysterious. Now she looked at them and felt as if she could read his thoughts.

"I think I want food first. Roast goose. Sugarplums. Stewed plums. Marzipan. And mince pie."

"And a cup of wassail," Dash added. "The steward makes ours from his father's recipe."

She licked her lips, and he did the same. They laughed together as the carriage stopped. Despite his wounds, which must be agony, Dash clambered down and reached up to help her. Trent followed.

All the servants stood outside!

As Maryanne's feet touched the snowy drive, someone shouted, "Hurrah! Three cheers for his lordship and her ladyship! And Happy Christmas!" Everyone cheered. Caps flew up in the air. Smiles and laughter and tears broke out all around.

But Dash rushed her into the warm house. "It is so good to be home with you," he said, and her heart sang. Henshaw followed, and Dash instructed him to ensure Lady Farthingale was cared for and drinks served for the servants. "And bring Maryanne food at once," Dash ordered.

Maryanne watched kindly maids lead Lady Farthingale away. She would ensure that doctors helped Lady Farthingale, ensure that the poor woman recovered from Sir William's cruelty.

"Maryanne!" Venetia rushed forward and hugged her. "Thank heavens you are safe."

Dash's hand slid around her waist as Venetia let her go. "Your brilliant sister saved herself."

"As you did, Venetia," Marcus added.

Venetia wiped away tears. "Of course, I knew she would. What else would one expect from one of Rodesson's daughters?"

"And I've lost my taste for adventure," Maryanne admitted. She leaned forward and whispered to her sister, "And Georgiana was involved but has been caught. No more erotica."

"I hope not." Dash laughed. "Though I'd like you to write it for me."

Startled, Maryanne swung round on her grinning husband. "Dashiel."

He waggled his dark brows, but before she could say another word, Anne embraced her. And so did Sophia. Both women hugged Dash, and Anne then flung herself against her husband's chest and openly wept. His grace, the Duke of Ashton, stood at Sophia's side.

Her mother stepped forward. Maryanne's throat dried, and she knew the tears would come. Her mother's eyes were red and swollen, and she cradled little Richard in her arms.

"I spoke with Venetia," Olivia whispered. "I am so very sorry if I hurt you, Maryanne. I always loved you. Always. You were so sweet, so quiet; you were such a treasure. You have always been my strength, my rock, so calm and happy and so willing to try to make peace for all of us."

"I know, Mother," Maryanne spluttered. "I realized how foolish I was."

"And your father has always loved you. I was the one who did not want him to be part of your life."

Blinking away tears, Maryanne turned to Rodesson.

"My beautiful girl," he exclaimed and joined her mother in hugging her.

Baby Richard stirred in his grandmother's arms; his lips worked. Tiny lips, glossy with spittle and marred by a little sucking blister. "My sweet little grandson," Olivia cooed.

Olivia blinked, and the winter sunlight touched tears on her mother's cheeks. Rodesson laid his hands on Olivia's shoulders. He nuzzled her cheek. "Let me take you to Italy, my love. Let me make up for all these years. Make it a gift to me on this special day."

How destructive it was to carry the pain of the past forever. It had burdened Dash with painful guilt. It had rendered his uncle weak and confused, a mere shell of a man. It had turned Sir William into a demented madman.

And here, her parents were seeking a new beginning. A new love. It was never too late, after all.

Rodesson drew back from the kiss and his eyes shone with hope. His hand cradled her mother's cheek.

"I will go," Olivia whispered. "I've always wanted adventure."

"And I promise to show you grand adventures, Olivia."

"Where is Grace?" Maryanne glanced about, but Grace's spun-gold hair could not be seen. Grace was the most like their mother, dainty and beautiful, and Maryanne suspected she had been the daughter to enchant Rodesson the most. He had painted for them all several times, pictures to be hidden away from curious eyes in the country village—not because they were rude, but because of the artist's name.

She remembered all those things now—the small things her father had done. A gift of ribbons, of paintings, of a doll with a painted porcelain face. She had dismissed all those things. Without making a grand gesture, how could her father truly have loved her?

Dash had risked death for her, had come to her rescue, had promised to pay her debts—all grand gestures. Yet it was the simple shared smiles that made for sweet memories and enchanted her the most.

"Grace is visiting with friends—in the country."

Was her mother just a bit evasive? But Olivia smiled and hugged her once more. "Thank heaven. For everything," Olivia whispered. "For you being safe. For you marrying a wonderful, wealthy viscount."

And for the besotted way Rodesson was looking at Olivia? Perhaps that, too. Maryanne glanced around. "Dash, your aunt and uncle are not here."

He looked questioningly to Sophia.

"They, along with your cousin, are preparing to leave." Sophia brushed back a white plume on her jaunty hat. "For once, they seem stricken with guilt."

"I need to speak with them first."

Maryanne felt Dash's hand at her elbow, and she moved away from her parents—to see them share a quick kiss and then glance guiltily around. "The kissing bough," Maryanne whispered to her mother. "In the ballroom."

Her mother blushed, but her hazel eyes twinkled.

Dash murmured, "I'd ask you to come with me, but you should eat."

"No, I want to go with you," she insisted, and she rushed upstairs alongside him, amazed at the way he took the stairs, considering the pain he'd endured. "Doesn't your back hurt? Do you really wish to see them? How can you be so strong?"

He clasped her hand in his as they reached the top of the steps. "You are with me. At my side. That's where I find my strength."

Maryanne expected a confrontation with his uncle, and she held her spine straight in anticipation, but Dash went to the door she believed was his aunt's.

And the gray-haired harridan opened it.

It is Christmas. You must be more charitable, warned an inner voice.

"So you survived, Swansborough," his aunt Helena observed. She had a plain brown gown folded over her arm.

"Indeed." He pressed forward into the room, forcing his aunt to retreat. "I'm extremely difficult to kill."

Maryanne followed him in, and he leaned over her to click the door shut as his aunt turned away. Frail shoulders greeted them. A neck with deep shadows along the tendons. His aunt shuffled toward her bed.

"I never agreed with hurting you, Swansborough," she said as she laid her dress on the counterpane. "Twice you survived accidents because I could not bear to watch a young boy be hurt. But then you grew—what sort of gentleman are you? Licentious and wild. Lavish with your spending, careless with your estate—"

"I hated this place because of the memories attached—memories you gave me," Dash broke in. "But I have never been careless with it; it has been improved, repaired, and cared for. All my estates are cared for. And I didn't come here to debate the merits of hereditary peerages." Dash moved toward the bed, his steps slow, his voice a deep, soothing murmur. "You have to tell them the truth. My uncle and Robert. They both must know what really happened to Simon."

Maryanne frowned. "Yes!" she cried. "Dash was not responsible—"

His aunt turned. Sheer panic touched Helena Blackmore's eyes. "I cannot. They'll hate me. Condemn me. His mistress lives in our house. He's mad."

Dash bent to Maryanne's ear and murmured, "My aunt was the one to arrange for the attack, the false ransom note, and the trap that killed my cousin."

"But why?" Maryanne glared at his aunt. How could this woman do such a horrid thing?

"To give my uncle his lifelong dream." Dash held up a quelling finger as Maryanne parted her lips. In truth, she didn't know what to say. She wanted to throw his aunt out of the house, but as she faced the woman, she saw at once how great a price she had paid. "But if your uncle doesn't know . . . ?"

Dash turned to his aunt. "I cannot keep this secret for you. My uncle thinks me a murderer. As does Robert."

Vehemently Helena Blackmore shook her head. Her hands shook. "I cannot do it. . . . They would despise me, and they are all that I have."

"It was a mistake." Even as Maryanne spoke the words, she could not believe she was offering sympathy and support to this woman. But she would. She saw the glow in Dash's glittering black eyes. The admiration.

"We will go together," Maryanne promised. "Face them together."

"Why would you?" Helena asked.

"It can be too frightening to confront the truth and face its consequences alone. When you arrived, in the drawing room . . ." Maryanne paused. She would not think of the vicious insults. "Both your husband and son love you. Both care about you. Your husband needs you. They both do."

She slipped her arms around the frail woman's waist and bit back an instinctive surge of anger—but not over the insults to her. Rather, over the horrid way these people had destroyed Dash's childhood. But there had to be peace. She might never let them over the threshold of Swansley again—she would *never* embrace them as family—but she understood that peace had to replace dark, consuming hatred.

Dash nodded. Maryanne tucked his aunt's gnarled hand in the crook of her arm.

* * *

"Where is Maryanne?" Rodesson asked as he filled his glass with brandy from Dash's decanter.

"Bathing." Dash propped his boots on his desk and eased back in his chair. He felt the point where it was in perfect balance, on its hind legs, and let it hover there.

"You didn't join her?" asked Trent as he finished his drink.

"Not with my back bandaged up." At least they hadn't bandaged his cock. Which grew, thickened, and strained painfully in his trousers. Closing his eyes, he imagined Maryanne in the bath—veiled by rose-scented steam, droplets of water running down her lips, the curves of her breasts. Droplets clinging to her ivory skin. Squeezing out the cloth and gently swirling it between her thighs, rubbing the roughness against her clit—

He forced the image to vanish.

He took the glass Rodesson handed him, sipped the French brandy. "I've had women tie me up," Dash mused. "I've been whipped, chained, paddled, bitten . . . I've even had hot wax dripped on me—"

"And you talked me into that one, you bastard," Trent complained, then took a long draught of his ale.

"But even chained up, I was still in control." Dash laughed. "Maryanne is the only woman with whom I've felt out of control. She ties me in knots—without using any rope. Twists me in circles. Turns me on my head. She stormed into my uncle's bedroom and forced both my aunt and uncle to agree to reconciliation. She warned my blasted uncle that he was not to punish my aunt over Simon's death, that they must work together to find the strength to endure it. She's remarkable."

Trent swung his glass so it collided with his. "Swansborough, it appears you have fallen in love with your wife."

"Of course he has." Rodesson tipped back his glass and took a drink. "She is my daughter."

Dash grinned, but that smile disappeared. "How is Harriet?"

He'd already sent messages to Bow Street, directed to Mr. Axby, who worked beneath Sir William. He was certain Axby would have already stopped Craven and rescued his innocent prisoner in London.

"Sleeping off laudanum," answered Moredon. "But she'll survive."

Dash set down his empty glass. "Then, if you will excuse me, gentlemen, I have something to ask my wife."

"Destroy all the black, my lord?" The voice of Dash's valet rose peevishly as Maryanne slipped into the parlor connecting her bedchamber and Dash's room. Her hair was loose and still a bit damp, though her practical flannel wrapper covered her from chin to toe.

"Get rid of it," Dash insisted from behind the partly open door to his bedchamber. "The shirts, the waistcoats, the cravats. I no longer have the desire to look like a combination of Satan and a mourner."

"Am I to save the tailcoats and trousers, my lord?"

Dash gave an impatient sigh. "Of course."

"And the chance to order new . . ." trilled the valet. "It brings a tear to my eye."

Suddenly Dash strolled into the parlor—he caught her eye and winked. Then closed the door firmly behind him, separating him from the busy valet. He strode into her room.

He was half dressed—in a white shirt open at the neck and buff trousers that caressed the lines of his thighs, the enticing curve of his rump. She drew a deep breath.

"But black is your signature, is it not?" she asked. "Every matron in London spoke of your devilish obsession with black. And I admit, it hurt me when you began wearing it again after our wedding."

"Maryanne—"

She held up her hand to quell him, to ask him to give her the truth. "I understand now, I think. Were you mourning Simon or your ruined youth?

"Both, perhaps." He sat on the edge of her bed and held out his hand. "I don't feel as though I am in mourning anymore. Not now that you have come into my life, Maryanne."

"That is so . . ." It was as if doves took flight inside her. To think she had made such an impact. It stunned her. "Wait right there."

He leaned back on the bed, propped on his elbow, all six delicious feet of him sprawled over her ivory silk sheets. And she shook in her slippers as she went to her wardrobe and dipped to slide out her secret from beneath it.

Maryanne's cheeks were hot as she returned to Dash holding her muslin wrapped package "I smuggled it in—and it was the very devil to do so. I couldn't risk having a maid find it during the unpacking. But I have a small compartment in my case."

Dash's mind ran riot. A whip? A large dildo? What would be Maryanne's secret? Slowly she drew the muslin down, revealing curled pages, and then finally she flicked the translucent material away to reveal a stack of paper with an ivory ribbon tied around it. She picked it up, cradled it, and then handed it to him.

Handwriting, tight and neat, covered the first page. The writing angled in every direction as though the notes had been added haphazardly and at different times. Then he picked out the words: *A Novel by M. Hamilton.*

"This is your book. You wrote all this yourself?" He patted the bed beside him.

"Yes." She laughed.

But it still seemed miraculous to him. That she had created a story and diligently set all these words to the page.

"No one has ever read it before. I've never shown it to anyone. I was always too afraid to let anyone see it. But I would like you to read it." She ducked her head, cheeks pink. "You see, it is an erotic story."

"Hell," he muttered, instantly erect, lusty, yet completely astonished.

"You must wonder why I did it," she hurried on. "And I really cannot say. I edited those stories for the courtesans who wrote for us, and I . . . I felt a compulsion to put down words myself. To tell a story. Of course, since it is an erotic story, I was hampered by a certain lack of experience." She stood by the bedpost, her arm curled around it.

Too shy to join him while he read her book? "Not anymore." He grinned, sat up, and spread his legs. "Come and cuddle between my thighs while I read."

"I don't know. You may find parts that are . . . silly."

"I doubt that, love."

"Or physically impossible."

God, he was hard with anticipation. As he turned to the first page, he watched Maryanne. A curl brushed her cheek, she looked so sweetly demure. Then he looked to the first lines.

I was brought into the ballroom by my guardian, his lordship. Gauche in my uncertainty, I feared only one thing—disappointing him. He had dressed me in a low-necked gown of white, gauzy silk, one that revealed my every curve when I stood in front of candlelight! A fanciful corset trimmed in scarlet narrowed my waist until it was merely as wide as the span of my hand. My breasts, youthful and firm, spilled over the top.

And his lordship had the advantage of height—he could see down my dress. That made me blush, yet excited me, too. I wanted him to look.

I imagined the scene before I stepped through the doors. Thousands of candles! Dazzling debutantes in soft, brilliant silk, breezing through the gathering like flickering flames. And the gentlemen. Surely there would be handsome gentlemen to charm lovely ladies.

Oh, the room was indeed bathed with light. But the women were nude. And bound with lengths of black silk. Rows and rows of nude, bound women crouched on their knees, waiting to pleasure gentlemen with their mouths.

Startled, confused, and oddly hot, I looked to my guardian. My heart beat faster as his lordship grinned, as unabashed at the sight of depravity and sin as the Devil.

"Welcome, sweet nymph, to pleasure—"

Entranced, Dash had to breathe deeply to slow his heart. "A sweet innocent in the power of a debauched rake?"

"It is not us." She jumped on the bed finally, vehemently shaking her head. "I didn't even . . ." A smile warbled on her lips. "I'm supposed to be 'Verity,' and the truth is that I did fantasize about you—for months before we 'met' at the hunt. But you aren't the devilish lordship in . . ." She sighed and crawled between his legs. "All right, you are."

Dash was touched to his soul.

"This is the point where I should put your story aside and make love to you until you scream my name and faint with passion," he teased. "But I have to admit, your story is too enticing to put down." And he read, " 'He walked me up and down the rows to observe the way the women delightedly sucked the men's swollen and rigid members. He remarked on the different techniques used by each courtesan. There were those that paid greatest attention to the head with lips and tongue and even teeth. And those that took the entire beast down the throats, as their eyes watered. It hardly seemed pleasurable, but it excited his lordship. His trousers tented out in front and—' "

"Stop," Maryanne admonished. "I hoped to sell many books and knew, of course, that I must depict male fantasies. But it sounds rather silly when you read it."

"I think you like making sport of male fantasies."

She smiled. "That is true."

He laid down the book. "Why not tell your fantasies? Why not reveal what a woman really wants?"

"Georgiana told me that a man would only want to publish fantasies that appealed to men—and our publisher, who actually typeset and created the books, was a gentleman, of course. That was why we had to be so subversive about showing how women reach orgasm."

Dash laughed. "I would like to know how to please you. How to give you your fantasies."

"But you already do." Brows drawn together, she pointed at the manuscript pages. "You are the hero of the story. You are my fantasy."

His heart simply ceased to beat.

"I love this," Maryanne whispered. "Being able to tease you. I would have never dared do this before meeting you."

"I can't believe that. You've always been bravely outspoken." He undid the belt of her wrapper, caught his breath as he flung open the sides and drank in the sight of her lovely, curvaceous, nude figure.

Smiling shyly, she fumbled with the buttons on his trousers. He helped her. "I wasn't though, truly," she remarked as she freed his cock. "I was only a saucy piece with you."

She stroked his shaft, and he dropped his head, eyes shut tight.

"Good," Dash murmured. "Because you, my love, are my fantasy. I fantasized about finding love, having a family of my own. A happy family. It seemed a dream I could never have."

He slid off the bed, darted around it with his hard cock jutting out. Her feet dangled over the edge of the bed, and suddenly, because he knew he should, he dropped to one knee in front of them, in the classic stance.

"What are you doing?"

"Proposing."

"But you already did."

"But I didn't ask the right question last time." Dash had hoped to form the right one, but his heart hammered too hard. "Maryanne, will you marry me and become my wife because I love you and because I cannot imagine living without you? You agreed to marry me out of duty. Now I'm asking you out of love."

"Oh, dear!"

Not the reaction he'd hoped for. "What?"

"I've forgotten what you actually said the first time. That's terrible, isn't it? You would think a woman would remember the words for the rest of her—"

"Maryanne, you haven't answered me yet."

"Yes, of course. Yes." Her voice wavered, rich and aching with joy. Tears sparkled in her large brown eyes. "Yes because I love you."

"I want to protect you for the rest of my life," he vowed.

But she shook her head. "The point of marriage is that we protect and nurture each other."

"Remember these words for the rest of your life, Maryanne. I love you."

She grasped his wrist and tugged him up, so Dash obeyed and joined Maryanne on her bed. "I'd like to read a little more of your story."

But she shook her head and playfully pushed him back on the bed. "I'd much rather act out our fantasies for real."

"One of mine is you on top," he suggested hopefully. And Dash groaned as she climbed on top of him and took his cock inside her, joining them.

She rode him, her body lit by sunlight, her face beautiful in pleasure. They arched together, slowly, languorously, and he wanted this—to spend a decadent afternoon in bed. Making love. Ah, he couldn't ask for a better Christmas.

He cupped Maryanne's face as she rocked on his shaft.

"You took away the pain of my past and showed me that all that matters is now and the future. Our future. Our family. And love."

And then she bent and kissed him.

Perfect happiness.

Forever after.

Epilogue

The door opened, and her abigail stepped back. Reflected in the mirror, Maryanne saw the girl dip in an obedient, if awed, curtsy, and then hasten to the door as Dash strode in. She understood the girl's trembling movements. He wore the most wicked smile. A heartbreaking smile.

"Lovely gown," he said. "Now take it off."

"Take it off? But we have supper guests. Have you forgotten there is to be a ball?"

"Sex first. Balls afterward."

"Sex! We can't have sex."

"I am both husband and viscount. I can command you to have sex. And I can't resist you or your lovely, remarkable, plump breasts anymore."

She sighed. Her breasts were huge now that she was feeding Charles, and Dash could not keep his hands off them. Though he had to be very, very gentle. "We'll smell of it," she protested. "It will be obvious to our guests—"

"We are married. We have a child—a beautiful, perfect son. Unless you had an immaculate conception, which leaves me out in the stable, I suspect they know how you came to have a baby."

Maryanne laughed helplessly as Dash pulled out a length of black silk from his pocket.

"What are you doing?" she protested as he prowled behind her and lifted the black silk to her eyes.

He draped the fabric over them, and she blinked, her lashes brushing softness.

"I love you," he murmured.

She stilled. Those simple words still had the power to make everything stop.

"Do you trust me?" he whispered.

"Yes, you know I do." She reached up and pulled off the blindfold. To her surprise Dash stood across the room holding a tiny wooden toy in his outstretched palm. It was a miniature horse with carved mane and tail, brightly painted with an endearing smile. Shyly Dash said, "I made this—for Charles."

"You made this?" She was astonished.

"You can write an entire book—I thought a viscount should be capable of carving a toy."

"It's lovely, Dash. Charles will adore it." She brushed at tears with the strip of silk as she imagined Charles's sweet, toothless smile as he clutched his new toy. "You are such a good father." And he was. He had been there at the birth to help her bring their son into the world. He had held her hand, encouraged her, soothed her, and gave her courage and strength.

As she'd squeezed his hand and pushed once more, then once more again, and "once more" for a few more times, she'd realized how deeply she trusted Dash.

"I know Rodesson was proud to have our child carry his name."

Maryanne took a shaky breath, trying to hold back tears. "And thank you so much, Dash, for being willing to do so."

He grinned. "I'm not afraid of a little scandal, my love."

"You do realize you will have to carve another of these—"

His brows shot up in astonishment, and she rushed to him and grasped his hand. "No, not for me! Not yet. For Anne."

"Anne?" He rocked back on his heels.

"She's expecting another child, Dash. She wrote me to tell me. She is already about six months along—she's been hiding it from you. She told me you would be impossible and commanding if you knew, so I should not tell you." Maryanne gave a shy grin. "But she will have to be angry with me—I can't keep secrets from you."

Impulsively she rushed to Dash, and he caught her to him in a strong embrace.

"I'm sure all will go well this time," she whispered, pressed to his hard body. "And I received a letter from Juliette—Lady Farthingale. She is with family in Hertfordshire and is recovering. It is slow progress—those three months had broken her—but I think she is finding her strength again."

Dash brushed a kiss to the top of her head. "Venetia and Marcus are expecting another babe. And your mother and father are enjoying the pleasures of Italy."

"And now it is Grace's turn," Maryanne added. "I hope Grace settles on a wonderful man and has a normal, safe courtship."

Dash groaned. "I doubt it."

"Let's go upstairs," she whispered. "And give Charles a kiss before dinner. And then we can come back here and make love."

She felt Dash's heartbeat speed up. Wearing a wicked smile, he took the piece of silk from her hand and dangled it before her eyes. "After all," he murmured as he bent to her mouth, "with a little bit of black silk, the possibilities are endless."

Turn the page for
Sharon Page's next book,
HOT SILK!
Coming soon from Aphrodisia!

Grace shrank back against the papered wall of the hallway, fighting the hot bile that clawed at her throat. He'd shared his horrible plans with Wynsome all along. It had been a joke, a wager, perhaps. And she'd stumbled right into it, a stupid, gullible girl.

How many other *gentlemen* knew? Did they all?

"She's a treat," Lord Wesley said with callous triumph. "Every bit as good as I conjectured, given that she was a virgin. A born trollop. And, as you will note, she makes my twentieth virgin of the year. Your blunt is at risk, Wynsome. I'll have bedded a hundred by Christmas."

She felt pinned to the wall by their appalling cruelty. This was sport to them.

"The rest of the club will be astounded. There's many who wagered more than they could afford, certain you'd never claim one hundred gently bred virgins."

The rest of the *club*? There were others, possibly dozens, of men involved in this? Men who would all talk of her ruination? This would destroy her. Oh God, what had she done?

All of society would know—every gentleman who had treated her as a gently bred young marriage prospect. Wynsome knew—would he tell the Earl of Warren about it? Would the handsome, white-haired earl sneer at her, calling her the horrid names he had used on her mother?

"What have you done, my dear?"

Grace gave a strangled scream at the deep male voice that repeated the very question she'd asked herself.

Devlin Sharpe had seen many frightened women in his day. Terrified women. Desperate women. He had seen the eyes of women as they stood on the gallows and waited for the platform to drop away.

But he'd never seen such a mix of fear and loathing and anger shooting from such beautiful and determined eyes. Of course, he did not think he'd ever seen such an intriguing woman before—an intoxicating, alluring mix of angelic golden hair, pretty features, and enticingly carnal curves.

He held the lovely blonde's gaze, aware from the way her eyes darted and her lips trembled that she intended to lie to him. "Don't lie," he warned. "Don't give me a weak story and try to run away. I want the truth. I want to know what—or who—has hurt you."

She straightened away from the wall and Devlin knew exactly what had happened. Her small fingers were curled around the crumpled sky-blue silk of her bodice, holding it up over her generous breasts. Beneath the wall sconce, her soft hair was gleaming gold and poured in disheveled curls over her shoulders and down her back. A tear still clung to her lashes of her red-rimmed green eyes. She smelled of sex.

Hearing his half-brother's mocking laugh from the study was the final piece of evidence. "Did he rape you? Or just seduce you?"

Furious at his damned brother, he'd let a snarl creep in and she drew back. "I should go," she whispered.

"Not through the corridors of a crowded house with your dress hanging off you. Come with me."

"Why?" Her golden brows drew together in suspicion. *Now* the woman was cautious.

"I can negotiate this house without anyone seeing us."

Obviously she could not understand why any man would wish to do her a kindness. She took another step away from him. "You . . . you are a highwayman, aren't you?"

"Of course I would never admit to that, Miss . . . what is your name, by the way?"

Since he'd first spotted her startling golden hair in the ballroom, and then indulged himself with a good look at the rest of her, he'd wondered. None of his father's servants had obliged him with a name—they'd been more interested in tossing him out on the gravel drive.

Pity they did not know the secret entrances to the house as he did.

"Your name," he repeated.

"If I do not tell you, it will be one less man who knows." Her lips formed a sneer at that, and he knew she meant her anger for herself.

What was it with some women that they absorbed their anger, instead of using it for some good? His mother had been like that—taking every blasted insult and slap his father had bestowed upon her and swallowing it up herself.

"I know my half-brother," Devlin stated, determined to place blame where it lay. "What did he promise you?"

She shook her head. "It hardly matters what he promised me. I should have known he did not mean to stand by his words. I, of all people, should know that—" She stopped abruptly. "Did you murder Lady Prudence's lover, or is that something you will also not admit to?"

Murder? Hell, so that was the way the gossipmongers had described it. Since that had been his reason for returning here, it struck him on the raw. "I shot him in a duel," he said brusquely. "It was all damnably honorable—and I lay stress on the word *honorable*. It was also deserved. Not legal, of course, but I doubt that will be the crime I'll ultimately swing for. It was not murder. I am not asking you to follow me for nefarious reasons, love—and I do need a name to call you, or you will have to listen to endearments all the way up the stairs."

She goggled at him, as young women so often did, but from the slight curve of her lips—immediately quelled—he knew she'd followed his quick speech. "Hamilton. My name is Grace Hamilton."

Devlin took a step backward and crooked his finger. "Trust me, Miss Hamilton. You cannot stay out here with your gown half off. And even if I button it for you—"

"I know. I look far too obviously like a harlot."

She'd tried his patience too far. More roughly than he should, he caught hold of her wrist and forced her to follow him down the hallway. She dragged her heels but had no choice. A thump of his fist against the appropriate molding produced a *snick* and he pried open the secret panel. "In there—there's a hidden staircase to the upper floors. I apologize in advance for the cobwebs and the dust."

Plain fear showed in her large, round eyes. Blast. "I have no intention of hurting you, Miss Hamilton. But I promise you, if Wesley took your innocence, he'll marry you."

She paused at the foot of the stairs. "You cannot force him to."

Devlin waved his hand to encourage her to get up the stairs. "A man with a pistol at his back can be forced to do anything."

But she laid a slender, bare hand on the rickety balustrade. "I don't want that. I don't want to marry him. I just want to . . . to turn back time."

"Sweeting—"

She stomped her slipper on the worn floor, the thump swallowed up by the stale air. "Don't. My name is Grace. I told you what it was and I want you to use it. Don't call me names like that."

A strand of a spider's web dangled in front of her face, but she flinched as he brushed it way. The way she'd recoiled made him want to rip out Wesley's sorry guts. Gently, he shook his head, wearing what he hoped was a soothing smile. "I cannot call you Grace. That is an intimacy a man like me is not allowed. I can call you 'love' or 'sweetheart' and live up to my audacious nature, or I can call you 'Miss Hamilton,' showing you due respect."

He'd hoped to relax her by making her laugh but she threw up her hands. Which meant her bodice gaped. He caught a glimpse of lush ivory curves with a deep shadowed valley between. His throat dried and his blood rushed down to his cock, making it instantly as hard as iron.

"I don't want due respect!" she cried. "Nor do I want to be an anonymous 'love.' I want—Oh, this is ridiculous. What does it matter what you call me? I can imagine what everyone else will call me."

With that, she turned and began to clomp up the stairs.

"A little quieter, Miss Hamilton," he advised, though he hated quenching her spirited anger. It was just what she needed—the best remedy for humiliation. "A little discretion will keep our secret a secret."

"I don't understand," she whispered ahead, to the dark and the cobwebs. "Why would you help me?"

"I might be a highwayman, but there are certain things I do not steal."

"Like a woman's virtue?" Disbelief rang in her voice.

"Like a woman's heart. Now tell me your story. All of it."